What readers are saying about
*Kangaroo Island*...

**5 out of 5 stars ... Riveting!**
*Kangaroo Island* is one of those books that I can't let go of. The characters are wildly colorful, vivid, and so real that I feel like I've become part of their lives. I hated ending the book because I'm going to lose track of my new friends and family! Tony is an exquisite writer and his descriptions of Kangaroo Island are so vibrant that the reader can smell the smells, feel the breezes, and experience the violence of the storms.

The more I read, the more convinced I was that this book needs to be made into a movie. The landscapes, the characters, the drama – an audience would eat it up. I can only hope that a sequel is planned because I don't want to stop the journey.

**Penny M**, Arizona, USA

In his sweeping novel, *Kangaroo Island*, a tribute to his homeland, Tony Boyle lays it all out in vivid, passionate detail. His eclectic chronicle of island living is a soaring epic of the lives of two families – a brilliantly woven tapestry of Australian character with its idiosyncrasies, extraordinary tenacity and deadpan humor – tempered by the stark irony of life under the clutches of an abusive patriarch.

An ultimate tale of redemption and promise, *Kangaroo Island* will warm your heart, even as it sends chills down your spine with its gritty depiction of the systemic isolation and chaos that alcoholism and addictive behavior can rain down on a codependent family.

**Thomas Myers**, USA

Tony Boyle's latest fiction is a finely crafted work as well as an excellent rollicking story set on Kangaroo Island, an actual island off the coast of South Australia where Tony grew up in the 1950s, 60s and 70s. The story covers the love between the two central characters who come from different religious and social backgrounds. It dramatizes the tensions that such differences cause in families brought up with such different values, but posits how love can triumph over such adversities. I also found it particularly insightful in its description of the difficulties that families have to deal with when the patriarch is an alcoholic.
    **Napier Mitchell**, Emeritus Professor of Communication, Queensland, Australia

There is something about Australian writers that allows them to create a fully dimensional picture of their subjects, the wild beauty of the country, the incredible tenacity and tenderness of their characters and the subtle depth of character it takes to survive and thrive in a sometimes hostile, often unforgiving life among gum trees, deserts, savage coastlines and often-distant neighbours. Mr. Boyle has this ability to place the reader squarely amongst his characters, putting them amongst the families and individuals who struggle bravely to overcome the tests of life and pursue their own happiness. Not since *The Thorn Birds* and *A Town like Alice* have I enjoyed the colour, scope and emotion of an Australian novel of such insight, pace and passion.
    **Leighton B Watts**, Australian award-winning poet, song writer and singer, Sydney, Australia

*Kangaroo Island* beautifully describes the island's magic scenery and lifestyle. Great characters and an intriguing story ... I can't wait for the next book.
    **Carmen Joseph**, Islander, Vivonne Bay, Kangaroo Island

*Kangaroo Island* captures the growing relationship of two young and vital characters with such depth and intensity that you feel as if their story is taking place in your own back yard. I couldn't wait to experience the unfolding of their story, but I was crestfallen when the book ended. Mr. Boyle sets a pace and creates an undercurrent of intrigue that reminds me of John Grisham at his best.
**Mark Graham**, author of *The Missing Sixth*, *The Harbinger* and *The Fire Theft*, Colorado

The Australian vernacular and accent rings true throughout *Kangaroo Island* and, along with the vivid descriptions of the Island and the interesting variety of characters really brought the book to life. I thought that Frank, a man who clearly loved his family but continually struggled with the demons of alcoholism was one of the most interesting characters in the book and gave some interesting insights into the life of an alcoholic. The ending of the book was exciting and unexpected and I'm already looking forward to the sequel.
**David Howard**, United Kingdom

This book is a must read if you want to be swept away! Travel to a place you have never been, *Kangaroo Island* in Australia, and recognize a piece of yourself. Tony Boyle does an excellent job of taking you on the graceful and gritty journey of two young adults who are discovering their passion for each other. The descriptions of the environment and raw emotions are palatable. You will see and smell the sites of Kangaroo Island as you dive in. The story has an authentic feeling that is easy to relate to. A wonderful story told by a great story teller, who sprinkles in his Australian wit. It is a real treat.
**Kathy**, Oregon, USA

**5 out of 5 stars … Easy Read.**
Outstanding book. Best I read in a long time. Easy read and easy to identify with the main characters. Exceeded my expectations.
   **Arnold C. Wegher**

**5 out of 5 stars … Fantastic journey reading *Kangaroo Island***
Tony Boyle paints a picture of Kangaroo Island through his eloquent writing style. Throughout the story I was picturing the beauty of the island and the culture of it's people who proudly call it home! I highly recommend this adventure … Go and buy it today.
   **Mimi Ryan**

*Kangaroo Island* is a genuine page turner. In between a stormy beginning and unexpected ending, the author, with amazing skill seamlessly weaves variety of subplots into a real life drama that rings true: a beautiful island made dangerous by great white sharks and poisonous snakes; feuding families connected by highly talented young lovers; an unrepentant alcoholic father engaged in drug trafficking and happily outwitting the local police; and last but not least – three intriguing love triangles.

This is one of those books that is not only a great read but also worthy of conversion to a full-length movie. I recommend the book to anyone who likes a combination of excitement, realism, surprises, a fast pace, and the challenge of correctly anticipating a story's ending.
   **Joe Masi**, desperately looking for something
   exciting to read. "I found it!"

*Kangaroo Island* by Australian Tony Boyle, is a magnificent work of art that captures the beauty of Kangaroo Island, a pristine environment off the coast of South Australia … Tony captures the beauty of life's struggles, the passion of true love, the pain and agony every individual faces in their life and the raw choices one faces between love, life and death … His writing style

is absolutely brilliant and the story will snare your heart ... I wept like a child during a few of the heart-wrenching scenes, but walked away invigorated when I read the last word of the last sentence. There are very few novels that provoke raw emotion on all levels. *Kangaroo Island* achieves this on a grand scale. This is one novel every individual should experience, it is a special gift.
**King Hurley**, Author *The Interview* and *Mondai Nai*, Colorado, USA

This wonderful book, *Kangaroo Island*, was like reliving my visits to beautiful, magical Kangaroo Island. The exciting story rang true, and I could hear the unique and quirky Australian accents as I read. I loved the way the author caught the voices of the characters. Of course he would, he's a Kangaroo Island product!
**Betty Austin-Ware**, Premier Aussie Travel Agent, USA

I have not read a book in some time that captured interpersonal relationships and tied them to a story in such a real and understandingly sympathetic manner. The author's understanding of the human condition hits home in a way that filled me up with love and forgiveness. Hell, this book healed me some. The story was fantastic! The imagery was amazing! What a fine read. Once I started reading, I could not put it down. I finished in just a few days.
**Brett Davidson**, Colorado

Tony Boyle's ability to get into the mind of the alcoholic, describing their emotions and behaviors was stunning ... for the alcoholic and those closest to them who suffer the most, Mr. Boyle's compassionate narrative offers hope, and beyond the demons a love capable of the greatest sacrifice.
**Bronwen Stow**, RN, Psychiatric Drug & Alcohol Emergency Room, Denver Health and Hospitals, Colorado

*Kangaroo Island* is a truly mesmerizing tale of culture, family pride and the everyday struggle of island life in this far corner of the world ... a sweeping epic tale of two families deeply entwined in a complex web of intrigue and suspense ... Tony Boyle captures the strength, beauty and charm of Kangaroo Island and her people ... I couldn't put it down!
    **Diane Chado**, RN, Mother, Reader,
    Kangaroo Island visitor, USA

Tony is a marvelous writer...I was captivated by the conflicts within and between the two families in Kangaroo Island ... Tony's descriptions of Kangaroo Island absolutely mesmerized me.
    **Ann Camy**, English Faculty (ret), Red Rocks
    Community College, Golden, Colorado

Tony Boyle's *Kangaroo Island* is superb writing...this Australian writer captures the essence of the island where he grew up ... his characters come alive in this wonderful first novel.
    **Jack "Lucky" Larsen**, E.D.D. English teacher (ret),
    Denver, Colorado

**4 out of 5 stars ... Great Read!**
This fast-paced story left me guessing about what could happen next. Found myself reading it on my lunch break. Well worth the time!
    **Tyler Larkin**

# Kangaroo Island

a novel

Tony J Boyle

Kangaroo Island by Tony J Boyle

Copyright © 2011 Tony J Boyle

All rights reserved. No part of this book may be reproduced or transmitted in any form or by any means, electronic or mechanical, including photocopying, recording or by any information storage and retrieval system, without permission from the author, except for the inclusion of brief quotations in review.

ISBN Number 13: 978-0-9793988-2-7

Library of Congress Control Number: 2013954136

First Print Edition New Title November 2013

Cover and interior design by Nick Zelinger, www.nzgraphics.com
Cover photo – Middle River, Kangaroo Island by Kathy Boyle
Author photo by Michael Ensminger

Published by Story Power Books LLC
Golden, Colorado

Visit our web sites at:
www.tonyboyle.me
www.kangarooislandnovel.com

Disclaimer: While the locations in this book are real, the story is a work of fiction and any resemblance or similarities of the characters to persons living or dead is purely coincidental

To:

Kathy, my brilliant partner, for her love, belief
and support;

Uncle Les: my counsel; a true blue Australian;
a quintessential gentleman to the end.
R.I.P… "Tell 'em I just conked out."

Michelle, Jamie, Cavell, Anne; Andy, Carmen, Julie,
Melanie; Scott, Karlee, Matthew, Lucas, Tye, Emma,
Riley, Jay, Harrison and Lewis for the blessings
and purpose they bring to my life;

And to my loving God, who 25 years ago led me to
the Storytellers Fellowship to make sense of it all.

# KANGAROO ISLAND

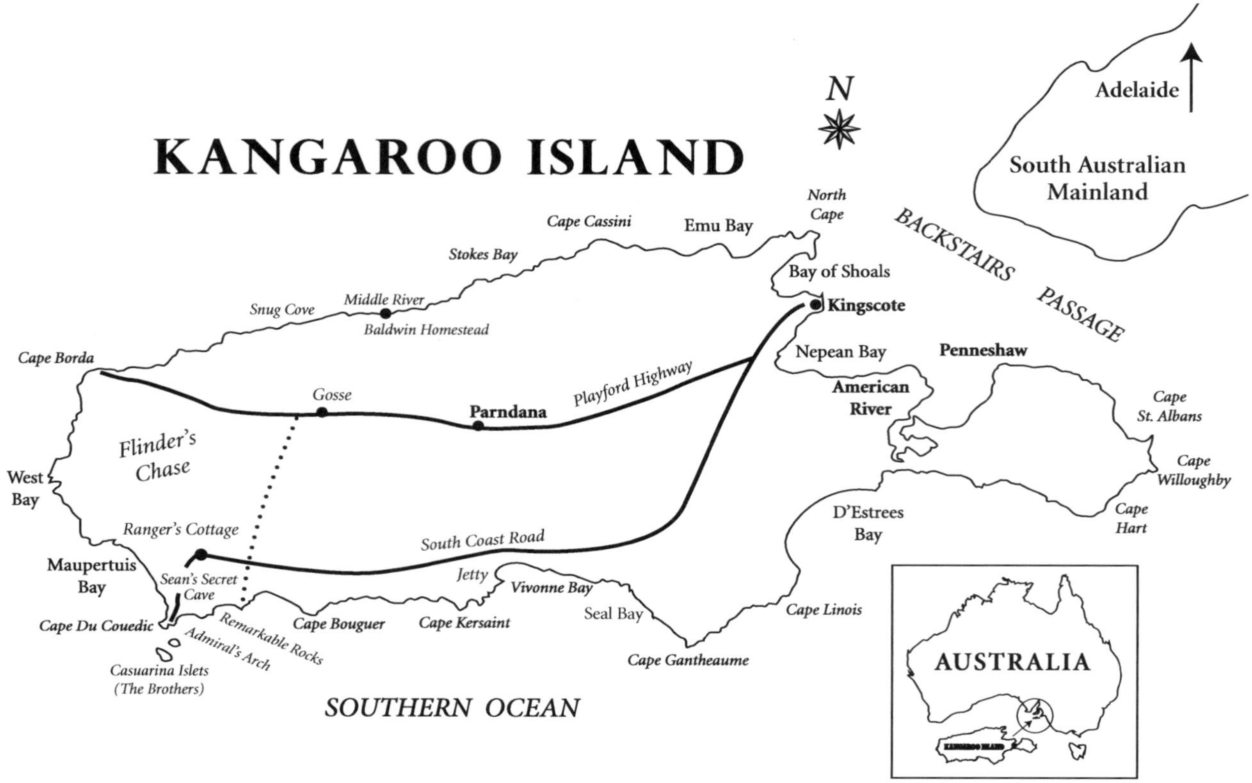

# PROLOGUE

On March 2, 1802, the British ship HMS *Investigator* dropped anchor in the magnificent bay of a big island located a few kilometres off the South Australian coast. After leaving Sydney months earlier to circumnavigate Australia, the explorer sailor, Captain Matthew Flinders, led his meat deprived crew ashore and slaughtered several kangaroos feeding on the coastal grasses that edged the sandy beach. A few days later, the crew's bellies full of the rich red meat and the ship's stores replenished, a grateful Flinders raised the British flag and claimed the rugged island for the Empire, naming it Kangaroo Island.

Pirates, whalers, sealers and escaped convicts came to the island after Flinders. Then, in July 1836, the ship *Duke of York* arrived from London carrying South Australia's first settlers. These hardy pioneers were the founders of the farming and fishing industries and the island's main town of Kingscote.

Over the next 200 years, the people of Kangaroo Island successfully developed the island's fishing, farming and tourism industries while managing and retaining its unique pristine environment. Kangaroo Island today is a highly promoted and well known tourist destination for Australian and International travellers with over 200,000 of them visiting each year.

The islanders are noted for their friendliness, hard work and commitment to their inherited environment. They have hundreds stories of lives lived, dramatic and soaring sagas, dialogue and narrative threaded with quintessential Australian humour that offers relief and levity even when they are confronted with the toughest of life's challenges. This is one of their stories.

# 1

It was August, 1988, winter time in the southern hemisphere. A powerful and dangerous south-westerly gale was roaring in from the Southern Ocean, attacking the thick, sandstone walls of the Cape du Couedic Lighthouse anchored firmly in the limestone rock at its base. The old tower had stood imperious and unmoved for over 80 years, its sweeping light warning passing ships to stand well out from the dangerous and isolated south-west corner of Kangaroo Island. The intense shaft of light from its rotating source swept through the rain and skipped along the top of the massive, white-capped waves that charged toward the coast. At the peak of their power, the curling giants thundered onto the rocks and exploded into plumes of spray that rushed up the vertical cliff walls until, losing momentum, they fell back into the sea to perpetuate the broad white line that defined the island's southern coastline.

In the scrubby brush crowding the landscape a kangaroo pushed back into the thick bush to shelter from the screaming wind and stinging rain. Lightning forked across the sky and reflected in the eyes of the trembling Joey peering over the lip of its mother's pouch. A clap of thunder followed, and the youngster dropped from view to the bottom of its furry sanctuary. The concerned mum immediately checked on the terrified youngster. Satisfied it was unharmed and protected in the warmth of her pouch; she lifted her head and stared out to sea.

To the west, fifteen hundred meters offshore from the cliffs of Seal Bay, a fishing cutter, its engine dead, struggled to stay afloat. For a moment, all seemed lost as the huge seas buried it under a wall of water, but the plucky cutter emerged seconds later when another wave lifted it to the top of its licking tongue; a cat teasing a mouse. An intense flash of lightning revealed the black letters on the bow of the timber hull, *Smokey Cloud*. In the wheelhouse, a boxy structure set on the stern behind the swaying mast, an anxious young woman wrestling desperately with the ship's wheel stared out into the storm.

Cassie Baldwin, fear and exhaustion threatening to overwhelm her, screamed into the raging gale, "I'll never give up! Never!" As if testing the girl's fierce resolve, an intense gust of wind hit the cutter abeam and pushed it broadside into a breaking wave, rolling the little ship toward disaster. She reacted instinctively and spun the wheel to port; the drag of the sea anchor caused just enough flow against the angle of the rudder to point the bow back into the massive waves, bringing them back from the brink of a death roll to push on through the spray of the next the cresting monster. She turned to snatch a look at the open hatch cover. A dull yellow glow marked its entrance. "Hurry, Matt, get it started, or…" She pushed the thought from her mind and turned back to keep *Smokey Cloud* pointed into the storm.

Her thoughts turned to her mother. "If you're out there, mummy, help us," she cried.

Blessed with the exotic beauty of her Spanish-born mother, the feisty young woman, her body strong and athletic from years of classical dance, competitive sports and working on her father's farming properties as hard as any man, stared ahead. She wiped her dripping nose on the sleeve of her sky blue sweater still soaking wet from the wild dinghy ride to the ship from the Vivonne Bay jetty an hour earlier. The blue contrasted superbly with the olive complexion of her skin and the rich brown of her hair pulled back into a ponytail. The wheelhouse and the wet sweater offered little warmth; her teeth were already beginning to chatter.

Waves continued to slam the hull. The wheel was wrenched from her grasp; its spokes savagely rapped her knuckles. A wall of seawater exploded against the wheelhouse window, a moment of sheer terror that set her heart racing. As she strained to see through the water-streaked glass, ghostly images formed in the shadows of the intermittent light show surrounding *Smokey Cloud*.

A wispy form appeared in the midst of the spray sweeping over the foredeck, "Mummy!" Tears formed in the young woman's eyes. Her thoughts flashed to a picture of her mother and the headline in an old Islander newspaper. 'Beautiful Spanish dancer, Kristina de Coronado, marries Kingscote's popular young mayor, Monty Baldwin.'

Kristina's image floated to the wheelhouse window. "I am with you, Cassie, always with you. God is watching over both of you. Keep fighting, all is well." Another wave of water exploded over the glass and Kristina was gone.

"No! Please don't leave, not again, no." Immediately, she experienced the same terrible abandonment she had felt when Kristina was killed; a growing sense of fear and despair was threatening to break her resolve to fight on. "For God's sake get a grip girl, get a grip!" she shouted.

She brushed the tears from her eyes and looked ahead. Lightning lit up the swaying mast and pitching foredeck seconds before it plunged into a wall of water, stalling the cutter. The abrupt stop jerked her forward over the wheel; one of its spokes caught her under the chin and sent her tumbling. Fighting for balance on the heaving deck, she pulled herself upright and, ignoring the angry red welt already beginning to swell, snatched back the spinning wheel.

"The radio! Where the hell is the radio?" Her eyes swept the console ahead of her. "Ah!" It was to the right of her head and bolted to the wall a little below the wheelhouse ceiling. She reached up, flicked on the switch, snatched the microphone from its cradle and pressed the transmission button. "Mayday! Mayday! This is *Smokey Cloud*. Does anybody read, over?" The receiver hissed and crackled. Again, she pressed the button. "This is *Smokey Cloud*. Can anybody hear us… engine down, sea anchor out, not holding…drifting toward the coast, over." A bigger wave hit, rolled the cutter violently and slammed Cassie back onto the deck. "Bugger!"

The radio crackled. "…*Cloud*. This…*Wave Dancer*…are you. We are off Point Ellen…contact…repeat. Do…copy, over?"

She struggled frantically to her feet. The spinning spokes of the wheel cracked her knuckles again. "What bloody next!" she cried, wringing her hand and grabbing the swinging microphone again. "*Wave Dancer*, this is *Smokey Cloud*, having trouble hearing you. You are breaking up. We are off Knobby Island, engine down. Sea anchor dragging, over."

The radio crackled again. "…find you. Hang on…*crackle*… we are…*crackle*…Fire flares, repeat…*crackle, crackle*…"

"Did you say flares, over?" She listened for the voice connecting her to hope, but there came only the scratching of static, the howling of the wind and the waves crashing over the cutter. She looked about the wheelhouse for the flares, saw the cabinet under the wheel and slid open the latch. In that moment, *Smokey Cloud* shook free of hundreds of kilos of seawater weighing down on her bow and charged up the face of the next wave.

The cabinet door burst open, spilling out flags, ropes, tools and a heavy metal box labelled "FLARES." A razor sharp hunting knife jammed in between the box and Cassie's left leg, slashed through her moleskin pants and cut deep into her thigh. Blood immediately began to darken the cotton of her off-white pants. Stifling the urge to scream, she fell and slid along the deck with the cabinet contents toward the rear of the wheelhouse. *Smokey Cloud* reversed pitch, saving her from crashing headlong into the open hatch that dropped into the engine room.

As the flare box started to slide by her, she managed to grab it and then wedge her body between the hatch lip and the timber wall. She opened the lid and looked inside at six cartridges, each wrapped in orange cellophane and set side by side in a shielded section isolated from the pistol. She snapped the lid shut and attempted to stand, grunting as the pain knifed through her thigh. Again, the cutter fell off the top of another mountain of water and again, Cassie crashed to the deck, dropped the flare box and slid to the front of the wheelhouse.

The radio crackled. This time, the voice was loud and clear. "*Smokey Cloud*, Cassie, this is *Wave Dancer*. We picked up your call. Put up flares. Do you read? Please put up flares, over."

Cassie reacted with a burst of new energy, grasped the railing above the forward cabinets and hauled her hurting body upright. Lurching drunkenly with the violent motion of the corkscrewing cutter, she supported most of her weight on her right leg and reached for the microphone.

"Understand…situation critical…will fire flares…please hurry." The main cabin light, already at half its usual brightness, blinked off each time the microphone button was pressed. Realization turned into a new fear. "Oh, no!" She jabbed down on the button for the last time. "Generator down…running on batteries…must conserve power. Out for now." She snapped the microphone back into its cradle and flicked the power button to 'Off.'

A series of loud bangs that came from the engine room startled her. Suddenly, the wheelhouse light went out and the ship was plunged into darkness. Cassie froze. She knew that she needed help to get the flares up. She had to get Matt.

Panting heavily from pain and fatigue, her threatening panic barely controlled, she remembered the flashlight hanging under the radio. A series of lightning flashes helped her find it. She took it off the hook and then crawled across the pitching deck toward the engine room hatch. *Smokey Cloud* topped another wave and then tipped over into a vertical dive. Cassie's quick reflexes saved her; she managed to reach out and grab onto the hatch cover lip, which kept her from sliding back and slamming into the wheelhouse's open cabinet door. As the game little cutter bottomed out in the trough, an exhausted Cassie dragged herself over the last few centimetres to the engine room hatch opening. Sweating and gasping for air, she paused to catch her breath. The pain from the damaged leg was suddenly overwhelming; the beam from the flashlight revealed the extent of the bloody mess. Horrified, she realized that she had to stop the bleeding. Among the litter on the wheelhouse floor were several flags, one of which she was able to snare by stretching out her good leg and dragging it to her with her toe. Despite the violent pitching of the deck and the stabbing pain that came with every movement, she was able to wrap the flag around her bloodied thigh and tie it off tight, so that it slowed the bleeding and served as a bandage. When she finished, she saw that her hands were shaking; tears started to roll down her cheeks again. She descended into a well of self-pity, as her mind flashed back over her short life.

For 10 of her 20 years she had worked hard on the farm, did well with her school studies, consoled her father after the loss of her mother, worked her bum off at ballet school and was invited to join the Australasian Modern Dance Company in Sydney. "All for nothing!" she screamed, tears pouring over her cheeks; then she vomited.

Disgusted, she hammered the deck with her fists. "No! No!" Anger finally overwhelmed the fear and the pain and a new energy radiated from her core, re-igniting her will to live and determination to fight on.

"Where the bloody hell are the flares?" She began searching the deck floor with the flashlight when another series of lightning flashes helped her see the flare box jammed between the hatch cover lip and the wall panel. Thank, God. She rolled onto her stomach and pointed the flashlight beam into the pitch dark of engine room.

"Matt!"

\*\*\*\*

"You bloody idiot!" The angry words were quickly drowned out in the roar of the storm. The engine room was barely lit by the single light bulb that swung wildly from the solid timber beam supporting the main deck; the smell of diesel fumes permeated the small space. A mixture of seawater and oily sludge sloshed noisily back and forth in the bottom of the open bilge. Mounted on heavy wood blocks bolted to the cutter's keel, a big Caterpillar marine engine distinguished by its traditional yellow colour, took up most of the space. The sound of a metal striking metal competed with the noise of the waves battering the hull.

Matt Ryan, tall and athletic, was squatting between the engine and the port side of the cutter's timber shell, a wrench clasped in one hand while the other gripped the overhead beam. The amber glow of the swinging light picked up the stressed features of the twenty-one-year-old face. A mop of thick, sandy-brown hair framed the high cheekbones and complimented the impish nose set between sea-blue eyes. A wave crashed against the hull, and his head smacked against the overhead beam. He thumped the offending timber with his wrench. "What was I bloody thinking? I should've checked the fuel."

The young man was growing more desperate. Transferring the emergency reserve of diesel from the jerry can into the main fuel tank and then disconnecting the fuel line to purge the air bubbles had taken too much time. The knuckles on his right hand were a blend of bright red blood and black oil, the skin on the back of his hand scraped bloody in his hurry to get fuel into the tank. He forced the fuel line connection into the injector assembly; the brass connector thankfully gripped on the first attempt.

Another monster wave crashed into the cutter's port side and slammed Matt into the steel fuel tank. Howling with pain as two ribs splintered, he dropped the wrench into the black sludge under the engine. "No!" Eyes watery from pain and exasperation, he plunged his hand into the filth; his fingers clawed along the splintery bottom. Another wave; he cried out, jerked his hand out of the oily slime and clutched his chest. Desperately, he turned to Saint Anthony, the patron saint of lost belongings. "Saint Anthony, please come around, something's been lost and cannot be found!" Sucking in a deep breath, he plunged his hand back into the sludge. Miraculously and immediately, he felt the shape of a familiar object as his hand passed over it. His touch was at first timid, terrified it was not the wrench; it was.

"Thanks, Saint Anthony!" he yelled, as he lifted the tool carefully from the bilge filth and clamped it around the connector. "Don't let me drop this again; just a couple more turns. Good," he gasped. "Now, you big yellow bastard, let's get you fired up."

Starting the giant motor was hell, as he fought through the pain of his broken ribs. Leaning over the engine, he pushed the compression lever to the "open" position, gritted his teeth, reached for the switchboard and pressed the starter button. The single light bulb dimmed as the batteries struggled to provide the power to crank the shaft. With the batteries quickly running down, but still short of the revolutions needed to start the big diesel a desperate Matt slammed the lever to the "close" position. The compression built; one chamber fired and then another.

"C'mon, c'mon," Matt prayed. A third chamber in the big engine ignited, coughed a couple of times and then died. The switchboard exploded in a flash of arcing blue flame as the fuses disintegrated. The engine stalled and *Smokey Cloud* plunged into darkness. The noise of the storm hammering the ship's hull and was suddenly loud and terrifying.

Images of an earlier terror flashed through his mind, one that had haunted him throughout his young life. He had seen it happening, as he passed her bedroom door. His mother, naked and bleeding, was spread-eagled across her bed with a man bent over her, fist raised. The man looked up; intense blue eyes, blurred and bloodshot from alcohol, fixed on him. He fled, terrified and ashamed. His last memory was the bloody image of his mother throwing up her arms to protect her body from the lunging brute that was his father.

He stared into the dark frozen with fear. A beam of light swept through the dark and startled him. Shading his eyes, he saw Cassie waving frantically for him to come up to the wheelhouse. He reached for the steel ladder and began to climb, each grasp, each step was a challenge to push through the pain from his broken ribs. When he reached the top, Cassie grabbed his wrists and pulled him into the wheelhouse.

"Ugh."

"Matt, you're hurt."

"Busted my ribs, Cass," he gasped.

Icy chills ran through Cassie's body. She took a deep breath in an effort to calm the rising panic that threatened to steal away the hope she had from her mother's words and the close proximity of *Wave Dancer*. "Matt! We're closing on the cliffs. *Wave Dancer* is looking for us. We have to put up the flares!"

Matt nodded and tried to sit up. He howled, clutched his chest and fell back to the deck.

"Matt, c'mon! We've got to get those flares up!"

*Smokey Cloud's* bow rose sharply to climb yet another wave, forcing the couple to slide down the sharply tilted deck and slam into the rear wall. Matt's head hit the heavy timber panelling and knocked him flat onto his back; the stunned and badly hurt young man groaned.

"Matt! Matt!" Cassie bent over her mate.

"Here, Cass, help me up, mate," cried Matt as he struggled onto his knees, but then toppled back onto his bottom. "Bloody head's spinning a bit; give us a minute, hey luv? If I can make it to my feet I'll be all right." He took a moment to focus and then braced. "Righto, mate, let's go." He pushed up onto his knees again. She quickly slid in behind him and pushed up with her hands under his backside.

"C'mon, c'mon! You can to do it! You can do it," she gasped, pushing and struggling to stand as he slowly straightened up.

The heavy glass panel in the sliding door splintered with the loud crack of a pistol shot, causing her to put added weight on her injured thigh. Cold seawater blasted through the broken window and washed over the wheelhouse floor. He had almost made it when Cassie's leg gave way, and she fell. Matt toppled and smashed his head on the hardwood timber of the deck. His last vision was the distraught face of Cassie looking down on him as he lost consciousness.

# 2

*Kangaroo Island: six months earlier, summer*

A cloud of dust and gravel billowed about Matt, as he slid his motor bike to a perfect stop alongside the dozen or so battered vehicles angled nose first into the dirt sidewalk in front of the Parndana Catholic Church. He quickly slid off the bike seat, smacked the dust from his white moleskins and hurried into the church of his baptism.

In Parndana, the main town located close to the centre of the island, dirt roads the colour of rust converged from every direction on the tiny oasis of a few shops, sport fields, a school and a cluster of neatly kept homes. The town's prominent landmark was the praying hands design of the church roof, rising twenty meters above the surrounding flatland. Catholics from the central and west end of the island, some travelling a hundred kilometres, gathered each Sunday to attend mass, shop and exchange yarns.

The voices of the congregation singing drifted through the open church doors and out into the already hot morning air. Two black crows flapped lethargically across the blue sky, cawing raucously until they disappeared beyond the scrubby tree line. The singing stopped and silence returned for a few moments before the altar bells rang out in three short bursts, signalling the beginning of the communion ritual.

Inside the church, the Ryan family took up the space in one of the twenty-two pews made from Tasmania's finest timber, Huon pine. The pews, with their trademark golden hue added to the holy ambience and were divided equally along each sidewall, creating a centre aisle for the congregation to shuffle up to the altar for communion. Regrettably, the timber's comfort did not reflect its fine look; bums ached and kids squirmed.

In the Ryan family pew, where a stainless-steel plate read *Donated by the Ryan Family*, Matt was strategically seated alongside six-year-old Sean, the younger of his two stepbrothers. He had a fondness for fidgeting and getting into mischief, and Matt saw to twisting the boy's ear if he misbehaved. Sean's older brother, twelve-year-old Patrick, the only altar boy at church that morning was assisting Monsignor Byrne.

Katherine Ryan, Matt's stepmother, sat on the other side of Sean. A devout Catholic, she wore her difficult life in the lines of her face and looked more than her forty-three years. However, her faith, the mass, communion, family and sacrifice gave her life salvation and purpose.

Matt's father, Frank, was seated immediately behind Katherine in the last pew at the rear of the church. A band-aid, stained and darkened by blood, covered a wound just above his right eye. Squinting through red and swollen eyes set in a lined and drawn face, Frank Ryan could easily have been perceived as a man approaching his mid-sixties, rather than the fifty-two years his military service record claimed.

Matt's peripheral vision caught Frank taking a nip of brandy from his silver flask. With a wipe of his mouth on the back of the sleeve of his flannel shirt accompanied by a noisy clearing of his throat, Frank shifted from his sitting position and onto his knees. As he returned the flask to his shirt pocket, he saw the look of disgust on the face of his eldest son. For a moment, the older man was embarrassed, his face flushed red with humiliation and then it quickly changed to anger. He glared at the boy. Matt felt a mix of conflicting emotions. Shame was the big one, anger and anxiety were there, too, churning about in his gut along with the sadness, the bloody depressing sadness and powerlessness, feelings he remembered living with from the beginning of time.

The moment was broken by the shriek of a girl jumping up onto the seat in front of Sean. Martha was one of the Fahey family's eleven children and big girl for her five years of age. The family ran a dairy farm, and the separation of delicious cream from the rich milk of jersey cows was an obvious treat enjoyed by the family on a frequent basis; they were all big— well, "healthy" was how the locals might have described them. Rosy Fahey, the girl's mother, was not amused by her daughter's hysteria or her frenzied tap dance on the golden seat.

Immediately grasping the nature of the girl's distress, Matt, barely able to contain himself, cast a furrowed brow in the direction of Sean. The boy squirmed and pretended innocence; a small white mouse, Snot, appeared, pink nose twitching as he sneaked back along the pew to his master. Gently taking hold of the tiny commando, Sean placed him in the pocket of his short pants and then looked coyly, through wide, emerald eyes, at his brother and protector; he grinned triumphantly. Matt, feigning stern disapproval could not quite contain the crease of a warm smile spreading across his face. He placed his arm around the boy.

As suddenly as the disturbance started, it was over, leaving the church silent and the Monsignor frozen in the midst of administering Communion to his altar boy. He was not amused and glared through bright, blue eyes at the congregation. He held the silver chalice in front of his chest. The sun shone through the skylight built into the praying hands roof, reflected off the sacred cup and split into brilliant rays of golden light. The effect was stunning, an apparition; it seemed the Monsignor had descended from heaven on the golden rays.

Katherine moved her rosary through her fingers one bead at a time with added intensity, her face radiant as she gave herself, body and soul, to her maker. Matt was looking across at his stepmother. He remembered she was quite the looker when she first met Frank. In fact, both of Frank's wives were stunners at their marriages. Life with Frank was not easy. Matt's mother bore the worst of it, the beatings as his alcoholism raged. Matt was too young to understand her suicide, but he knew that his father had something to do with it.

After a calculated pause to signal annoyance for the disruption of his Mass, Monsignor Byrne placed the wafer on Pat's tongue and motioned with a nod of his head for the congregation to come forward and receive their communion. Matt stood and followed his stepmother and stepbrother into the line leading to the altar. Frank, smelling of alcohol, stepped in behind his son.

Matt approached the altar, kneeled before the priest and took the host on his tongue. While it melted away, he prayed, "Dear God, please bless Cassie, my mother, Katherine, Pat, Sean and Mad Tom." He made the sign of the cross, stood, turned around and almost bumped into Frank who it seemed was deliberately blocking his passage.

Matt stared coldly into his father's eyes. *It should've been you.*

# 3

The temperature was already 39°C, stinking hot, but not hot enough to deter the congregation from gathering in groups outside the church to catch up on local gossip, Sunday's after Mass ritual.

"Mad" Tom Donaldson, a bachelor from the west end of the island, was a local character who always attracted an audience of kids after mass. That was pretty much the extent of his socializing, although he would always attend the church's annual barn dance. His Sunday wardrobe had been the same since he purchased it new for Matt's mother, Matilda Ryan's funeral 15 years earlier; a '60s purple shirt that had a broad collar with turned up tips, unmatched green tie and a light-grey suit with bell-bottom trousers. It was at the funeral that the committed bachelor became a father figure and mentor in Matt's life.

A tribe of kids, including Sean, clustered around the sixty-five-year-old eccentric. The kids loved him. Considered by the locals a gifted storyteller and "a bit of a character," Tom's dark eyes glowed with excitement and wonder as the kids pleaded with him to start on a new story. "Come on, Tom, come on; get on with it." "Geez, Tom, we've been wait'n all week." "Yeah, pull ya finger out, Tom and stop pissing around, will ya?"

Tom grinned. "Now don't you be cheeky, you little bugger, or I'll have to tear your tongue out." He waited while they settled.

"Yeah, well anyway, last night I'm out with a couple of the dogs, taking them for a run, see, and making my way toward the fishermen's jetty at Vivonne. I guess it must've been around one in the morning," he said in a conspiratorial tone, as he tousled Sean's hair. "Anyhow, a truck pulls up to the jetty, see. Two blokes get out and start unloading these bags onto the rail-cart."

Tom's voice switched to a melodramatic pitch, appropriate for developing mystery and building tension. His eyebrows furrowed. "Then, out of the gloom, a fishing boat slides in alongside the far end of the pier, keeping away from the light of the jetty lamps, see, and ties up. Now, these two blokes, see, one of them taking a swig out of a bottle of grog, push the cart along the rails to the cutter and start throwing the bags aboard. There is a heck of a lot of shouting and cursing going on, and then one of them stumbles and falls, arse-over-head into the boat, and he's got a death grip the bottle like it's the last one left on earth." Tom's voice growls on the word 'death' as he reaches out to wrap his fist around the imaginary bottle's neck.

Sean's eyes widened. Matt, who had been apologizing to the Fahey girl for Sean's prank and was at the same time listening to Tom's story, joined the audience. "Did you see who the blokes were loading the cart, Tom?"

The storyteller, his face encircled by a mop of wild red hair and matching beard, winked at the questioner. "No, Matt," Tom lied. "The light was bad, and I was a long way off. The bloke that fell into the boat, well, he walked back down the jetty, see, nursing what looked like a hell of a whack on the head, had a bit of a limp up, too. Funny thing, though, he was still carrying and taking swigs of grog from the bottle. He'd held onto it all along, didn't spill a drop." Tom laughed. "I think he was a bit pissed."

Matt knew Tom was lying, but he was grateful; the wise old bastard knew how to keep his mouth shut. One thing about Tom, he had no love for the coppers. They had come out to his property once and questioned him about spying on tourists staying at the Vivonne Bay back-packers hostel. They had no proof and Tom told them to "get stuffed, I'd never do anything like that," so the island's acting sergeant of police, Reg Woodson, slammed his fist into Tom's gut and left him flat on his back, gasping for breath.

"Anyhow," continued 'Mad' Tom. "I did make out the name on the cutter. It was the *Smokey Cloud*."

# 4

Monsignor Byrne walked out through the church doors, a ball of energy that belied his eighty-one years, the earlier look of rebuke from the altar gone and replaced with a bright smile. He took a deep breath and looked over the flock that he came to know and love intimately. He emigrated from Ireland to Australia as a young priest, and on arrival in Adelaide he was immediately sent to a parish in the South Australian outback where he settled in right away. The refreshing 'down to earth reality' of the country people appealed to him and when the Bishop of Adelaide asked him what parish he would like to minister before he retired he chose Kangaroo Island, the annual destination for his holidays and retreat. "Tis on the island where I feel a special closeness to God, and tis there where I want to retire my body to its final resting place," he had told the Bishop.

The Monsignor winked at an attractive young woman he had baptized in his church 18 years earlier. "T'was a nice shot ya made to win the game yesterday, Maureen," he said, referring to the tennis match in Kingscote the previous afternoon. "Ya be keeping up the good work, now."

"You can count on it, Monsignor," the tall red-headed girl with emerald green eyes answered in a voice loud enough for Matt, who was standing nearby to hear. Maureen, pretty, tall and athletic, enjoyed the attention of the local lads with whom she flirted furiously, but it was the elusive Matthew Ryan with the angel blue eyes she was after. "Are you coming to the parish barn-dance at Gosse Hall next Saturday night, Monsignor?"

Monsignor Byrne smiled a warm confirmation in response to Maureen's inquiry, fully aware of the web of seduction fashioned for the intended victim. He had watched the same rituals over the generations that filled his churches; the raging hormones of young, vibrant blood demanding gratification; God's glorious design for ensuring mankind's survival. The monsignor chuckled; *what a brilliant ploy this wonderful pantomime that keeps our churches full.*

He moved from group to group, exchanging greetings, shaking hands, hugging babies, all the while closing on his targets, Frank and Katherine Ryan. His concerns were the well-being of all his flock, but it was the Ryans who caused him his greatest anxiety.

"Hello, Katherine, Francis," said Monsignor Byrne. Frank nodded and shifted his feet uneasily, as he strained to listen to Mad Tom in the midst of the kids. "Tis good to see ya both are here today."

"I miss coming when we can't make it, Monsignor, but there are times when Frank is up to his neck with so much to do," Katherine responded.

"Yes, I noticed. Still needing the wee nip then, are we, Francis?" The priest looked at Frank with care and concern, but there was also a hint of sternness in the tone of his voice.

Frank grimaced. "Medicinal purposes, Father. Ever since I fell off the lighthouse platform and…" Frank's sentence was cut short by a sharp interjection from Matt, who had crossed to them from Tom's group along with Sean, his shadow.

"...and blew your back out. You've always got some medical problem going on, Dad, hey? G'day, Monsignor," said Matt, his voice on the word 'dad' laced with sarcasm. Frank braced and stared at his oldest son, threatening.

The monsignor quickly intervened. "Matthew, I've been want'n to catch up wid ya all week." He winked and nodded his head. "I've got something for ya, so run along and wait for me in the sacristy, will ya?" he said in his heavy Irish brogue, breaking through the tension and pointing in the direction of the sacristy.

Monsignor Byrne turned back to the Ryans and Sean. "Oh, and Sean, I hope ya caught up wid ya little friend. I don't want him scaring any more of the ladies, now. Off to the sacristy wid ya brother; I've got something there for ya. I'll be along in a minute, but I want a few words wid ya mother and father first." He winked at the boy.

Sean ran after Matt who was waiting at the sacristy door, watching the priest and his parents. Shame and anxiety fed Matt's anger, knowing that Monsignor Byrne was talking to his father about his drinking. He watched Frank kick the dirt, scowl and turn to walk back to the family truck, a beat up Landcruiser.

The monsignor continued talking with Katherine. Matt saw her attempt to smile, to make light, he guessed, of Frank's behaviour, an inbuilt response they all had when Frank's public face would embarrass and shame them. Matt's mother was just the same. The kindly old priest hugged Katherine then blessed her. As she walked to the Landcruiser, the priest turned, smiled, clapped his hands and, with a light spring in his step, walked to the boys. With a hand on each of their backs, he gently shepherded them through the door of the sacristy.

Inside, the air was cool. The smell of incense still lingered and caught in the boys' throats, causing Sean to cough. "Sit over there and give me jest a little minute here, Matthew," said the monsignor, pointing to a richly padded, red velvet chair.

He turned to Sean. "Now, Sean, I've got something for ya and Patrick." He opened the vestment closet and pulled out two brand new fishing rods. "Here ya go, then. I know ya boys have been trying to catch the big snapper off Admirals Arch. Well, now ya got a good shot at get'n 'em."

"Jeez, thanks, Father," said Sean, excited.

"Holy Mary Mother of God, boy. Ya don't be using the holy Lord's name in vain, young man. Be off wid ya and find Patrick. I want to have a few words wid Matthew."

Sean was all smiles as he ran out the open door with a firm grip on the fishing rods, yelling for Patrick at the top of his voice. Monsignor Byrne smiled, closed the door and sat in a half-size pew opposite Matt. The old priest had known the young man since the day he visited Matilda Ryan in the hospital after she had given him birth. He remembered her smiling and proud, looking beautiful holding her first born child; seven years later she took her own life. A highly respected teacher of early grade children, she had written many essays about the island that made newspapers and magazines around the country. Matt had inherited his mother's looks, her ice-blue eyes and her talent for writing. The old priest was well aware of the cause of the sadness that haunted the blue eyes looking back at him.

He reached for Matt's hands. "Now tell me, lad, how's the writin' coming along?"

Matt was quiet, still upset with his father. The priest waited, silent, Matt's hands in his.

"Not real good, Monsignor. I try to find a quiet spot each night, but Dad yells and beats up on Katherine a lot and bullies Pat and Sean. It's only when I'm there that he doesn't whack into them. He's drunk most the time these days, and I'm scared to death he'll damage the light, or even shut it down. You never know what'll set him off. Being around him is like walking on eggshells."

The monsignor struggled to find meaning and inspiration. "It's hard for ya all, I know, Matthew. Who knows the ways of the Lord? But, I do know this, he's blessed ya wid a special talent, a very special talent, indeed. You carry tremendous power, power to influence, to even change the course of human history for the better and sometimes, sadly, for worse. Ya have it, Matthew, and it needs be to nurtured and put to good purpose."

The boy sat quietly for a few moments, gathering his thoughts. The priest sat still, holding the boy's hands, looking into his eyes, waiting patiently.

"You know I love to write, Monsignor. Once I start, it seems no time at all when I'm completely in the…in the zone. Something always interrupts: the Oldman yelling, my typewriter jamming, a fishing cutter calling on the radio for information, or the hourly weather report due and Frank, who gets paid to do it, is bloody well flaked out."

"I hear ya, boy, but ya have to keep at it; ya got to work through all that. Pray to ya God for strength." He smiled. "And there's no need to be swearing in the House of the Lord, Matthew, or at any other time for that matter."

"Sorry, Monsignor," said Matt. He chuckled. "But I recall when you and I were building the rock wall at the church entrance a few years ago. Remember? A rock slipped after you'd spent a lot of time wiggling it into place, and you said the 'f' word. I was about twelve at the time, and you shocked the hell out of me."

"See what I mean? Ya remember events and details. You've a sharp mind, boy, and ya a bit of a wit; it's the mind of a writer ya have," said the monsignor, chuckling, building the boy's self-esteem at every opportunity. "Well, at least it did ya some good, shocking the hell out of ya, did it? Now, I want ya to take a look at this."

The Monsignor moved to a bench made from a heavy slab of redwood. Above the bench, Matt's eyes were drawn to the beautiful stained-glass window alive with rich, vibrant reds, blues, greens and yellows, forming the image of Jesus praying in the Garden of Gethsemane, his disciples clustered in the background. Matt had studied the picture many times when he was an altar boy. Later, when he started to write his own stories, the story of betrayal and denial captured in the clever placement of the collared glass became evident, as did the lesson he took from it. *It didn't matter that were you the Son of God, they still got you.*

From underneath the bench, the monsignor retrieved an oddly shaped brown case and placed it on the bench top. He snapped back two clasps, opened the lid and lifted out a word processor.

"This is for you, Matthew. It's a tad old, but the little beast works well."

Matt's eyes brightened. "Wow." He ran his hand over the discoloured plastic case and examined it closely. "Seems I've seen this somewhere before," he said, scratching his head. "Look, I don't think I can accept this, Monsignor." He tapped a key and pondered some more. "Well, I could if you let me pay for it…I mean…the church always needs money, and I've got some cash coming in."

"It's a gift, boy, given to the parish with the express instruction that it be given to ya for ya writing. The only contract ya enter into is that ya use it for at least an hour every day, no matter what's going on in ya life." Monsignor Byrne placed his hand on the boy's shoulders. "Ya see, Matthew, there are people in the parish who believe in ya, and there's a secret admirer, a non-Catholic would ya believe, who wishes to remain anonymous."

"Bloody hell, I don't know what…Okay, tell everyone thanks, will you? I'll try not to let you down, Monsignor."

"Don't be letting ya-self down, Matthew. One more thing, the Australian National Writers' and Poets' Competition that I entered ya into, the 2000-word essay along wid ya poem, is expected to be into the judges in Sydney just two months from now, in the middle of April or thereabouts. The details for completion of ya entry are due in two weeks. Bring them along to Mass next week, and I'll make sure they're in on time."

"Jeez, Monsignor, I haven't even finished the outline yet."

Monsignor Byrne cocked an eyebrow and waved a finger.

"Sorry, Monsignor, it's a bit of a habit. I have a poem, but I don't think its right for the competition, too abstract. I need a new idea," he said, packing the word processor into its case and moving to the door.

"Look about ya, lad, Kangaroo Island is a wondrous place. There's plenty to write about here. Ya mother did some wonderful articles. Trust in God, he'll inspire ya if ya ask him, or try his angels; just start to write. Trust ya instincts and do the work. Just write, write, write; off wid ya now." He patted Matt on the shoulder and opened the sacristy door. "And Matthew…"

"Yes, Monsignor?"

"One last thing; I had a few words wid ya father. He wasn't too happy, but he won't be bothering ya about ya writing, I'll tell ya that. God bless ya, boy." The old priest blessed Matt and then turned back into the sacristy and closed the door behind him.

Matt walked toward the family truck. Frank was sitting behind the steering wheel, the surly look still on his face.

"Matt! Matt!" a voice yelled. Pat appeared, running around the corner from the main street. "Cassie's in town, at the store."

"Bloody good stuff, Pat, thanks. Here, put this in the truck, will you?" He handed Pat the faded brown case and ran to his bike, kicked the motor to life and roared off in the direction of the store, a fishtail of dust spewing from the spinning back wheel.

# 5

"Nice job, nice job, Winston," said Cassie, slapping the sweaty neck of the big chestnut gelding, its flanks heaving from exertion. She turned in the saddle and stared back at the long white beach they had just raced down at a reckless, sand-flying gallop. The air was already warm. The sparkling seawater, blue and pristine, washed onto the sand, cool and inviting. She glanced at her watch. "Darn. Sorry, Winnie, not this morning, mate, it's time to get ready for church." She turned to the rolling hills that ran along the north coast of the island; the family homestead, huge and formidable, dominated the top of Constitution Hill, the highest point overlooking Snellings Beach, better known as Middle River by the locals. She sat quietly for a few moments, surveying the scene familiar to her since birth. Smiling, she spurred Winston lightly on the flanks and urged him toward the hill and homestead.

The homestead, built in the mid 1800s, overlooked the twenty-four-kilometre stretch of ocean separating that part of the island from the mainland. The views were spectacular, the homestead, impressive. What started out as little more than a stone cottage had grown into a massive building with walls a half-meter thick, built from the natural limestone carried by horse and cart from the pits on the family's south coast properties near Vivonne Bay and Cape Kersaint. Everything about the Baldwin homestead was expansive: the eight bedrooms, the mammoth kitchen annexed to the large dining room where a long, solid, redwood table sat up to thirty people; but, the piece-de-résistance was the huge living room with its front window, extending for the entire length of the wall. The views were breathtaking. Rolling hills formed grassy spurs that dropped away to the pebbly beaches edging the sea. Slightly to the east, waves broke in a white flurry of foam along Middle River's long sandy beach. At its eastern end, the river struggled to break into the sea, a sandbar blocking its passage and usually prevailing until the winter rains forced it to give way.

Monty Baldwin was standing on the front veranda looking toward the beach, watching for Cassie while taking in the view that had always inspired him. His great grandfather, Harry Baldwin had left England with his young Welsh bride 150 years earlier. When he set out to sail around the island he got as far as Middle River. He rushed back to Kingscote and enquired about the availability of land at Middle River. Monty was standing on the land that was the very start of the Baldwin family's property acquisitions and subsequent agricultural business success.

As the sun's reflection danced off the surface of a flat sea, Monty shaded his eyes to watch Cassie ride over the brow of the homestead paddock. He smiled and noted her saddle posture, upright, elegant and textbook perfect. "Kristina taught her the basics," would be his common refrain when someone remarked on what an accomplished rider his daughter had become.

"Cassie!" he called. "Hurry it along, there's a good girl, it's time to get cracking. You know how the pastor hates late arrivals interrupting the service."

"Be there in a jiffy, Daddy. Quick shower and I'll be ready." She tapped Winston with her spurs and trotted off in the direction of the stockyards and the stables.

Monty watched her ride by, pensive, contemplating the coming departure of his daughter for Sydney. Cassie had always been the closest of his three children. Even when she was little more than six months old, he would take her in the Ute on his daily inspection of the farm, holding her in the crook of his burley left arm while she pointed, wide-eyed and giggling, at the sheep running away from the path of the intruders. When Kristina died in the plane crash, Cassie was only six-years-old. She became Monty's anchor and he credited her with saving him from a growing dependency on alcohol for relief from the pain of his loss. He considered Kristina his soul mate, a partner he could not imagine living without. He smiled, as he watched his now grown daughter turn into the stables, and his heart swelled with pride; she had done well in all she took on: a very good horsewoman, a talented dancer and above all she had the heart and chutzpah of her mother. *Kristina would be proud.* He turned and looked back to the beach.

Nearly fifteen years had passed since Kristina, in the prime of her life, had been killed, taking off from the property airstrip in the Baldwin's Cessna. A mother of two boys and a daughter, full of energy, in love with all of her family and happy, she was living in her own words, "A blessed life." Monty stared at the beach on which he and his wife had made love, on that same brilliant white sand, a vivid contrast to a perfect body; smooth, dark skin endowed with the beautifully sculptured contours of a Venus. He had explored every part of her, every minute cell and blemish, and there was nothing of her he did not love passionately. She was his life.

He had watched the Cessna gather speed as it raced down the gravel airstrip, begin to lift off and then suddenly plunge nose first into the ground and explode. Kristina's body, thrown meters from the wreck, lay writhing in the agony of a terrible, flaming disintegration. Monty, eyes wide and wild, ran desperately through the green carpet of lush spring grass. He reached her, breathless. "Kristina! Kristina! No! No!" he cried. The stunning brown eyes widened in a moment of recognition and then locked into an opaque stare. His hands became small, ineffective paddles, helplessly beating, beating, beating at the flames. Her flesh bubbled, blistered, and melted into raw, red tissue. The flames burned his hands and blistered his face. His urge was to tear the skin from his body, to wrap it around her and smother the flames with his love. Mercifully, in moments, she was gone. Sobbing, he turned to see Cassie, tears streaming down her cheeks, bewildered and transfixed by the horror.

It had been tough enough for Monty when Cassie had gone off to Adelaide to attend college and ballet school, but now, she was leaving home to take up the career path and life her mother had set her on. He walked back to the house and into the living room to where a cup of tea languished next to his favourite recliner. He sat down and lifted the cup to his lips, sipping at the warm liquid, holding it in his mouth for a moment or two before swallowing, feeling the warmth of its journey where it finally settled in his stomach. Raising his cup to the life size painting of Kristina that hung on the feature wall built from river rock, floor to ceiling on the right of the fireplace, he whispered reverently, "To our Cassie's success, my Love."

Minutes later, Cassie breezed into the room towel drying her wet hair as she crossed to the mirror set on the mantelpiece above the fireplace, a huge stone construction that took up a good third of the sitting room's south wall. She let the towel fall over her shoulders and began brushing her hair into a pony tail.

As Monty watched, he saw in her the same mannerisms of his wife, the posture, her long, arched back, shoulders held square and upright, her prominent and finely toned behind, her knee-length brown skirt that fell smoothly from her narrow waist, and from which her bare legs and gracefully developed calves emerged; she was the mirror image of her mother.

Honouring Kristina's wish that Cassie developed her prodigious dance talent, Monty sent her to train at the best schools in Adelaide. Their recent flight to Sydney and her successful audition for a place with the Australasian Modern Dance Company was a mix of joy and sadness for him. He sighed and sipped the last of his tea.

"I'll miss you."

"I'll miss you, and all of this," she replied, smiling and whirling around with her arms outstretched. She pirouetted to his chair and kissed him lightly on the cheek. "Where's Jordan, Daddy?"

"He's going to follow us on his motorbike. He got into some trouble last night, so I don't want you to get upset when you see him. He looks a little worse for wear."

"Not again!" She walked back to the mirror and tied back her hair. "We're going to have to do something about his drinking before he kills himself, or someone else." As she ran the brush through her pony tail, she could see Monty's reflection in the mirror and was taken aback by the sudden realization of how much he had aged. She considered her reflection, angry. Since the *incident*, Jordan had been a constant cause of pain and trouble for the family. His drinking had worsened to the point that Monty was planning a family intervention before Cassie left for Sydney, but Grant, her older brother, was in Europe on business for his law firm, so Monty had decided to wait for Grant's return.

"When the hell is he going to grow up? It's not fair on you. I'm going to have a few words with him, Daddy. This bloody crap has to stop."

Cassie had just finished speaking when Jordan limped into the room; a large cut was evident above his left eye. Tall and slender, the twenty-four-year man would be described as pretty rather than handsome were it not for the grotesque scar carving its way from the corner of his right eye to the corner of his mouth, the result of the *incident*. The family still referred to the event as the *incident*, even though his near-death was the result of a stupid choice made two years earlier. The angry red crevice of the scar was made more distinct by the paleness of his skin. He had not inherited his mother's olive complexion, but the colour and texture of the skin of a British aristocrat. His mouth, unfortunately, was fixed in a permanent sneer, a feature discouraging advances from even those who might be inclined to offer him friendship.

"Talking about me, I suppose. Nothing good to say, of course," he charged.

"Oh, for goodness sake, Jordan, give me a break," Cassie said, looking at him in the mirror while continuing to brush her hair. "Stop feeling sorry for yourself. It's about time you grew up and made something of your life. That stunt you pulled was two years ago. There's still a lot you can do."

Jordan ignored her scolding. "I suppose you're preening yourself for the Ryan kid. It's about time you woke up to the fact that the Ryan family is in no way the sort of people you ought to be getting involved with. Matt Ryan has a reputation with the ladies, and rumour has it that he has quite an investment in some rather sordid goings-on. I told him the next time I see him with you, I'll beat the living daylights out of him."

Cassie whirled around, planted her feet and made fists of her hands. Her dark brown eyes flashed a cold stare at Jordan, as she readied for battle.

Monty cut her short. "Enough, Cassie, enough, there's no time for this. Besides, it does no good, you know that."

Cassie looked at her father with a mix of defiance and concern. She was sadly aware that the pain and resignation in his voice reflected not only disappointment in his son, but also the disapproval of her relationship with Matthew Ryan.

# 6

The 250cc Kawasaki trial bike slid through the intersection east of the church; Matt was almost thrown from the seat when the back wheel gripped the strip of black asphalt running the length of Parndana's short main street. A few commercial buildings, constructed of corrugated iron, brick and timber, fronted each side of the road. A first-time visitor might have thought that Parndana was not much of a town, but the locals would argue there was plenty of action behind the seemingly austere facade.

Excited, he roared toward the general store where many of the parishioners were standing on the pavement, still talking, hands brushing continuously at the small, sticky bush flies trying to settle on their sweating faces. Others were already inside the general store, shopping and sheltering from the blazing sun.

A broad grin spread across his face, as he kicked down a couple of gears with a showy display of throttle control. He slid to a stop beside the Fahey family truck, from which eleven yelling kids were scrambling over the sides of the cattle crate to line up for their regular Sunday ice cream treats. Rosy Fahey was midway through the process of backing out of the truck cabin, not an easy task for her. Slowly, she lowered her generous frame through the open door and began to probe for the road with her foot. Matt's dramatic arrival scared the hell out of her, and with a howl of alarm, she crashed to the hot asphalt. Luckily, her well padded backside cushioned the fall, damaging only her dignity. Matt was shocked, but quickly recovered and then, red with embarrassment, he rushed to her aid. As he tried to lift her, she delivered a rash of invective. To his relief, members of the family crowded around, and with a mighty team effort, hauled her to her feet.

Mrs. Fahey's usually jolly face, flushed red with effort and anger, rounded on Matt. "What the heck is the matter with you Ryans? First, Sean taunts my daughter with that damn mouse, and then you scare the hell out of an old lady. You ought to know better. You'll finish up like your father. A no-hoper and a drunk..." She stopped, realizing she had gone too far. "Oh, for goodness sake, I'm sorry, Matt. I didn't mean..."

Matt was already turning away from her. Angry, humiliated and oblivious to a wry Monty Baldwin watching, he stormed into the store ignoring the store patrons gathered about in the newspaper and bakery section. He did not see Cassie look up from the pages of *Dance International*, a publication the local store's magazine section ordered especially for her. She hurried after him.

The wine and beer racks were in the back of the store. A colourful cardboard display promised good times go with a glass of South Australia's West End Bitter. For Matt, the beer would ease the churning in his gut that was fed by a fear of his unworthiness being exposed, the legacy of shame and inadequacy, a consequence of being raised by a violent and alcoholic father. Matt did not want to be a drunk. He did not want to be like his father, but just as he had once overheard his dad telling his mother that the booze was all that could shut out the voices and images of the war in his head, so it was for Matt when he tried his first drink, he was immediately imbued with a sense of well being and confidence.

"Stuff 'em all." He reached into the stacked beer, picked out a carton of the fabled brew, turned around and found himself looking into the brown eyes of his Cassie.

"Hi, Matt." For fifteen years, they had been best mates, since first and second grade at the Parndana Area School; even then their relationship was special. In their late teens their relationship began to change. She was falling in love with him. She knew he had a special talent and a beautiful, generous sensitivity, but he had been seriously wounded when his mother took her own life. Cassie did her best to build his self-esteem and encourage him with his writing. What worried her more than anything else was the way he would drink.

She reached out, took the carton and placed it back in the display stack. "You don't need this, Matt. Most people are laughing about what happened out there right now, even Mrs. Fahey. She kissed his cheek and chuckled. "You should have seen the look on your face when Mrs. Fahey plopped on her bum."

Matt studied her for a moment, and then laughed self-consciously. "Yeah, I really made a mess of it, didn't I? I was in a bit of a rush to get here after Pat told me he saw you. I didn't think that would be until this afternoon."

"Well, we weren't coming in this morning, but Daddy had some business with the pastor, something to do with Jordan. You know the story, so here I am," explained Cassie, taking his arm and guiding him back to the newspaper and cafe section.

Rosy Fahey was at the ice cream counter. "That's eleven doubles, oh, and you'd better make it two singles for Jack and me."

Matt crossed to the counter. "Mrs. Fahey, I'm sorry for scaring you out there. It was bloody stupid what I did."

The woman smiled and wrapped her arms around Matt, squeezing him tight into her large breasts. "No, Matt, it's me who needs to apologize. I was the silly one. You know, I watch the way you look after your step-mum and brothers. You're a good boy. Your mum would be proud of you." She released him. "Hello, Cassie, dear; my goodness, you two make a handsome couple."

Cassie smiled, "Thank you, Mrs. Fahey. I hope you have a wonderful day." They started toward the door. "We're still meeting this afternoon, aren't we?"

"You better believe it," said Matt, feeling much more at ease. "Hey, I'm going to bring something special for you to look at."

She squeezed his hand. "About time; I was beginning to wonder…" The roar of a motorcycle throttling down into a lower gear rattled the shop windows.

"What the bloody hell…" Matt looked outside and saw a familiar bike sliding to a stop at the curb. The rider was dressed in black leathers, black boots and a black racing helmet with a dark, reflective visor snapped shut over the rider's eyes. Matt tensed. "I don't want to be the cause any trouble here, but if he gives any lip I'll…"

"He's my brother; I'll handle him," said Cassie squeezing his arm.

Monty saw Jordan arrive and interrupted his conversation with the store clerk at the magazine stand, picked up his newspapers and crossed to his daughter and Matt. "Hello, young Ryan. You were in a heck of a hurry when you came in here, um," he said in a voice affected with an educated correctness. "Got yourself into that bit of a kerfuffle with Mrs. Fahey, um? Absolutely irresponsible to be riding like a maniac through the main street at anytime, let alone when there are kids all over the place."

"You might tell him that." Matt nodded toward the approaching Jordan.

"I think it would save a lot of trouble if you were on your way, young man. You could slip out there," Monty said pointing toward a side door.

"Oh, cut it out, Daddy. Matt will leave through the front door when he is ready, and I will leave with him."

Jordan pushed through the main door, saw Matt and Cassie and limped over to them, trouble written all over his face. "I thought I might run into you."

"Yeah, well this is your lucky day; here I am, Big Shot."

"Jordan, please don't cause a scene. Matt and I were just leaving," said Cassie.

Jordan ignored her. "You have a cheek, Ryan. I keep telling you not to hang around my sister. You don't get it, do you? I don't like you, or your family; nothing but trouble, all of you. You'd do us all a favour if you kept to your end of the island."

Matt bristled, but managed to hold in check the urge to retaliate. "Look, I want no quarrel with you. You can please yourself how you feel about my relationship with your sister, that's your problem, but," Matt's voice turns icy, "my family is another matter. You'd be smart to keep your trap shut about them. They've done you no harm." He turned his attention back to Cassie. "I'm out of here; we'll catch up later, Cassie."

He kissed her gently on the cheek, nodded to Monty, "Mr. Baldwin," and stepped around the smug and smiling Jordan.

"Smart move, Ryan," said Jordan. "And if I was you, I'd keep the hell away from my sister."

Matt shrugged his shoulders and walked out into the hot sun as his father, stepmother, and two stepbrothers pulled into the curb in the Landcruiser. Sean stepped out, looking uncertain and embarrassed, and walked toward the store. Matt understood exactly what was bothering the boy. Ryan Senior never went into the store when his account was overdue. He always sent one of the boys in for his tobacco and papers.

"I'll take care of it, Sean," said Matt, stepping in front of the boy.

"It's all right," mumbled a sullen Sean, as he went around Matt and on into the store.

Within minutes, an angry Wally Wright, the storeowner, banged through the doors and made straight for Frank's truck.

"You ought to be ashamed of yourself, Ryan, sending young Sean in to get what you haven't the guts to ask for yourself. I'm tired of you being behind with your bill, so from now on you'll get nothing here unless you pay cash." He looked at Katherine sympathetically and sighed. "I'm sorry, Mrs. Ryan, I really am, but I have a business to run and a family to take care of, too."

Matt wanted the earth to swallow him. The people standing around who heard Wally were embarrassed for Katherine and the boys. Sean ran to the truck. Cassie watched from outside the door of the store. She tried to smile and waved a 'don't worry about it' message to Matt.

Frank pushed his head out of the truck window and yelled at Wally, "I'll have your money to you by the end of next week, you wasp prick." He leaned further out of the Landcruiser, waving his fist furiously, "And, as far as I'm concerned, you can shove your store up where the sun don't…"

Abruptly, everybody's eyes were drawn upward. The air filled with the scream of a jet-turbine engine. The police helicopter from Adelaide lifted over the trees and banked to circle the town twenty meters above the ground. Matt looked up; the flushed face of Sergeant Reg Woodson stared at him through the chopper's downside door.

Frank was yelling at Sean to get in the truck; Patrick pulled him into the back seat. The raging lighthouse keeper reversed to the centre of the road, slammed the gear lever into first and roared off along the town's main street, eventually bouncing onto the gravel road at the town limits where the truck disappeared in a swirl of dust.

Matt walked quickly to Cassie. "This afternoon at three… usual place," he shouted into her ear. He gave her quick hug, ran to his bike, started the engine and chased after Frank.

A smirking Jordan joined Cassie and Monty. "At it again, are they? When are you going to learn, sis? Those Ryans are nothing but bloody trouble."

# 7

Sergeant Woodson grinned, as he watched the Ryans speeding off in the direction of the South Coast Road. "We got right up Frank's nose," he said into the microphone. "We'll catch up with them later. That's one advantage of being on this damn island, sooner or later people run out of road."

Constable Robert Dunning pressed his earphones a little tighter to his ears. Kangaroo Island was his third posting since graduating from the police academy in Adelaide four years earlier. Two weeks had passed since he was transferred from South Australia's Upper North, the land of his ancestors, where the red desert and blue sky blended into extraordinary orange ochre that went on and on way beyond the horizon.

"What have you got against Ryan?" asked Dunning.

"He's nothing but trouble. Frank thinks because he went to 'Nam' he's a hero. Alkie is what he is, and that kid, Matt; he's going the same way."

"Vietnam did a lot of blokes in, boss, doesn't hurt to cut them some slack."

"Bleeding hearts don't do well on my team, Constable Dunning." Woodson turned to the pilot. "Head for Middle River, Sergeant, we'll get to the Ryans at the lighthouse later, that's where they're going, home. I want to check on what boats are out along the North Coast first; Marino's got to be around the bloody island somewhere."

As the chopper thundered over the rolling landscape, Dunning, sitting behind Woodson in the front seat next to the pilot, felt uneasy. Sergeant Woodson, he observed, probably reaching into his early 50s, was a short, stocky fella with an expanding paunch that pushed at the mid-section of his blue uniform shirt. The rolled-up sleeves exposed thick, muscular arms extending to the largest and thickest hands Dunning had ever laid eyes on, and his neck was short and thick as a tree trunk. Set close together in the heavy, jowly face, two beady black eyes revealed nothing remarkably intelligible except for the chilling stare, the eyes of a cobra, cold and deadly. Tough old bastard, Dunning thought.

A few minutes later, the helicopter was circling over Middle River and the Baldwin homestead. The enormous house was at the forefront of a complex of several other buildings. A long, narrow shed of iron and steel took up almost the entire back area of the homestead paddock. A six-stand shearing shed, stockyards and stables stretched to the west, while on the eastern side, a cluster of silos for grain and feed storage completed the homestead complex.

"That's where the 'Island Baron' lives," said Woodson into his microphone. "He's head of one of the wealthiest grazing families in South Australia. You'd do well to stay on the right side of boss-man Monty Baldwin. He holds a lot of sway with the big boys in Adelaide."

Dunning nodded and his mind flashed back to an ugly encounter with Jordan Baldwin who went to the same college in Adelaide. While Jordan exuded all the airs of the privileged class, Dunning had come from very humble beginnings. His father was a blue-collar bloke from the north of South

Australia where he worked in the Leigh Creek coalmines. He married a mixed-blood Aboriginal girl from the Port Augusta mission despite contrary advice of family and friends. Robert's birth was the crowning event of their love. While his facial features were most like those of his father, the mix of his mother's dark colour with the white skin of his dad blessed him with a skin tone of an exotic light chocolate.

Harry Dunning decided the day his son was born that he was going to get a good education, and Harry worked overtime regularly to earn the money to make it happen. Happily, the talented kid responded to Harry's guidance and disciplined regime. Opportunity came through their combined efforts and he was awarded a scholarship to attend Kings College, a prestigious Presbyterian boarding school in Adelaide. He did well, and Harry was the proudest parent in 'the Creek.' Unfortunately, the hard mining life took its toll, and he developed lung disease from the coal dust, forcing him into early retirement. Although travelling was hard on him, and Leigh Creek was 400 kilometres north of Adelaide, he still made it to important college events.

It was the biggest college game of the year for Kings, an Aussie Rules football match-up with their archrival, Rostrevor College, an all-male Catholic boarding school run by the Christian Brothers. Dunning was easily the best 'footy' player on the King's team. He was fast, courageous and spectacular, and for the first time in eight years Kings had a chance to win, just one point behind the Catholic champions with a minute left to the final siren. On the run and clear of his opponent, he was in good position to receive the ball from a pass by Jordan and win the game. He was running toward the bleachers where his father was standing with his mother, cheering wildly, when he saw Harry stiffen and fall to the ground. The ball hit Dunning on the chest and bounced into the arms of an opponent. They lost the game by the one measly point, a rare and historic opportunity, gone.

As it turned out, his father was okay; his diseased lungs were the problem. Too much excitement, not enough oxygen and he had blacked out.

When Dunning finally made it to the dressing room, a furious Jordan was waiting. "So what the hell happened, mate," he said, jabbing his finger into Bob's chest. "Go walkabout, did we? Part of the tribe mentality, hey?"

"Let it go, Jordan," said team captain 'Chesty' Barnes. "His dad took a turn. We'll have another go next year."

"A pox on next year," yelled Jordan. "We had it in the palm of our hand, and this darky let it all go down the gurgler."

What happened next was so quick that nobody had the chance to intervene. 'Darky' was a word Dunning had heard many times before, a derogatory term used to insult aboriginals. Normally, he didn't react much, but this time, Dunning took the insult as a slur on his mother.

Before Jordan knew what hit him, he was on the floor nursing a bloody nose. Chesty was holding Dunning back as Jordan struggled to his feet and slammed a cowardly blow to his enemy's stomach. All hell broke loose and by the time they were pulled apart, both boys were a bloody mess. Dunning was called before the school principal. Monty Baldwin, always politically astute, put in a good word and saved him from being expelled.

The helicopter straightened and headed toward the sea. "He's got a real stunner for a daughter," said Woodson, "Reckon if you play your cards right, you might do well for yourself, young Bob. Nice farm to go along with plenty of fun in the hay, eh?" The more the young constable got to know the sergeant, the more he…

"Here we go," barked Woodson into Dunning's earphones. The chopper dropped sharply under the brow of the cliff line. Dunning's stomach lifted to his mouth and then settled when the pilot levelled out at a good 120 kilometres-per-hour at 100 meters above the water. As they charged west along the north coast, Woodson looked for boats or signs of suspicious activity among the many caves weathered into the cliffs. Some minutes later, the aircraft banked sharply and swept into Snug Cove, the last haven for small boats and fishing cutters before the exposed north-western corner of the island gave way to the vastness and peril of the southern ocean. The cove was more than 500 meters across, but its narrow neck was a perfect barrier for protecting and sheltering craft from rough seas. Three boats were quietly at anchor in the calm, crystal-clear water, the shadows of their hulls prominent on the white, sandy bottom, menacing, eerily reminiscent of the great white sharks that frequented the waters around Kangaroo Island.

Woodson howled with delight, as he pointed toward one of the fishing cutters. In the same moment Dunning recognized it, too. The rugged hull of the sturdy boat rose to a narrow point at the bow where a little below the gunwale, painted in large black letters, was the ship's name, *Smokey Cloud*.

# 8

Landing a helicopter on the Snug Cove beach was difficult and dangerous, but the pilot, giving way to Woodson's direct orders, managed to settle the craft on the widest strip of sand available without burying the main rotor blades into the sand dunes lining the beach just meters from the water's edge.

As the noise from the turbine faded, Dunning unclipped his seat belt, opened the door and almost toppled into the water lapping the helicopter's offside landing skid. Woodson exited on the sand dune side and, clutching a megaphone in one hand, scurried around the front of the aircraft waving furiously at *Smokey Cloud*. Sergeant Woodson, the warrior, did not notice the water splashing over his polished brown shoes. He was ready for war.

"*Smokey Cloud*, stand to. This is Sergeant Reg Woodson of the South Australian police!" he yelled through the megaphone. "We are to board your vessel; send your dinghy to pick us up immediately."

Three men standing together at the rail of *Smokey Cloud* looked toward the beach.

"*Smokey Cloud*, I am ordering you to send us your dinghy," bellowed Woodson.

Dunning watched as the men split up. One moved to the bow and began raising the ship's anchor, while the other two disappeared into the wheelhouse.

"You know what, boss," yelled Dunning. "They're going to bolt for it."

"Get the ducky, Constable," yelled the sergeant, taking his mouth away from the megaphone for an instant. "Stand to, *Smokey Cloud*. I am warning you; do not run!"

Dunning dragged a tightly bound rubber package from the cargo door of the helicopter to the beach and quickly snapped open the restraining straps. A quick turn of the tap on the compressed-air cylinder screwed to the wood bottom of the package and connected to an inflation teat, in seconds, transformed the package into a rubber dinghy big enough for two people.

Black smoke billowed from *Smokey Cloud's* engine exhaust. "Come on, come on, get a move on, Dunning," yelled a frantic Woodson. "They're getting away."

Dunning turned back to the chopper and snatched the small outboard from the cargo space. Spinning around, he dropped to one knee and slammed the motor onto the rear mounting plate, pushed the dinghy into the water, jumped into the stern seat and began pulling the outboard's starter cord. The tiny motor coughed, spluttered a few times and then settled into a routine idle. Light blue puffs of smoke from the exhaust drifted across the cove while Woodson splashed through knee-deep water, rolled over the gunwale and fell into the rubber boat, almost swamping his tiny warship before it had travelled a meter.

"Let's go," the pumped up Woodson shouted, and then settled into a kneeling position facing forward, hanging onto the rope attached to the bow. "Give it to her, Bobby boy, give it to her! Try to run from me, you bastards!"

Even Dunning was beginning to feel the thrill of the challenge. A smile began to spread across his face, as the comedy of their situation, the tiny vessel almost bereft of freeboard, putt-putt-putting over the water at a mere four knots, approaching a vessel beginning to assume the proportions of a battleship, struck him as insane.

The two policemen closed to within twenty meters of *Smokey Cloud*. The man on the bow ran back to the wheelhouse. Another huge black cloud of diesel exhaust plumed into the hot afternoon air. Below her stern, the propeller began thrashing the water and *Smokey Cloud* slowly moved forward headed for the open ocean and away from the closing ducky.

Dunning was aware of the wash of boiling water rolling their way. Woodson, too, could see the looming danger and frantically signalled his constable to turn away, but Dunning was reluctant to swing the tiny craft broadside to the wash, fearing they would roll over. Woodson jerked crazily on the bow rope, trying to pull the nose around.

"For God's sake, Dunning, turn this bloody boat around before we finish up fish bait!"

He had barely finished the sentence when the wash hit them, swamping the dinghy and leaving the two men sitting in the flooded vessel, the water up to their waists. Luckily, in part due to Dunning's quick thinking, throttling back and keeping a straight course, the inflatable did not turn over and dump them into the deep water. Their sodden clothing would have taken them straight to the bottom. Nevertheless, with their boat now 170 meters from shore, heavily waterlogged, and as Dunning quietly noted, a receding tide taking them toward the open sea, they were in serious trouble.

The thought of great white sharks, frequent visitors to the cove at that time of the year, sent a shiver along his spine. *Why the hell didn't we just take the helicopter?* he thought, looking derisively at the back of Woodson's bald head.

"We'll have to swim for it, boss," shouted Dunning, as he gingerly attempted to remove his clothing, trying not to upset their distressed vessel.

Woodson stared toward the beach to where the helicopter pilot was waving frantically and pointing at something close to the shoreline. "Good God!" yelled Woodson, shading his eyes and pointing as he pushed back into the ducky's centre almost causing it to capsize.

Dunning sucked in a lungful of air as he turned and saw the large, dark shape cruising slowly along the sandy bottom between them and the beach. "We're in a bit of strife, Sergeant."

With their attention fixed on the shadow, both men were unaware that *Smokey Cloud* had stopped, or that the cutter's dinghy was being let down over the side. Nor did they see two of the crew jump easily into the small boat, start the outboard and close to within a few meters of the policemen's ducky before Woodson saw them.

"You wanna tow to the beach, Mister Woodson?" called a heavily accented voice. A short, burly man with a heavy dark beard and bushy eyebrows, under which peered two black eyes over a mouth creased into a into a grim smile.

"You're not so smart, Sammy," snarled a very nervous Woodson. "You're going to spend a night or two in the slammer after I get my hands on you. I told you to heave to, and you disobeyed a lawful order."

"I never understanda a word you say, Mister Woodson, I thought you were giving us a friendly wave. You getta a little wet," taunted Sammy Marino, the fishing cutter's jaunty skipper. "Now, do you want I shoulda bring you in, or do you wanna to do it yourself?" he asked, nodding in the direction of the black shadow cruising along the sandy bottom.

Dunning was quick to reply, "Mr. Marino, we will be forever indebted for your kindness. Now get us the hell out of here, will you?"

"Ah, you are a man of respect, Constable. You mussa be the new one. I have only just heard of you. Robert Dunning, eh? I am Captain Samuel Marino, the best of alla fishermen in the Southern Ocean."

"Yeah, you go fishing, all right," responded a sarcastic Woodson. "You got away with it this time, Marino, but look out. I've been on your coat tails a long time. I'll get your lousy hide eventually and nail it to the bloody jail wall."

Sammy laughed while his crewman threw a line to Dunning, and then turned for the beach, pulling the ducky with them. Dunning's heart started to beat a little faster when it became obvious that their route was going to take them over the path of the cruising shadow.

"Watch out for the fish," yelled Dunning, his voice beginning to crack as he watched the shadow turn at the end of the beach and head back towards their crawling caravan. Sammy did not respond, and Woodson, still sitting at the front of the drowning inflatable, began to panic as he realized, too, that they were going to intersect with the shadow before they got to the sand.

"For God's sake, Marino, do something," shouted Woodson, as the shadow closed on the ducky. He tried once again to back away from the front of the boat, but this time he upset the balance, and he and Dunning were dumped into the water.

The shadow immediately streaked toward the open sea. Sammy and his crewman broke into gales of laughter, as the sputtering policemen scrambled the last few meters to the beach.

"Hey, Reggie, you just frightened a biga stingray, babee. He won't hurt you unless you stepa on him, you know," Sammy shouted through his laughter. He stood up in the bow of his dinghy a few meters from the beach and studied the two soaked men. His face tightened, and his black eyes fixed on the sergeant.

"Mr. Woodson, you are welcome to comma on my boat as a guest, but don't ever try to order me around or board me with outa invitation or a warrant. This is bloody Australia, mate, a free country with a bloody law for everyone, meaning you, too. Until, maybe, we meeta again; arrivederci!"

He extended a salute, which could have been broadly interpreted as "giving the finger," turned and sat in the bow of his boat. His crewman opened the throttle of the outboard and, with a cloud of blue smoke trailing on the top of the water, aimed for the *Smokey Cloud*.

Dunning stared after the boat for a few seconds. He had heard stories about Sammy's generosity: funding for kids programs, buildings for recreation, and he was a hell of a big donor to the Catholic Church. Despite knowing Sammy was under investigation for alleged offenses against the crown, Dunning chuckled; he liked the man and was somewhat amused at how the Southern Ocean's self-proclaimed greatest fisherman got under his sergeant's skin.

They stripped to their underwear while the pilot packed and loaded the inflatable into the chopper. Woodson, brooding and angry, threw one of two blankets to Dunning. "Put this around you," he said, as he wrapped himself in the other. "Fill out a report on the incident when we get back to Kingscote and file a property loss form for the megaphone. And, I want a warrant issued for the arrest of Marino charging him with obstructing police officers in the course of their duty."

"C'mon, boss, he just saved our necks."

"He's lucky I'm not charging him with attempted murder. I want that paper on my desk first thing in the morning, Constable. Okay, let's get out of here." They climbed into the helicopter and Woodson mumbled instructions to the pilot. Dunning made out a few words, West Bay and the du Couedic Lighthouse.

The roar of the turbine eventually drowned out the whine of the starter motor. Abruptly, in a mix of swirling sand and flying spray, the helicopter lifted off the beach. As they climbed over the bay and above the cliffs, *Smokey Cloud* was already well out to sea and set on a course to the north-east. Dunning knew that inevitability there would be a showdown between Woodson and Marino. What troubled him, as he looked at the little cutter getting smaller and smaller on the growing expanse of ocean, was the uneasiness he felt in the pit of his stomach; *Smokey Cloud* and her skipper, Sam Marino, were set on a course that could only end in a disaster.

# 9

A trail of dust hung behind the speeding Landcruiser, as it bumped and rattled along the South Coast Road. Matt, arms aching from the tension of his tight grip on the handlebars, was far enough behind to avoid the worst of the flying gravel kicked up by the family truck. Despite having ridden on the treacherous ironstone surface countless times, keeping the speeding bike upright was little more than one slight over correction away from disaster.

Minutes later, the two vehicle convoy was clattering over the cattle grid entrance into the Flinders Chase National Park. Spreading from the north coast to the south coast on the west end of the island, Flinders Chase and its neighbouring parks were home to an amazing diversity of native animals: kangaroos, wallabies, wild goats, wild pigs, cuddly koalas, spiky echidnas, cute platypus, various reptiles, including the deadly black tiger snake, and the rare Cape Barren geese. Thousands of small, colourful birds darted in and about the trees, enlivening the landscape with myriad twittering and melodic song. Disturbed by the rushing vehicles, black cockatoos and the smaller red-breasted galahs screeched noisily, as they lifted from the tall gum trees. Crows, cunning and vulgar, their raucous squawking obnoxious, scavengers that would pick out the eyes from newborn lambs, searched the road for any reptile, wallaby or possum left dead or broken in the wake of Frank's desperate bid to beat Woodson to the lighthouse.

Hundreds of wildflower species flourished throughout the rugged landscape: purples, pinks, whites, yellows, blues, and greens added spectacular texture to the thick carpet of low scrubby brush. Leafy crowns of soaring white gum trees growing along creek beds snaked through the rolling topography, ending abruptly where the island coast held back the Southern Ocean. Precariously, dopey koalas dozed in the forks of towering gums for most of the day, as their unique digestive system slowly broke down the toxic eucalyptus leaves, their staple food source.

The Ryans passed by the ranger's cottage, the tourist centre and its ancillary structures, and then turned sharp left toward the southwest corner of the Chase and Cape du Couedic. As they topped the plateau, Matt slowed. A broad vista of trees and scrub dropped away ahead of him, and through its centre a ribbon of road snaked all the way to a blue sea. Barely visible, the astonishing "Remarkable Rocks" balanced precariously on their granite base, teasing spectators to ponder their permanence. To the west of the "Rocks," where the road disappeared into the ocean, stood the formidable Cape du Couedic Lighthouse, guardian of the many ships that passed by the island's southwest corner.

Matt stopped and watched the Landcruiser thread its way toward the cluster of buildings preceding the lighthouse, their home. He drew in a deep breath of the scented air, held it a moment to let the eucalyptus clear his head and then sighed. He realized how strong his connection to Kangaroo Island was, and he was going miss what would always be the place he called home, if he went to Sydney. He watched an echidna waddle and swagger from a yucca bush growing by the road. The spiny anteater became aware of him and hurriedly scratched into the sandy loam to protect its soft underbelly. Matt smiled and turned back to the stunning view.

He had moved with his father to the lighthouse after his mother's suicide. Frank lost his north coast farm: low commodity prices, tough seasons, the bankruptcy and, yeah, the alcohol was probably the biggest factor. Because the farm was part of the "Returned Soldier's Land Settlement Scheme", the Returned Servicemen's League made representations to the government minister in charge of the scheme for consideration of a special circumstance, a family tragedy, to allow Frank a reprieve, an opportunity to keep his land. Instead, he was offered a job by the federal government to manage the lighthouse at Cape du Couedic. It was probably for the best in the end—a government job with regular pay and retirement benefits.

Frank managed to get off the booze for a couple of years, dry knuckled it through the period of withdrawal. He met Katherine Roden, a nurse at the local district hospital in Kingscote. She was a highly regarded professional and well liked by the islanders. They found it hard to believe when she started to go out with Frank, the alkie. Still, eventually, they were fooled and so was she that Frank had overcome his drinking problem for good, so she married him; after all, he was a good-looking bloke and could be quite the charmer. Patrick came along and things seemed to be going pretty well, but it did not last. How could it? Frank had the disease; he was an alcoholic. Soon after Sean's birth, the old curse and its demons   returned to haunt him, and he was on the booze again.

Matt watched the prickly animal warily resume its journey toward the safety of the scrub. Satisfied, he re-started the bike and turned onto a barely discernible hiking trail that branched off from the gravel road and headed northwest. He pushed along, as quick as he dared, dodging overhead branches of low lying brush until, 10 minutes later he came to the top of a cliff 150 meters above the ocean and stopped. Ahead of him and to the south was the massive Southern Ocean; glassy conditions prevailed and made for a perfect day of diving on any one of the many wrecks that had founded on the dangerous coast surrounding the island. He thought of his last dive on the wreck of the *Portland Maru*, a Japanese grain ship driven onto the rocks along the North Coast during a deadly storm forty years earlier. In 20 meters of water he had been half way down to the broken wreck when he saw the Great White circling; he made it back to the boat topside and had not dived there again since.

A flash of light from the north caught his attention; a helicopter appeared to be circling West Bay. He knew it had to be Woodson probably taking advantage of the unusually calm water to spot the *Vennachar*. The *Loch Vennachar*, a 1550 ton three-masted iron clad sailing clipper, reported to be carrying gold bullion, foundered with the loss of all hands during a fierce storm in September, 1906. If there was gold, it had never been found.

Matt pushed on along the cliff line south toward the lighthouse, as fast as was safe, before turning into the scrub where the track descended steeply to a creek running through the middle of a one hectare basin. Massive gum trees, well spaced, formed a leafy canopy overhead. Even on close inspection from the air, the basin floor was hard to see. In its midst, off to the side of the creek, a small humpy was well camouflaged with bulloak bush and gum bark blending in with the natural colours of the forest floor. When he shut down the bike's engine the only sounds were the soothing murmur of rustling leaves. But not for long; in the distance he caught the sound of the faint whoop-whoop-whooping of helicopter blades coming his way, the noise growing louder by the second.

He scrambled into the humpy and took the bike with him.

# 10

Looking out through the front canopy of the helicopter, Dunning was able make out the desolate form of the Cape du Couedic Lighthouse that rose from the barren south-western corner of the island 15 kilometres ahead. As they flew a few meters above the cliff line, and while his keen eyes continued to search each side of the aircraft, he reflected on the flight from Snug Cove.

After leaving the cove, they had flown along the north coast, tracking west. Dunning was thrilled by the aerial view, the towering cliffs dropping sheer into an unusually calm sea, and the wild goats exposed on the steep inclines, feeding on the natural grasses of the coastal hills, scattering as the helicopter thundered overhead. They had landed at the Cape Borda Lighthouse, a neat, square, white structure built to protect all manner of seafarers passing the north-western corner of the island. The lighthouse keeper's wife had dried their clothes and served them afternoon tea. They took off again and flew west. Dunning noticed that even on the calmest of days, an occasional boomer, a monster wave, "a rogue," would appear from nowhere, hidden among the mild swells rolling in from the southwest. They were the waves the rock fishermen had to watch out for; many a life had been lost to the sudden appearance of a towering rogue.

At West Bay, they hovered low over the water, drifting back and forth across its width. Woodson told him the *Loch*

*Vennachar* story as he searched the rocky bottom, looking for signs of the wreck, but the incident at Snug Cove had cost them the best viewing time. "Supposed to be gold on it," he said. "None has ever been found." A breeze from the west had already picked up, rippling the surface and making it impossible to see the bottom clearly.

Woodson, still angry from his unsuccessful encounter with Marino, complained that it was very rare to get a day calm enough to see the bottom at West Bay; only one or two came along in any one year. He was even more pissed off by the time they had left the bay; he now had an extra score to settle with Sammy Marino.

The helicopter rushed on in the direction of the du Couedic lighthouse. Dunning continued to search the terrain for signs of human activity, but he saw only the tracks of wild animals. Woodson looked over his shoulder at the aboriginal policeman, this time an evil grin creased his face from ear to ear.

"We're going to have a little fun here, Constable. We'll drop under the level of the cliffs, scoot around the arch and fly into Weir Cove and then come up over the top of the cliff from behind the old storehouse ruins; should scare the hell out of them." He laughed and turned back to look at the ground along the top of the rugged cliffs.

Moments later, he stiffened, suddenly alert and excited. "Hold it. What the hell is that?" He pointed to a fresh track heading into the scrub. The pilot slowed the helicopter and hovered a few meters above the apparent trail. "Follow that," the sergeant ordered, pointing into the bush.

"Probably wallaby or goat trails," responded Dunning, unsure why he kept quiet about seeing the tire track. "They're all over the place."

"Looks a bit more than that to me; I've got a hunch we might be onto something," Woodson insisted. "It looks like a tire track to me, and it's heading straight into that basin."

"Well, there'd be fresh water there, boss. The wildlife has to drink somewhere."

The pilot headed the helicopter over the top of the basin.

"I can't see a thing down there. It's like a jungle. You see anything, Constable?"

"Animal tracks, water hole; nothing out of the ordinary," Dunning said. In the brush on the basin floor, his sharp eyes picked up what looked like some kind of structure, one he recognized. He knew it was a humpy. He reached forward to tap Woodson on the shoulder, but stopped. He had no idea why he decided to keep what he saw to himself; he had always been good copper keen to get the bad blokes. Perhaps, it was his growing insight into his boss's mean streak and vindictiveness. Scare the Ryans with a schoolboy prank; what was that about?

"All right, we'll have to come back in a ground vehicle and check it thoroughly. It's a perfect spot for a cultivation hide," said Woodson. He nodded to the pilot and pointed toward Cape du Couedic. "Let's go and stir up the Ryan mob."

# 11

Frank's hectic drive along the rusty ironstone road through the Chase ended abruptly when he brought the Landcruiser to a skidding stop in front of one of three stone cottages lining the road 120 meters from the lighthouse. A rough limestone track cut through low scrubby brush for another 150 meters to Admiral's Arch, an incredible structure fashioned from the limestone over thousands of years by wind and pounding waves, eventually forming a huge arch under the rough and cratered headland. On the rocks around the Admiral, hundreds of fur seals rested from their eighty-kilometre fishing sorties out into the Southern Ocean, while their younger off-spring frolicked and flirted in the restless waters around them.

To the east of the cottages a sea mist rose from the incessant breaking of huge waves on the rocks at the bottom of the rugged cliffs of Weir Cove. They curved all the way to Kirkpatrick Point where on its granite headland balanced the Remarkable Rocks, which hinted of a Stonehenge mystique in the mist shrouding its giant, craggy boulders. Even the mild breeze stirring the air seemed to suggest a lament from a Celtic pipe.

Next to the Ryan cottage set in the southwest corner of the tiny cluster of buildings, Frank slid from his seat in the truck and began barking orders. "Pat, get your bum down to the lighthouse and grab that bag of grass from under the stairs. Hide it in the stores cottage and hurry up about it, those coppers will be here soon. Sean, you come with me."

Pat scampered off to the lighthouse. Frank and Sean hurried to the cottage in the northwest corner, the storehouse. As they reach the wire gate, Frank slid back the catch, skinning the knuckles on the back of his hand. "Bugger," he swore and hurried on to the door only to find it padlocked. "Damn!"

"The truck, boy, the keys; get 'em and be bloody smart about it."

Sean scurried away, yelling to his mother who was on her way to the cottage veranda with the brown case. "Dad needs the keys, Mum!"

"They're still in the truck, Sean."

As he turned back to the truck, an ear-splitting scream shattered the stillness. Rearing vertically up and over the cliff and the old store ruins, the police helicopter roared toward the cottages. The noise from the turbine echoed off the cliff walls, scaring the life out of Katherine and Sean. She froze. Sean's heart crowded his mouth, and he reached for his mother's hand. Frank tensed; the whoop-whoop of the chopper brought flashbacks from Vietnam. He ran toward his family, angry and ready for war.

"Mongrels!" he yelled and waved his fist at the descending helicopter.

Panting heavily, he reached Katherine and Sean. Dust and small stones stirred up by the whirling blades peppered them until the chopper settled on the road between the cottages and the engine was shut down.

Woodson and Dunning climbed out and stepped onto the roadway. Sean's dog, an Australian kelpie named Barney, was connected to a wire dog run set up in the back yard of the home cottage. He was barking savagely and straining at the end of his leash, wanting to have a go at the coppers.

"Shut that bloody dog up," yelled Woodson.

"Up yours, Woodson," said Frank, fists clenched at his side. Barney bared his teeth and snarled.

"Well, well, well, same old Frank, hey? It's been a while, hasn't it? Haven't changed a bit, hey?" said Woodson, striding to where the family was standing. He slowly looked them over and then indicated Dunning with a nod. "I don't know that you have met our new constable, so let me introduce you to Constable Bob Dunning, an expert in matters related to illicit plant cultivation and smuggling. You know all about that, Frank, don't you?" He paused, posturing. "Come on, Frank, production, procurement and distribution, that sort of thing, hey?"

Dunning was surprised by his boss's threatening approach, especially with Mrs. Ryan and the young boy present. He stepped forward and offered his hand to Katherine. "Pleased to meet you, Mrs. Ryan, Mr. Ryan," he said. "And who's this young bloke here?"

"This is Sean, Constable," replied Katherine, regaining her composure. "He's the youngest of our boys."

"Yeah, that's right, and I wouldn't get too close to these kids, Constable," said the sergeant. "Like feral animals, these kids; scratch your bloody eyes out, give 'em half a chance."

"You'd be the mongrel of the year, wouldn't ya, Woodson? Come flying in here in your fancy chopper, scaring my wife and kids half to death," said the belligerent Frank, blue eyes narrowed through hostile slits. "Don't scare me none. flew 'em in Nam; heard you bailed your sorry arse out of contention to serve by pleading domestic policing crap. You're a limp prick, copper; don't scare me none at all."

Woodson reddened with anger. "Why you…"

Dunning intervened and grabbed Woodson's arm, just in time. "Easy, boss, we've got nothing on Frank, no evidence that would stand up in court."

Woodson took a breath and then smiled maliciously. "Well, Frank, things change and I'm the only game in town for you now, which brings us to the why of our visit today. The story goes that you and your eldest kid are growing weed around here and that you are a collection agent for Sam Marino and his mob in Victoria."

"Long bloody way from here; you think I walk on water?"

"Mate, we have good information about what's going on," Dunning offered in a conciliatory manner. "It's a bloody serious matter, cultivating marijuana for commercial purposes. I know, we don't worry if you have a plant or two for your own use, and we'll even look the other way if it's a few more. Look, you come clean now; we can make it a lot easier on you; we are really after the big blokes." He paused. Frank remained quiet. "For God's sake, Frank, get yourself too far into this and you'll end up in jail."

"Let me make it plain to you, Ryan," interrupted Woodson. "We have good information; if you're not hiding anything, you won't mind us taking a look around, will you?"

"You got a warrant?"

Woodson looked at Dunning.

"No, but the sergeant has a point. Why would you want to stop us?" asked Dunning.

"I'll tell you why, Constable," said Frank, his anger building. "I'll tell you this. I, along with a bunch of me mates, some of whom didn't make it back and others who are so screwed in the head they're good for nothing anymore, went to Vietnam and laid it on the line for what we thought was right. We get back here, and we have the likes of you blokes interfering in our lives, trying to enforce stupid bloody laws designed to protect the special interests of a few arse-holes. That prick, your boss, is the sort of mongrel we despise, and there's no way in the world I'd lift a finger to help, period."

Frank's argument was familiar to Dunning. His people often had to bear the prejudice of bigot coppers enforcing white men's laws that rarely respected the traditions and laws of Aboriginal culture. He felt a surprising empathy for the troubled Frank.

Woodson's reaction was predictably the reverse of Dunning's. "You're a drunk, pure and simple, Ryan. Like many of your sodden mates, the whole war thing is an excuse to opt out of taking responsibility."

Frank's eyes fixed a blank and terrible stare on the sergeant. He sucked in a deep breath, trying to stay under control, but his mind began to spin, his knees weakened, and the familiar icy breath of his demons blew through the emptiness in his gut. His mind flashed back to Vietnam.

His best mate "Wombat" Hodges was sitting in the command position atop his armoured personnel carrier. He and "Wombat" were roaring into battle side by side and the hostile fire from the enemy, well dug in on the ridge ahead, was flying all over the place. Frank looked across at his mate and gave him a thumb up and a big grin. Seconds later, Wombat's upper body disappeared in a cloud of crimson mist. Frank went berserk; with tears streaming down his cheeks, he accelerated his vehicle to full speed, charged into the enemy line and engaged in what became an orgy of lunacy and slaughter.

Dunning saw what was coming in time to grab Frank as he launched himself at the leering Woodson. "Frank, Frank!" Dunning yelled and wrapped his arms tight around the old soldier's arms. "For Christ's sake calm down or I'll have to handcuff you."

A seizure gripped Frank, and he began to topple. Katherine rushed to her husband, as Dunning lowered him to the ground. She called out to Patrick who was returning from the lighthouse after hiding the bag of grass in the scrub, "Patrick, get your dad's brandy, quick!"

Patrick knew the routine and ran into the house. He knew where the liquor was kept, in fact, he knew most of the hides where his father planted booze around the lighthouse and the cottages: in trees, under bushes, in toilet basins, stashes in and around the generator shed and even in the bedroom where there was no attempt to hide it, keeping it under the bed for when the demons came in the early morning hours.

"Here," said Katherine, grabbing the brandy from Patrick, as he ran up to her. "Frank, drink this," she ordered, holding the bottle to his lips.

Frank needed no arm-twisting, and he took the bottle in both hands. Shaking violently, he poured the dark brown miracle into his mouth. The liquid surged through him, spreading its warm glow, finally spilling into his gut and drowning the howling demons. The affect was instantaneous; his body relaxed, the shakes stopped and a silly grin spread across his face. He looked into the eyes of the young constable. "Thank you, Mr. Dunning. You, sir, are a gentleman."

"You Vietnam blokes had a hard time of it, Frank. I know a mate of..." The unmistakable high-pitched howl of a Japanese trail bike approaching from the north interrupted.

"It's Matt!" shouted an excited Sean. Matt slid the bike to a stop next to his mother. Frank, with Dunning's assistance, got to his feet.

"You all right, Dad?" Matt asked, taking in the situation, knowing.

"Yeah, I'm all right; just had a bit of a turn, that's all." Frank looked back at Woodson. "You arrived just in time to wave these blokes goodbye, Matt."

Matt struggled to keep his anger in check. "Yeah, right... um, saw the chopper landing, so I got here as quick as I could. I mean, we don't get to see a chopper landing here...err...ever, do we?"

"Where have you been, son?" asked Woodson.

"Making my way back from church, Sergeant," replied Matt politely. "I took the scenic route, same as you."

"So, you're Matt, hey? I'm Bob Dunning. I've heard a lot about you at footy training in Kingscote. They reckon you're pretty damn fancy." Dunning reached out to shake Matt's hand. "Call me Bob," he said, and they shook hands.

"Yeah, I've heard a lot about you," said Matt. "I was told that you were invited to sign with the League."

"Right, but I knocked it back because I like my job. Speaking of which, we're here on business. There's information come to us that some of you folks down this end of the island are cultivating marijuana for commercial purposes. You know anything about that?"

"Stop pussy-footing around, Constable, this young bugger

is right in the middle of it all," interjected the sergeant. "He knows damn well what the drift is on this deal."

"There you go again, Woodson," said Frank, "always having a go at putting the wood on someone, whether they've done anything against the law or not. It's about time for you to piss off!"

"Not before your kid tells us where he's been and what he's been up to," threatened Woodson. "And you keep your mouth shut, or I'll take you in for threatening a police officer."

"Calm down, boss," said Dunning. "Let me handle this." He turned to Matt. "How about you show us where you've been, Matt? We'll look around, and if there's nothing going on, we'll get on our way. Chance for a ride in the chopper, too, hey?"

"I would like to do that for you, Cons…err…Bob, but I'm already running late for a get-together with me girl."

"He's going out with that nice young Baldwin girl, Mr. Dunning," Katherine offered. "You know the family from over at Middle River?"

Dunning nodded. "Yes, Mrs. Ryan, I know of them."

"I can take you out there sometime next week." Matt checked his watch. "Yeah, well I'm out of here, or I'm going to be late."

"All right, Matt, I'll be out here first thing tomorrow, how will that work for you?" said Dunning.

"Okay, I suppose; see ya then, hey?" Matt propped his bike against the fence and hurried off into the cottage to change his clothes.

Sergeant Woodson stared at Dunning. "That's about the dumbest deal I've heard in a long time, Constable. The kid will have everything cleaned out by the time you get out here tomorrow."

Dunning ignored his boss and turned to Katherine. "Sorry about all this, Mrs. Ryan, but we have a job to do. Will you and the boys be okay?"

Katherine nodded. "Of course, Frank's really a good man, you know."

Woodson shook his head in disgust, turned and walked back to the helicopter. Barney snarled.

"Frank, it's none of my business, but I've heard a few mentions about your fondness for the grog and how rough that is on your family. If you want help, I've know a few blokes who have whipped their addiction. Frank eyed the young constable warily. The helicopter's motor began to whine and the blades began to slowly rotate. "Think about it, hey?" Dunning shook hands and ran to chopper.

For the second time in the day, Dunning wrestled with a growing premonition of disaster, as he looked down on the Ryans staring up at the departing aircraft.

# 12

Matt glanced at his watch. It was two-thirty and another twenty minutes of hard riding to go before he reached the turn onto the track into Cape Kersaint. The fierce afternoon sun had the temperature soaring toward 35 degrees Celsius, 95 degrees in the old Fahrenheit measure, unusually hot for Kangaroo Island, but the air rushing over his body was some relief. His thoughts turned to the earlier events of the day.

The encounter with Woodson was a close call, and Matt was aware that the mongrel copper would not let up until he had them in jail. It was a good thing Dunning was there. He seemed like a good bloke, but as his Oldman had said to him many times, you could never trust a copper.

The bike hit a patch of bull dust, and Matt's thoughts flipped to survival. The dramatic cut in speed lifted his backside off the seat and almost threw him over the handlebars. A few heart stopping moments later, he regained control and slowed to a safer speed.

Matt had lived through many tough times with Frank. He took his share of hidings. It was the beatings that he witnessed his mother getting that made him hate his father and then caused him confusion when he felt a natural love for him. It was only a year ago that Frank had punched Katherine in the face in the kitchen. Matt was there, and he launched into the drunk. After a long and brutal fight, Frank finally got the best of Matt. But, from then on Frank seemed to have grown a healthy respect for his son, and he was more careful about throwing his weight around. Katherine took the two younger boys and stayed away for a week in Kingscote until a remorseful Frank showed up and begged her to come home to the lighthouse. He had not laid a finger on her since, but when Frank was on the booze the threat was always there.

Cassie wanted Matt to live with her in Sydney, but he was reluctant to leave Katherine and the boys while Frank's drinking was getting worse. He worried that when Cassie got to Sydney, she would eventually forget about him. After all, she would be in a world of privilege where glamorous choices would be hers for the choosing. His deepest fear, though, was that he was no match for the Sydney 'posers', the pricks in tights she would work with who would be all over her. "The bastards!" he shouted into the wind.

The bike kicked sideways in a rut of gravel. "Stuff it!" he yelled, opened the throttle and roared on down the road, frustrated and angry.

A kilometre on, he slowed to turn off the South Coast Road and onto the Cape Kersaint access trail. He stopped at the boundary gate, which was closed and had a sign hanging in the middle with a warning, 'Private Property-Keep Out'. He saw the familiar and fresh truck tracks in the sandy loam, a signal that Cassie had passed through and was probably already at the beach. And, there was the fresh track of a motorbike heading into the property. *Why the hell would he be here?*

Matt was soon speeding along the narrow track running next to the boundary fence, separating the scrub from a paddock of mustard yellow stubble, the straw debris from a harvested barley crop belonging to the Baldwins. Ahead, a shearing shed, stockyards and a small stone cottage were clustered in the corner of the next paddock. He roared through the open gates of the stockyards. Jordan's black motorcycle was leaning against the wall of the cottage.

The ridge ahead was covered by low dense scrub, broken only by glimpses of creamy, white limestone, identical to the landscape surrounding the lighthouse. The track deteriorated into a rough, barely discernible impression on the ground. He scrambled over the outcrops of crumbling limestone and the exposed black roots of mallee trees, working the throttle furiously, trying to avoid the branches that occasionally slapped his face and scratched his bare arms and legs. From the top of the main ridge a rugged carpet of rolling green scrub spread out ahead, split through the middle by the faint line of the track winding all the way to the blue of the Southern Ocean 10 minutes ahead. Excitement mixed with apprehension, as he pictured Cassie waiting on the beach.

Finally, he arrived at the top of a sand-dune overlooking the Cape Kersaint Beach, fifteen meters below, and pulled up next to Cassie's truck. Shading his eyes from the sun, he saw the lone figure lying face down on a towel near the water's edge. She raised her head and waved. *Bloody psychic, I swear to God.* He grinned and waved back, quickly changed into his swimming trunks, ran, rolled and slid down the sand dune, finishing with a sprint across the beach to splash spectacularly into the surf.

Cassie watched. *Hmm; the Sydney ladies will like you.* She thought about that scenario for a minute. *Bitches better not try to...*

His tan body cooled, Matt splashed out of the water, jogged over to Cassie and kissed her lightly on the lips.

"You are such a hunk."

"I am? Yeah, that's right, thanks, mate. You're looking a bit of all right yourself, hey?" He dropped on to the towel laid out next to her. "Sorry I'm late. That helicopter dropped in at the lighthouse. Dad got all bent out of shape as usual. Katherine and the boys…well, it was pretty awful. I wish she would take the boys and get the hell out of there." He looked out across the 3,500 kilometres of wild water that extended all the way to the ice of Antarctica.

"Everything will work out, Matt. I know you worry. You saw some terrible stuff, but Katherine is a good mother, and she'll do what's right by her boys. After all, she knows what happened to your mum when she stuck around your dad for too long. Maybe, when you come to Sydney that will shake him up a bit; he's not a bad man."

"Yeah, but he can't do without the grog."

"You have to think about your life, too, mate. My mother used to tell me life is a precious gift that rushes by too fast, and it is up to me to take hold of it, to make the most of every moment. Mummy died in her prime, but she crowded a lot into her short life and, by God, she made most of her moments."

"Yeah, I remember your mum when she first came to the school. Mother said she was special, the best teacher she ever knew and a wonderful dancer; both mums made their mark, hey? Strange how they died about the same time; what the hell was that about?" His voice was soft, tinged with sadness. "Bloody waste, hey?"

Cassie was quiet. Matt was aware of the sound of the surf: the warmth of the sun, the colour of native wildflowers emerging from the green brush skirting the brow of the sand dunes around the curve of the beach, and the waves tumbling onto the white sand, receding and leaving wet, shiny patches for a few seconds before vanishing. *Life.*

"Growing up here is a hell of a gift, Cassie. I want to write about all this someday," he said, his arm sweeping a wide arc over the beach.

"Yes, well, you make sure you get all the paperwork in," she replied, cupping her head in her hand, as she delighted in the sensuality of curling her toes in the warm sand. "The monsignor is going to a lot of trouble for you."

"God, you're beautiful." He gently ran his finger over the fullness of her lips and then looked into her eyes. "I love you," he whispered, his voice husky.

She pulled him tight into her body, nuzzling his ear and kissing his neck, tasting the salt on his skin. He took her head in his hands and gently kissed her.

"I love you," she whispered, rolling onto his chest and crying out with delight, as the rush of heat through her body responded to his growing passion.

"I love you, Matt. I will always love you."

# 13

The lovers splashed from the water naked and sprinted across the sand to their towels where they collapsed kissing, laughing and hugging. Then, with a cry of sheer joy, Cassie leapt to her feet and launched into a routine of classical ballet movements: *arabesques, pirouettes, fouettés,* and *entrechats,* all of which were extremely erotic and provocative to a delighted Matt.

He clapped enthusiastically, enthralled and aroused again. At the end of her routine she sprang on him, rolled him in the sand and finished up straddling him, crushing her lips against his, panting from her rigorous choreography. "Phew, I need a little more conditioning, especially for what's ahead in Sydney."

"I have the perfect remedy for that." He took her in his arms, gently positioned her over his thighs and, again, they became one.

When they had thoroughly given of themselves, they lay stretched out on their backs, holding hands, not speaking but soaking in the extraordinary minutes of bliss both were experiencing, listening to the crashing of the surf while they stared up at the cloudless blue canopy. Matt was the first to sit up. He reached into his backpack, brought out a burgundy leather journal, leafed through the pages and stopped at the one titled 'Life'.

"Okay, this is the poem I have now. I was going to use it for the competition, but now I feel I want to write something about what I experienced with you," he said, placing his hand on his heart.

"Yeah, I'll look forward to it, but I want to hear what you have written now."

As he read, she was drawn to his eyes scanning the lines, watching them sparkle through changing shades of blue, reflecting the contrasting colours of the sea and sky. She listened, suppressing the urge to reach out and touch the full lips that so often had met hers in glorious moments of union, watching as he mouthed perfectly each word of his poem with the same passion.

He went on to finish and then looked up from the journal, grinning self-consciously. "So, what do you reckon?"

She launched herself at him, pushing him back onto the sand, crushing her lips against his again, kissing him until she was almost breathless. "I love it, Matt, and I love you."

He squirmed under her weight and then pushed both of them back into a sitting position onto the towels. "Whoa. I love you, mate, but the bloody sand, it's hot."

"Oops, sorry, but I had to get to those hot lips of yours." She reached around and vigorously brushed the sand off his back. "I think you are brilliant."

"Thanks. I've got another that's been on my mind about us. When we come together like just now, all sorts of incredible thoughts come to me. I want to write about that."

"Well, I think what I just heard would be good enough for the competition, so the one you write about us would need to be especially good."

He chuckled and winked mischievously. "Well, what I have in mind might just heat up some of the old stuffed shirts a bit. I'll either win the competition, or they'll toss it out for being too hot." He laughed and tickled her under the chin. "I'll have it done before you leave for Sydney, and you can tell me what you think."

"I want you with me, Matt. I want you get away from here, to experience more of the world and develop your talent. The monsignor tells you the same thing." She attempted to imitate the old priest, "Ya've been blessed, Matthew Ryan. Ya need ta get away ta learn more, ta get out into the world and share ya gift."

He laughed a joyful kid's laugh. "You're funny when you do that; you sound way to British to be Irish, though."

"Hey, I'm an Aussie, mate, and proud of it." She laughed and then became suddenly earnest. "You know what I worry about most, don't you? I want you to stop messing around with the marijuana, helping out your dad. I don't like it. You could finish up in jail. Your life would be ruined, Matt."

"I've told you before; it's none of your business, Cassie. If the Oldman gets caught and goes to jail, what the hell happens to Katherine and the boys? Besides the money's good and it will help me get my own farm. And, hey, I never touch the stuff, myself."

"Well, thank, God, for that! You know there are times when you drink too much. Look at your father, he's an alkie; you want to finish up like him? I certainly don't want to finish up like your poor mother!"

Matt was stunned; lost for words, he looked away toward the ocean. Cassie had tears in her eyes. "I'm sorry, Matt; I shouldn't have said that, I'm sorry." She reached out to him. "I would never do that to you. I'm sorry."

He gently pushed the hair back from her forehead. "I'm not an alkie, Cassie. I'm not like my father; I will never be like my father. I would never, never hurt you." He took her in his arms and kissed her.

"You have to give up helping your dad with the smuggling; get away from here; come to Sydney; see what it's like."

"I love this island, Cassie, and I do want to be with you, that's God's truth. Anyway, I told dad I wanted out of the whole marijuana deal, the growing and the collecting. He asked me to hang in for one last load in August, and said it would be Sammy Marino's last trip. I said okay, one last load and that's it; I would leave for Sydney right after Sammy was loaded and on his way. I guess that's if you'll still want me."

"Oh, Matt, sometimes you frustrate the life out of me. I will always want you to be with me. Sydney; you'll love it there, I know it. And, there will always be Kangaroo Island and the farm to come back…What is it?"

Matt, distracted by a flash of light from the top of the sand dunes, suddenly jumped to his feet and pulled on his Speedos.

"Get dressed, Cassie, quickly; someone is spying on us. I'm going to find out who the hell it is."

"No, Matt. Let them be." But, Matt was already running toward the dunes. "By the time you get there, whoever or whatever will be long gone," she yelled after him.

Matt was in no mood to ignore a 'Peeping Tom', particularly' if it was Jordan. He reached the top of the sand dune, panting furiously. Nothing! On the beach, Cassie had already dressed and was hurrying toward the track leading up to her SUV.

A loud roar caught Matt's attention. Dust swirled around the black motorbike, as it slid to a stop beside Cassie's vehicle, 20 meters away. Matt's face, already flushed from the tough sprint up the sand hill, turned blood red from rage. With a wild, savage howl, he charged forward to confront his enemy. Cassie topped the sand hill and immediately took in the situation. There was Jordan sitting astride his bike, stunned and immobilized by the maniac steaming toward him.

"Matt!" yelled Cassie. "Stop! Stop now!"

As if a brick wall had suddenly shot up in front of him, Matt propped and stopped. He stared at Jordan, nostrils flaring, eyes cold and hostile, sweat streaming over his heaving frame.

"What on earth has gotten into you, Matt?" Cassie demanded.

"That prick brother of yours was spying on us," yelled the war-ready warrior. "He'll go running to your dad, spilling his guts."

"What's he on about, sis, hmm?" interjected Jordan, gaining courage from his sister's power over Matt. "I just arrived. Ah, so you two have been at it, hey?"

A suddenly deflated Matt looked stupidly at Cassie. He turned back to Jordan. "I thought…"

"Well, well, look at the two of you. You're right, Ryan, Dad's just going to love hearing about this. His prized daughter screwing on the beach like a minx with some nobody, a feral Irish kid," taunted Jordan. "Yes, somebody was spying on you. No, it wasn't me, but I'm sure Mad Tom will have another tale to tell at next week's Catholic stir. Well, don't let me keep you." He threw Matt a mock salute and roared off back along the track.

Matt and Cassie watched in silence until Jordan disappeared over the scrubby ridge.

"Oh, shit, he's going to run to your father and…"

"Shh, I'll handle him," she said, holding a finger to his lips.

"Well, I'm coming with you. You're not doing this on your own."

"No you won't, said Cassie. Its better I do it alone. I can deal with him. We can talk; he's not crazy all the time. In fact, you and he have more in common than you realize. He's been hurt, too, and like you, he's bloody impulsive,"

"I'd like to believe that, but I know he's got a malicious streak in him. You watch out, and if you have any trouble I want to know about it."

The sun was dipping below the horizon. "Time I left, my love; I'd like to be home before Jordan."

Matt wrapped his arms around her. "By the way, the church barn dance is next Saturday at Gosse. I'll call during the week."

"You better, and just you keep at your writing; it's what the Irish do best," she said, laughing and kissing him hard one last time. "You *will* write a great novel."

"I'm an Aussie, mate," he countered, mimicking her earlier claim on the beach. She laughed, started the SUV's motor and waved merrily out of the window as she rattled off along the bumpy bush track, heading for Middle River and the homestead.

As he watched the red tail lights disappear over the ridge, Matt tried to ignore the icy breath of anxiety beginning to blow through his gut. "Bugger it."

He walked to his bike. "Let's call on Tom, hey?"

# 14

By the time Matt's bike was bouncing over the steel cattle grid entrance to Mad Tom's property, the last of the day's light had gone. He sped by the two massive white posts set to each side of the grid, passing the white rail fences angling off for a couple of meters where they slotted into the heavy strainer posts that anchored the wire fences stretching off into the darkness to surround the property, marking its boundaries. *Nice work, Tom*, noted Matt, a common thought every time he visited the farm. Despite Tom's lack of care and attention to his personal appearance, his farm and the way he ran it was one of the island's best, second only to the Baldwin properties.

The bike's headlamp lit up the dirt track leading to the homestead. Wallabies scattered, disturbed from their nocturnal routine of feeding on the pastures beyond the tall Norfolk pines lining the 200-meter-long driveway. He rounded the final curve, shut down the engine and let the bike roll to a silent stop at the gate of the homestead yard. A cicada's grating shrill broke through the silence for a few seconds and then ceased abruptly. A slight breeze rustled through the leaves of the eucalyptus trees scattered about the darkened house. His eyes flicked to the treetops and beyond, to the black, inky-black sky, background to a million sparkling gems, the Milky Way and the Southern Cross. He switched his attention to the house.

"Bit early for him to be in bed," he muttered, as he opened the gate and then quietly walked to the veranda. A chill ran up and down his spine. Gingerly, he stepped onto the porch and reached out to knock on the door. A barely audible squeak, like the sound of the wheel rounding a poorly greased axle, caused his heart to miss a beat.

"Looking for me?" said a gravelly voice from the darkness.

Matt squinted into the gloom and made out Mad Tom sitting in his favourite chair, rocking slowly back and forth, his head tilted toward the treetops. A red glow brightened, as Tom took a hit from his pipe.

"Why don't you pull up a chair?"

"Hell, Tom!" Matt crossed to another rocking chair set alongside Tom and cautiously sat down. "Frightened the crap out of me, you did. Do you have to be so bloody creepy?"

"Who's being creepy? It was you who crept in here, like a bloke sneaking in to cut me bloody throat". He laughed, "Ah, I'm just joking. You know, you can hear everything for miles on a night like this, see. Listen for a moment; hear the surf hitting the beach out there; nothing like sitting out here, quiet-like and just thinking. A bloke spends too much time running around like a blue arse'd fly and never takes enough time to think, to maybe give a little thanks to the Big Bloke each day for all he's given him."

Tom rose from his chair, walked behind Matt, stopped, bent over and whispered, "Especially for a young bloke, who had a beaut time of it today, hey?" He straightened, moved on to the refrigerator at the far end of the veranda, pulled out four stubbies and went back to Matt. "Here, get these into you, young fella. After all the energy you've given up today, you'll feel better for it, hey?"

Matt ignored the offer. "So it was you peeping on us today. Bit bloody sick, isn't it, spying on people like that?"

Except for the sound of his breathing, Mad Tom was silent and still. The hair on the back of Matt's neck tingled. The noise from the rustling leaves, stirred again by the gentle southerly breeze slowly taking over the warm air, was magnified a thousand times to the tense young man.

Eventually, after a few long seconds, Tom snorted, drew up a mouthful of phlegm, swirled it about his mouth, and then spat it out in a well-practiced fashion into the darkness beyond the veranda. He stepped around to the front of Matt's chair and looked him square in the eye.

"Now, there's no need to be rude, young fella. The truth is I was walking the dogs through the sand dunes, something I do, as you know on a regular basis and I see you and Cassie on the beach. I didn't watch but a few seconds," he said, offering the two of the stubbies again. "I knew what you were up to, see. Mate, you're like a son to me, and I like that Baldwin girl, always did. She's a fighter and classy young lass, too. Pity she's not Catholic, but that's not as important today as it was in my time. There's a lot of good coming your way, lad, just don't stuff it up, see. As I just said, I didn't hang about perving on you, as you put it. Besides, I could hear Jordan's bike coming, which is why I flashed you with me glasses to warn you, see."

Matt began to relax, took the stubbies from Tom, popped the top on one and took a long drink of the cold liquid. In an instant, the amber magic hit the spot. "Thanks, Tom," he said, pausing to take another drink. "Yeah, I had a run-in with him after he showed up. I don't think he saw anything, but he threatened to tell his Oldman we were at it. Cassie's gone after him. He told me he reckoned it was you, so he wasn't crapping about that. Damn it, Tom, I don't want this to get out."

"Well, you need to find a more private spot in the future. Other people besides you go down there, see, and they're usually locals. No, I won't be saying anything to anyone, but God knows who Jordan will talk to when he's on the grog. He was an uppity enough young pup before nearly killing himself in that barrel roll down Kohinoor Hill, but now he's a lot worse. It's like he's on a suicide quest." Tom put the stubby to his lips. "What a bloody waste, if you ask me. What's worse is that the rotten little twerp doesn't seem to give a damn what trouble he causes others who cross his path."

Tom took a long draw on his pipe, slowly released the smoke and watched it drifting off into infinity. "Bloody awful, it is. You can see it wearing away at his Oldman. It's a good thing Cassie's around, but she'll be gone soon. He'll miss her, that's for sure."

"I'll second that, it's going to be bloody rough without her around." Matt's stomach took a couple of turns, as he thought of Cassie's fast approaching departure. "Tom, how come you never got married? I mean, well, don't you, don't you get lonely sometimes?"

"No. No, I'm never alone, Matt. The bloke upstairs is always around, see? Anyway, there's plenty of life going on about me all the time, so I really don't miss…" Tom's voice softened; he recalled a time when there was someone in his life. He was young then. She was a beautiful Irish Catholic girl with a full head of long, red hair and the pale-bluest of eyes, so powerful, so penetrating, that when she flashed them at him, he would have died for her there and then if anything threatened her. It took him a long time to get over his hatred of God after he watched her waste away from the cancer. A few tears found their way down the weathered cheeks of the tough old bachelor. He reached down to the veranda floor, replaced the empty stubby with a full one, took a long swallow and regained his composure.

"Take a flower. You ever picked one and looked at it; I mean really looked at how it's put together, taken a real close gander? Well, next time you do, look closely for the myriad colours that make up its hue. It's a flaming miracle, see." Tom's enthusiasm grew. "Ever wonder about the delicacy of its composition, hey, so vulnerable? Yet, no matter what nature throws at it, see: storms, fires, whatever, it comes back to charm us year after year with subtle, seductive fragrances that tease our senses and stir our emotions, turn on our desire to love, hey, Matt?" He chuckled, obviously happy to be part of it all.

"Jeez, Tom, I know you read a lot, but...mate, you could be a bloody poet, beautiful the way you see things, just bloody beautiful. I never get sick of looking at what's around us here, blessed we are. This has to be the best place in the world, hey."

They both sat silent, drawing in the extraordinary night. The young man and the old bachelor, surrendering to the soothing coolness of the evening breeze brushing lightly over exposed skin, each lost in his own thoughts, but in the most exquisite of settings, as one in their experience of God's grace.

Mad Tom chuckled. "You know, that girl of yours is a looker, hey? What I saw, the two of you together, pure art, pure bloody art, hey? She can dance a bit, too."

Matt looked at Tom; a wry smile creased his face. "You saw a bit more than you let on." He laughed, "You are a bloody perv you old bugger, aren't you? Bit of a romantic, too. Yeah, I bet you had a few ladies charmed up in your time, Tom." He chuckled, as he lifted off the lid of the second stubby, the amber fluid from the first successfully killing the gut worms, replacing them with a warming 'all is well.' "Cassie's a looker all right," Matt said, beaming.

# 15

"Good evening, Cassie," said Monty Baldwin. Cassie had entered the huge living room from the kitchen to where Monty was sitting in his favourite armchair, well worn with a greasy dark discoloration showing on the seat of the light leather covering from years of collapsing into it after coming in from the paddock. He spent a lot of his time in the chair, looking up at the portrait of Kristina and thinking about their times together. "How was your afternoon?" Cassie placed a pitcher of iced water and two glasses on the coffee table adjacent to Monty's chair.

"Mummy loved this room," she said, sensing her father's sadness. When Kristina was alive, family and friends would gather for after dinner chats, parties, performances, games and loads of fun in the 'big room.' He missed that, she knew. The life-sized painting of her talented mother reminded him of those earlier days, and now the departure of the daughter who carried him through the pain of his greatest tragedy was suddenly imminent.

"She did, she did, indeed, but no point dwelling on that, tell me about your day. Come on now, tell me."

She smiled warmly, and then laughing danced to the back of his chair and threw her arms around his neck, smothering him with kisses and hugs.

"Oh, it was wonderful, Daddy. I went to Cape Kersaint. It was hot, but the water was cool, and I went for a swim. Matt met me there, and we talked and danced on the sand and talked and…the sea was beautiful. The air was filled with the smell of wild flowers and salt and pure…it was all so…alive, vibrant… like dancing in the arms of God."

Monty stiffened. His head filled with the experience of his loss of innocence with Kristina. It came to him all at once, the realization shocking him; his daughter was no longer his child. She was a woman, and she had been with the Ryan boy on the beach; just as he had been with Kristina. Monty's thoughts were a stream of overlapping voices and images. He freed himself from the arms of his daughter and hurried to the open front door, desperate for fresh air.

Cassie followed, concerned and confused. "Daddy, what's wrong? Are you all right? Can I get you something?"

"Yes, um, please, some water," he replied, hardly daring to look at her.

She returned to the coffee table, poured a glass of water and took it back to him. "Here, Daddy, drink this."

He drained the glass in one gulp. "Thank you, Cassie. I'm sorry…I…it's just that sometimes you become your mother. You bring her back to the here and now."

"You scared me, Daddy. I know you have been worrying a lot about me leaving. I worry about leaving, too, and you left here alone; perhaps I shouldn't go."

"That, my dear girl, is the last thing you ought to be thinking." Monty certainly did not want her to stay at home. It was last thing he wanted especially now after what had happened, he had to get her away from away from the Ryan boy. His daughter, as far as he was concerned, had no idea of problems that the boy would have to face, as he matured; the legacy of his dysfunctional upbringing; the curse of the Irish, the alcohol. You only had to look at the father to see where the son was heading. *Hell, no; not with my baby; not on my bloody watch.*

"Tell me, Daddy, when you…truly love someone…and you want to live with them for the rest of your life…"

"Not now, Cassandra. Not now," interjected Monty, angry about where his daughter's conversation was heading. "The important question now is how you can best develop the talent you inherited from your mother. And that, it seems to me, is to follow through with the dance company in Sydney."

"Yes, of course, and I love to dance, you know that. But can't it be both?"

"It can, but later, later. You have to develop…focus. You cannot divide your attentions. And besides, you will meet people from all walks of life who have much more to offer than…"

"Matt!" she cried out. "Oh, Daddy, what are you saying? You taught me to respect people for who they are, to look into their hearts. Matt is beautiful and talented and sensitive and, yes, deeply wounded by the loss of his mother. He is a good, good man. He stays here to protect his brothers and stepmother." Her voice grew more strident by the word. "He is courageous, and I love him, and I will always love him."

"Enough, enough for now, Cassandra, before we say things we may regret," said Monty, almost shouting.

The ringing of the phone interrupted. They looked at each other. "Jordan," said Monty. "What now?"

"I'll get it." Cassie stepped into the living room and picked up the phone on the writing table next to Monty's armchair. "Hello…Yes, it is." She listened. "Is he all right, Constable?"

"Is it Jordan?" asked Monty.

Cassie nodded. Minutes passed, as she listened to the new constable. Finally, she said, "In the morning then, okay." She returned the phone to its cradle.

"What is it? What happened?"

"That was the police, Daddy. Everything is under control. Jordan's not hurt, other than a few bruises." She threw her hands in the air. "He's bloody hopeless.

"Well, tell me, where is he? What about the police? Is he in jail?"

"Not yet, but he will be. Constable Dunning called from the Parndana Community Club. He is taking Jordan to the Kingscote jail for the night. Apparently, he reached over the bar and hit the manager after he refused to serve Jordan another whiskey. Some of the other drinkers tried to eject him, but he went crazy and knocked over old Rosy Fahey who was carrying a tray of drinks to her table. Beer went flying, and the other drinkers got stuck into Jordan. Someone called the police and Constable Dunning, who was already in the area heading south, showed up. Anyway, he's got Jordan handcuffed and is on his way to the Kingscote jail. He said we can pick him up in the morning after the court hearing."

A disconsolate Monty shuffled to his armchair.

"I'll make us some tea, Daddy."

Monty appeared not to hear. "Last night trouble, again tonight. Why whiskey? I have told him, stick to the beer, and you won't get into trouble. I've told him that over and over," said Monty in a voice barely audible.

"It's not just the whiskey, Daddy. If it were beer, it would be the same result. Jordan is sick, mentally and emotionally sick, and he's an alcoholic. I am afraid for him, for others around him and for us. Look at you, sick with worry. We are going to have to have him committed."

"No, not that, Cassie, we are family and family takes care of its own. I'll call his brother when he gets back from Europe later in the month and see if he can spend a few days here after you've gone. Tomorrow, you go to Kingscote and pick up Jordan. I'll go out to Stumpy Flats with Harry and get on with the crutching."

"Didn't you tell Harry to go on to the scrub line tomorrow to repair that hole in the fence at Jumpy Creek?"

Monty nodded. "Damn, I forgot."

"Don't worry, I'll call him tonight and get him to come straight to the homestead. I'd better get the smoko and lunch ready. Jordan won't be here to take care of that, of course."

"Come here," he commanded. "Give your father a hug."

She went to him and hugged him, pressing her cheek gently against his ruddy face. She felt the roughness of his whiskers against the smoothness of her skin, a familiar sensation that rushed her thoughts back to the days after her mother's death when she would settle onto his lap in the evenings, trying to lessen the pain of his loss and hers.

"Cassie," he whispered into her ear. "I'm sorry. I want what's best for you. Go to Sydney, work hard and let destiny guide you. If it is God's will you be with this boy, there's nothing can stop it."

Cassie ran her fingers through the Oldman's thinning hair and kissed his forehead. "Yes, and you make sure you don't think you're God."

They studied each other for a moment. Monty shook his head and saw again Kristina's steely determination reflected in the steady brown eyes of his daughter.

"I am powerless," he said, struggling for a touch of levity. "I am at the mercy of another goddess."

# 16

Matt opened his eyes, yawned and squinted into the early morning sun bursting through the bedroom window. The alarm clock read 7:30. He suddenly remembered that Dunning was coming out to Humpy sometime that morning, probably early.

Kicking back the blankets, he slid out of the bed and crossed to the open window. Stretching away to the southeast, a panorama of colour highlighted the separation of land from the sea through a pattern of greens, rusty browns and myriad blues. Remarkable Rocks, the ever-present symbol of the island's enduring character, its precarious balancing act splendidly captured in the morning sparkle, stood prominent on the balding granite cliff of distant Kilpatrick Point. Beyond, the Southern Ocean flooded to the horizon where it gave way to the powder blue pastel and orange tint of the emerging new day sky.

Exhilarated, Matt drew in a deep breath of the pristine air, stretched, rolled his upper body around the axis of his hips and slowly breathed out, the first part of a regular routine most mornings followed by a series of exercises for ten minutes, a shower and then breakfast.

Katherine was already busy in the kitchen. "Morning, Matthew. I've put on some eggs and bacon for your father and the boys. I can throw a couple on for you, if you'd like."

"No, thanks, Katherine, I'll stick to my usual." He filled a bowl of favourite cereal, muesli, and then drowned it a with a princely helping of fresh, full cream milk pulled from the 'tits' of the family cow, Maria, milked by Katherine every morning.

"Your father will be in shortly. He wants to talk to you about getting Humpy sorted out."

"I bet he does," Matt said, slicing up a banana and the dropping the pieces onto his muesli. The energy level in the kitchen rose to another level when the two boys burst into the kitchen.

"Well, well, well," said Katherine. "It's about time you boys showed up. Your eggs are cooking and the sandwiches are ready on the sideboard, over there. Pack them into your school-bags now before you forget; you have ten minutes before it's time to leave. Did you do your hair, Sean? I think not. Come here." Almost in one movement, a hair brush was in her hand, sweeping through the young boy's thick, blond hair.

The boys took care of the sandwiches and then scrambled to race each other to the table, impatient for breakfast. Katherine set three plates. "Frank, get in here, your eggs are done," she called through the open kitchen door.

"Do you and Cassie kiss?" a giggling Sean asked Matt.

Katherine swept two eggs from the frying pan and slipped them onto Sean's heavily buttered toast. "Mind your tongue and eat this up quickly. You'll be a lucky boy one day if you can find a nice girl like Cassie."

"Do you love her?" asked the undeterred Sean.

"Suppose so, mate," Matt said, chuckling, "but you'd better concentrate on putting that breakfast into your tummy. We have to leave for the school bus in a few minutes, and Tom can't wait about for us, so get a hurry-on, hey?"

"Yeah, love is all well and good," said Frank on entering the kitchen, "but you are not their kind, fella. Oldman Baldwin won't have a bar of you joining his uppity mob, so as I've said before, you'd be better off forgetting about her."

"Oh sure, that's what you'd like, hey? Can't stand the idea of anyone being a little bit happy." said Matt, keeping his anger under control for the sake of family peace. "It's none of your bloody business, anyway. Hurry up, you blokes. I have to get you to the school bus first, and then I want to be at Humpy before the coppers arrive."

"Right, I wanted to talk about that." Frank looked haggard. He had obviously been pissed all through Sunday. "I heard on the two-way this morning that Jordan got into some bother at the club last night, shooting his mouth off and whacking Davo from over the bar. The copper got him and tossed him in the Kingscote lock up for the night. Yeah, it was young Dunning. I got a bit of time for him, savvy young bloke; he'll have his hands full at this morning's court hearings. My guess is he won't be out here until this afternoon. Good thing for you, seeing as you got out of bed so bloody late."

Matt held his tongue and ignored the gibe, relieved by the policemen's delay but mindful of Cassie's concern about her brother's drinking. He looked at the kitchen clock. "C'mon, you blokes, time to get moving." He scoffed down the last of his cereal and started for the kitchen door. "See ya, Katherine, thanks for breekee; Sean, Pat, c'mon." The two boys stuffed down what was left of their breakfast and chased after him.

"Hey, a thank you would be nice," Frank called after them. "Geez, I work bloody hard to put tucker on the table for you lot." Matt and the boys were already outside and out of earshot.

"Bloody Matt ought to know better; ungrateful piece of work."

"Perhaps if you weren't so full of grog most of the time, Frank, and going off at him the way you do, he would appreciate you more," said Katherine, hurrying after the boys.

From under the shade of the back veranda, she waved. "Drive carefully, Matthew, and you boys behave yourselves." They waved back, Sean distinguished by the heart warming, cheeky grin spreading across his face. Katherine's eyes followed the trail of dust rising from behind the Landcruiser, watching it trace the twists and turns through the green carpet all the way to the top of the distant plateau, until it disappeared from view only a couple of kilometres from the ranger's cottage, the turnaround point for the Parndana school bus. "Keep my boys safe, Lord, all three of them."

"Katherine, Katherine, hurry up, luv. We've got the place to ourselves. Plenty of time for a little bit of the old slap and tickle, hey?"

Katherine sighed and walked back to the cottage door. Despite the troubles that came with Frank's disease, her love for him was part of her being, their marriage sacred. "Coming, Frank, coming."

# 17

Cassie slowed the Pathfinder at the outskirts of the island's main town, Kingscote. The morning had been hectic, up at five and into the kitchen to pack the lunch and smoko for the day's crutching. Harry arrived early and helped feed the horses. Monty apologized for being unusually curt the night before in what little time they had for conversation. His mind was mainly preoccupied with what to do about Jordan. She told Monty she would drop Jordan off at Stumpy Flats after she picked him up from Kingscote; he could work off his hangover, penning sheep and sorting through the soiled wool.

She swung the SUV to the right at the top of the town's main access road where the new recreation centre dominated the intersection's northwest corner, the most popular building after the two pubs. It was, also, a constant reminder of the generosity of the principal donor, fisherman Sammy Marino. The road dropped down into the seaside village of Kingscote, population around 1,750 permanent residents, expanding many times that during the busy tourist seasons. The town nestled in the top part of the western curve of Nepean Bay; the shoreline swept away to the east and arced to the north where the red bluffs and sandy beaches turned sharply toward the town of Penneshaw where the waters of Backstairs Passage separated the eastern end of the island from the mainland, 18 kilometres distant.

"Dear, God, I love it here."

At the bottom of the hill, she turned right again and drove slowly along the town's main street. The locals were already well into the business of their new day: picking up mail from the post office, lining up for coffee and newspapers at the Deli, chatting with friends, opening stores and sweeping clean the pavements. Islanders, blessed to be living in the thriving country town of Kingscote, Kangaroo Island, which in these modern times was still one of the world's best kept secrets, a consensus sentiment common among most locals and visitors alike. The smell of fresh sea air, pastry and coffee floated through the cab of Cassie's vehicle. The dashboard's clock flipped over to 8:45, fifteen minutes before Jordan's court appearance, just enough time to meet with the constable before the hearing. She drove slowly through to the next intersection and onto the police station situated prominently on the northeast corner.

Bob Dunning was at his desk looking through the front window when the SUV nosed into the curb. He watched Cassie step out and noted how her light blue blouse tucked neatly into the narrow waistband of her tight fitting moleskin pants accentuated the very feminine line of her slim body. Impressed, the tall, young constable opened the front door and met the natural beauty with a smile. "You must be Jordan's sister. I'm Bob Dunning."

"That's right, Constable," she said, an edge of irritation in her voice. "I'm Cassie Baldwin. I'm a few minutes early, I know, but I was hoping I could have a few words before the hearing starts."

"Of course, and call me Bob. Come this way, it's a little more private." He ushered her along a narrow corridor to a small interview room at the back of the building. "The boss, Sergeant Woodson, I believe you may have met him, he certainly knows your father, would have been here this morning, but he had to pick up the superintendent from Adelaide HQ at the airport; they are probably already on their way south to Flinders Chase. So, that leaves me to take care of today's cases. There are only two; Jordan's will be the second."

Dunning flipped the switch to the fluorescent lights and offered Cassie a seat on one of the three chairs around a bare table and under a small window high in the wall.

"Interrogation room?" Cassie might have been less caustic were it not for her thoughts about Woodson on his way to Flinders Chase. Matt had told her that Dunning was coming out to du Couedic in the morning, and he had not volunteered the reason, but she knew anyway. She declined the offer of the chair.

"Sorry," said Dunning, a little taken aback by the sudden, icy tone in Cassie's question. "This is all we have unless I use the sergeant's office, and it is rather a mess, I'm afraid."

"Why doesn't that surprise me?" said Cassie. Dunning grinned and shrugged. "I don't think he's anything to grin about, Constable. I met your sergeant the day he came out home to lobby Daddy on some political matter. The creep practically undressed me when Daddy was looking the other way; horrible creature.

"I'm sorry that happened to you."

"Well, he won't ever get on the property again. Now, tell me how we can get this matter with Jordan cleared up. My father wants him out of here today. He is sick; I think an addict and needs treatment. The family will take full responsibility for him."

Dunning found Cassie's direct approach refreshing, but he was still a little overwhelmed by her beauty. He forced his thoughts back to the role of policeman. "I booked him for disorderly conduct, not disastrous. David Hill, the club manager, did not want to press charges for assault, so that saved him from a more serious situation. I think we can get the magistrate to let him off with a warning, a fine and damages. You should be on your way in no time. But you are right, Ms. Baldwin, he needs treatment. He could end up killing himself, or some other poor innocent bugger. Sorry, but that's how it often pans out."

Cassie was beginning to warm to the young constable. "My sentiments exactly; thank you, Const…err…Bob for being so considerate. I'm frustrated right now, worried about Jordan and my dad, so forgive my bad manners. And call me Cassie, please."

"No worries. I was at King's College around the time Jordan was there. We weren't in class together, but on the same football team. Maybe, you and I can get together and talk about it sometime, I would like to help." He glanced at his watch. "Oops, can't be late; I don't want to stir up the magistrate, unnecessarily. You can come in, if you like."

"Okay, but can I quick use your phone?"

Dunning smiled, "I called Frank Ryan to let him know that the sergeant was on his way out to du Couedic earlier. Katherine Ryan told me about you and Matt; so, I guess your call might be to him, hey? Well, not to worry, I met him yesterday, impressed me right off actually. I'd like to help keep him out of trouble, and he might be heading that way from what the sergeant tells me."

"Your sergeant's full of bullshit, Bob, and I think you know it. Matt's had a tough life, but he's a good person, ask Katherine or his stepbrothers."

"Whoa, I'm on your side. I've heard around that all of the family could do with a break or two; they have a lot to deal with in Frank. Still need to use the phone?"

"No thank you, Bob." She laughed. "I like you."

# 18

Ironstone gravel scattered over the dried brown clovers of the Flinders Chase Visitors park paddock, as the powder blue sedan broadsided around the turn leading away from the ranger's cottage and onto the road to Cape du Couedic. The distinctive yellow school bus from the Parndana Area School was stopped at the front gate of the cottage where a group of the Chase kids were climbing aboard, among them the Ryan boys.

Woodson saw that Matt was talking to Mad Tom, but he was in too much of a hurry to get to the suspect marijuana plot to stop and talk. He was not happy; his boss from Adelaide HQ, Chief Superintendent Holloway, was with him to do a quarterly appraisal, his appraisal. His probationary status was a result of the disciplinary measures imposed for suspected cattle-duffing activities at his previous posting in the southeast of South Australia. There was a lack of solid evidence to make any charges stick, so he was demoted and sent to the island for a chance to rehabilitate his career. Holloway told Woodson the reports about his progress were not good and warned him that unless there was a major improvement in the next quarter, he would be recalled to Adelaide to spend the rest of his career hosing out cellblocks at the city lock up.

Woodson was especially anxious to find the suspected evidence of marijuana at the plot before the Ryans cleaned it up. "That was the Ryan kid back there, boss. We get him and his oldman, Frank, it'll be a major blow to the marijuana cultivation and procurement operation on the island and it will shut down bloody Marino from transporting the stuff to Victoria."

Woodson was confident a big bust could get him back onside with the department. He pushed the accelerator to the floor.

"Slow it down, Sergeant, or you'll finish up wrecking a new police car, and that will get you in a hell've lot more trouble than you are already in, I can tell you that." The bend in the road at Matt's lookout over the expanse of scrub to the lighthouse at Cape du Couedic was suddenly upon them. "Watch out, Woodson!" screamed the Chief Superintendent.

The warning was too late. The car was already beginning to drift on top of the ironstone rubble when Woodson caught sight of the fresh bike track heading into the scrub toward the area of the suspected crop cultivation. *Damn, must be Frank out here already.* With a sudden and impulsive move, Woodson made the error no Islander raised driving on the island's ironstone roads would ever make, he hit the brakes and swung violently toward the track. Forces were now operating beyond the control of the driver. Sliding sideways at almost a hundred kilometres per hour, the vehicle ploughed into the heavy gravel curb lining the road. The sedan lifted over its left front wheel, corkscrewed into the air and rolled three times, finally coming to rest upside down deep into the bush.

The superintendent's last and momentary view, before everything became a tumbling, noisy crunching of metal and breaking glass, was of Remarkable Rocks balancing on their granite base at the edge of a very blue Southern Ocean.

A dreadful silence descended on the scene of the destruction. A few minutes passed, and then the stillness was broken by the raucous cawing of black crows arriving and settling in the branches of the stringy bark trees, their eager eyes checking out the wreck.

# 19

Frank was wary, a trifle jumpy approaching the cultivation site at Humpy Creek. He cut the bike's motor and drifted to a stop a few meters short of the canopied clearing. Sitting absolutely quiet astride the bike, he listened for any unusual sounds and studied the bush at the perimeter for any movement of leaves, animals, or birds that may have signified a human presence. The phone call from Dunning soon after the boys had left for the school bus was a worry. It had been a message for Matt that Dunning would not be able to meet him, and that Sergeant Woodson was on his way out instead. Frank was especially alert, suspicious because Dunning was after all a copper and really had no reason to give them a break.

Finally satisfied all was clear, the wary Frank picked up the half-bag of oats from the pillion seat and carried it into the cleared area, checking as he walked for any illicit plant material, plastic wrapping, cigarette butts, or anything incriminating left from the harvest of the previous week. The rain, the rooting of wild pigs and an assortment of animal tracks had left the ground looking like similar clearings found all over the park. Only the plastic hoses, fertilizer and camouflage nets stored in the humpy were a danger now. "I'll shove this stuff off the cliff," he muttered.

Frank was dragging a piece of the humpy's rust collared iron roof when a loud series of thumping noises echoed through the ravine and stopped him. "What the hell was that?" He cupped a hand to an ear, listened intently and looked at his watch. He waited, motionless for a couple of minutes. He heard nothing unusual; no noise, no sound of an approaching vehicle came from the road or through the bush.

Using the materials from the humpy, he quickly threw together a wild pig trap and then scattered oats over the rooted ground, laying a trail into the centre of the trap, where he dropped the bag and what was left of the oats. After a quick ride to the cliff to dump the hoses, net and fertilizer, he returned to check again he had missed nothing that could land them in jail.

"Good, that should fix the buggers," he said, chuckling. "See if you can get me on anything here, boys." The old, mischievous sparkle in his blue eyes, a disarming characteristic before the war, the alcohol and the nightmares, returned as he delighted in the thought of putting another one over on Woodson.

The moment of levity passed as quickly as it arrived, and the throbbing headache returned with a vengeance. He pulled a bottle of Black Label brandy from the saddlebag and took a long, deep draw from the brown remedy. In seconds, the headache was gone, the icy hole in his gut, thawed.

Pushing along the scrubby track at a brisk pace and attacking the occasional cluster of bulloak with an extra twist on the throttle, his cursing echoed through the ravine when the odd sappy branch whipped across his face. As he neared the main road, the crows lifted out of the trees *en masse*, their screeching loud enough to be heard above the noise of the motorbike. "What the bloody hell…!" Frank braked, looked up and down the road and saw the huge gouge in the gravel along the line of the scrub.

"Hell!" The flattened scrub was obvious; he slid off the bike and was about to walk into it when the familiar roar of the Landcruiser fast approaching the bend stopped him.

Matt saw Frank, slammed on the brakes and leapt out of the truck. The skid marks into the broken bush told the story; he did not need to ask.

"There's a car rolled over in the scrub," yelled Frank.

"Oh, shit! It must be Woodson and Dunning. They went flying by the cottage while I was talking to Tom. I thought you said…"

"Dunning called after you left to say that Woodson and his boss from Adelaide were on their way out here. I've already cleaned up the plot. Wait here while I check this out, Matt; it might not be pretty." Frank followed the tracks into the scrub, hurried over the flattened scrub and pushed through a section of bush undisturbed where the sedan had flipped over the top.

Then he saw it. "Damn." He crossed to the body that laid face down on a flattened section of the scrub. The head was shockingly crushed; he checked for a pulse, nothing. "It's all over for you, Superintendent," he said and made the sign of the cross.

The snapping of twigs alerted him to the approaching Matt. "I told you to stay back, Son."

"I thought you might need some…" Matt saw the crushed head of the body dressed in a police uniform and froze; his face turned to the colour of chalk.

"This is a dead man, son. Take a close look; it probably won't be the last one you'll see."

Matt was close to vomiting. "Where's Wood…," he said, fighting to keep from vomiting up his breakfast.

"He's probably in there." Frank took off his jacket and laid it over the dead policeman's head and upper body. He then moved quickly to the wrecked sedan. "It's him, all right," he called, reaching into the interior of the vehicle, and checking Woodson for signs of life. "He's alive, but barely, upside down in his seat belt, hanging like a rag doll. Quick, Matt, over here, I'm gonna need your help with this bloke."

Matt crossed to Frank, looked into the front of the sedan and vomited.

"You'd better pull yourself together fast, lad. We gotta get this bloke out of here in a hurry."

"I'll be right," Matt said, wiping his mouth. "What do you want me to do?"

"I'm going to lift him to take some of the strain off the seat belt buckle. As soon as the tension eases, get that buckle undone."

Frank strained to take Woodson's weight. As the tension on the belt eased, the heavy sergeant threw up a mouthful of phlegm and blood over the struggling rescuers. Matt grappled with the belt release buckle, his hands now slippery with blood. "I can't get it."

"Stay with me, Matt, you're doing okay," said Frank, grunting. "I'm going to give an extra heave, so be ready to snap that buckle. Okay, now!"

Frank shoved; Matt tugged and pushed on the catch. The belt came apart and Frank collapsed under the weight of the falling victim, which probably saved Woodson from further injury. They dragged the big man from the car out onto the flattened bush; a crimson froth bubbled from his mouth.

"He's going to die, if we don't get air into him," said Frank, turning the gasping sergeant's head to the side. "Get me a knife or a screwdriver from the truck, whatever you can find, but be quick or we'll lose him. And I need a tube, a straw anything narrow and hollow will work."

Matt scampered back to the truck and rummaged through the toolbox.

"Hurry, hurry," he heard Frank yelling in the background. Fighting to stay calm, he found a thin electrical screwdriver with a pointy nose. He clawed through the contents of the glove box, looking for a hollow tube; nothing.

"C'mon, hurry it up, boy! Frank shouted.

"There's nothing bloody in here!"

"Have you looked behind the seats?"

Matt scratched through the tools behind the seats and, again, found nothing that would work as a straw.

"For God's sake hurray it up, boy, find me bloody something!"

"Shut up, will ya! I'm looking everywhere in here!" shouted Matt.

Desperate, tears in his eyes and his hands shaking, Matt scrambled across the cab to look under the front seat. At last, he saw something, two dirty drink straws almost hidden from sight among the beer cans and a half-empty brandy bottle. With the pliers and straws in hand, he scurried back to Frank and the dying policeman.

Frank took the screwdriver and in one deft movement punched a hole through Woodson's neck with the pointy end. The sergeant's eyes opened wide with terror, and he lashed out at his rescuer with flailing fists.

"Hold the bastard down, Matt; he thinks we're trying to kill him, not that the thought hadn't crossed my mind."

Matt held down the sergeant's arms while Frank took a straw and pushed it into the bleeding wound; almost immediately, the deathly pale patient began sucking air into his lungs.

Matt looked at his father, amazed. Frank caught the look. "Picked it up with Special Forces in 'Nam," he said grimly. "Okay, we'll have to lay him out on the tray of the truck."

The men were panting heavily by the time they got Woodson to the Landcruiser.

"How the hell are we going to get him up there?" asked Matt, looking at the tray that was over a meter from the ground.

"Catch a breath or two, and then we'll lift him," replied Frank.

"I don't like our chances; it's a bloody big lift."

"Listen, Matt, we have to get him on the truck, or he's done for. Now grit your bloody teeth and lift."

Matt wrapped his arms under Woodson's legs. The sergeant let out a loud howl, which caused the straw to fly out of the hole in his throat, spraying Matt with blood. Woodson began to slip from Matt's grip, but Frank, with instinct born of previous crises, dropped to his knees, took the policeman's full weight and with a mighty grunt hoisted him onto the flatbed.

"The straw, boy; quick, give me that straw."

Matt, coughing and hacking, was on the verge of throwing up, again. He desperately searched the ground around him.

"It's stuck on the front of your shirt, in the blood."

Matt plucked the bloodied projectile from his shirt and handed it to Frank. Woodson began to shake violently.

"Damn, he's seizing." Frank pushed the straw back through the hole. The shaking intensified; Woodson's head, arms, legs and feet repeatedly hit on the steel tray. Frank slipped a woolpack under his head and pushed down on his shoulders. Eventually, the shakes ceased. Matt bent over and let go what was left of his breakfast.

"C'mon, Matt, enough of that, you gotta drive, let's get going."

Matt straightened up, "I'll be right," he snapped back.

"Maybe, this will make a man out of ya. C'mon hurry up and get on the radio; let the hospital know what's happened and tell them to send the ambulance. We'll meet 'em somewhere along the coast road. Tell 'em this bloke's ready to croak."

Matt was already crashing through the gears of the Toyota, as Frank lay down over his patient and thought of all the reasons he loathed Woodson. He was tempted to rip out the straw protruding from the bloodied throat. For the first time since he had gone through intense first aid training in the SAS, he wished he had forgotten what they taught him.

# 20

Jordan's disorderly conduct charge cost the family a heavy fine, court fees and an order for payment to the Community Club of Parndana for the property damaged. In a lengthy dressing down of the wayward Baldwin, the local magistrate warned that Jordan needed to adopt a more responsible attitude in keeping with the family's good reputation. If he finished up in his court again the consequences for his antisocial behaviours would be far more serious. He would find himself in jail, period.

"I'll be outside," said Jordan, walking toward the police station's front door.

"Lay off the grog, Jordan, or you'll be back here again and I won't be able to do a thing to help you."

"Nobody asked you, Dunning. You'll do well to keep your nose…"

"Shut up, Jordan. If it weren't for Constable Dunning's help, you'd be in jail for the next thirty days. Now, wait for me outside."

Jordan stared at his sister, turned to the door and stormed outside.

"I'm sorry, Bob. He's a huge worry for the family, especially for daddy; what he needs is professional help. Daddy's talking about an intervention after Grant, my older brother, gets back from Europe," she said and handed over the check for the fine and the damages.

"Thank you. Alcoholism is tough on families, Cassie. In my job I've had to deal with a lot of the consequences, most them tragic. I tried talking to Jordan earlier this morning, but he's never gotten over our school days at Kings. Maybe you and I can get together some time and…Well, I might have a few ideas that could help, and I know a few people in AA."

"That's kind of you, Bob, but it will need to be soon; I'm leaving the island in a couple of week's time to join a dance company in Sydney."

"Yeah, I saw the article in the Islander. Congratulations, a hell of an achievement; it'll make the islanders proud, that's for sure. Doesn't surprise me, though, you certainly have the body to…your body looks…err…you have the perfect look."

Cassie grinned, enjoying Dunning's awkwardness. "Hard work and luck, but the tough part is leaving the island."

"There aren't many places left like this with their natural beauty intact, especially after the white blokes get hold of it. The islanders, though, seem to appreciate what they have and have done a damn good job of managing their land responsibly." He handed her a receipt. "I'll be on duty at the barn dance at Gosse next Saturday night. If you're going, maybe we can catch up." The telephone rang, and then rang again. "I'd better get it. Excuse me a sec, will you?"

He picked up the phone. "Kingscote Police, Constable Dunning." As he listened, the smile on his face faded. "He's dead? Good Lord…What…The air ambulance is on the way…Kingscote, right. How bad is he…I see…right…Frank Ryan and his son are bringing him in…right…just off the du Couedic road…Yeah, I'll notify headquarters. Listen, no one is to disturb the scene until…Yeah, of course, you can place a blanket over him. Don't let anybody tramp all over the place, that's all…Good, and tell them to take it easy on that road."

Dunning looked over to Cassie, his face pale. "This is bad, real bad, that was the hospital. Woodson rolled the police car on the du Couedic road, and the superintendent is dead." He paused and took a deep breath. "The sergeant's in a bad way and might not make it…How the hell do you roll a police car?"

"I heard you mention Frank and Matt; are they okay?"

"Yeah, they found the wreck and are bringing in the sergeant. The ambulance just left the hospital and will meet them somewhere along the South Coast Road. The Flying Doctor has been alerted and is about to leave Adelaide airport; it should be here in about an hour."

"Can I do something to help? Actually, I would like to ride along."

Dunning thought for a moment, and then nodded. "Sure, Matt is bound to be shaken up and you'd be a help by just by keeping me company, but I warn you, it's going to be a tough situation out there."

"Thank you, I'll get sandwiches and drinks. Jordan can take the truck back home."

"I have to phone headquarters. Be ready to leave in…say, fifteen minutes." He paused for a moment, reflecting. "I liked the super, he was a good bloke; treated me like a…he helped me out a lot."

"I'm sorry, Bob." She said softly and then hurried out through the front doors.

"You're a good'n, Cassie," he called after her.

\*\*\*\*

Thirty minutes later, Cassie was vaguely aware of the stringy bark trees flashing by her window, and the black ribbon of road with the painted dashes that formed a continuous white line rushing under the front hood of the police wagon. Tired from her very early start to the day, she struggled to stay alert, but the fatigue was overtaking her. She had been through what the Superintendant's family was about to experience. You got up in the morning to a new day, every day, life started over and you didn't really know what was going to turn up. The day Kristina died started out just great, and then suddenly, horror, blood, fire, smoke and lives altered in a heartbeat, changed forever.

Cassie had never really gotten over the death of her mother. She loved all she had learned and experienced with her, her beauty, charm, grace and style; it was how she moved her body through space and time that made her special. Whenever Cassie danced, she felt her mother's presence in every movement; Kristina's spirit, gently coaxing the muscles of her lengthening limb to stretch and combine with the perfect arching of a soaring foot, naked toes pointing, pointing, stretching to just, just reach into heaven. "Lift, Cassie, lift and stretch and point. There it is; magnífico, my sweet little ballerina."

She was not naïve to her mother's imperfections, oh no, especially when she reflected on them, as she matured. She was not always the perfect mother, no. She had a blistering temper that was for sure. She could scream and bitch to get her way, enough to embarrass a raging banshee, but when the upset was over, she would laugh, a glorious, beautiful, belly laugh that infected everyone around her. The memories sustained Cassie and embedded in her psyche the iron will and chutzpah to reach beyond the ordinary, to claim and use.

Cassie opened her eyes, suddenly aware that she was in the police wagon. She looked over at the young constable who was focused on the road ahead. She already liked him. She had little experience of aboriginal people except for a minimal contact with those that had attended the ladies private school in Adelaide. It seemed to her that Bob Dunning was not like the usual young policeman that came out of the South Australian Police Academy. Of course, there was the obvious difference in skin colour, his was a creamy chocolate, and he had already demonstrated a good heart with his handling of Jordan's court appearance, but what really fascinated her was what might be tucked away behind the handsome features hinting of his ancient ancestry, a mix of modernity and instinctual mysticism.

As they swept by the turn-off to Vivonne Bay, she looked out to the south, beyond the low scrub, to where she could see the Southern Ocean all the way to the horizon, its blue surface choppy with white caps from small, breaking waves, signalling a stiff breeze beginning to blow in from the south-west and Antarctica. She had always been drawn to the wild beauty of the Southern Ocean, even though it had almost taken her when she was nine. She had fallen overboard from her father's boat *Wave Dancer* and nearly drowned before Monty dived in after her and plucked her from the water.

Suddenly, the great sea she was looking at turned violent, the sky darkened, the waves grew huge and frightening; forked lightning scorched the water sending up tiny puffs of steam. She grabbed at her throat, choking, gurgling, drowning…

"There's the ambulance," said Dunning, his voice cutting through the nightmare, saving her. "Are you okay?" Dunning slowed, as they came up to the ambulance and the Ryan's truck. "You don't have to get out. I can take care of this," he continued, misunderstanding the alarm that showed in Cassie's face.

"No, no, I'll be fine. I flipped into some kind of nightmare, bloody weird." She watched a paramedic pulling an empty stretcher from the ambulance. Matt and his father were standing in the back of their Landcruiser where the doctor was bending over Sergeant Woodson.

They stopped adjacent to the ambulance. Dunning and Cassie slid out of their seats. "How bad is it, Doc?" yelled Dunning, as he hurried to the Landcruiser. "Oh, shit, is he going to make it?"

Woodson, who was barely conscious, recognized Dunning's voice. "Get 'em; go check it out. It's there, I know," he croaked, venomous. Dunning was reminded of a snake, its head severed, but still continuing to bite at anything that moved.

"He'll make it, Bob, thanks to these blokes," said the doctor. "But we need to get him to Adelaide as quickly as possible. He'll be laid up for a good bit. Another centimetre and the glass would have ruptured his jugular."

Cassie looked past Woodson to Matt. Blood and vomit caked the front of his shirt. Their eyes locked. He gave her the 'bit of a bloody mess, hey?' look, his face grim, stressed.

"Are you hurt?"

"Naa, I'm all right, his blood, my chunder," he replied, tapping at the mess on his shirt.

He jumped from the truck, and she hugged him. The scent of his aftershave overpowered the smell of the vomit and reminded her of the day before. "I couldn't bear it, if anything happened to you," she whispered into his ear. "I love you."

"Yep," he responded quietly, "me too."

"This is horrible."

"Yeah, bit bloody rough, especially about the dead bloke. There's going to be big trouble; he was one of the big bosses over from Adelaide."

"Thanks for what you and your dad did, today, Matt. We owe you," said Dunning, approaching and shaking Matt's hand. "I'll have to get a statement from you and Frank, but we can do that later in the week. I need to go on out to the accident scene now, check out if I can determine what happened and take care of the Super's body until the second ambulance arrives. Thanks for your company, Cassie; I guess you'll get a ride with Matt."

"Yes, and thank you, thank you for your help with Jordan."

"All right, I'll be on my way. See you at the dance, Cassie."

"You bet." Dunning left.

"What was that about?" asked Matt with a hint of jealously edging his voice. "I can see you two like each other already, hey?"

"Don't be silly. He helped out big time with Jordan, that's all."

"Drop the bullshit, you blokes," interrupted Frank. "Give us a hand here, Matt; we have to get this heavy prick onto the stretcher; be a pity to drop him, wouldn't it?"

# 21

As the sun lifted off the horizon, an enchanted Matt watched a group of lively fur seals race, leap and splash in the lick of seawater that reached under Admirals Arch. Another group played on a huge slab of smooth rock that sloped at a 45 degree angle to the water's edge. Playful seal pups tumbled and slipped on the misty-wet surface, eventually to plunge gloriously into the narrow tongue of cold water that ran back out into the open sea. Matt's soul resonated happily to the familiar smell of saltwater and rotting seaweed, and the ever-present hiss and splash of tumbling waves that crashed onto the jagged rocks at the base of the Admiral. In his darkest moments, it was here he came, to his Admiral, to seek refuge, renewal and inspiration. He placed a notebook and pen on the flat rock in front of him and looked out across the ocean, reflecting on the events of the week.

Already it was Saturday, and the death of the policeman on the previous Monday seemed a distant event. Woodson was expected to make a full recovery and according to the island intelligence, usually amazingly accurate, although often not without some degree of embellishment, he would be back on duty in six weeks. Constable Dunning did not come out to inspect Humpy, but instead, took their statements over the telephone and again thanked them for their assistance at the accident scene, insisting that the sergeant would most definitely have died without the Ryans intervention.

He had caught up with Cassie on the telephone on the Thursday night. Her life was, as always, busy: helping with the crutching, feeding sheep, exercising Kingston and religiously honouring her daily two-hour dance routine in the stable loft studio. It was when she mentioned the things to be done before she left for Sydney that he winced.

He turned from the ocean view and sat in his usual place, the comfortable writing-chair rock that overlooked the seals' playground. His attention was drawn to the movement of two adolescent pups, a male and a female swimming almost as one, their bodies entwining, coupling and rolling in unison, their large brown eyes wide with wonder, expectation and excitement.

The pleasant sensation of hot blood rushing through his body caught him unawares, as his mind replayed the images of the graceful and erotic movements of his Cassie dancing on the sand at Cape Kersaint the previous Sunday. He smiled and laughed aloud as the female pup rose to the top of the water, her tail beating up a flurry of foam, her front flippers slapping together in joyous applause for the gawking admiration of her male suitor, floating on his back before her. Without warning the happy playfulness under the arch changed dramatically when a dark presence entered the space and the cavorting switched to a race for survival.

The older group of seals rushed for the rocks. The lovers' eyes grew wide with panic and for a long moment they froze unsure of what to do. The massive dark shape moved swiftly along the tongue of water toward them. Too late; the youngsters swam desperately toward the sloping rock, the male slightly ahead of his mate, and scrambled up the slippery surface. At first it looked like they had made it, but the huge form of the great white shark, riding on its own momentum surged onto the rock close behind them and took the young female in its mouth, the exposed teeth sawing and chomping through her mid-section, cutting her almost in half. And then the monster lost momentum, stalled and slid back into the water with the bloody mammal still struggling hopelessly caught vice-like in the killer's perfect mouth.

Matt and the surviving seals were spellbound. The shark sank and swam slowly back to the open ocean a red trail briefly marking the horror, but it quickly dissipated and the amphitheatre returned to its wild normalcy, except for the distraught mate and a pondering Matt. In a quick, brutal moment, nature's process was graphically demonstrated, the life of the seal for the life of the shark.

Words began to ticker tape through his mind: passion, fire, rage, heat, alive, dark, life, lust, battle, death. He reached for the notebook and began scribbling more words, crossing them out, replacing them and rearranging their order to fit the structure of his chosen poetic form, a sestina. Feverishly, he worked around a final six, each one marking the end of a line in each of six stanzas.

At last, he had the first draft of the first stanza. His mind groped for a title; on top of the page he wrote, "Lust: Life's Fiery Centre."

"God, Katherine! You startled me."

"I'm sorry." She looked past him to the ocean. "This is such a wonderful place for inspiration, isn't it?" She smiled. "I've been here a few minutes and wanted to say something, but you were absorbed in your work, I didn't want to interrupt.

You get really focused, don't you, when you are being creative? Can you tell me something of what you are writing?"

"Oh, I don't think…I'm trying to put something together for the competition."

"Is it a poem?"

"Well, yeah, sort of."

"Can I read it?"

"It's only the first draft…oh well; I don't suppose it will be a problem, hey?" He tore the page from the notebook and handed it to her.

"Thank you." She took her time and read it twice.

"Wonderful, this is powerful. I have never really thought about relationships in this way; it seems you are writing about the connection between lust and love, both having the same primary goals: pleasure, pain, procreation, human survival. Is that what you are driving at?"

Matt was taking in the action of the waves that relentlessly pounded the Brothers and the Admiral, year after year, circling them with a permanent periphery of white foam. "Yeah, I saw two seals cavorting together under the Admiral, something of a mating ritual, when a shark took one of them. Something beyond the brutality of what happened got me thinking about the relationship between life and lust; sex, food, the driven savagery of the shark and the idea just popped into my head out of nowhere about lust being one of life's imperatives."

"Hmm, God is always talking to us. We just have to listen for his voice." She took a deep breath. "This is the perfect place to write, isn't it? I feel safe here, free and close to God."

"Yeah," He paused, deep in thought. "They eat fish to live, the seals, you know, just like the shark, which was following its instinct to survive. The act, brutal as it was, carried a certain beauty and justification. Do you think we live like that, have to live like that, at times soaring, tender, loving, serene, but also, like the shark, savage and brutal?"

"I'm not one for such weighty concerns, Matthew. I think God's plan is ideal for each of us, and it's simpler to leave matters to him." She looked at her watch. "You'd better run along; the boys can't be late for tennis."

He got to his feet, ready to walk back with her to the cottage. "No, you go on ahead. I'll be along in a minute," she said, looking beyond him to the Casuarina Islets, the solitary Brothers, the du Couedic guardians who were the first to challenge the persistent violence of the great southern sea. A few clouds drifted across the face of the sun, turning the bright morning a sudden gray. A rush of wind blew in from the south. All at once, the air was chilly.

Matt prepared to leave and saw that Katherine appeared to be talking to someone. He paused, curious, listening and the tone of her voice scared him. "Please, Lord, keep my boys safe."

# 22

Out in the boonies farmers were isolated, their work physically demanding and good returns for their efforts challenged by price fluctuations and unpredictable seasonal factors. The wives often pitched in to get the outside work done, and the kids, too, after the school bus dropped them off in the afternoon. There was the stock to feed: sheep to pen at shearing and crutching time, crops to plant, hay cutting, harvesting, grape pruning and everyday chores, milking the house cow before and after school along with firewood to cut for the kitchen stove. The weekend was a prize, an opportunity to kick back a little, catch up with neighbours and locals, and pick up a snippet or two of gossip along with a visit to the general store in Parndana, Kingscote, Penneshaw, or American River to shop for supplies.

Sport played a big part in the community's social life, too, and Saturday was sports day. The locals, including the kids, tested their skills against other island districts and the rivalry could be intense. It was not uncommon for a few wild jabs to be exchanged in the heat of a close footy game, but at the end of the day, socializing over a few beers at the local watering hole mended any animosity that lingered from the field.

For the West-Enders, the small township of Gosse was the centre for their sports and social activity. Well, Gosse was hardly a town, but that was what the map said 'Gosse Township'. It consisted of a community centre building, football oval, clubrooms, tennis courts and basketball courts. There was no store, and it was surrounded by thick scrub inhabited by kangaroos, wallabies, snakes, goannas and other fauna and flora. Almost hidden in the scrub, the town could easily be missed by a speeding tourist along the Cape Borda Road, and that was often the case. Until the early 1950s, before the soldier settler development scheme got underway, the west end of the island was mostly an uninterrupted landscape of trees and scrub from south to north, except for two rough pioneering tracks that snaked along two of the coasts, one southwest to Cape du Couedic and the other northwest to Cape Borda. Gosse was a part of the Federal Government's Returned Soldiers Land Resettlement Scheme created for Australian soldiers who fought in World War II, which qualified them for the opportunity to settle and farm the virgin land.

With the clock ticking past six o'clock, the bar and lounge areas of the community centre were already crowded. Thirsts primed from combat in the afternoon heat, tennis and cricket players along with spectators and kids were 'dropping down' copious quantities of beer, rum and cokes and raspberry-lemonade mixes. Three bar attendants were flat out like lizards drinking, trying to keep up with the demand. Two women were furiously processing orders for counter dinners shouted to them through the kitchen opening by cheeky players, kids and mothers. "Pepper steak, a serve of whiting, and five plates of chips for the kids," yelled one mother with a kid balanced on each hip. "Hey, Meg," a young, red-haired, freckled face cricketer, still in his whites and balancing a tray of schooners of beer, shouted, "Throw a rump on for me when you've got a sec, will ya? Medium rare would be about right."

"You'll be waiting all night if I wait 'til I'm not busy, Bluey. Where's the please in your vocabulary?" scolded Meg, as she picked out a prime rump steak from an alloy dish holding twenty-plus superb cuts. "It'll be ready in a few," she yelled back, throwing the steak onto the sizzling hotplate, sweat streaking down her pudgy cheeks and then turning to the next customer.

A continuing flow of early arrivals for the church barn dance swelled the crowd to over 200 animated revellers. Two young cricketers from the host club leapt over the bar to help the swamped servers. Organized chaos best described the Saturday evening ritual, as those with topped-up schooners, froth slopping over the top and sliding down frosty glasses, an image that could bring a red-blooded Australian male to tears if deprived of the amber fluid for too long, spilled outside to make room for the growing crowd.

Matt was walking across the oval from the club rooms when ahead of him he saw a group of young kids shouting and yelling. Becoming clearer as he got closer, two of the youngest kids were fighting for possession of a small bike. Sean was hanging onto the front handle bars and tugging viciously to pull the bike away from a bigger boy who was holding onto the rear wheel; Sean's bare feet were clawing the gravel, and he was yelling viciously. "Let go, let go, I got it first!"

The other boy, who happened to be Sean's best mate, nick-named 'Butch', was crying and yelling, "It's my bike; give it back!"

"Let go, shithead, I got it first." With that, Sean jerked the bike free, mounted it and tried to escape, his little feet pedalling like crazy. 'Butch' took off after him. Matt saw that things were going to get way out of hand. He took three quick steps, reached out and grabbed Sean off the bike before 'Butch' got to him first. Sean was not happy, but realized he could be in trouble.

"Whose bike is it?" asked Matt.

"It's his," answered Sean. 'Butch' was now quiet. Nobody fooled with Sean's big brother.

"Okay, so give it back to him and say you're sorry."

"Sorry," said a surly Sean, as he handed over the bike.

"All right; now, 'Butch', put your bike somewhere safe, and then you come inside with Sean and me, and I'll get you both a raspberry drink, hey?"

Matt and Sean waited while 'Butch' disappeared to hide his bike. Sean looked up at his hero, a smug look on his face. "I'm a good fighter, aren't I Matt?"

Matt grinned, "Yeah, you're a good fighter, mate, but you don't want to fight your best mate, hey?"

"I bet he gives me the bike next time I want it."

'Butch' arrived and the three of them headed into the Community Club lounge. Frank was at the bar; Matt caught his attention and raised two fingers to indicate a drink for the boys. He sat at the table Katherine and Pat had secured for the family; a table away from the bar and in front of a window opened to the southwest where a light, cool breeze helped keep the temperature reasonably comfortable in the crowded room. Frank was right at home, leaning on the bar lined with noisy drinkers, and managing to get a quick one away while waiting for his order to be filled. Matt watched his father place the empty glass back on the bar.

Frank, now in the jovial stage of his drinking day, smiled and winked impishly at Matt. The server set the drinks on the bar: a rum and coke for Katherine, a beer for Matt, and a couple of raspberries for the three boys. Frank peeled a hundred dollar note from a roll as thick as his fist and passed it to the young cricketer behind the bar. He pocketed the roll of notes and change in his baggy jeans and waved Matt over to help carry the drinks.

The thirsty boys quickly emptied their glasses. "Can we go now?" squealed an impatient Sean, gasping for breath while banging the glass down on the table.

Frank was sitting beside Katherine with his arm draped over her shoulder. "Yeah, all right, but before you go, take this." He reached into his pocket, pulled out two crumpled twenty-dollar notes from the change and handed one each to the boys. "I want you lads to have a good time tonight. Buy your own dinner and leave your mum and me alone, hey? Now, piss off." The boys scampered away to join their mates, chuckling.

Matt was used to his father's generosity, usually on payday every two weeks, or from the cash he received from the business twice a year, and then after he had consumed a few ales to counter his usual irritability, he slipped into a philanthropic frame of mind.

"I suppose you reckon some of this is yours, hey?" said Frank, reaching back into his pocket and drawing out the roll of hundred dollar bills.

"A couple of hundred would help out right now. I'll get the rest off you next week when I pick up the ute."

"Did Harry get that bull-bar on? You'll hit another 'roo sooner or later; bastards are all over the place."

Matt was still angry with himself for not slowing down where it was common knowledge among the islanders that hundreds of kangaroos and wallabies crossed the South Coast Road from the scrub on the south side to the pastures on the north where they fed every night. He had hit a big buck 'roo there a couple of months earlier, which caused three and a half thousand dollars damage to his vehicle. What had angered him at the time was that the 'roo jumped right back up and bounded off like nothing happened.

"Yeah, he put on an aluminium one, tough as steel, but a lot lighter. He reckons you save heaps of petrol."

"Good," said Frank, peeling off three hundred dollars and handing it to Matt. "There's a bit extra in there, buy your Shelia something nice."

"Geez, you're laying it on a bit thick tonight, aren't you?" teased Matt.

"Don't use the Lord's name in vain, Matthew," said Katherine, gently scolding her stepson.

The conversation was interrupted by the roar of a motorbike skidding to a halt outside the window next to the Ryan table. Astride the bike, a dashing figure dressed in black leathers and a black helmet, his face hidden behind the helmet's reflective visor, peered through the window at the Ryans. Matt glared into the visor, but saw only the reflection of his strained features staring back at him. Jordan Baldwin revved the engine to an unbearable screaming and held it there for a few seconds, taunting his enemy before shutting it down and dismounting. Kids appeared from all directions to crowd around their Darth Vader hero.

Frank's congeniality evaporated. "That prick is asking for it, always causing a bloody stir." He tipped back his chair to get up. "I'm gonna have a few words with him."

"No! Not tonight; don't start anything here." Matt placed a hand on Frank's chest. "He's drunk and looking for trouble with us, with me, really. He'll come unstuck on his own."

Frank glared at Matt, fighting for self control. He tossed down the rest of his drink, pushed back his chair and stood up. "Okay, but you better make sure he keeps well away from me, son. I won't put up with any bull from him, pommy upstart. It was the likes of him and his father that threw our people into the holds of filthy ships and transported us out here, the few of us that didn't die on the way out, that is, and they still try to keep us under with their money and fancy gerrymanders, so stuff 'em." He stomped angrily to the bar.

Matt shrugged; Katherine sighed with resignation. "Your father really is a good man, Matt; been through a lot, Vietnam and all. I pray for him; I pray every day that he will find peace and be happy."

Matt nodded and turned toward the bar and his father. *Oh shit, there's gonna be trouble here before the night is out.*

# 23

Matt took a long swig from his fourth stubby and looked at his watch, five after nine. The barn dance was in full swing and the local lads, already boisterous from the effects of South Australia's favourite West End beer, were crowding about the main doors, snickering and gawking at the local beauties sitting along the walls: chatting, pointing, staring, flirting and giggling. The band started playing another bracket, and the older couples were quick onto the floor.

Feeling comfortable, relaxed and looking forward to Cassie's arrival, Matt pushed further into the hall, chuckling at the snippets of conversation coming from among the well lubricated males. "Phew, she's a beauty, mate." "Geez, Stumpy, 'ave a go at her, bloody beautiful, hey?" "She's home from college, mate. Reckon the girls from there are real goers, too, hey?" "Go'n, go'n, ask her."

From the elevated stage at the far end of the hall, the band's 40s and 50s era music was stirring up the now crowded dance floor of sweating bodies swinging to a hyped-up quick-step. Kids of all ages and sizes were sliding in the sawdust spread on the floor to make it slick and fast, skidding dangerously around the feet of the hustling couples. Sean was in heaven, slipping and sliding from one end of the hall to the other in a stylish crouch, a cheeky grin spread across his face, bumping into other kids and sending them flying off into the sidewalls. Matt chuckled and thought about Snot in Sean's pocket. He knew the tiny mouse would be on the floor as soon as Martha showed up.

The band was made up of five local blokes who played piano, violin, drums, guitar, trumpet and saxophone, and they were going all out. Molly Owens, a jolly, middle-aged woman with huge breasts amply displayed in the low cut of her cotton dress and blessed with a voice that could lift the roof of an amphitheatre, was singing her heart out. Tradition dictated the band be kept well oiled, and the Irish Catholic church hosts were not remiss in maintaining a generous flow of the local brew within arm's reach. Maxi Feldman, seventy years old, bald, cheeks ballooning as he sucked, spat and blew through the reed of his mouthpiece, sweat pouring off his ruddy head, boogied about the stage, his notes exploding through the building and out into the warm night air, signalling "it's a party time in here, you lot."

Eventually, the bracket ended. The dancers cleared the floor, leaving the kids to create even greater chaos as more of them crowded onto the polished boards to do "broggies" and yell and squeal with gleeful malice. Much to Sean's delight, Martha arrived and joined in the bedlam. However, before Sean could act and pull *Snot* from his pocket, Martha, quick to exact her revenge for the previous Sunday's humiliation, slammed into him and sent the boy cannoning into the women sitting along the wall. Laughing, two high school girls picked him up, dusted him off and made the kind of fuss that women all over the world seem to make over cute little boys. Martha, hands on hips and feet set apart in a defiant pose, looked at the disoriented and vanquished little warrior with a triumphant 'get even' smirk.

Matt laughed and turned to look along the line of women. The beautiful redhead staring at him touched off a tingling sensation that electrified his body, its intensity catching him off-guard. Maureen gave an especially alluring smile and waved, indicating she wanted to dance. His intuition warned that a dance with her could lead to trouble, big trouble. He flashed back a reluctant smile, shook his head with a "you'll get me into trouble" look and pointed to his watch.

Maxi called a fox trot for the next dance. Clasping his saxophone to his chest with one hand and filling his empty glass from the jug of beer resting on the piano with the other, he lifted the jug to his lips and guzzled down the contents without taking a breath. Cooling and oiling his parched and rusty throat, the amber draft washed through his delighted system all the way to his gut. With a satisfying belch, he wiped his mouth with the back of his hand and burped into the microphone, juiced up and ready to boogie. He grasped the saxophone's reedy mouthpiece between his teeth with the glee of a youngster grabbing onto the nipple of its mother's breast and launched into the next number.

With their courage fired up by the same miraculous potion, the young blokes scooted across the hall to grab a 'Sheila,' going after the 'good lookers' first. Matt tried to quell a sudden anxiety when the lovely redhead stood and began walking across the floor toward him. Smiling, she reached out to Matt, but a dark figure cut in front of her, took her hand and whisked her into the midst of the dancing couples.

Despite his gimpy leg, Jordan, with a sudden exuberance of flair and flamboyant conceit, demonstrated that he was no mug on the dance floor. Provocatively, he whirled his dazzling partner through the sawdust, sweeping close by Matt who could not ignore the perfect body of the beauty all the way from her red stiletto, open-toed shoes, supporting her long, sexy bare legs and perfect thighs to where they slipped tantalizingly out of view under the hem of her short tartan skirt.

"Oh, God help me, she's a bloody looker, all right," he muttered, as he noted the time on his watch, 9:15. Cassie had told him she should be there by 9:30. She was picking Monty up from the airport and had to drop him off at the homestead. He turned away from Maureen and Jordan and pushed back through the males crowding the entrance. Maureen watched from over Jordan's shoulder, smiling, and a glint of mischief in the emerald sparkle of her eyes.

Feeling the need to relieve himself before Cassie arrived, Matt walked beyond the parking lot and into the scrub to where the bushes were thick enough to screen him from public view. Unzipping his fly, he freed his best mate from the pressure of confinement, sighed with relief and delighted in the bliss of peeing unencumbered in the open space, a benefit of living in the bush easily taken for granted, but for the occasional reminder that came from a visit to the suffocating constraints of any city. In keeping with his usual habit, he looked up at the black canopy dotted with myriad stars that formed the Milky Way, a misty constellation familiar to those who lived under the southern sky. As always, he was fascinated by the unfathomable immensity of the universe. A meteorite shot across the sky, burning brilliantly for a few seconds before disintegrating.

*A metaphor of life; what a ride, riding this rock 'round and 'round our little part of the universe, hardly more than a speck of dust in the vastness of...of...what? Infinity; blows my mind every bloody time.*

He looked down at the source of his relief. "What'd you reckon, mate? Is that our life? A quick flash and then...it's all over. We sure as hell need to make the most it while we're here, hey?"

Suddenly, two arms circled his waist from behind, "I'll go along with that, no worries. Can I help you out with your mate down there, Matt?"

"Geez, Maureen! What the hell are...?

Maureen pulled him around, hugged him tight to her body and pushed her tongue into his mouth. Her passion rushed through him like a firestorm and triggered an immediate response in his exposed 'member', the early beers dissolving any lingering resistance to Maureen's surprise entrapment.

"C'mon, Matt, I've wanted to do this for a long time," she panted and lifted her skirt.

The effect on Matt was explosive. With all self-control taken over by his unprincipled mate, he sped toward disaster.

"Whoa, whoa, Matt, ease up or it'll be all over before it started."

Her breathy request was enough to cause him to stop, to think; to think long enough for images of Cassie to enter his head: Cassie dancing on the beach, Cassie unbelievably happy, Cassie, her eyes glistening, her beauty overwhelming. A horrifying and sickening sense of guilt ripped through his gut, and he stepped back.

"What are you doing? I don't want you to stop, just slow down a little." She moved to put her arms around him.

"No, no, back off, Maureen, please. I don't want to do this," he said pushing her away and quickly tucking his errant member into the relative safety of his pants.

"Well, well, well. Look at what we have here. Seems I've shown up at an inappropriate moment?" A sarcastic, slurring Jordan stepped through the cluster of thick bulloak. "At it again, are we, Ryan?"

"Jordan!" Matt was instantly filled with a crushing sense of dread. Maureen froze. Jordan was smirking, triumphant.

"It's not what you think," said Matt.

Jordan laughed. "Give me a break, Ryan; you were at it, all right, *hard* at it. I saw with my own eyes, and you tell me it is not what I see. I wonder what my ever-so-gullible sister will make of it when I tell her."

"You rotten bastard, Jordan, you followed me!" screamed Maureen.

Matt waved the girl away. "I'll take care of this, Maureen. You get out of here."

"I'm...I'm sorry...sorry, Matt. That bastard..."

"I said I'll take care of it. Now go on...go on back to the hall."

She turned, but the heel of the stiletto on her left foot caught in the exposed roots of a young wattle tree and came off. She took what remained of the shoe off, screamed with rage and threw it at Jordan.

"You rotten mongrel, Jordan, this is all your fault!"

"Maureen, get the bloody hell out of here!" shouted Matt.

"All right, all right, I'm going." She took off the other shoe and threw it at Jordan. "Here's the other one, ya mongrel!" she yelled. "They'd probably look just right on you anyway." She left and pushed through the bulloak back to the hall.

Despite the seriousness of his situation, Matt could not help thinking of its irony. Here, under an extraordinary canopy of stars in the scrub on tiny Kangaroo Island, riding this amazing rock called earth through an infinite universe, the very fact of its reality testing the most brilliant minds, a contemplation so complex, so deep, God seemed the only explanation. Yet, juxtaposed with all of it, two males faced off over something pathetically trivial in the grand scheme of things. And, as was often the case, human behaviour overrode the grand journey with a pointless self-absorption and right-eousness.

"Got you cold, Ryan," said Jordan, sneering.

Matt was silent and guilt ridden. As he looked into the face glaring back at him, he saw depicted the mask of tragedy from the two-sided logo of the theatrical arts, the one reflecting pain, anger, fear and sadness, the feelings he knew so well. Compassion fuelled his empathy and stayed his first impulse to attack the threatening Jordan. He talked quickly, urgently. "Listen, Jordan, I've never had anything against you. We have a few things in common. We both lost our mothers around the same time, and we went to the same primary school. Oh, I knew you were never really one of us ordinary kids, you grew up rich, but we all got on okay. It was after your bloody fool stunt, you turned mean, crazy, or something, didn't you? Twenty-two years of age and you climb into an empty 44-gallon oil drum and roll down Kohinoor Hill. One hundred and fifty meters before you're thrown out; and how long were you in the coma? Twelve days? The money was on you dying, nearly killed your Oldman. Stuffed up your leg, ruined your sporting career and almost took your face off, all for what? Maybe, down deep in your gut you just wanted to fit in, to be one of us ordinary blokes, hey? Is that what you were thinking when those dip-shit Rankin brothers called you a gutless wonder and talked you into climbing into the barrel?"

Jordan was caught off-guard, confused and distracted by Matt's unexpected approach. The quick downing of a dozen or so beers at the dance combined with the reliving of the *incident* cut through the layers of protection he'd kept in place to keep him safe from being humiliated and hurt again.

"You okay, Jordan?"

Jordan snapped back to the present and snarled. "I don't know what you did, Ryan, you had me going for awhile. You're a smart bugger, all right, but you can't con me. Cassie is going to know all about your fooling around."

"For heaven's sake, Jordan, I don't give a damn about me. What's the matter with you? It's Cassie you'll hurt most."

The look on Jordan's face told Matt all he needed to know. "You bastard, Jordan, it's her you want to hurt, isn't it? Even more than me, you sick…"

Jordan closed his fists and took a wild swing at Matt, but Matt was ready and managed to sway to his side, mitigating the force of the fist that just clipped his chin. Angry and now out of control, Matt charged headfirst into Jordan's stomach, taking him to the ground and slamming his head into the dirt. He grabbed his stunned adversary around the throat with both hands and squeezed. Jordan struggled fiercely, but he could not break the hold; his face was turning purple, and then he stopped struggling, his eyes rolled back and a terrible rattling sound emerged from his throat. Shocked, Matt realized he was killing Cassie's brother; he pulled his hands from the man's throat and stood up, horrified and scared by what he had almost done.

Jordan was coughing, wheezing, fighting for air and thoroughly frightened. "You're crazy, Ryan, crazy. You tried to kill me," he croaked.

"For God's sake, Jordan, stay away from me." Panting heavily, Matt stood over his enemy. "Stay away from me. Stay away and keep your bloody mouth shut about any of this." He stepped off into the bulloak and made for the hall.

Jordan watched Matt disappear into the bush. "I'll get you, you Mick bastard; I'll get you for this," he squeaked through a bruised throat.

# 24

Cassie was driving fast, way too fast for the perils inherent along the great Cape Borda Road, but she was running late and eager to see Matt. Tired from an unusually busy day, she did not see the kangaroo on the side of the road until the very last second before it jumped out in front of the Pathfinder. She swerved violently and narrowly avoided the animal, but her SUV slid sideways, dangerously out of control from the ball bearing-like effect of the ironstone gravel under her tires. Instinctively, she turned the front wheels against the slide, saving her from a certain rollover and, her angel working overtime, eventually slid to stop centimetres from a massive white gum tree by the side of the road. Dust swirled through the hi-beam of the headlights and quickly settled, an eerie silence replacing the clatter of flying gravel bombarding the body of the SUV moments before.

Breathing quickly, almost panting, she sat clutching the steering wheel, hands shaking, looking out beyond the windshield, fighting to regain composure. She took a deep breath, shut her eyes and concentrated on relaxing, letting the tension drain with every slow exhale. Her mind was soon reflecting the events of the day.

With Monty away for the day in Adelaide, Cassie had been busier than usual: feeding the dogs, dropping hay bales into the ram paddock, feeding grain to the 2,000 ewes in the way-back paddock, taking Winston for his workout through the hills before finishing with an easy canter along the beach before his favourite exercise, a swim in the surf. By skipping lunch, she was able to keep to her afternoon routine of working out in the studio. Each day at the same time, her favourite time: two hours plus of music, stretching, and dancing through a series of choreographed exercises until she was exhausted and exhilarated, all at once. As a child, she would watch her mother for hours dancing in the very same studio, enchanted; watch her arms, so elegant in their movement, especially when raised over her head in a classic *en couronne*; be enthralled, as she swept, floor-foot classically *en pointe*, a gloriously sculptured leg stretching upward in a perfect *grande battement*, extending her foot in a perfectly curved arch, reaching above and beyond the level of her wild, dark hair wet with sweat.

"Come, Cassandra, try it," Kristina would say in her Spanish-accented voice, reaching gently to take the tiny five-year-old hand and help her balance while she stood on *demi-pointe*, stretching *her* leg and arching *her* foot to almost match the perfection of her mother's *grande battement*. She would have been happy to spend all afternoon in the studio, but Monty was arriving on the evening flight from Adelaide, and she had to pick him up.

"Sweet Jesus, thank you for watching over me." She reversed onto the road and, in a bold display of defiance floored the accelerator, spun the back wheels in the gravel and fishtailed for fifty meters down the road in the direction of Gosse. "Keep a lookout, girl," she said aloud, chuckling while snatching a look at the clock set into the dashboard, its glowing green digits showing 9:15. "It'll be 9:30 by the time I get there; not too bad, considering."

As she drove, her thoughts turned to her father. He had looked worn-out when he stepped off the plane. She had been trying for a long time to get him to give up his Freeman Club board position. Politics held no interest for her, but Monty was passionate and active about his Liberal Party involvement.

"The Kangaroo Island discussion was tough," Monty had told her. "The right wing is pushing for the liberal government to enforce the state's drug laws. They want the police commissioner to target the island aggressively because of the marijuana growing here, and they say it is getting way too far out of control. The pharmaceuticals are the ones behind it, really—afraid of how the big push that's going on now for the legalization of medical marijuana might affect their product sales."

"I thought you were against the idea of legalizing marijuana?" Cassie questioned.

"Yes, and I'm still against it; we have enough problems with alcohol, Jordan being a prime example. It's the timing I'm not happy about. Right now, a significant percentage of the farmers are close to going out of business because of the low wool and meat prices. As you know, that is having a very serious affect on the rest of the island economy. Cultivating a small amount of the marijuana and sending it to a mainland distribution outlet could mean the difference between keeping the farms operating, and losing the lot to the bankers. This is not the time to harass the Islanders; they have enough to contend with and, anyhow, it seems that support for marijuana cultivation for medical pot is growing. I think it will eventually become a legal reality."

Cassie saw a small wallaby on the side of the road and slowed. She passed safely and returned to her thoughts. Monty was having a harder time with her leaving than he was letting on. Of course, she was having her own misgivings. Kangaroo Island had been the biggest part of her life for twenty years. She knew she would miss the farm, the daily rides on Winston and the freedom of living a mostly uncomplicated life on one of the earth's most precious and pristine locations. She did not want to let her father down, and the truth of the matter was that she loved to dance and she was very, very good at it.

Surprisingly, the separation from Matt was less of a wrench. Deep in her soul, she knew, yes, knew that they would be together. A power greater than her, a Higher Power, was working in their lives, a Power that she had been acutely aware of after her mother's death. When she got right down to it, though, she did fear for Matt; no, not about losing him, but about the low sense of self-worth he at times exhibited. The battering he had taken as a kid had left him little self-esteem, and he needed love and nurturing. Tough love, too; he had a tendency to wallow in self-pity, a characteristic she told him served no useful purpose, and that the most productive way to get over it was to do something for someone who was in real trouble. She grinned; *God knows I love him*. Of course, it was not one sided; he had awakened her to another part of herself, the urge to fulfil a hunger deeply rooted, but so essentially woman, to become a mother. It would be Matt who fathered her children; you could take that to the bank.

The welcome glow of diffused light above the trees surrounding the Gosse Community Centre signalled she was close to the turn-off to the gravel track leading into the township. As she turned into the parking lot, her headlights swept over the large crowd that was drinking and laughing in the temporary beer garden set up alongside the hall. She slowed for a mother, crossing to check on her child asleep in one of the vehicles strategically parked in a dark area of the car lot. While looking for a spot to park the Pathfinder, she saw Matt walk out of the scrub and merge into the spill-over crowd at the hall entrance. She smiled and turned into a space between two station wagons and only a few meters from the main doors, hoping the light from the beer garden would discourage the males from urinating in the vicinity of her vehicle, all the while aware that as the night wore on and they got drunker modesty became less of a consideration, anyway. Mrs. Fahey was the one to sort them out. When she caught them peeing around her car, she would yell, "If that's all you have to showcase, you would be better off to keep it hidden and save yourself the mirth of the women I know who love to gossip." Rarely did a male ever pee near Mrs. Fahey's car unless he wanted to make a point.

****

A visibly upset Matt pushed his way through the crowded doorway of the hall; he was angry with himself mostly because of his stupidity, encouraging Maureen, responding to her flirtation with his own.

"Fair go, Matt," said one of the young drinkers, spilling his beer, as Matt bumped him.

"Sorry, Bluey."

"That's one you owe me, Mate; next time you're at the bar wouldn't be too soon."

"Don't hold your breath," replied Matt coldly.

Bluey was tempted to respond, but decided against it. Matt was looking pretty pissed off. A quick scan of the room told him that Cassie was still on her way.

"Ya looking deep in thought there, young Matthew," said a friendly, familiar voice. The sight of Monsignor Byrne triggered the guilt he felt about what had happened with Maureen. He would have to tell the priest in confession, and the old bloke would want to hear every detail.

Matt thoughts flashed to the question the priest had asked him one night after benediction when they were changing out of their altar attire? "How's that girlfriend of yours?" he had said. "Have you two had sex yet?" Matt was shocked, but the follow-up was a real doozy. "Well, be sure ya use a French letter if ya at it, then." Matt didn't think priests even talked about sex, but the worldly monsignor believed that, if he was to be effective among the young males in his flock, he needed to communicate to them on a level that would have them feel comfortable to share anything troubling them.

"Ah, not really, Monsignor," Matt lied, not daring to look the priest in the eye. "Big crowd; I hope the parish makes a killing tonight."

"We'll do just fine. We're gettin a share of the grog take, so that'll push up the night's overall profit." He placed an arm around Matt. "Come along here now, and I'll buy ya a beer; ya look like ya could do with one. It'll give us a chance to chat about the coming competition. I trust ya working hard on ya projects?"

Matt nodded a 'yes'. As they walked into the supper room, Maureen entered from the door of the female toilets.

She flashed Matt an adorably innocent smile and stopped, blocking their path and then gave the monsignor a cheeky wink.

"Don't you look the catch of the night, Monsignor? Are you having a good time?"

"I am, and ya look like ya enjoying yourself, Maureen, along with everyone else, it seems."

"Yes, and I think it's going to liven up a lot more before the night's out, Monsignor." Winking provocatively at Matt, she pirouetted and sashayed barefooted into the dance hall.

"She's a wild one there, Matthew, and she's definitely got ya in her sights, there's no mistak'n that look. Ah, the power of young hormones, and there's plenty of them dancin' about this place tonight, I'll tell ya that. Ah, she's a good Catholic girl, I know, and she'll settle down and make a good mother," he offered, years of ministry reflecting his understanding of the human condition.

"I wouldn't know about any of that, Father," said Matt warily.

\*\*\*\*

Cassie made her way toward the door, as the police wagon from Kingscote swung onto the township road and made its way slowly toward the hall, its headlights on hi-beam lighting up the crowd in the beer garden. Like moths attracted to a lamp, a few of the well-lubricated lads turned to welcome the new copper with a stream of good-natured mockery.

"You're a bit early, mate; the footy season don't start for another couple've months."

"Yeah, bloke, we gotta get the snakes cleared off the oval before the first game yet, too."

"On the way home, watch out for Macca's pet goanna on Hendy's corner. The bastard gets out on the road, occasionally, and you got to watch out you don't hit one of its legs; do you right in, that would. If you aim for under the belly, you'll get through all right."

The locals howled with laughter. A grinning Dunning reversed the wagon into a parking spot that allowed him oversight of the entrance and the most active outside areas, including the beer garden. He saw Cassie appear from the parking lot, heading for the hall entrance.

Cassie threaded her way through the crowd milling outside the hall entrance. Her presence was not lost on a group of admiring males, many of whom she knew from school and sport gatherings.

"Yep, g'day, Cass," said one young fellow, somewhat intimidated by the tall, elegant young woman, but finding some beer-assisted courage to actually speak to her.

"Hello, Nugget," she said, smiling. "You look like you're having a good time."

She moved on, leaving a heroic Nugget swooning. "Ah, Jeez; cop that, did ya, Blue? I'm in bloody love, mate."

"Yeah, you and half the mob here tonight," replied the flaming red-haired Bluey, tossing the last of his beer down his thirsty throat. "She's on with Matt, mate, lucky bugger. Here, give us ya glass, and I'll top 'er up."

Maxi's band was beginning a new dance bracket when she finally made it into the hall. Pausing on the fringe of the dance floor, she looked among the dancers for Matt. Her eyes passed over the band to the supper room door, adjacent to the stage, where she caught a glimpse of Monsignor Byrne inside talking to someone partially out of her line of sight, but looked like it might be Matt. She started for the supper room when a tap on the shoulder caused her to turn.

****

"Now, tell me more, how's ya writing coming on?" said the priest, pouring two glasses of beer from a jug kept full by the local parishioners. He handed a glass to Matt and lifted the other to his lips. "Here's to ya writing, lad." He swallowed the beer in one magnificent gulp. "A beautiful drop from the Lord his-self that dances on the tongue of a t'irsty man, Matthew; both a curse and a blessing, but 'tis surely hit'n the right spot at this blessed moment."

Matt emptied his glass. The effect was instant, the worms retreated. He motioned for a refill. "I think I'm doing all right, Monsignor. Dad was a lot quieter last week. I got the processor up and running, thank you, and I'm doing better than the hour-a-day you wanted, so I've been able to make some real progress. My essay is about Kangaroo Island and, well, having lived here all my life, it gives me something I'm intimate with at least. Bit like recording the facts and trying to make an interesting story out of it all. Then this morning, I started a poem that got me excited; a sestina, a French form of poetry that I kind of understand and like to work with…helps stimulate my thoughts. Now don't choke on me, but I'm calling it 'Lust: Life's Fiery Centre.'"

****

"G'day, Cassie," said a smiling Robert Dunning. "I hope I'm not intruding."

"Oh, Bob, hi, no, of course not. I saw you drive up a few minutes ago and heard the locals give you a bit of a roasting," she said, gushing slightly, unable to ignore his dark good looks and the dashing figure he cut in his khaki uniform and light-brown Akubra hat, the South Australian police badge precisely centered on its blue and white chequered hatband. The pistol holstered high on his brown police belt added just the right touch of macho authority to his presence, and there it was again, that unmistakable hint of aboriginal ancestry in the structure of his face, suggesting an ancient wisdom deep within from which to draw. She noticed some of the young women who were sitting and standing around the hall, staring at him.

"I only just got here; I'm looking for Matt. I think he might be in there," she said, pointing to the supper room, "talking to the monsignor."

"Well, don't let me hold you up; I'd like to see you before you leave."

"It's okay; I'd rather not interrupt Matt if he's talking to the monsignor. Want to dance?"

"I'd love to," said Dunning, "but I'm on duty and regulations…"

"Don't allow it." She flirtatiously feigned heartfelt sorrow. "Where is the justice, but next time, no excuses? So, what do you want to talk about?"

The music stopped and Maxi reached for the microphone. "Ah, I see our new constable, talking to one of our prettiest girls, Cassie Baldwin. First time out here to Gosse, I believe. Welcome, Constable Bob Dunning. We out here on this end of the island would like to wish you the best, appreciate your service, and, err, mind the goannas on the way home, hey, big as dinosaurs out in this neck of the woods." The crowd howled with laughter. "I'm told you're a pretty classy football player, too."

"Thanks," the embarrassed constable called back. "I'm looking forward to playing, especially against the Western District Football Team. I'm told you blokes are a tough crowd."

"Just don't get too fancy when you play out here, Bob. Macca's goanna is the club mascot, and he's got a bloody foul temper, I can tell you, 'especially if the team's losing. And you can't control the bugger, neither, when he gets really pissed off," yelled one of the young players from the dance floor. The crowd roared with laughter again.

Chuckling, Dunning waved to Maxi and the crowd. In seconds, the band was going all out: Maxi's trumpet was spitting out the notes, dancers were whirling and the kids doing their usual thing; broggies all over the floor. The women left sitting along the wall during the earlier part of the evening were up and dancing with the young fellows too shy to ask before the effects of the grog kicked in to crank up their courage. Maureen was taking a more than casual interest in the two celebrities when one of the young cricketers got her up to dance.

****

The monsignor's blue eyes sparkled. "I can't wait to be read'n it. Now, have ya got the forms filled out? Ya supposed to bring them to mass tomorrow, so I can get 'em off to the Institute in plenty of time."

Maxi's gravelly voice suddenly boomed from the dance hall speakers and cut through their conversation. "Ah, I see our new constable out there, talking to one of our prettiest girls, Cassie Baldwin..."

Matt did not hear the rest of the sentence. Maxi's voice faded into a dull drone in the background of his tumbling mind. *Dunning?* The demon battalions were back, gnawing at the lining of his gut. *No, she wouldn't...* The threatened young man grabbed the fresh glass of beer from the table and gulped it down.

"What is it, boy? Ya look like ya swallowed a snake."

****

As the dancers bumped and gyrated to Maxi and his band's wild quickstep and jive, Dunning, Cassie still at his side, was enjoying the attention. "That caught me off guard. Hey, what's all this about Macca's goanna?"

"Macca's a local farmer's son who was always bragging about how big he grows things. He reckoned that when his turkeys got out on the road, everything was okay as long as the turkey had its legs open; the cars could drive right under its belly, same as with the lizard. He was always coming up with something. The latest was his tomatoes growing so big they had to be loaded onto the truck one at a time with a forklift."

"It sounds like they've got a hell of a sense of humour out here."

"Don't let it fool you. They can take and give out a lot of bull, but there is line you don't cross. The people out here will give you the shirt off their backs, but you cross them and they'd just as soon feed you to a great white. Your boss, Sergeant Woodson, doesn't get any help out of them."

"Yeah, I already experienced that out at the Ryans."

The music was getting louder. Sweat was flying off Maxi's bald head as he leaned back, the saxophone angling horizontally from his mouth while his 70-year-old pelvis gyrated spectacularly.

"Cassie, the last time we spoke, I mentioned that I'd been to college with Jordan. He and I don't have much in common except for football, but your dad did me a good turn once, and I can see your brother is heading for big trouble, so I'd like to help. I know some professionals who are very good with people who have problems similar to Jordan's."

"That's thoughtful of you, Bob; I appreciate the offer, I really do, but my father looks at Jordan's problems as a family matter, and as far as he's concerned the family will take care of it, and Dad can be very stubborn."

"Like his daughter, too, from what I hear," Dunning offered. Cassie laughed.

\*\*\*\*

"Gotta go, Monsignor, gotta go. Thanks," Matt said, avoiding the priest's eyes and placing the empty glass on the table before moving unsteadily through the door and into the dance hall.

"Ya look after yerself, Lad," the monsignor called after him.

"C'mon, Monsignor, what are you doing standing there with a beer in one hand and nothing to eat in the other?" A beaming Rosy Fahey put an arm around the priest and hustled him toward the tables overloaded with an assortment of homemade desserts. "Get something into you, Father. Gaud, you're getting so skinny you'll be flat out casting a shadow before too long."

When Matt passed through the door and into the dance hall, he saw Dunning and Cassie standing close to each other, talking and laughing. Sweat broke out on his forehead, his hands felt clammy and anxiety claimed him again. He had always reacted the same way when he felt vulnerable, when his most concealed thoughts emerged to tell him that he was not enough, could never be enough, particularly when it came to Cassie. *I need a bloody drink.* He stopped next to the stage and saw the half-full jug of the band's beer set on a guitar case, unattended. Grabbing the jug with both hands, he poured its contents down his throat, but to his consternation the usual affect of immediate relief from the 'panic attack' was nothing, no relief.

None of the unfolding drama was lost on Maureen, as she whirled about the floor with her drunken partner. She had watched Matt come in from the supper room and quaff down the jug of beer. Her attention, after returning from the bathroom had focused on the arrival of Cassie. How delicious it was to see the new and stunningly handsome policeman ingratiate himself before the well-heeled princess.

****

"Cassie," said Dunning, his demeanour becoming serious, "Jordan came out of the scrub a few minutes ago, looking very drunk and heading for the beer garden, trouble written all over him. Maybe, you could have a word with him before I have to get involved again. The magistrate will throw away the key if he has to appear before him again."

"I'll handle it." She placed her hand on Dunning's arm, "Thank you again, Bob; I'll have a chat with him right away."

"Look, it can wait. Matt is…"

"I'll be back, after I've spoken with Jordan. I want to nip this in the bud before he does something stupid."

"I'll come with you. I should make an appearance at the beer garden, anyway."

They moved toward the entrance, pushing through the group of young blokes, who immediately started up on Dunning again. "Hey, Bob, the girls have a bloody top basketball team here. They might give you a spot, if you're nice to 'em." "Ground's like concrete out here, mate, not like that pansy turf you played on in Adelaide."

"They're all full of piss and wind, Constable. From what I hear, we're going to have to put Matt Ryan on you to keep from tearing us apart."

"Well, we'll find out soon enough. Now don't you lads get too pissed and drive. It's going to take your team at its best to beat us when we get out here," said a chuckling, yet serious Bob Dunning.

Cassie and Dunning finally made it outside, unaware that Matt was watching.

# 25

Maureen watched Cassie and Dunning leave the hall arm in arm and then turned her attention back to Matt. She unwrapped from her dance partner and left him abandoned in the middle of the floor, wondering what the hell he had done, but drunk enough not to care. "Well, stuff you, then," he mumbled to no one in particular and then aimed unsteadily for the door and another beer.

Maureen crossed quickly to Matt, took him by the hand and jerked him onto the floor into the midst of the crowd before he could protest. "Matt, I'm not up to anything. I just want to apologize for what happened outside; I didn't know Jordan was lurking."

"It's over, forget it."

"I mean it, Matt, I'm sorry," she whispered, her cheek lightly touching his, her breath warm and scented with the spicy aroma of red wine. The tempo of the music changed, as Maxi ditched the saxophone and picked up his violin. Molly Owens started singing a heartrending version of "Angel of Music" from the *Phantom of the Opera*, not the usual fare for the locals, but one eagerly anticipated whenever Molly was on.

Maureen nuzzled Matt's ear. He pulled back. "C'mon, Maureen, cut it out; I'd better go."

"You can't leave me standing here, Matt; at least wait until Molly finishes her song," said Maureen.

"Okay, but cut the cuddle stuff, Moe."

"Sure…just for tonight though, mate. Did you sort out Jordan? He frightens me a bit, always causing trouble."

"Jordan? Yeah, we reached an understanding, I mean, I hope we did. He was crazy drunk…probably dope in the mix. What the hell, it really doesn't matter, anyway."

"What, what do you mean, 'it doesn't matter?' Oh, I get it, Cassie and the handsome Dunning. I wouldn't worry about that, Cassie would never have anyone but you while she's here on the island." Her voice carried a touch of derision. "Of course, in Sydney…I tell you, Matt, if anything happens…I mean, if you ever split up with Cassie, I'm here for you."

"What?"

"Well, Sydney is a long way from here, full of good-looking blokes, and she'll be in the middle of it all: the theatre, the ballet and the boys in tights. And there's bloody old Monty, too. Do you really believe he would ever let his daughter hitch up any Islander, let alone one from out this end?"

"Meaning me, of course, hey?"

He studied the gorgeous redhead. *Sly bitch*. He shrugged and broke into a self-effacing smile. "Ah, nothing, I'm just carrying on like a mug," he laughed, the grog at last beginning to work its magic. He kissed her lightly on the cheek. "You're a good sort, Moe. If it wasn't for Cassie…"

"I'll have you one day," she interrupted, a touch piqued. "You're too good a bloke, Matt. She'll be nicking off to Sydney soon, meeting all those city bull-dust artists, and that'll be the end of it."

Molly came to the end of her song. After the applause, the noise level in the hall faded dramatically to a low murmur.

The crowd of lads around the entrance had vanished. Outside, someone was shouting; a mix of cheering, screaming and angry voices signalled there was a fight going on in the beer garden. Sean appeared at the door, wide-eyed and obviously looking for his big brother. He saw him, took off waving furiously, slid heroically through the sawdust, a man on a mission, and had to grab Matt's leg to avoid a collision with Maureen.

"There's a fight, Matt," Sean said, puffing, his voice excited. "Dad and Jordan are into it. That copper was trying to stop them, but…you better come quick."

"Bugger it, here we go again." Matt was already moving to the door. He rounded the outside corner of the hall and there, in the midst of the crowd, was Frank and Jordan trading blows in a completely out-of-control and bloody fist fight.

Cassie was close to the two fighters, frantically shouting at them to stop. Dunning was sprawled in one of the chairs, looking decidedly uncertain as to his whereabouts. Then, frustrated by her inability to stop Jordan, Cassie jumped onto his back just as Frank took a wild swing. Jordan managed to duck the blow, unfortunately leaving Cassie's lovely face fully exposed to the rounding fist. Luckily, Frank's punch, its power mitigated by his imperfect aim and lack of reach, smacked her cheek a glancing blow with just enough impact to topple her from Jordan's back, leaving an angry red bruise under an instantly swelling eye.

Matt flew into a rage and launched an attack on his father with a fury that threatened homicide. "Damn you!" he yelled amid a flurry of punches to Frank's body, sending the drunk reeling back to crash heavily and slam the back of his head on the hard cement. Before the semi-conscious Frank could recover, Matt was on top of him, continuing to land punches until his strength and anger began to wane. "You bastard; you're a drunk, a hopeless bloody drunk, Dad."

Tears streamed down his cheeks. A pair of strong arms reached under his arms and pulled him away from Frank. "Easy does it, Lad," said Mad Tom. "God knows, he deserves a hiding, but it'll bring no good to any of us if you kill him." Matt gave Tom an angry look, broke his grip and turned to Cassie who, having regained her balance, was fiercely confronting her brother. "God, Jordan, you can't stay out of trouble, not for a minute. How can I go away and leave Daddy…"

Matt pushed between them, holding his clenched fist close to Jordan's face. "Don't give me an excuse, Jordan. You're in enough trouble already, pal. You'd better wait over there, the copper is going to want a word with you!" he yelled, pointing to one of the beer garden chairs.

Jordan was seething, considering another attack, but this time it was Matt he was targeting.

"I wouldn't, mate, no," Matt growled. He turned to Cassie, his back to Jordan and reached out to her bruised cheek and closing eye, touching them gently. "Oh boy, are you going to have a shiner."

"It'll heal," she said, shrugging and looking at him with an expression that said, 'Life's full of surprises'. "Well, my face, that is. At least he missed my nose; a flattened nose wouldn't look good on a ballerina." She smirked and then winked at him with her good eye before crossing to Dunning, who was looking a little better, but still waffling incoherently. "We're going to have to get him back to Kingscote. He'll probably want to arrest everyone, if he works out what happened, so we should pray he won't remember any of it tomorrow."

Jordan retreated and sat in one of the chairs, sullen, but chastened, suddenly aware that he was in very deep trouble.

Cassie went over to where Katherine and the Monsignor were kneeling next to Frank. "Mrs. Ryan, I think you'd better get Frank home right away; it would probably be better that Constable Dunning doesn't see him again tonight." Sean and Patrick were standing on the fringe of the crowd, upset. "Hey, Sean, Patrick, are you two all right?"

Patrick took Sean's hand. "Yeah, we're okay thanks, Cassie," said Patrick hesitantly. "Aren't we, Sean?"

"Yes," said the little man bravely, his voice barely audible.

"I'll do that, Mrs. Ryan," said Mad Tom, as Katherine tried to get Frank onto his feet. "C'mon, old fella, come along quietly now; you're in a ton of trouble, and you'd better hope the young copper doesn't remember too much tomorrow." He swung Frank's arm over his shoulder and shuffled off in the direction of the Ryans' Landcruiser. "Hey, Sean, help me out, mate. Pat, you go on ahead and get the truck started."

The weary little group made their way in the direction of the parking lot. "Thanks, Tom," Cassie called after them. A deep sadness griped her. She had known the family since she was a child. Frank frightened her. She had seen him smack Matt around the head when Frank was drunk, and she had often heard the terrible stories about Matt's mother coming to the school with a black eye and bruises on her body. "Those kids make me want to cry, Matt. Bloody alcohol, what you lot go through."

"That's why I can't leave them; they're my family, and the boys need me around for a while yet."

"I know it's hard for you."

"It'll work out." He tried to smile.

She sighed. "Guess you'd better get Dunning's wagon."

The crowd was already breaking up, some heading for the bar, others to the hall where Maxi and his band had launched back into a new bracket. There were those that milled about voicing their opinions in the aftermath of the disruption. "The young copper is going to be pissed when he figures out what happened." "That Jordan needs to be put away before he kills someone." "Jeez, Matt went nuts. I thought he was going to kill Frank." "That bloody Cassie is tough, see the way she went after Jordan?"

Cassie went back to the dazed policeman. "I need the keys to the wagon, Bob. We are going to have to take you home."

"In the wagon, gorgeous," he replied, a clownish grin spreading across his good looks, although the swelling on his jaw and cheek were beginning to distort its usually square features.

"You won't be so jovial in the morning, I bet. Keys are in the wagon, Matt," she shouted over her shoulder. "No, sir'ee, you'll be wanting a few answers, and after a look in the mirror a little blood, too, I think, Mr. Dunning."

Matt brought the paddy wagon to the gate of the beer garden, helped Dunning to his feet, hooked an arm around him and struggled toward the van. "Jordan, get off your bloody arse and help here with this bloke!" shouted Matt. Jordan, forever antagonistic, gave Matt the finger.

"Jordan, get over here and help," called Cassie. Jordan, every movement telegraphing his disdain for Matt, slowly got to his feet. Eventually, they got Dunning into the police vehicle and buckled him into the passenger side seat. Cassie walked to the rear of the wagon and opened the cage door. "Get in," she ordered Jordan.

"You got to be kidding. I've got the bike, I can ride home."

"Pigs might fly," said Cassie. "You're drunk. We'll drop you at Stumpy Flats on the way to Kingscote, and you can stay there the night. Now, get in, or I'll make sure the constable files charges against you myself. It was you who hit him, remember?"

A belligerent Jordan stood his ground. Matt grabbed the front of his jacket, put his leg behind the man's knees and shoved; Jordan immediately fell to the ground. "I've really had it with you tonight, mate," said Matt. "Now do what your sister said and get in the bloody wagon."

"Oh, I wouldn't get too high and mighty, Ryan. I've a few things to say that I'm sure you wouldn't want my sister to hear."

"Last chance, Jordan. Either get in, or I'll leave you here and let the constable know who belted him," said Cassie. Jordan realized Cassie meant business and reluctantly crawled into the back of the van. She shut and bolted the cage door, and then Matt walked her to the Pathfinder.

"Stumpy's a bit out of the way, but I don't want to leave him here. I'll follow in my car while you keep Dunning amused. We'll drop Jordan off and…ah…we'll need to get Bob to the hospital and have him checked out, I suppose." She kissed Matt softly on the lips. "I want you to come back to Middle River tonight. I'll call Dad from Kingscote and tell him to prepare the guest room."

"I don't know about that, Cassie."

"Leave it to me, Dad will be fine. He thinks that once I'm in Sydney, it'll be different. I'll meet lots of other people and…"

"Yeah, I heard the same thing earlier tonight," said Matt.

"Who said that?"

"Maureen, she got me up for a dance after you left with Dunning."

"God, she's a bloody tart."

"I was in the supper room, talking to the monsignor. When I came out, I saw you with Dunning, laughing and…"

"And you thought I was chatting him up, and then she came after you to add some fuel to the fire. Bloody hell, Matt, I would never betray you; you should know that by now."

"I'm not all that bloody secure about some things."

"Well, you haven't been given much reason to trust anyone, have you? Your dad, your mother…"

"Hey! Hey!" It was Dunning peering at them from the police wagon's lowered passenger side window.

"Calm down, Bob, I'm on the way," Matt called.

"We had better get going," said Cassie, kissing Matt, an unmistakable hint of mischief lurking in the sparkle of her good eye. "Oh, and by the way, you can tell me what Jordan doesn't think you'd like me to know after we get these boys taken care of. You went quite pale when he said that."

"It's nothing important," said Matt, stepping back from the Pathfinder, the all too familiar sensation of the threatening worms beginning to stir.

# 26

The seventy-minute ride to Kingscote went without incident except for one heart-thumping moment when Matt and Dunning nearly hit a kangaroo at the Seal Bay turnoff. They had dropped Jordan at the Stumpy Flats cottage, a thirty-minute diversion off the Borda Road. Of course, the still drunk Jordan had behaved in his usual bellicose manner, abusing Cassie for being heartless, and waving his fist at Matt promising retaliation of such severe measure that his future prospects would end abruptly at the gate of the state jail. "That is where you belong, and that is where you will stay for a very long time, you Mick prick."

Bob Dunning was a completely different story. They took him to the hospital, where it was decided he should be kept overnight for observation. He swore undying appreciation for Matt and Cassie's assistance and an open-ended declaration of eternal friendship to be called upon if either of them ever needed help. "And, you can bloody well take that to the bank."

After the nurse had scolded Dunning for swearing, she assured them that he would wake in the morning with little more than a pounding headache, and so long as he took it easy for a couple days, "the constable should be fine." Then she turned her attention to Cassie's swollen eye and bruised cheek. "No serious damage," she cheerily reported after a thorough examination, "but I'd slap a bit of butter on it if I were you, fix it up in no time. Hang on a bit; I'll get some from the kitchen."

Cassie telephoned her father from the hospital. He was furious with Jordan and concerned about her black eye. His only reaction to Matt staying overnight was that he would fix up the guest room, clearly intimating that was where the boy would sleep. She left a note in Dunning's vehicle, explaining that they thought it best they drop him at the hospital to be checked out for any possible concussion issues.

\*\*\*\*

It was after midnight when they finally left Kingscote. Forty-five minutes later they were sitting on the sand at Middle River beach. Suspended high in the midnight sky above the northern horizon, the full moon's ivory reflection shimmered along the top of a flat sea separating the north coast of Kangaroo Island from the mainland's Southern Yorke Peninsula. From the unusually calm water, tiny wavelets formed along Middle River Beach and splashed onto the sand, creating long, luminous lines from one end of the beach to the other.

"I'm going to miss this," said Cassie, nestling into Matt's arms where they were sitting on a blanket spread over the sand next to the Pathfinder, a meter from the water's edge. The night was still warm, barmy; the cool southerly breeze of the South Coast yet to arrive.

"For sure," whispered Matt, brushing her bruised cheek gently with his lips. He was aware of her breathing, its rhythm, the rise and fall of her chest almost matching that of the splashing wavelets.

"Maureen is full on, hey?" Cassie, tense at first when Matt told her about the episode with Maureen and Jordan, was beginning to relax. She looked into his face, chuckled and then shifted her gaze back to the ocean.

"Look, Matt, I'm not surprised by it. Maureen has been a hot tart since she started to sprout tits, and I've known all along she's been bulling for you. Hell, you're a handsome devil, and she'd like nothing better than to notch you up along with the others. The harder it is for her, the more she wants. Pardon the pun." They both laughed. "No, she'll figure out a way to have another go at you, particularly now that I'm leaving."

"Screw Maureen; I love you and that's the end of it."

"Good, but watch her. She snuck up on you tonight, and you nearly blew it. Pardon the pun, again," she said, unable to control a fit of giggling.

"You're something else," he said, laughing and kissing her forehead. "I reckon you do fancy that Dunning bloke a bit, though, hey?"

She smiled, teasing, "He'd be a good backup, if you misbehave."

"You know how to cut a bloke to the quick." He held his hands to his heart, feigning a mortal blow.

"I'm not impressed." She sat up, suddenly serious. "Jordan, I'm so tired of his antics. It's time for Dad to give him an ultimatum. He either puts himself into a treatment centre, or we have him committed."

"I can't see him going along with either of them."

"We'll see about that."

She leapt to her feet and immediately began to unbutton her off-white cotton dress, a neck to knees summer dress with small reddish flowers printed into a light-weight fabric, transparent enough to see the contours of her body silhouetted in the light of the moon behind her. "C'mon, you, time for a swim."

In seconds, the dress was a pile on the sand, and she was running, skipping and splashing into the water. Matt stripped and ran after her, his face beaming. They splashed about, danced and played catch, brushing each other, teasing, touching and kissing until thoroughly aroused; they rushed back to the blanket.

Twenty minutes later, after the final glorious merging of their energies, they rolled onto their backs, spent, but exhilarated, staring at the sky. "I love you, Matt."

"Yeah, I love you." He sighed. "I'll miss doing this when you're gone." They were quiet; minutes passed, both reflecting on their coming separation.

"Cassie, I…"

She pressed a finger to his lips. "Hush, hush, my sweet, be quiet and no more thinking. Let's enjoy the moment and keep it as something very special between us. Here," she said, pointing to her heart and then touching his, "is where we hold each other. I love me, and I love you. That cannot end unless we choose differently, no matter how great the distance separating us. God's greatest gift after giving us life, my love, is we get to choose how we live it."

"You blow me away, girl, you really do. You're so together. I'm fearless, almost reckless about some things: footy, fights, driving too fast, yeah and behaving like a clown, I suppose, but deep down, and I hate this, I'm scared, Cassie, scared to death, and I don't know why. I just am."

"Matt, your life has been…"

"No, I can't blame the Oldman, or my mother's suicide; that stuff's over. I have to get on with my life, take responsibility for…"

"You have what it takes, Matt. You are a good person, brilliant and talented, too. Finish your writing projects; get them into the competition. The world's out there waiting, my love; embrace and soar, my mother used to say." She began to dress. "I'm afraid sometimes, too. At times when I think about mummy's death, my faith in God is tested. And, if anything happened to you, or what if the world was to take you from me when you become famous?"

Matt watched her drop the dress over her head, watched her pull it out and over her perfectly sculptured behind from where it bunched in the sweeping arch of her lower back. A twinge of guilt tweaked his mind. He had sometimes imagined what success in the big wide world might do to him; a lot of blokes had run off the rails.

"I'll kill myself first," he declared.

"Ah, don't be so Shakespearean. I'll love you whatever happens," she said, laughing.

"How do you do that?"

"What?"

"Read my mind?"

"Oh, my psychic powers," she gently teased, waving her hands like a clairvoyant behind a crystal ball. "No, you are so delightfully and beautifully transparent."

Matt shook his head, a broad smile underscoring the blueness of his sparkling eyes. "Maybe it's what's called feminine intuition; is that scary or what?"

"Enough. Into the car, you, and take me home. I'll cook breakfast in the morning and then drop you at Mass. I might even come into the church myself, if the Catholic God's Monsignor Byrne doesn't throw a fit at the terrible protestant heathen leading his bright young writer to a perishing eternity in hell," she said, the developing fun of their conversation washing delightfully through her heart. "Hmm, that reminds me, he'll not be happy if you don't have the entry papers for the competition in the morning. What time is Mass?"

"Eleven; I'll call Katherine and have her bring them."

The ironstone road from the beach to the Baldwin homestead was impressive. Cut into the side of the steep Constitution Hill, spectacular beach views opened up from the road that wound steeply up the 250 meters to the top. When the Pathfinder had reached halfway, the dark outline of Althorpe Island appeared on the horizon, the solitary beam of light from its lighthouse flashing a quick identification sequence every few seconds. The sand on which they had just made love, brightened by the moon, continued to welcome the pearly lines of breaking wavelets. The road took them to the edge of the universe where the sky, crowded with millions of sparkling jewels, merged with the rolling hills.

"Stop, Matt."

"Here?"

"Yes."

"C'mon," said Cassie, sliding out of her seat. He joined her by the fence at the edge of the road. Startled, two wallabies scattered through the pasture, and then paused, cheekily observing the observers before breaking away to hide in the scrubby brush beyond.

"I love it here, Cassie."

"This will always be our home," she whispered, not wanting to disturb the peace, deep in thought. "Yes, we'll come back one day and raise a family. They'll have this and the life that goes with it, I swear."

"What about your dancing career?"

"Can't last forever; I use what I know to teach the island kids at the schools, just like mother."

The moon slid under the first of the clouds, arriving with the breeze from the south. The sky darkened, the air cooled and Cassie shivered. Matt drew her tenderly into his arms.

# 27

"I told you to keep quiet!" Frank reached across the breakfast table and cuffed Sean's ear. "That's not what happened. And get that bloody mouse out of here, or I'll step on it."

Sean scooped *Snot* from the table and into his pocket.

Katherine, at the kitchen sink, picked up a rolling pin and turned on Frank. "You hit that boy around the head again, Frank, so help me God, I'll wrap this around yours," she hissed. "You don't know what happened; drunk and blacked out, as usual."

"I remember Matt coming at me. The piss-ant, wait'll I get my hands on the bludger. Didn't come home last night, did he? Scared to death, I bet," raged Frank.

"He got a few good whacks into you, Dad," said Sean, challenging him and then scampering out of the kitchen before Frank could grab him.

"Come back here, you little bugger." He slammed the table with his fist. "Why don't you bring your kids up to show some respect?"

"They are your kids, too, Frank, and you have to earn their respect. You hardly qualify for that since getting back on the drink."

Frank scowled. "That's the trouble around here; you're always having a go at me in front of the boys." He skewered a piece of sausage with his fork. "Yeah, well anyway, where *did* Matt stay last night?"

"He called from the Baldwins this morning, asking me to bring the entry papers to the writing competition into Mass. After the fight, he took the police wagon back to Kingscote. Cassie followed in her car, and they went to Middle River after they dropped Constable Dunning at the hospital."

"Bet her Oldman loved that. What the hell happened to the copper?"

"There you go; I just said you were in a blackout. Jordan hit him and knocked him out while he was trying to break up the fight. You could be in a bit of trouble, Frank."

"Why? It was the Baldwin twit who hit him, you just said. I remember now. Dunning should've stayed out of it. Baldwin was looking for a good hiding from the time he got there, and you know that. You heard him shouting we were just a mob of feral no-hopers, and that he'd fix Matt for good if he kept hanging around his sister. I still got a bit of family pride left in me, Katherine," said Frank, feeling somewhat self-righteous. "I was on the verge of giving him a good licking, too."

The phone rang. Katherine picked it up, listened briefly, and then handed it off to Frank, who was lightly touching the sore spots on his face, especially his nose already scarred and twisted from past battles. "Ouch," he grunted. "Sam."

"What?"

"Nothing, Sam," answered Frank. "Matt's getting to where he can handle himself pretty damn well; kid packs a hell of a wallop."

"Thatsa one reason I'm calling you, Frank. Peter, my manager at the sportsa centre in Kingscote called me justa now to say the new young copper, Dunning isa his name, I think he said, nicea young fella, met him last week, finished up in hospital and thata you had something to do with it."

"Now, hang about, Sammy. It was the Baldwin kid who hit him."

"Yes, but you were in a fight with him…"

"He dishonoured my family name," interrupted Frank.

"Momento, Frank. Listen, we hava too much at stake to create unnecessary problems with the law. They're onto us, but hava no evidence. I hada a close call a week ago when thata bloody Woodson showed up in his helicopter. I'm told he's getting healed pretty bloody quick, tough fella. Anyway, we are gonna lay low for awhile."

"Righto, Sam. Sorry I stuffed up," said Frank, relieved to be out of trouble. "When will you be back? The last of the season's pick will be done in a couple of months."

"We'll be back for a load in August. Now, I know thatsa a while away, so you pick up whata they have, pay them, that'll keep everyone happy, and then ahide it under the old storehouse ruins. Tell them to hava the rest ready by August; I wanta full load."

Katherine was busy putting away the last of the breakfast dishes, trying to ignore Frank's conversation. Patrick, ever the peacemaker, the priest as Matt referred to him, gave his mother a "don't worry" look.

"We'll be leaving for Mass shortly, Patrick. Find your brother and the two of you be ready to go. Frank, we've have to leave for Mass."

Giving Katherine a sharp look, he covered the mouthpiece with his hand. "Will you shut up, woman, I'm discussing business here."

"Business! Ha, monkey business, if you ask me," she said, pulling off her apron, throwing it over the towel rack, and storming out through the kitchen door, shouting over her shoulder. "We'll be waiting outside."

"Thatsa no way to talk to your wife, Frank," said Sam, overhearing the exchange. "Getta yourself off to Mass, we'll talk later and…"

Frank interrupted, "Before you go, Sam, there is one more thing; money. It'll cost to pay the growers, and I don't have that kind of cash."

"I'll have a $150,000 for you by the middle of the week. You cana pick it up from Peter. Get to Mass, Frank, and you aska the good monsignor to bless his mosta generous of fisherman, hey?"

"Yeah, right, Sam." Frank dropped the phone into its cradle, walked outside to where Katherine and the boys were sitting in the Landcruiser waiting, and feeling much better already—more money on the way—despite his hangover and the bruises on his face and body.

Sean was sitting in the back of the cab, trying to be as small as possible. Frank saw him through the driver's side door. Lifting his body up as far as the cab would allow, and with his arms reaching up and over the boy, Frank growled like an attacking bear. Sean was mortified and pushed further back into his seat.

"Arrrgh," roared Frank, before breaking into laughter. "You've got some spunk, you cheeky little bugger. I'll let you off this time, but watch out in the future, hey?"

# 28

Matt was relaxing on the front veranda of the Baldwin homestead, enjoying the cool morning air. It was early, and the sun's blazing rays were already bouncing off the ocean mirror and beginning to heat up the new day. Then it was dark.

"Guess," said a voice from behind. Cassie kissed him lightly on the cheek and removed her hands from his eyes. "It's me, handsome," she chortled gaily, pirouetting to the front of the veranda, stretching with fingers fully extended, reaching for the pale blue mantle streaked with wispy, white clouds sweeping over her head. "Isn't this amazing?"

He looked beyond her, beyond Althorpe Island to the mainland. "Perhaps we should stay here, Cassie. Maybe, there's really nothing out there that we don't already have."

"Probably, my love, but we have to go out there to know how much we have here. If we didn't find out for sure, wouldn't we always be wondering?"

"Good morning," said Monty.

"Morning, Mr. Baldwin."

"Good morning, Daddy," said Cassie, throwing her arms about him and kissing him lightly on the forehead. "Oh, Daddy, isn't it the most wonderful of mornings?"

"It is one of many, Cassie. That eye doesn't look too wonderful."

"It'll be fine by the time I leave for Sydney. Nurse Shirley said to put butter on it, and it would clear up in no time."

"I hope so. Now run along and make us some tea, there's a good girl. Matt and I need to have a little private time for a man-to-man chat."

"Oh, I see. Just you be on your best behaviour, Daddy." She rolled her eyes at Matt and then padded on bare feet toward the main doors, looking delicious in her mauve satin bathrobe. She paused behind Matt and gave him a reassuring hug; then she was gone.

Monty looked out to the sea, silent. Matt studied the Oldman's face, noting his strong features and the firm set of his square jaw; *Cunning old bugger.*

Monty cleared his throat. "Matt, I overheard you and Cassie. First of all, I want you to understand that she will not be staying here a day longer than planned; she is to go to Sydney. Her acceptance into the dance company is a wonderful opportunity, and I do not want her swayed or distracted from exploring that break. Her mother would have wanted the same." He lowered himself into the single seat hammock, hanging from one of the veranda joists.

Matt listened, waiting for the hammer to drop.

"Cassie told me she asked you to go with her to Sydney. Umm, for many reasons I suppose, along with the idea that she loves you, of course; adolescent infatuation, maybe. Well, I'm pleased you said no, at least not yet." He paused and looked into the younger man's eyes. "Stay here for the winter, lad. Let her be for a time and see what happens," he said, testing.

The Oldman and the young man held each other's eyes. The silence was overwhelming.

Matt took his time, pushing back at the building anxiety that threatened to weaken a respectful and appropriate response, carefully thinking through what he wanted to say. "Look, sir, I don't want to appear rude, but the truth of the matter is that you would rather Cassie find someone more her equal and more to your liking. My father told me it would never work, but I don't accept that." Monty shifted in the hammock, a little taken aback by Matt's directness. "And I don't accept that now just because you imply or hope it won't work out. The fact of the matter is that Cassie and I are right for each other, and I also believe that the outcome is up to the will of a power far greater than yours or mine." He paused, surprised by his calmness and show of strength, taking time to consider his next words. "Come spring time, if all is well with my family, I will be leaving the island for Sydney to be with Cassie, if she still wants me with her."

Monty sat very still, watching the boy's face. A few long moments ticked by. "Cassie told me you are a writer, Matt. Well, if you write as well as you speak, then, maybe, you will make your mark. I will hold you to the six months when Spring is here. After that, if the two of you still want to move your lives forward together, well, I won't stand in your way."

*Yeah, right.* "Fair enough, Mr. Baldwin," he replied, a wry grin creeping across his face.

"Come and get it," Cassie called from the kitchen.

"Well, good, that's settled. Now, let's eat. I'm sure our favourite woman has prepared her two best men a feast," *And make the most of it, lad. This little romance won't last; I'll make damn sure of that.*

In the middle of the kitchen, laden with fruits, cereals, milk, and cream, was a heavy wooden table built from the massive ghost gums that lined the banks of Jumpy Creek. "This kitchen," said Matt "brings back a lot of memories."

Cassie smiled, "Yes, we have had some good times here. Don't hold back, help yourselves: eggs, bacon, sausage and toast will be ready in a few minutes. Tea, Daddy?"

"Yes," said Monty, who sat in one of the chairs and motioned for Matt to do the same. "I remember when you used to come here as a little tacker, Matt; when your family had the block up there on the hill. Shame you had to lose it. It's a good piece of dirt. We're in the process of buying it now."

"I heard." While Cassie poured his tea, he remembered.

It seemed that it was only a short few years had passed since Matt's mother was alive in the Baldwin house, at the same table, talking with Kristina; the lovely, kind Kristina, rattling on about the classes she and Matilda had taught at the Parndana Area School, and occasionally breaking into Spanish with her bubble-over enthusiasm. Matt and Cassie would sneak their tiny hands over the top of the table and reach into the biscuit tin. Kristina and Matilda would smile at each other, not letting on that they could see what the two youngsters were up to. They all had fun together; it was peaceful in the Baldwin home.

Not far along the road was the farm, the Ryan farm. It was there, at the house dam where the police were looking at a line of sleeping pills neatly arranged on the white clay below the windmill. There was a small dinghy with a neighbour and a policeman in it, methodically throwing a hook attached to a light chain into the murky water, pulling it in, throwing it out and pulling it in, until after an hour of repetition, it tightened. "I've got something," shouted one of the men in the boat.

Matilda Rose Ryan, nee Gordon, nurse and venerated schoolteacher at the Parndana Area School, born into the Protestant Church, but converted to Catholicism to marry Francis Ryan, her eyes closed, laid serene in her coffin in the praying hands Parndana Catholic Church, drowned, suicide, in the dam she had always feared.

"Get back here and sit down, Matt." The drunken voice bellowed and ripped through the heart of the young boy standing by his mother's casket, praying. The seven-year-olds eyes, defiant and vengeful, turned from his mother to stare coldly across the void at his father.

"Hello, Matt, Matt, anybody home?" Cassie's voice broke through the anguish and hatred he was feeling in that moment.

"Oh, I am sorry. I drifted back to the days when my mother and I used to come here together." He remembered that Kristina had died shortly after his mother. "She loved coming here, loved your mother." He paused. "Life hardly seems fair, two good women, hey?"

"There is more than enough tragedy in life to go around," said Monty. "Life wasn't meant to be easy, seems I remember Prime Minister Frazier once saying." He paused and gestured to Matt's plate. "I think Cassie wanted to know if you'd like sausage with your eggs and bacon, lad."

"Yeah, yeah, that would be great, thanks." Cassie loaded two sizzling pork sausages onto his plate.

"Welcome back," she said, teasing. "We lost you there for a bit." She smiled warmly. "I'm glad your home, with me, here."

The smell of the bacon and eggs reminded Matt that he was hungry, and he attacked the loaded plate with relish, dispatching the contents in short order. A request for seconds had Cassie promptly reloading the plate.

"You had better call Katherine, as soon as you've eaten; it's already eight o'clock." He glanced at the fancy clock with the Roman numerals set above the big wood stove.

"I did, early this morning. What time will you be ready to leave?"

"Quarter after ten," said Cassie.

"Great. Now, if I can borrow a pad and a pen, I'd like to work on the sestina before we leave…in the gazebo, if that's okay?"

"Good idea." Cassie retrieved a pen and pad from her father's study. "Go for it."

"Thanks." He cleaned up the last piece of sausage and gravy. "Come down when you're ready; I'll give you a look at what I've got done so far. Thanks for the brekky; you're a hell of a good cook, and thanks for putting me up for the night, Mr. Baldwin."

"All right, then. Keep yourself out of trouble, now, young fella."

Matt nodded, smiled warily and left.

"I'm going to Mass today, Daddy. You're welcome to come along, if you want."

"Humph, thought I raised you to be a good Presbyterian. Spent all that money…"

"Now, Daddy, you know my views. I prefer *my* God, not dogma, but I'm happy to go to any church where there's a loving God."

"Humph," growled Monty again.

Matt made his way through the front doors and followed the grey slate path to the lip of the steep hill overlooking the ocean. Where the path ended, a series of limestone steps dropped a steep two meters to the gazebo Monty had built for Kristina for study and meditation. Solidly constructed from treated timber and lattice panels, the soft earthy colours of its paint blended perfectly with the landscape. A light-green metal roof provided shelter from all of the usual storms, but had yet to be tested by the most vicious of gale force winds.

Meticulously tended shrubs and bushes circled the structure; red flowers blossomed from hibiscus, white flowers from gardenias along with the pink and purple of rhododendrons and azaleas. Pink staechelin roses snaked in and out of the lattice panels and twisted around the pine log supports all the way to the conical roof.

Het sat at the round table inside, settled and closed his eyes; his mind quickly slipped into semi-consciousness. After a few minutes, he began to feel a sensation of pins and needles creeping over his body. He heard a rustle, the sound a full skirt makes when the wearer moves, the sound of a dancer swaying her hips, shoes rat-a-tat tapping on a hard-wood floor to *flamenco!* He opened his eyes. An eerie chill raced up his spine, his heart was pounding and a hot flush surged through his veins. "Kristina!" His mind was suddenly alive with images of her and a young Monty, playing around a small campfire on the beach. They were running, laughing, dancing, swimming and coupling. He heard a laugh and looked about the gazebo. "Kristina!"

Suddenly, black clouds swept in from the southwest, chilling the air instantly, forcing the young lovers to dress, to huddle closer to the fire. Fanned by the arriving south-westerly wind, the sparks from the flames flared into the darkened sky, rushed across the top of the water and disappeared into eternity, taking with them a floating Kristina. Matt's mind snapped back to full consciousness. He was not amazed by what had happened. He had heard of many other islanders having visions, premonitions; Kangaroo Island was known for mystical phenomena that manifested in myriad forms.

His heart raced with excitement, and he slammed the writing pad onto the table, snatched the words and images tumbling over and over in his mind to feverishly scratch them onto the paper before they deserted him. Two more stanzas began to take shape. Cross out, reword, reconstruct, correct, spell; an intense, continuing process at once frustrating and soaring, drawing from instinct and the inspiration that he knew came from the metaphysical world and, in this moment, from Kristina.

A distant voice sang through his feverish activity. A loving embrace from behind closed around his shoulders and the sweet, warm breath of an angel coaxed him gently into the now.

"Matt, Matt, my darling, it's time to leave," she whispered into his ear.

He slowly turned to her, smiled, and nuzzled her arm. "She was here, Cassie. Kristina, she was here, I saw her dancing. She gave me this." He jabbed the pad with his finger. "I'll have the rest of it finished before you leave next weekend."

She continued to smile. "I was hoping she would come. It's in this space where she created some of her best work. She tells me you are very talented."

"You've seen her?"

"She visits often," said Cassie.

"You never told me."

"I was waiting for the right time."

"I felt this incredible energy, and then…you look just like her," Matt said, still excited. "It seems I have two women looking out for me."

"I'd like to read it."

"Next week. I'll have it ready before you leave. C'mon," he said standing, taking her hand and laughing gleefully. "It's time to conquer the world."

# 29

Constable Bob Dunning's head was throbbing, but he convinced the local doctor to let him go home to the cabin by the water on Brownlow Beach, telling him he would rest easier there and heal quicker. The doctor gave the okay, along with a proviso that he rested and gave it a couple of days before returning to duty.

When he walked out into the bright sunlight, he began doubting the wisdom of his request, but despite the fuzzy head and unsteady walk, he managed to make it across the road to the police wagon where he saw the note.

"From Cassie, would be my best guess," he mumbled. He reached inside to retrieve the neatly folded piece of paper from the dashboard console. As he backed out of the vehicle and straightened up, his head spun and only by holding onto the driver's side door saved him from toppling over. He steadied, gingerly let go of the door and walked slowly and purposely toward the edge of the bluff, five meters away. The view out over the fisherman's jetty and the wide strip of water to the mainland, a shadowy landmass on the distant horizon, was stunning. He took in several deep breaths and popped a couple of the pain medication pills the doctor gave him.

The fresh air soon worked its magic, and he began to feel a little better. He opened the note and began to read.

*Dear Bob,*

*As you read this, I hope you are feeling much better. Someone whacked you last night, could have been accidental, but I don't think anyone knows, really. Anyway, you weren't quite with it, so I thought you ought not to be driving. Matt offered to bring you into the hospital. I hope he hasn't broken any laws by driving a police vehicle. If you need to get in touch, it will have to be before next Saturday when I leave for Sydney.*
*Cheers,*
*Cassie Baldwin*

He stuffed the note into his tunic pocket. *Nobody has a clue what happened? Yeah, right.* He chuckled and gently felt the swelling around his jaw. "That bloody Jordan got me a beauty, all right. It'll be his last; I'll be ready next time. Yeah, and you know what happened all right, Cassie, my lovely. I have a fuzzy recollection that you were trying to pull Jordan off Frank when you copped one, too."

With the pills doing their work, Dunning decided to ignore the doctor's advice and take a quick run around town before checking into the station. Driving down the main street with the window down, the scent of coffee and pastries drifting out of Roger's Deli was too much to resist. He nosed the wagon into the pavement, stepped out, nodded to the early Sunday morning coffee drinkers sitting around the outside tables and went inside.

"G'day, Bob," said Roger. "You're looking a bit seedy this morning, mate; coffee?"

"Yeah, and kick in one of those cream buns, too. And no more smart-arse comments, hey?"

"I heard early this morning. Here you go," Roger said, passing the coffee and bun across the counter top. "On me today, Bob."

"Much appreciated."

"No worries. Oh, crap, here comes 'Scratchy'. He's been looking for you all morning. You're in trouble, Constable."

Roger ducked out to the back of the shop.

'Scratchy' Dougherty looked decidedly pissed off, as he walked up the ramp and into the deli. "I waited up all night at the station door for you, Mr. Dunning. Had a rough night, and I'm bloody hungry, too."

'Scratchy' was one of those people found in most country towns, well known, a little short of a dollar and usually not much of a nuisance. He earned his nickname after an irate husband came home early one afternoon to find Scratchy with his wife, 'at it' on the back veranda, so he filled Scratchy's backside with buckshot, as he scampered for cover over the back fence. Ever since the local doctor took half a day to pluck the lead pellets from Scratchy's buttocks, he had developed a nervous reaction that had manifested as a constant scratching of the pitted and itchy reminder of the man's indiscretion. Hence, one of the local wags called him 'Scratchy' and the name caught on.

Scratchy barely made a living distilling eucalyptus oil on his small scrub block at Emu Bay, a beautiful north coast beach a few kilometres out of Kingscote, despite putting in a solid five-day work-week. On Saturdays, he would hitch a ride into the township, get drunk and then book himself into the police cells for the night on a drunk and disorderly charge. Sunday morning, tradition, along with government regulation, dictated a healthy Australian breakfast for the inmates, after which the on-duty constable would drive him out to his block.

"Give me a break, Scratchy," said Dunning. "You already know what happened to me, so cut the bull dust." He called out to Roger, who was doing his best to remain inconspicuous in the back room that was his office. "Roger, give Scratchy a full breakfast, will you? I'll fix you up later. Now, Scratchy, I'm going up to the station to check on a few things, so you wait here until I come back, and I'll take you home. And, mate, you better eat outside, you're a bit on the bloody nose, mate."

Back at the police station, the red light of the answering machine was flashing. Dunning pushed the play button and listened. Most of the messages were the usual fare: cows wandering the roads, two dogs killing sheep and a group of teenagers swimming naked in the town's seawater pool at mid-night. The message from headquarters was one he could not ignore. The local hospital had notified them of his admission, and he was to report immediately on being discharged.

Three calls were from Woodson, all brusque; each one, especially the last, irritated the hell out of him. Woodson said he wanted to start planning a major operation to clean up the marijuana cultivation problem, and see to it that the Ryans and Sammy Marino were put away for a very long time. The message ended with the number of his bedside phone and an order to call back right away.

The affect of the painkillers was wearing off, and the headache was returning with a vengeance. He managed to radio headquarters and get in the expected report. The next call was to Woodson who answered before the first ring had finished.

"About time you got back to me," said Woodson, his voice rasping and his breathing laboured. "I heard about last night. Don't ask me how; I keep my ear to the ground. Stupid young bugger; I tried to tell you to watch out for the Ryans."

"It was Jordan Baldwin who hit me."

"Not what I heard, but never mind that now. The point is that we are going after the Ryans and Sammy Marino, big time. There was a meeting in town here, yesterday. The state's top politicians told the brass to make a lesson out of what's going on over there," growled Woodson.

"Is that right?' replied Dunning. "Well, it's quiet here right now. After that big shipment went out a week ago, there's nothing to go after other than a few blokes who may have a plant or two left around the place, but nothing incriminating." With his headache worsening by the minute, Dunning reached into his trouser pocket, pulled out a packet labelled 'Codeine' and tried to open it with one hand, the other cradling the phone.

"That's why I'm calling you, I want you…"

Dunning, his patience quickly fading, interrupted, "Hang on, will you?" He dropped the phone, used both hands to release two tablets, popped them into his mouth and picked up the phone again. "Yeah?"

"What happened?" asked Woodson.

"I've got a throbbing headache. Look, boss, tell me later; I have to get home and put my feet up. Oh shit, I have to run Scratchy home first."

"Won't hurt you; you young blokes are bloody soft these days. All right, all right, here's the drum in a nutshell. Do not follow up on last night, got it? We want to back off and give these blokes the feeling that the pressure is off. I figure that Marino won't be back until toward the end of winter, August, September, sometime in there. In the meantime, we poke around and see who is growing the stuff besides Ryan, find out where they're storing it, and then we go for the big bust when Marino comes in to load up. There'll be a team on call from Adelaide when we're set. This is going to be big, Bobby, my boy. Good for you and me."

The Codeine had yet to kick in, and Dunning's headache was getting worse by the minute. "Yeah, well that's bloody terrific, boss," he said, barely able to disguise the sarcasm. Not wanting to let Woodson wallow in his grandiose scheme to screw the Ryans, he continued. "By the way, I'm picking up a couple of blokes from the accident investigation branch on Tuesday. They want to inspect your accident site. Seems the speed I estimated you must have been travelling at, in my report, is at a marked variance with yours."

"What the hell did you tell them?"

"I estimated eighty kilometres per hour. We both know it was faster than that though, don't we? More like 110, 120 would be closer to the mark, hey?

"What are you driving at?" demanded Woodson.

"You told them sixty, which was the speed you should have been travelling. No, I'm giving you a break, Sergeant. They don't take kindly to coppers killing their superintendents, especially the good ones. You owe me."

# 30

It was early Saturday morning. Although, the sun was still low on the horizon, the day was shaping up to be another sizzler. The absence of the evening's normal southerly breeze over the last week, along with unusually high temperatures hitting the old century mark, meant no respite from the heat. Even the thick limestone walls of the Ryan cottage were unable to keep the inside rooms cool, making it difficult for anyone to get a good night's sleep. The night before, Matt barely slept at all. His mind kept running over the events of the week and the jarring reality that the time for Cassie to leave for Sydney had finally arrived.

He was relieved that Bob Dunning did not pursue the events of the previous Saturday night. Maybe Cassie was right when she suggested he probably would not remember much. The phone call to thank him for his help did not convey that impression, though. Dunning's suggestion that he stay out of trouble, that there were people who would be very happy to see him and his father go to jail, troubled him. Something was in the wind and it did not bode well for the family. Dunning mentioned Woodson was recovering quickly and would be returning to duty much earlier than expected. *We should've let the mongrel die.*

The week was tough on Matt physically. The Hamilton shearing started on Wednesday, and he had not used a handpiece for months, so he was out of condition for the physical and mental stress of standing and bending over sheep for a solid eight hours. Shearing sheep was piecework; the shearer was paid for his final tally of sheep at the end of shearing, called the cut-out. As if the work was not hard enough, the shearers put more pressure on themselves by competing against each other for the eight hours, every day, five days a week, for the highest tally. It was extra tough on a shearer out of condition, especially when the weather was stinking hot.

Matt had picked up his blue ute from the repair shop in Kingscote on the Tuesday. It was a relief to have it back. Harry did a nice job and the new aluminium 'roo bar would protect the radiator from unavoidable kangaroo encounters. The insurance company picked up most of the tab, but it still hurt when he had to pry open his cash box for the $500 deductible.

Cassie had convinced him to stop for dinner at Middle River that night. Jordan was there, and he behaved in a rather cordial manner, which Matt found somewhat disquieting. Jordan agreed to check into a drug and alcohol treatment facility at the Royal Adelaide Hospital after Cassie left for Sydney. Matt was suspicious of Jordan's motives, but he was prepared to give him the benefit of the doubt, as long as he stayed off the booze.

He and Cassie spent some time together in the gazebo. It was after four in the morning when he finally left. Of course, he would be at the airport by midday on Saturday, he promised. Yes, he would bring the sestina.

Matt was deep in thought, partially mesmerized by the rhythmic slap, slap, slap of the seawater lapping the rocks under the arch. From his perch on the Admiral's cape, he sat on the smooth sloping slab of rock, the very spot where the young female seal had screamed her last breath before life's cycle took her. His mind wandered over the week's work on the sestina, three stanzas and the last of the six-liners, finished. One more left to go, the three-liner, the one that made sense of it all, a summary of the whole.

Suddenly, inspiration electrified him. "It fits, it all fits," he shouted, jumping to his feet and throwing his arms toward the roof of the craggy arch, disturbing the seals, causing some of them to panic and dive from their rocky lodges.

Taking up his pen from its granite perch, he wrote feverishly, oblivious to all but the voices and images whirling around in his mind, until he was finished. He studied the work carefully, and then became aware of the absolute tranquillity about him. Even the lapping of the water had stilled, and the seals now quiet, lazed about on their rocks, spectators, all participants in his magical epiphany. He looked up from his work to experience what had become a new world, transformed for him through the practice and confirmation of his art.

"Are you okay, Matt?" said Pat. He had not noticed the approach of his eldest stepbrother. "I'm sorry; I didn't mean to intrude, but I was walking on the Admiral, and I heard you yelling. Is everything okay?"

"Yes, Pat, everything is absolutely fine," said Matt, smiling and brushing the tears from his cheeks. "Dear, sweet, Pat; my brother, the priest to be, hey?"

"Lord willing. Breakfast is ready. Ah, mother said Sean and I could go to Kingscote with you, if that's okay?"

"Of course; we'll be calling into the airport on the way, though. Cassie leaves today, so I know she'll be glad for the opportunity to say goodbye to you two blokes. You can practice your priestly duties and console me after she leaves. What time is tennis?"

"Yes, we'll all miss her. We have a bye, no tennis."

"Aw, yeah, right. You know, Pat, you'll look great in a black cassock and white collar. You're a handsome bloke; all the girls will be flocking to Mass. Rome will love you." He laughed and then waved his hand in an arc indicating the huge expanse surrounding them, eyes sparkling. "You know God, Pat; all this is God. You can take this God to the world, and they'll know you know God." He placed his arm around his stepbrother's shoulders and guided him along the rough limestone path toward the lighthouse and the cottage. "Where's Sean?"

"He got up early this morning, and said he was going to his secret cave. He still won't tell anyone its exact location."

"Yeah, over by Weir Cove, though, isn't it?" said Matt. "I don't like him going over there on his own; it's bloody dangerous."

"I know, but it's kind of a refuge for him, especially when Mum and Dad are fighting," They continued along the path. "There he is on those rocks."

"I see him." Matt paused for a moment. "Patrick, the yelling you heard? I got a glimpse of the top Bloke this morning."

"Awesome. I reckon he is always there for us. We just need to say g'day and listen, hey?"

"G'day, Matt," said Sean. He was sitting on a pile of stones set off to the side of the lighthouse's auxiliary engine shed. "Mum said we could come with you to Kingscote."

"Jesus, God!" Matt tightened his grip on Patrick's arm, freezing them both to a standstill. "Don't move, Sean. Don't move a muscle."

A black tiger snake was coiled on a large slab of limestone, centimetres from Sean's arm. Sean no more than flinched on hearing Matt's warning, but two meters of venomous reptile was instantly alert, threatened, the open mouth exposing its glistening and deadly fangs. In a lightning move, the coal black devil struck at the boy and buried its fangs deep into the flesh and muscle of Sean's forearm. The snake whipped back and recoiled, leaving a red and painful swelling at the bite site and a deadly neurotoxin spreading into the boy's bloodstream. It readied to strike again.

Sean uttered a terrifying howl that triggered a surge of adrenalin through Matt's blood stream. Moving quickly, he snatched the boy away from the snake and spun him into Patrick's arms. Then, balancing on the balls of his feet, he moved to confront the tiger. Primordial rage fed every cell in his body, setting up in him an overwhelming urge to crush his brother's attacker. He deftly avoided an attempted strike, slipped quickly behind the rearing reptile, grabbed its tail, whirled it around his head and cracked it like a whip. It dropped to the ground, its back broken in several places, mortally wounded.

Sean was screaming. "It bit me, Matt. It hurts," he sobbed, beads of sweat forming on his little face that was already turning a deathly white. "Help me, Matt, help me; it hurts."

Taking the boy from Patrick and cradling him in his arms, Matt ran toward the cottage. On the verge of panic, he yelled, "Run ahead and tell Katherine, Pat. Then get the snake, put it in a bag and throw it in the back of the ute." He turned his attention back to Sean. "It'll be all right, little bloke. It'll be okay, I promise. Love you, mate, love ya," he said, panting from exertion, fear fuelling his urgency.

As they approached the cottage gate, Katherine was already running from the house with Patrick. Barney, tethered to the stringy bark tree in the corner of the cottage yard, was barking frantically

"Lay him on the couch, Matthew. Over there, on the veranda," she ordered, pointing, her years of experience as a nurse kicking in. "Get some bandages from the medicine chest and find a flat piece of wood that will work as a splint." She took the small boy's wrist as Matt laid him gently on the old couch. "I want you to keep as still as a rabbit hiding in a bush from a fox, Sean. You are going to be fine." The look on her face belied her knowledge of tiger snakes and their deadly venom. They had to get him to the hospital quickly; his best hope, antivenom treatment, critical within the hour.

"Patrick, wake your father, quickly."

"I'm here," called Frank, hurrying through the back door with bandages in hand. "I heard the commotion. Matt, get the ute. Katherine, take Sean and go with Matt. I'll call the hospital; Pat and I will throw a few things together and follow." As Katherine pressure bandaged the bite and wrapped the whole limb, Frank stroked his young son's head. "Chin up, mate, you're going to be okay, I promise." Tears trickled over Frank's weathered cheeks.

Matt picked up a long, flat length of boxboard from under the veranda and broke it slightly shorter than the length of Sean's arm. He handed it to Katherine and rushed off to the shed to get the ute. Katherine placed the makeshift splint along the boy's limb and wrapped another roll of bandage around it to restrict movement.

Patrick tossed the dead snake into the back of the Commodore while Matt slid into the front seat and turned on the ignition. The petrol needle read 'half-full', enough and with some to spare to make it to Kingscote, ninety kilometres to the northeast. The big V-8 motor throbbed to life and in less than a minute, it was sliding to a stop at the cottage gate. Katherine climbed into the passenger seat, took Sean from Frank and settled the boy onto her lap. Sean, tears moistening his eyes, was fighting to keep from crying.

"Topped this up, you might need it," said Patrick, passing a full canvas waterbag to Matt through the window. "I'll bring a change of clothes for you."

"You're going to have to go like a bat out of hell, Matt," said Frank. "You don't have much time.

"She'll be right, won't it, Sean?" Matt said, hoping more than believing, looking at the little man's brave face and fighting to keep his rising panic under control. He slammed the ute into drive and floored the accelerator, throwing up dirt and gravel behind the spinning rear wheels.

Katherine held the porcelain lip of the waterbag to Sean's mouth, and managed to get him to swallow a small amount of water. The ute slid around the corner where less than a week before the police superintendent had died. Katherine gave Matt a quick look. "Keep it going, Matthew, keep it going! He's going into shock; drive as fast as you can."

The speedometer was registering a 120 kilometres per hour when the Commodore rattled over the Chase cattle grid and onto the main South Coast Road. The road immediately widened, but its surface remained the deadly roller-bearing gravel of rusty ironstone. Dust loomed from a vehicle ahead; they closed quickly. Despite the absence of a clear view beyond the vehicle in front, Matt pulled to the right of the road to pass.

Katherine screamed, "Look out!"

Matt automatically swung the wheel violently to his left, sliding in behind and brushing the rear bumper of the car in front; flying gravel battered the headlights and windshield of the slowing Commodore. A road-train burst out of the dust, thundered by, lights flashing and horn blazing, missing the Ryan vehicle by centimetres.

"God is with us," said Katherine, sucking in a deep breath. "Keep it going, Matthew."

"The road drops into Gum Creek; I'll get a clear view from there."

The car in front dipped over the lip of Gum Creek valley. Matt could see the road ahead for several hundred meters to where it scooped into the creek and then climbed away to the crest of the next spur. He moved to the right of the road and again pushed the pedal to the floor, speeding quickly through 140, 155, to 160 kph. They moved quickly next to the other car, almost scraping its side. Matt focused directly on the road ahead, the speeding Commodore dancing delicately on the edge of oblivion, straining to give way to its tendency to slide in the treacherous gravel. Only Matt's skill saved them, as he delicately corrected every movement toward disaster with minuscule adjustments of the wheel. So close were they to the right side of the road that Katherine ducked instinctively when overhanging branches of bulloak slapped the windshield. Matt's mind registered that the car he was passing was Max Hamilton's, the owner of the sheep he was shearing the day before. The utility bottomed out on the creek bridge, a resounding thud shuddered through the tough frame before it roared up the other side toward the crest of the spur.

****

Max Hamilton was white as a ghost. "That's young Matt Ryan. What the hell is he up to? He could have killed us all. I'll be having a few words with him when he shows up on Monday."

His eldest daughter Julie leaned over from the back seat. "Mrs. Ryan is with him, Daddy. She has Sean on her lap; they've got trouble."

****

Worry and fear were making canyons in the lines of Katherine's face; she was on the verge of panic as Sean's breathing was becoming more rapid, shallow and desperate. The boy screamed. "God have mercy on him," she cried. "The venom is working fast; he's going into a seizure."

Sean lapsed into semi-consciousness, and his body became gripped in a series of jerking muscular contractions. His back arched and the spasms increased in intensity, causing his feet to kick hard into the driver. Matt ignored the involuntary onslaught and concentrated on keeping the speeding utility on the road. Ahead, he saw the black surface of the tarred portion of the South Coast Road, which meant that Kingscote was about 12 kilometres away.

"I'll have to clear his airway," yelled Katherine above the noise of the roaring V-8. She opened the glove box and searched frantically, looking for a hollow tube, straw, anything she could use to open a passage in Sean's throat and get oxygen into his lungs. "Nothing!" she shouted desperately.

"The pressure gauge, use the long-stem pressure gauge," Matt yelled back, reaching over her, snatching the tool from the glove box and handing it to her. "The two ends come off; the guts will shake out."

Sean's convulsions stopped; he lay limp in Katherine's lap. She fumbled feverishly with the gauge, got the ends off and shook out the internal parts. Trying hard not to cause damage, she pulled his head back to straighten out his throat, inserted the steel tube and gingerly worked it in as far as she was able. Seconds ticked by, and then the little bloke stirred.

The ute bounced onto the blacktop. "Thank, God; not far now, Katherine."

"You're doing great, Matthew, keep it going, keep it going."

The road stretched out straight ahead for a couple of kilometres. He pushed the pedal all the way to the floor. The V-8 surged forward with a throaty roar. In the distance and speeding toward them, Matt saw the red and blue flashing hazard lights of an emergency vehicle. He started to flash his headlights.

****

Constable Dunning had received the call from the hospital. "Young Sean Ryan has been bitten by a tiger snake. Matt and Katherine are on their way with him; the situation is critical." Dunning was on the way out of the police station and on the road in seconds. Fifteen minutes later, he could see a vehicle coming toward him and flashing its lights. "That has to be him; hell, he's moving." Pushing down hard on the brake pedal, he slowed and then swung into a squealing u-turn, straightened and gunned the Commodore's Police Special V-8 Interceptor through 100, 130, 140 kilometres per hour.

The image in the review mirror grew quickly larger until Matt was within three or four car lengths of Dunning, both vehicles now racing toward Kingscote at 175 KPH, police siren screaming and hazard lights flashing. They thundered through the intersection where the roads from Parndana and the airport converged with the main road to Kingscote.

"Just a few more minutes, Katherine."

"Keep going, keep going as fast as you can; he's fading fast and needs that antivenom now, or we'll lose him."

At last, with blue smoke billowing from protesting tires, they rounded the bottom corner of the main road into the Kingscote, sped up the frontage road to the hospital and finally screeched to a halt under the emergency awning where the hospital staff was waiting. A doctor opened Katherine's door, took Sean, quickly transferred him to a gurney and whisked him toward the main entrance, the nurse hurrying alongside checking the boy's vitals, Katherine chasing after them, as they went through the casualty room doors.

Bob Dunning walked back to where Matt was leaning over the hood of the ute, exhausted, tears trickling down his cheeks. "You okay, Matt?"

"Dunno, Bob, he's looking pretty crook. I don't know if he'll make it."

# 31

An orange hue spread across the sky to the east. Cassie was on her way to the gazebo for a few minutes of meditation. With her hair pulled back into a ponytail, she looked stunningly fresh and elegant country in her white riding breeches, knee-length boots and bright lemon blouse. Arriving at the gazebo, she was surprised to see her father settled in his chair, sipping from a cup of hot tea.

"Ah, thought you might pop down here for a minute. I brought the teapot, fresh brew and a spare cup; pour you one?" Monty asked, tapping the top of the steaming pot next to the extra cup on the table.

"I didn't expect to see you up this early. Yes, please, Daddy. Hmm, warming up already; it'll be a stinker by noon. Adelaide will be brutal." She sipped the hot liquid. "Ah, lovely; thank you."

"I'll miss you."

"I will miss you." She smiled and looked out to the Althorpes. "And, I'm going to miss all this."

"It'll belong to you one day. I've made up my mind about matters affecting all three of you: you, Grant, Jordan, all of this," he lifted his head to indicate the property, "and the other interests that make up the family estate. Grant is not interested in keeping the place going and said you could handle it. I was a little piqued, though, when he said, 'Cassie can dance, but she'll get over that; two or three years in the city will drive her crazy.'"

"Mummy thought Grant was the insightful one. I will tell you this, Daddy, I intend to be successful; my passion is as great as it has ever has been."

"Good. All this," he looked about him, gesturing. "I don't dare leave it in Jordan's hands, God love him, and I'm not getting any younger, so I've decided to set up a trust with enough cash to pay out the boys over the next twenty years. It will be up to you to decide what you do. I would hope that you keep the place going. You won't have to make those decisions for a quiet a few years, yet. I've still got a bit of get up and go left in me."

"No doubt about it." She looked at him steadily. "I'll keep my options open, Daddy, but I promise you this, this estate will be kept intact with the Baldwin name a part of it," she said, practical and to the point, understanding how painful the process despite his brave face and attempt at humour. She took a sip of tea. "If it turns out that a few years in the city is enough, if I'm good enough, of course, to last that long, I could teach the kids here to dance, just like Mummy…" Her voice trailed away.

"Your mother loved watching you dance from the time you put on your first pair of ballet shoes. Ah, you are so much like her, fiery and…and somewhat prone to going off and doing things your own way, like the Ryan boy thing, hmm?" Monty paused, knowing he was on dangerous ground and needed to choose his words carefully. "Matt comes from an unstable background, a dysfunctional environment headed by an alcoholic father and a mother who, sadly, committed suicide. He has a lot to work out, and he may never get that done, Cassie."

"Oh, Daddy, I can take care of myself. You know that, or you wouldn't have me take over the family properties. Matt is going to leave the island. He has to and I encourage him. He'll develop his talent, and find his way and then I believe he will eventually want to come back here. Anyway, what did you know of Mummy when you met her? Nothing, she came from Spain and that's about all you knew, but you listened to your heart, didn't you?"

He picked up the teapot and topped up his cup. *Damn girl is way too smart for her years.* "More?" He held up the pot and motioned toward her cup.

"No thanks," she said, draining the last of her tea. She placed the cup on the table, crossed to Monty and hugged him. "I love you, Daddy; I worry more for you than I do Matt. You know, once Jordan has settled into treatment, you should leave Harry in charge and come out to Sydney again for a long break. The crutching will be over and Harry can manage things just fine. Besides, you have that friend in Sydney. You should look her up…err…Belinda, isn't it?" He nodded. She kissed him on the cheek, rough with its greying stubble. "I have to run along. Winston deserves a good workout before I leave, and it will be a while before I ride him again."

Monty patted her hand. "Actually, that's a good idea; I might do that. Yes, I'll get you settled, and then pop back again in a few weeks." He looked at his watch. "It's almost eight o'clock. Off with you; we need to be leaving by eleven."

Cassie ran up the stone steps to the slate path and paused to take a last look at the stately homestead, her home of twenty years rooted solidly in the earth, its thick stone walls impregnable, familiar and comforting. She was grateful.

She entered the stable, and Winston's head poked out from the stall, inquisitive, looking at her. She stroked the white blaze running the full length of his nose and reached for the bridle hanging from the hook next to the stall door. Preparation for the daily ride almost always played out the same way, but today was different and Winston seemed to sense it. Usually, when Cassie attempted to bridle him, he acted up, tossing his head, teasing. This time, though, he was quiet, brooding, and she was able to slip the bridle over his head easily.

After brushing the big chestnut's back, she lead him to the saddle room, a converted stall with a well-drained cobble floor where the horses stood for a hosing down after a workout. Several saddles straddled evenly spaced pegs at the rear of the stall. A royal blue saddlecloth with an embroidered gold band running around the edge stretched over Cassie's saddle; a Spanish riding saddle. The de Coronardo family crest of scarlet red and gold embroidery, depicting a Conquistador brandishing a sword above his head while astride a rearing horse, stood out in the left corner of the cloth.

She ran her hand over the embroidery, relishing the rich texture and fine artisanship and then threw it over Winston's back before turning to the saddle. A gift from her mother, she paused to marvel at the fine, intricate carvings in the leather. With her finger, she traced the pictures formed within a complex pattern of emblems that showed a horse and rider progressing through various stages of dressage.

By the time Cassie got to the beach, the sun was higher in the sky, and the day was well on the way to being a scorcher. The surf was moderate, breaking with its familiar rumble and then running on up to soak the sand briefly before retreating to rejoin its source. Cassie urged Winston forward into knee-deep water. Almost immediately, he started stomping and splashing with his front hooves, often a signal that he was about to roll on his back. She pulled sharply on the reigns, trying to keep his head from dropping. Too late, he rolled, throwing her into the water, but clear of him. She surfaced, sitting in water up to her chin, laughingly chiding him, but enjoying the enforced cool-off. Winston regained his feet and stood, waiting for his rider, looking down at her with what could be best described, as a quizzical expression. She checked over the wet saddle, satisfied herself that all was well and then re-mounted.

Like a bolt out of the blue, she was suddenly aware of where she and Winston were standing. She laughed: the wild wonderful laugh of a person happy and in love. This was where she and Matt had made love a week ago. She whirled the big horse around to face the far end of the beach and kicked him into a flat out gallop yelling, "Go, Winston, go." Her excitement soared, as she laid flat along his powerful frame, yelling "faster, faster" into his ear, slapping each side of his neck with the overlap of her reigns, pounding over the sand at a hair-raising gallop.

Monty was waiting on the front veranda when she rode up. "I watched you, saw you come off in the surf and then gallop the length of the beach and back; it looked like you were having a wonderful time."

"Yes, fantastic." She laughed and dismounted. "Winston was quite pleased with himself, the brat. The saddle is soaked and there is sand in the carvings; I'll have to brush it down and give it a good coat of saddle dressing right away."

Jordan, looking fresh and already dressed for the airport, joined Monty on the veranda. "Don't worry, Sis; I'll take care of it. Take care of your boots, too, if you like," he said, crossing to her. "Here, let me have him."

"Really?"

Jordan grinned and took the reins. "I owe you, Cassie, I owe you a lot."

"Well, thanks. I'll come with you; I have a few things to get from the studio. You're looking good this morning, Jordan, I'm impressed. Amazing what a week off the drink can do."

They walked into the stables together, Winston ambling along behind.

"Cassie, I'd like to come up to the studio?"

"You haven't wanted to do that for years. Are you sure?"

"Yes."

"Okay. Come on up, but take care of Winston first, okay?"

Jordan led Winston to his stall while Cassie took the steep loft stairs to the studio. The familiar aromas of the coating protecting the polished hardwood floor and the rubdown liniment spilt around the sofa hung in the air. She pulled aside the multicoloured silk drape hanging from the top of the door, went to the sofa and began the usual struggle to take off her boots, made even more difficult this time because of their soaking and the suction affect created around her feet. Jordan arrived.

"Want help?"

"Thanks," she replied, offering him a leg. He wrenched the boot free, took care of the second one and then surveyed the room.

Years had passed since he was in the studio. He remembered Kristina's delight when she first danced on the floor after Monty and Harry finished building it.

"Funny, it feels alive; like it's full of electricity. I've never felt that before."

The room was big. Floor to ceiling mirrors were positioned the length of the long wall. A *barre*, a rail for support when doing exercise routines, ran the length of the same wall. Reflecting in the mirrors were four life-size posters hanging next to each other along the opposite wall, each depicted a different form of dance and movement.

In the first, a male ballet dancer was mid-flight through the arc of a *grand jeté*, his movement captured in its greatest moment of perfection and exhilaration. The next poster offered a very different form of dance; Australian Aborigines raised red dust from their stomping feet, as they danced stories in a corroboree in front of the sacred rock, Uluru, a magnificent backdrop in the red Australian desert. In the third, a young woman was seen in the middle stages of an Irish jig, knee raised, toe pointed, arms and hands held rigid to each side of her body. The fourth portrayed the end to a long day of rehearsal. One male and two female dancers stretched out on the floor exhausted, while a weary ballerina balanced on her left leg as she bent, caught in the moment, removing her ballet shoe from a red and blistered foot.

Across from the sofa, a stereo system and speakers were set on top of a small bookcase. Wall shelves filled with books on dance, exercise and biographies ran off from each side of the bookcase. In the far corner, a huge glass display cabinet held an assortment of trophies, photos, flamenco and ballet shoes, and a rack of costumes hanging beside it.

Hanging on the wall beside the stereo was a life-sized photograph of Kristina, frozen in a moment of dance, jondo-flamenco. Her arms reached back in a sweeping motion above her head, her dark hair, pulled severely into a tight bun, framed the classically beautiful face. Her brown eyes, intense, looked out from the centre of the picture, on fire, alive. Even the click, click, clicking of the castanets she held in her hands seemed to reverberate through the studio.

Cassie heard Jordan suck in a deep breath. He walked to the glass cabinet. "May I?"

"Sure."

He opened the glass door, reached in and removed the pair of black flamenco shoes that were resident next to Cassie's first pair of *demi-pointe* ballet shoes, a gift from Kristina shortly before she died. The flamenco shoes were scuffed and worn, but still in good shape. He turned them over to where dozens of nails were imbedded in the soles and raised heels.

"These are the pair she has on in the photo?"

Cassie nodded. "She wore out lots of others."

"She, um, was quite something, hey?"

"She was the best."

Jordan's eyes glistened.

"Go ahead, let it out; it'll be good for you," said Cassie.

"Can't, Cassie, can't, too much water under the bridge. She, um, well, I don't want to get into that." He handed her the shoes. "These fit you?"

"They should."

"Will you put them on and dance like her?" He gestured toward Kristina's portrait.

Cassie looked up at the wall clock.

"Just a few steps, Cassie; please."

"Okay. Put on the album with the image of the three gypsies with their guitars." She strapped on the shoes and crossed to the *barre* to stretch and warm up. When she had finished, she opened the cabinet and picked out a pair of castanets. "Okay, let's go."

Jordan lowered the stereo needle onto the vinyl. A couple of seconds of hissing was replaced by the plucking of strings, the wailing of the gypsy trio, stamping feet and the slapping of guitars. Cassie, innocent and beguiling, began to move her arms about her head and upper body, slowly clicking the castanets and stamping the heels of her shoes on the polished wooden floor. She increased the intensity of her performance with the building tempo of the music and the mesmerizing wailing of the gypsy musicians.

Her eyes flashed across the line of posters. Always, they inspired her, filled her with thrilling bursts of raw energy translated into complex and aggressive emotions communicated through flying feet and swirling arms. She snapped her head to her right and snatched a glimpse of her mother's portrait. Kristina de Coronado, her eyes staring out into the studio locked into her daughter's, willing her presence and power into the young woman's flying movement. A fiery lust flared through Cassie's psyche and body, pushing her to a greater level of intensity in a wild, passionate, creative choreography.

The click, click, clicking of her castanets picked up with the tempo of the music, building until their speed matched the rapid clattering of a machine-gun. Her shoes matched the tempo of the castanets, their action, stomping and stamping, becoming a blur of motion, beating out a blood-scorching rhythm of primitive heel and toe tap. Her hair flew untamed about her head, streaming strands whipped across her face, escalating her allure. Her persona was transformed; a temptress on the edge of ecstasy; the guitars and singing crescendo and then end abruptly with a single loud hand slap on the lead player's guitar.

Cassie, with a full-throated yell, "I live," froze, one hand flung back over her head, the other tucked into her hip, a foot anchored to the floor while the other lifted onto its ball, allowing her knee to bend and point directly down stage. She was, for the moment, an image of Venus, transfixed in the imperious pose of an aristocratic goddess and in that moment, all at once, flushed, excited and spent.

"Bravo, bravo, magnífico, mi fantástico, Cassie," yelled Jordan, standing and clapping enthusiastically, tears streaming down his cheeks. "It's amazing; Mother lives within you." He hugged her.

Cassie responded. "It is wonderful to see you enjoying yourself, Jordan. It seems so long since you smiled. Staying away from the alcohol this past week seems to be working a miracle." She paused, stepped back and took his hand in hers. "I'm glad you're going into treatment."

He looked up at the photo of his mother. "I hated her, you know, towards the end, before she died. She wanted me to be different, a man's man; she would not let me dance. I was jealous of you."

"Yes, I knew that, and it seemed to get worse with your drinking. That can be put away into the past, Jordan. Mother got it wrong about you, and you suffered because of it. There were times when she drove me so hard, when my feet were so blistered that it was agony to walk let alone dance. I hated her then." She placed her hand on his arm. "We love you, Jordan; you're family, even though you worry us sick a lot of the time. Listen, commit to treatment and get well, stay well, and keep away from that bloody booze."

She looked up at the clock. "Ten o'clock already; time to go. We have an hour before we have to leave for the airport. You go ahead, I'll catch up. I'd like a few minutes here alone."

"Of course, thanks, Cassie."

"Oh, come on, cheer up," she said, unbuckling the straps of her shoes. "It's not the end of the world." She laughed. "It's rather the beginning of a new one, really, isn't it; for both of us?"

"I hope so," he said, trying his best to smile, unsure.

His footsteps faded away from the bottom of the stairs. Cassie went to the cabinet and returned her mother's shoes to their special place. On the bottom shelf, the split-sole pearl ballet shoes caught her eye. They were her favourite pair, the first pair given to her by her mother when she was five years old. They opened her to another beautiful dream, one of the many created by Kristina before she died.

She looked to the photo on the wall. "Thanks, Mummy." Then, smiling, she padded barefooted to the exit, stopped, looked back and gestured for her mother to follow. "Come on, Kristina, time we got on with what you started here."

# 32

Matt watched Dunning drive off from the hospital to check on a report of a broken window at the Kingscote Area School. With Woodson out of the picture for the time being, Dunning was the only policeman on the island, meaning that for twenty-four hours a day, seven days a week, he was on call; even with the island's low crime rate, routine duties alone were enough to keep him busy. Matt's early experiences of the police were pretty much limited to the brushes his father had with Woodson, who represented the despised face of authority. To be sure, any encounter Frank had with the police was usually hostile, but when Dunning showed up, he was wary and little confused by the policeman's friendliness. Frank had always contended that none of the bastards could ever be trusted. Nevertheless, Matt found Constable Dunning more and more to his liking. His pondering was interrupted by the arrival of Frank and Pat, pulling up behind his ute in the Landcruiser.

"How's he doing?" yelled Frank, as he slid out of the driver's seat to join Matt, Pat close behind. Frank looked dreadful, pale, drawn and troubled.

"They're working on him in the Casualty Room. Katherine is with him."

"I'm going in there." Frank placed his hand on Matt's shoulder. "Look, good work, Matt, the way you took care of that snake and getting in here as quick as you did; you kept your head and Sean's in with a chance because of you."

"It was Katherine who kept him alive; did something like you did with Woodson to get air into Sean, except she used the tire gauge and went down his throat with it."

"Team effort is what it takes, lad." He hurried off to the hospital entrance and disappeared inside. As he rushed down the corridor, a nurse came out of Casualty.

"Sean in there?" asked Frank, pushing through the doors before she could answer.

Katherine was standing back from the triage table. The local doctor was pushing a needle into a vein in the crook of Sean's arm. "Nice job, Katherine, your improvising kept him alive," said the doctor. "He has a good chance of getting through this."

"Frank," said Katherine, turning as he entered and then reaching for his hand.

"How is he doing?" Frank took her hand and squeezed it.

"We don't know yet," said the doctor, looking up at Frank. "It depends on how he responds to the antivenom."

"Oh, God," Frank replied. He reached out to brush back the cowlick from Sean's sweating forehead, choking back a threatening flood of tears. "You gotta save him, Doc, he's just a little bloke, you know." He kept brushing the boy's hair from his forehead.

Everyone was quiet. Katherine stood and took Frank by the arm. "Come on, Frank, let's go out for a bit." He resisted. "Come on," she coaxed gently, "let the doctor and nurses do their job." She led him from the room.

Matt was pacing about the visitors' waiting room, and Pat was sitting, reading the Islander when Frank and Katherine entered. Seeing Frank in tears shocked and frightened the boys.

"Is Sean dead, Dad?" asked Patrick. Matt was mortified, unable to make a sound.

"No, no," said Katherine, wrapping her arms around Pat. She motioned at Matt. "Come here." She wrapped an arm around him. "Boys, he's in pretty bad shape. The truth is we don't know if he will come out of it, but he's a fighter, and he is in good hands. As long as he is breathing, he's in with a chance."

Pat said softly, reverently. "He's made it this far; he's going to be fine, I know it. I know it." He started to kneel. "Come on; let's say a rosary for him."

They kneeled, all of them including Frank, using the waiting room chairs to rest their heads in their hands. Pat led them. "Hail Mary, full of grace, the Lord is with thee. Blessed are thou among…"

Twenty-five minutes later, the doctor came into the room. "We have him stabilized." The Ryans all stood. "He seems to be responding to the antivenom, but we won't know for sure for a few hours. I have arranged for the air ambulance to take him to the Royal Adelaide Hospital later this afternoon; they have the resources to give him the care and attention he needs. He'll be better off there."

"Can we see him?" asked Frank.

"Let's give him a couple of hours before you go in, Frank. I have arranged for the kitchen to bring you sandwiches and drinks. Katherine, I think it would be best if you went with him on the flight."

"Of course."

"I need some air," said Matt. "I'll be outside if you need me."

With myriad images spinning through his mind, Matt crossed the road in front of the hospital, to the edge of the bluff and stared out over the calm water, his stomach crowded with the awakening insurgents. A white pelican, its wings flapping powerfully, launched from its perch atop one of the wharf's tall light poles. Once airborne, the bird stopped flapping and descended in a graceful glide to skim the top of the ocean water. It lowered its feet and snatched, with a splash Matt could hear all the way on the bluff, at the seawater. The bird began to flap again, its long, wide wings pushed rhythmically through the air with powerful, leisurely sweeps, up and down, up and down, up and down. It gradually gained height, its track taking a wide arc over the glassy water toward the narrow strip of rocky foreshore, a desperate, struggling mullet trapped in the grip of its clawed feet. *A seal for the shark; a fish for the bird; a death for a life; and Sean…why?*

"You never know, hey?" Frank said, joining Matt. "I mean, you know it's coming, sometime, but you just don't know when. Here today, gone tomorrow. Take this; it's one of the sandwiches from the hospital."

Matt took the sandwich and manages a half-hearted bite. "Thanks." He looked at his father and shook his head. *I'll never work you out.*

"Seen it all, I have. Nature's creatures have it tough, brutal, hey? Hell, they don't hold a patch on what the human species get up to. Should have seen 'em at work in 'Nam, bloody slaughter all over the place, it was. Bits of body, blood and guts everywhere hanging off trees, women, kids, bloody awful, and what'd we do it for? You know, it's ironic; we're the lot given free will and knowledge of a God."

The pelican landed on the narrow stretch of beach, dropped the struggling fish onto the sand and then scooped it into its webby mouth.

"Isn't ya girl leaving today?" asked Frank.

"Yeah, I guess she'll be wondering where the hell I am."

"What time does the plane leave?"

"Twelve-thirty," answered Matt.

"It's five to twelve. If you get going now, you could make it out there before she leaves." Matt gestured toward the hospital. "There's nothing you can do for Sean right now. He's in good hands; we can't see him for another couple of hours, anyway. You'll be back by then."

"I'll never work you out, Dad. You're a prick most of the time."

"Get out of here, or that bloody plane will be gone before you get there."

Frank watched the boy scamper across the street to his ute. *Thank God, you don't have to live in this bloody skin, son.* Frank looked at his watch, again. *One or two won't hurt.* He headed off in the direction of the town and the Ozone Hotel overlooking Nepean Bay a few minutes walk away, thirsty.

# 33

Kingscote's large regional all-weather airport a few kilometres southeast of the town was the only commercial airport on the island and a very busy one especially in the summer months, the premium tourist period. A small building, adequate most of the time and set up against the tarmac fence, housed the check-in and reception services. Several small charter planes crowded much of the space on the tarmac where they waited for the return of their tourist passengers who expected to see all there was to see of the huge island in a day. A 50-seat turbo-prop aircraft belonged to the airline fleet that provided regular scheduled services to the island; a giant alongside the smaller aircraft, it was being readied to load passengers and their luggage for their trip to Adelaide. A pilot walked around the monster bird, looking into the wheel wells, kicking the tires, the required ground check before the short, twenty-five-minute hop to the big city.

Monty swung the Ford sedan into the airport entrance, clattered over the cattle grid and drove to the parking lot. Cassie was first out of the car, looking gorgeous in a lightweight, blue cotton dress, contrasting splendidly with her dark tan. She held tight onto her broad-brim straw hat, which was threatening to lift off her head in the light breeze, and looked over at the people milling about the airport building.

"Looking for Matt, hey?" said Jordan. "He's not here; can't see his ute."

Monty was lifting the luggage out of the trunk. "He'll show up. Jordan, give a hand here."

Cassie lifted out her small carry-on and moved off in the direction of the airport building, worried. A vehicle rattled over the cattle grid, and she turned to see another tourist bus.

Monty and Jordan joined her at the check-in counter with the rest of the luggage.

"Morning, Mr. Baldwin," said the clerk, nodding his head in greeting. "Cassie, Jordan, so all three of you are off to Adelaide today, hey?"

"Yes, Jim," said Cassie. "Do you have a customer phone I can use, please?"

Jimmy pointed to a phone on the corner of the counter. "No worries, it's the company phone, just dial 'O' for a line out."

"Thanks." She dialled the du Couedic lighthouse number, but no one answered. "He should have been here by now; something is wrong, I know it."

"We will be boarding in five minutes, Mr. Baldwin."

"Thank you, Jim," replied Monty, taking the boarding passes.

"Daddy, something has happened to Matt; I'm sure of it."

"Yes, he should have been here by now. I'll give the police station a call, if you like."

"Please, Daddy."

After three rings, an answering machine responded. "This is the officer in charge, Constable Bob Dunning. The station is temporarily unattended. Leave a message, or if the matter is an emergency please call 000."

"Bob, Monty Baldwin here, we are at the airport and young Matt Ryan was to meet us, but he has not turned up.

Just checking to make sure everything is okay. If there is a problem, call us and let us know, will you? We are staying at the Adelaide Hilton tonight."

"Mr. Baldwin, I'm sorry, but I have to ask you to board the aircraft now, sir," interrupted Jimmy.

"Yes, of course." Monty placed his arm around Cassie's waist and shepherded her toward the door. "Sorry, my dear, he probably had a tire blow-out, or some kind of breakdown. It can happen anytime on these roads."

"Something awful has happened; I don't feel right leaving like this."

"There's nothing we can do now, Cassie. We have to get on the plane. I told Bob Dunning where to get in touch. But, my bet is he has a flat tire, or something minor like that."

"I hope you're right, Daddy," said Cassie, her voice strained.

She kept looking over her shoulder as they made their way across the tarmac. Minutes later, she was buckling into a seat next to the window. The aircraft propellers began to rotate and were soon spinning at high speed after the turboprop engines ignited with their familiar, high-pitched scream. The pilot let off the brakes and the plane began to move slowly forward. Cassie stared out the window toward the entrance to the airport.

****

Matt roared away from the hospital. By the time he had flashed through the town's outskirts, he was already doing ninety-kilometres-per-hour, breaking the speed limit set at sixty, unaware of the police vehicle approaching from the school road that intersected with the main highway.

The red and blue flashing lights of the pursuit car quickly caught him up. "What the hell, now!" Matt yelled, thumping the steering wheel and pulling over to the left shoulder of the highway. He opened the door and stepped out, just as Dunning pulled in behind the Commodore and got out of the pursuit vehicle, looking extremely angry.

"What the hell are you doing, Matt, speeding through town like that. That's a busy intersection back there and right by the school; you could kill someone."

"I'm trying to get to the airport before Cassie leaves."

"That's no bloody excuse, mate. You got young Sean in hospital already, haven't you? That's enough, isn't it? It is for me. I don't want to be dragging you from a wreck dead, or someone else from the town for that matter."

"I'm sorry, Bob. I'm not thinking straight."

Dunning shook his head, "Look, I'll let you off with a warning this time, but if I catch you at it again, I'll book you hard. Now on your way, and stay within the bloody speed limit, will you?" He looked at his watch. "You can still make it. They rarely leave on time." He began to walk back to his car, paused and turned back to Matt. "Don't take my friendship for granted, Matt. I am a policeman. Just don't cross the line, all right, I've got a job to do."

"Yeah, right; right, Bob, sorry." Matt hurried back to his car, jumped into the driver's seat and roared off, the rear tires throwing up blue smoke. Dunning shook his head, returned to his vehicle and turned around to head back to Kingscote.

Creeping over the speed limit, Matt cursed himself for running afoul of Dunning. The encounter set him back five minutes; he pushed on the pedal a little harder. The car clock was showing 12:30 when he approached the airport turnoff. Two minutes later, he banged over the cattle grid, his heart sinking; the plane was beginning to taxi from the tarmac. "Bugger me bloody dead!" he cried out.

****

"There he is," said Monty. A blue vehicle bounced over the airport cattle grid and rushed to a sliding stop at the tarmac fence. Cassie watched through the small aircraft window, letting out a sigh of relief. *He's okay, thank God.* Her *bloke* jumped out of the ute and waved. Smiling, her face pressed against the window, she waved again, hoping he could see her.

****

Matt scanned the line of passenger windows. He thought he saw her, but he could not be sure, because of the angle of the aircraft and the reflection of the outside light denied him a clear view. But, the perky nose he thought he could make out, and the slow wave of her hand across the plastic, it had to be her. He waved furiously, love and anguish overwhelming him all at once.

Then she was gone. He railed briefly, slammed his fists against the hood of the Commodore, kicked the front tire and then cursed when a stabbing pain shot through his foot. "Bloody hell, bloody hell!" he yelled, hopping about on his good leg and shaking the hurt out of the other.

****

The aircraft turned to line up on the runway, and he slipped from her view. She did not see him bang the hood of his ute with his fists, or kick the front tire.

\*\*\*\*

He watched the plane line up for takeoff, weary, sad and lonely. The scream of the turbo-props built to full power. The pilot eased off the brakes and the plane lunged forward, quickly gathered speed and then, deliberately, it lifted into the air over the bush boundary, climbed quickly, arcing north to eventually track toward Adelaide. His eyes followed until the plane became a speck in the sky and disappeared into a bank of dark clouds, carrying his best mate, his love. Anxiety began its deadly creep. He remembered the copy of the sestina lying on the seat, retrieved it and began reading:

> *Oh, in this moment do I long for my river where the waters surge*
> *In tumultuous victory over the earth's impede—and where the heat*
> *Of conquest so stirs the heart to beat and keep this warrior alive*
> *To vanquish mortal fear and destroy the eternal dark.*

# 34

Matt walked into the hospital waiting room where Pat was watching the Australian versus West Indies cricket test on television.

"How is he, Pat?"

"Mother is with him; Mad Tom was here earlier. He said he would be back later. You can go in, if you like."

"Are you okay, mate?"

"I've been watching the test match. If you asked me the score I probably wouldn't be able to tell you."

"Yeah, I know what you mean; I've been feeling crook in the gut all day. Hang in there, Pat; I'm going in to check on him." He went into the corridor that led to the emergency room and was about to push through the swing doors when a nurse called out from the end of the long corridor.

"In here, Matt, we moved Sean into intensive care."

"What's happening to him, Linda?" Linda was from a farming family on the east end of the island and her two brothers played football in the Island League competition; the 4,000 plus islanders were a tight community.

"He's doing a little better. The antivenom seems to be working."

"Is it okay to go in?"

"Gosh, yes, of course. We're all praying for him, Matt."

"Thanks, Linda."

Katherine was sitting alongside Sean's bed, dozing. Sean was breathing with the support of a ventilator. A saline solution in a clear plastic bag bedside his bed, ran through tubing that connected to a needle in his wrist. A number of thin electrical wires attached to small adhesive patches stuck to parts of his chest and fed into an EKG machine. A green line registered his heartbeat on a monitor screen, a sharp ping accompanied each beat, and a printer ran continuously recording the vital signs on a chart. He was deathly pale.

"Is he going to be okay, Katherine?"

Katherine woke, instantly alert, and reached for Matt's hand. "He's doing a little better, Matthew. He's in an induced coma; the doctor didn't want him waking up and fighting the treatments."

"He will make it, won't he?" asked Matt, barely able to get the words out for fear of the response.

"He's getting the best of care. Doctor Wilson is confident, but we have to monitor him closely. One of the dangers is that antivenom can cause a heart attack, but he is responding. We are leaving for the airport in about an hour."

He released Katherine's hand and moved closer to the bedside. "Hey, you're going to be good as new, mate," he said, picking up Sean's hand. The boy shifted a little and grimaced. "Hey, did you see that, Katherine? I reckon he heard me. You little, bloody bewdy, hey?"

"I told you I reckon he'll come through," said Pat, as he walked into the ICU and heard the last of Matt's words. "He's tough, and God is looking out for him." He paused and cleared his throat. "Err…do you know where Dad is?"

"You haven't seen him?" asked Matt.

"He said he was going outside to speak to you the last I saw him."

"Yeah, well he did, about two hours ago." He shook his head. "Ah, no, don't tell me he's down at the pub."

For a second Katherine's eyes flashed with anger, but then she shrugged and sighed. "It's his way of dealing with things. You'd better get him, Matthew."

Matt headed for the door. "I'll be back." He signalled for Pat to follow.

"Make sure your mother has her bag with her when she goes to the airport," he said quietly, walking along the passage toward the hospital exit. "You can come with me when we leave to follow the ambulance. The Oldman isn't going to be worth a damn, but I'll bring him back here."

"What's the use, Matt?"

"That's his kid in there, and he ought to be here."

The Ozone Hotel was one of two watering holes in Kingscote. Both were popular, and the patrons often moved back and forth between them several times over the course of a day. Matt peered into the main bar, but Frank had left. "Yeah, he left fifteen minutes ago; said he was going to the Queenscliffe, Matt," a local fisherman offered, squinting over the top of froth-topped beer.

Minutes later, Matt pushed through the swing doors of the saloon section of the Queenscliffe Hotel. A few thirsty blokes were bellying up at the bar, having a chin-wag and downing schooners of the cold amber. Frank, sitting at the far end by himself, was placing an empty glass back on the bar top, gesturing to Sparky Johnson, part-time electrician and barman, to "fill 'er up."

Matt, doing his best to keep his anger under control approached Frank warily. "What the bloody hell are you doing in here? Jeez, Dad, Sean is up in the hospital fighting for his life from snake bite, and here you are in the pub getting pissed. What sort of a mongrel would you be, hey?"

Frank reacted angrily, "Yeah, well I was just coming, wasn't I? Only had a couple, and if you think you want to do something about it, have a go."

The bar crowd fell silent.

"Who'd you say got bit, Matt?" asked Sparky.

"Sean, my brother; the Doc reckons he'll make it, but he's not out of the woods yet…flying him to the Royal Adelaide this 'arvo."

"What the hell are you doing in here, Frank?" yelled a voice from among the drinkers. "You ought to be up at the hospital with your kid and your wife."

"Why don't you shut ya mouth, ya bloody drongo, and if you want to make something of it, I'll be outside."

Frank slid unsteadily from the stool and pushed Matt out of the way. Matt spun off the bar bench and grabbed his father by the arm. "That's your way to solve everything, isn't it; give 'em a good hiding? That's what mum copped every time she had a go at you about your boozing; bloody killed her in the finish, hey, ya bastard."

Frank was on the verge of lashing out at Matt when a large hand grabbed his wrist. "Don't do it, Frank," said Mad Tom, "you'll be sorry later." Frank turned and faced Mad Tom ready for war. They stared at each other, and then without a word Frank pulled away from Tom's grasp, pushed through the swing doors and out into the street.

"Thanks, Tom," said Matt.

"All that matters right now is young Sean, Matt. Go after your dad and take him up to the hospital. I'll be up there in a few minutes."

Matt left, angry, disgusted and embarrassed.

"Give our best to Sean and Katherine, Matt," yelled Sparky. "We'll all be pulling for him." The noise in the bar resumed as the drinkers began discussing the latest Ryan disaster: "Tough little bloke." "Ryans' is been through it all." "Frank's an alkie; mad as a cut snake since he got back from Vietnam." "Yeah, first wife committed suicide." "Bloody sad it is; the whole business."

Matt quickly caught up with Frank. "You lying bastard; you were setting up in there for rest of the day. What the hell is going on in that head of yours?"

Frank avoided the question. "Look, calm down, I needed a couple beers to settle me nerves, that's all, and now here we are on the way back again, no harm done, right? There was nothing could be done anyway, but wait. You said he's gunna make it, right?"

"No thanks to you. You could've stayed with Katherine; she's Sean's mother, for God's sake. Don't you think she needs a little support from her husband? Bloody hell, like I said earlier, I can't work you out." They came to the Matt's vehicle where he had parked it in front of the Ozone. "Get in," he said, pointing to the passenger side door.

He drove straight back to the hospital, and arrived as Monsignor Byrne was pulling in to the parking lot. The agile old priest was at the door of the ute before Matt finished unbuckling his seatbelt. "I got in from Cape Torrens a few minutes ago," he said.

The monsignor was an avid naturalist who became incommunicado for up to a week each month to camp out along the north and west coasts of the island, looking for fossils, rocks and animal skeletons. He was in the midst of writing his third book about his beloved island, *Kangaroo Island's Fascinating Historical Relevance*. Because it was Saturday, he was back in time to prepare for his Sunday sermon for Mass and to hear confessions held later in the afternoon. His first phone message on arrival back at the presbytery was the shocking message from Frank, informing him of Sean's snake bite.

"Where is Sean, Matthew; how is he doing?" asked the Monsignor. Frank approached the priest and was about to speak when Pat appeared at the hospital entrance.

"Monsignor, Mother said for you to come right on in, please."

"I'm on my way, Patrick"

When Monsignor Byrne looked at Frank's face, he caught a hint of shame in the man's bloodshot eyes. "Frank, let's go inside, shall we? I'm tink'n 'tis a good time for a rosary; you too, Matthew," he said, placing a hand on Frank's back and shepherding him towards the hospital entrance.

# 35

The cool breeze finally arrived, blowing in from the southwest, relieving the stifling heat of the unusual week of weather for Kangaroo Island. The sun had set, leaving behind a familiar pink hue spreading across the fading pastel blues of a sky moving slowly toward darkness. Matt and Pat were sitting on the front veranda of the cottage, watching the wind ruffle the face of the Southern Ocean waves lining up to attack the unyielding cliffs of Cape du Couedic. Frank was in the lighthouse, reporting the local weather to the bureau over the radio.

"I'm glad he's in the Children's Hospital. Mother sounded a lot better, too. He's going to be okay, I know it," said Pat.

"Yeah, close one, hey? Poor little bugger's going to be pretty crook for a while. I can do without another Saturday like today. We all can."

"Mother said he would be in hospital for a week, if everything goes all right," said Pat.

"Yeah, but we're going to have to watch him over the next six months; the symptoms can recur anytime, the doc said, especially in a little bloke. Barney's having a hard time of it." Barney, sitting at Matt's feet, looked up at the mention of his name.

"When I let him off the chain, he ran straight to Sean's bed and started whining." The phone rang. "I'll get it." Patrick hurried into the house and returned a couple of minutes later. "It's Cassie."

Matt hustled into the kitchen. "G'day, mate. I'm sorry I didn't make it to the airport before you had to board."

"Thank goodness you're home, Matt. Oh, dear God, I was horrified when I found out what happened to Sean. Bob Dunning answered a message Daddy left, and he told us. I was relieved when you arrived at the airport, but I still knew something was wrong, that something awful was going on."

"Yeah, it scared the hell out of all of us, but he's going to be okay. Miss you, bloke."

"Thank God, poor little chap. Miss you, too; I'd love to give you a hug right now." She paused. "We checked Jordan into the alcohol rehabilitation clinic this afternoon. I hope it works; he's been behaving so much better not drinking all this week. Anyway, Daddy and I are about ready to leave to visit Sean and Katherine. Is there anything he would especially like?"

"That's terrific of you, Cass, thanks. He likes chocolate a lot; bring him a Cadbury's Dairymilk and he'll be your friend for life. Give him a big hug from all of us, will you?"

"I will; along with a big sloppy kiss." She laughed.

"That'll buck him up. What time do you get into Sydney tomorrow?"

"Lunchtime; I have to be at the dance studio early Monday morning, ready to go." Matt heard Monty's voice in the background. "That's Daddy; the cab is here. I'll call again before we leave in the morning." She was silent for a moment. "I love you."

"Yep, love you, too." They lingered, listening to each other breathing, not wanting to go.

"Tell Patrick I'd like to talk to him longer next time, and say hello to your dad for me. Tell him you're all in our prayers." The click of her phone signalled their conversation was over.

Matt wandered back to the veranda and settled into the old sofa. "Cassie and her dad are going over to the hospital to see Sean and Katherine, said we are all in their prayers."

"Oh, that's nice; I like her, she's a really kind person, Matt."

"Yeah; look, I'm going for a walk over to the Admiral. Barney can come along, too; he's really having a hard time about Sean." He motioned to Barney, who was lying flat out on the concrete. He raised an eyebrow and looked at Matt. "C'mon, before it gets too dark; a walk will do you good. Sean's going to be all right, but you're going to have to take good care of him when he gets back, hey?" Barney stretched, got to his feet and ran after Matt, switching his tail in eager anticipation of sniffing out and chasing kangaroos, wallabies and any other assorted wildlife where their scent marked their passing.

Matt took the long way to the Arch, skirting the lighthouse deliberately to avoid running into Frank. On the cliff above Weir Cove, he looked over at a fishing cutter swinging on its anchor below. Barney tore about the bushes and limestone outcrops, sniffing for the animals that may have dared to trespass on his territory. Every now and again, he lifted his hind leg and fired a shot of pee onto a bush or rock to mark and reaffirm his claim. At the bottom of the cliff were the remnants of the old jetty, used to land supplies for the lighthouse keeper, his assistant and their families in the early days when ketches were the only transport for people and cargo before the land route from Kingscote was established. The boats would carefully tie up to the jetty, load the basket and then winch it to the top of the cliff. The supplies were then transferred to the stone storehouse, long since a crumbling ruin, behind the winch housing. Sometimes storms made it impossible to tie up alongside the jetty, and the supply drop could be delayed for days or even weeks.

In the distance across the cove, he could see Remarkable Rocks, and as he had from the times when he was as young as Sean, he marvelled how long the huge granite marbles had stayed in place and wondered when the day would come that they finally rolled into the ocean. He looked to the south, to where the islets, the sentinels, surrounded by white foam, stood out spectacularly from beyond Cape du Couedic's rugged thrust into the Southern Ocean. He grinned at Barney who was still busy staking out his territory. This was the place where Sean had his hideaway, but nobody else except probably Barney knew its secret location. His attention honed in on what the smart kelpie was up to when Barney peered over the edge of the cliff and began to whine.

"Barney! Yes, of course. Go on, Barney, seek and find Sean's place. Show me." Barney pawed at the edge of the cliff, throwing sand and small rocks back along his flanks, his whining growing progressively louder until it turned to yelping, and him running madly around the same spot in circles. "No, Barney, not down there, I want you to show me Sean's secret place." Barney stopped, but kept looking over the cliff and barking loudly. "Ah, c'mon you silly bugger, he can't have it down there, too steep, no way to get down."

The breeze that came off the ocean stiffened. He shivered, feeling uneasy and spooked, sensing a presence, an energy trying to tell him something. Then, it was gone. "Bugger this," he yelled in frustration, "we're out of here." Barney was still barking and looking down at the jetty. "C'mon, Barney, we're leaving."

There was little light left when they reached the Arch, but Matt settled down in his favourite spot. Barney raced around the rocks, disturbing seals and causing them to seek refuge in the water. After demonstrating his dominance and wet from his splashing, he returned to where Matt was sitting and vigorously shook the water from his hairy coat, dousing Matt before stretching out on the flat rock beside him.

"You better watch out, swimming in that water down there. Great whites like dog tucker," he said, remembering the seal taken there. He ruffled Barney's head and returned to his pondering; the water and the seals, unable to get the imagery out of his mind; the foreplay, the young seals, stunningly exotic, teasing, moving inevitably toward copulation, and then without warning, the shark stuffed it up, brutal. *Life!* His mind was full of the mix of colours, lots of red, blood swirling, crimson mixing with blues, aflame with the sun's fire, yellows, reds, and orange. *That's it!* Inspiration and excitement swept over him; his mind exploded with images of performers dancing in vigorous, sensual movements: red, blue, and orange colours mixed in fiery ribbons of light, casting dramatic and changing portraits of life, as they danced its story. Matt knew he had to write a short story using all these elements coming together to a moment of fiery copulation. "Maybe, maybe Cassie and her company could choreograph all the elements coming together." *Fire, Fire in the Centre.*

# 36

Sydney was big, brash and magnificent, an international city, crowding around the waters of one of the finest harbor's in the world. A bustling cosmopolitan city, home to over four million people, offering the very best of what the world had to offer, and for those who strived to excel, opportunity.

Looking out from the large scenic window of her Lavender Bay terrace house, Cassie could hardly contain her excitement. "This is sensational; what a view, Daddy."

Monty, smiling, followed her through the open double doors that lead to the patio. The warm, humid weather, typical for a Sydney summer, was comfortable enough for the two islanders to be outside to enjoy the fresh air. Lavender Bay was on the north side of the harbor, across from Sydney Cove, and this day for Cassie, the scenic wonder before her was even more beautiful and alluring than her Middle River.

In the sweep of the bay, dozens of small and medium-sized yachts pivoted around their moorings, rocking back and forth in the wash of vessels that thronged the harbor on any given Sunday. The wire halyards of the rigging clacked against the boats' metal masts, sending a constant mix of discordant sound over the harbor, but as Cassie was soon to discover, lending an individual and identifiable character to each of the boats.

Looking across the water to the south side, she marvelled at the grandeur of the Sydney Opera House, set like a fortress on the sandstone rock of Bennelong Point on the eastern flank of Circular Quay. Bennelong Point, named for an Aborigine befriended by Captain Arthur Phillip, Sydney's first governor. He had a hut built for the "highly intelligent" native on the point. In March 1791, in a gesture of gratitude, Bennelong arranged a concert for the governor who, along with his party of twenty-four men, women and children, danced to the accompaniment of beating sticks and stomping feet.

Two hundred years later, Bennelong's spirit carried on in the thousands of concerts performed in the Opera House built on the very site of the native's old hut. Adjacent to the signature white sails, the Sydney Harbor Bridge soared above the water to link the north and south sides of the city.

"There, Daddy, there to the right of the bridge pylons," said Cassie, pointing to a line of renovated warehouses on the south side. "The third one is the company's theatre and studios."

"Yes, of course; it is one of the reasons I bought this place for you. A few minutes by ferry from Blue's Point wharf to Circular Quay, a brisk walk to warm you up, and there you are ready to dance. Of course, the views from here are spectacular, too."

"What a lovely way to go to work." She hugged him, peeping over his shoulder to watch the yachts and cruisers compete for space under the bridge and around the opera house. "How fun; thank you, ever so much, Daddy."

He stepped back, chuckling. "You look splendid. Now, I expect you'll want some time to settle in, maybe put your feet up and relax for awhile, so I've arranged to spend the afternoon with an old friend of Kristina's whom I hadn't seen for a long time. Belinda Cohen, the lady you met here in Sydney with your mother shortly before she died. She still lives in Rose Bay, on the south side." He glanced at his watch. "It is 12:30...umm, how about I get back around six and take you to dinner? There's a charming little restaurant, Sails, right on the water below us." He pointed to a roof partly hidden by two large fig trees, some of the branches extended over the water. "That's it, where the ferry berths at Blue's Point; it specializes in fish dishes. I've tried their whiting, not quite the King George whiting of the island, but pretty darn good just the same."

"That would be lovely. Yes, just lovely." She grinned. "Can I order you a cab, Daddy?"

"Oh, I almost forgot, follow me."

He led the way down the stairs to a lower level, where a set of stone steps led off from the kitchen and descended into a two-car garage. At the bottom of the stairs, he ushered her into the garage ahead of him. The first thing she saw was a bright red Mazda RX7. Monty reached for a set of keys hanging from a hook next to the door. "Here we are." He handed them to her and gestured toward the Mazda. "Yours; it's not new, 35,000 kilometres on the clock, nothing really; get you around beautifully. Belinda found it for you," said Monty, beaming.

"I love it," she said, opening the front door of the two-seater and sliding behind the wheel. "Stick-shift, too; perfect, Daddy, perfect, you spoiler, you." She jumped out from the seat and hugged him again.

"God knows you've earned it, girl. Besides, I don't want you to have to think about anything other than your career."

She laughed. "Sometimes, Daddy, your motives are quite transparent."

"I'm not quite sure I understand."

"Oh, yes, you do, but the deal is six months, right?"

"Cassandra, you are your mother's daughter, that is the truth. Now, do you think I might borrow the keys?"

****

Cassie closed the door of her wardrobe, the last of her suitcases empty. On the bedside table, she placed her favourite photo of Matt, a close-up of his handsome features and blazing, blue eyes that looked out over a cheeky grin. She smiled, responding to the warmth of the energy radiating from his photo.

Her new home was a smart, Sydney, three-level, three-bedroom, remodelled terrace house, tastefully furnished throughout with rich textured Persian rugs spread over polished hardwood floors. The refrigerator was already full of food and drink.

She poured a grapefruit juice, prepared a plate of cheeses, dry cookies and fruits and then made her way to the deck. Relaxing into the chaise chair, she began nibbling at the snacks, soaking up the warmth of the sun and letting go of the anxieties of the last twenty-four hours.

*Strange.* It was only the day previous that she had left Kangaroo Island, and already it seemed light years away, all a dream. Matt called before she left Adelaide and asked about the visit with Sean. "Oh, he's so brave, such a little fighter," she told him. When Matt told her about *Fire in the Centre* she was excited, not just about the concept and the challenge he presented to her, but the fact that he was busy acting on his creative impulses.

She drifted into a state of bliss where images of bodies, silhouettes against myriad colours, stretching, extending and leaping to the sounds of didgeridoos, clicking sticks, guitars and drums, stirred her primitive passions and desires. The sun was hot on her bare legs. *Fire in the Centre; bloody raunchy stuff, mate.* Then, she was asleep, the voice of her mother whispering through her subconscious. "I'm with you, my darling. Here, we begin the dance; always, I am with you."

Cassie woke to the voice of her father. "Cassie, Cassie, wake up; I have someone I want you to meet." Monty was standing next a woman in her mid-fifties. She was tall, her posture, carriage and physique were obvious, a classical dancer.

"Cassie, this is Belinda. You met her once when you were just a tot; probably don't remember, hmm?"

"Oh, Monty, of course the poor dear doesn't remember. My goodness, the image of her mother, isn't she?" Belinda bent over and kissed Cassie on the cheek. "Hello, dear, it is so nice to see you again. Your father has told me all about you. Lovely." She smiled. "I danced with your mother when she first came to Australia. She could have gone on to become a celebrated artist, but your father took her from us." She looked back at Monty. "Oh, Gad, they are just going to love her, my dear man. This one will be the toast of Sydney in time, no doubt." She turned back to Cassie. "You'll soon forget all about that island of yours, I'll promise you that, dear."

Cassie was a little overwhelmed and immediately on the defensive. She got to her feet and gave Belinda a cursory handshake. "Actually, I do remember something of our first meeting, Belinda. If I recall correctly, you whisked me from the waterfront wall of your mansion, on which I was balancing rather unsteadily, to save me, I believe, from toppling into the harbour. I suppose I owe you a debt of gratitude, but it was the whack on my bum from your hand I remember most vividly." She tossed a glance at her father. "Daddy, I am a little surprised that you would be discussing my life on the island with Belinda, and my guess is that a good part of it would be about who Matt is in my life, right?"

Monty flushed with embarrassment. He shrugged, disconcerted, and cleared his throat. "You don't have to be so rude, Cassandra."

Cassie turned back to Belinda. "Yes, well, you started off beautifully," she said and pointed into the house. "Thank you. Yes, and for the car, too, perfect. Now, we will get on wonderfully, if you understand that my personal life is not up for meddling. I will be on the lookout for any scheme you or Daddy may concoct to undermine my relationship with Matt, so having said that, I'll go and slip into something appropriate for dinner. Please excuse me. I'll be ready in a few minutes." She left.

Monty was beside himself. "I do apologize, Belinda. I can't remember her ever being so rude. Forgive her, she's probably worn out."

"Oh, don't be silly, Montgomery. What a spirit. She is wonderful, her mother's daughter, no question, wonderful." Belinda was smiling and animated. "Yes, she is going to take this city by storm." She held Monty's hand and gave it a pat. "Now, don't you worry about a thing, this is all going to work out just how it should. She and I will get on famously, believe me."

# 37

The Monday evening ride on the ferry back to the Blue's Point landing was as glorious and fascinating as was Cassie's ride over in the morning. Like most evenings, a sea breeze worked slowly up the harbour from the Pacific, replacing the stale city air. As the Hagherty ferry's wooden hull slapped through the wash of other busy ferries taking home city workers, the spray of seawater occasionally lifted over the bow, splashing and cooling Cassie's gleeful face. A train roared overhead on the Harbor Bridge, prompting her to look up to the spidery web of steel girders that formed the arch curving away to her left and right, and which eventually punched through the granite towers supporting them on the north and south sides.

"The locals call it the 'ol Coat Hanger," said a deck hand, as he leaned over the gunwale, taking a last drag on a burned-down cigarette. "You're not from here, are ya?"

"What a vulgar name for such an elegant structure," she replied, addressing the rough, thirty-year-old decky. "I am now. I'll be travelling on this most days."

"Ah, good, get to know ya a bit then. Know a few good pubs around here, take you along some time?" he said, a cautious upward inflection judiciously accompanying the tone of his question.

She laughed. "I don't think so. My boyfriend is the jealous type, and he's young and strong."

The decky's response was a sarcastic grunt of disbelief. "Yeah, right." He moved on to prepare for the next landing.

The effects of the long day were starting to catch up with her; two lengthy sessions of class and rehearsal, one in the morning and one in the afternoon, each of three hours' duration. The rocking of the boat and the fresh salt air gradually lulled her into a drowsy contentment, and she reflected on the first day at the studio.

\*\*\*\*

It had been interesting. She was amazed at how much she could learn in one day; the nuance of movement, how the tiniest adjustments in posture and technique could improve balance and make a huge impact on a performance. She had no idea how many dedicated people it took to run a professional dance company.

At dinner the previous night, she also learned Belinda Cohen was the company's biggest and most influential patron, the founding member. How, after a successful career as an international artist, she had to retire because of injury. She married a wealthy Jewish financier and started the company, convincing a still performing and talented ex-partner, Timothy Barton, to join her as the artistic director and principle choreographer. The company became hugely successful and internationally renowned. Aaron, her husband, died, and Belinda withdrew from managing the company, reducing her shareholding substantially and selling the greater part of it to Timothy.

Over dinner, as Belinda talked about the dance company, her love of dance and about the love and friendship she had for Kristina, Cassie began to come to the realization that she had a lot in common with Belinda. And then, when Belinda had apologized for her inappropriateness of perhaps meddling in Cassie's private affairs, the last vestiges of Cassie's concerns about Belinda evaporated. Monty looked somewhat nonplussed, but then, and she had smiled at the time, her daddy had never really been able to understand the women in his life.

****

The harsh bump of the boat against the Kirribilli wharf startled her. A number of the passengers, many carrying briefcases, disembarked. She was thoroughly impressed with magnificent grandeur of the large apartment buildings; some of them converted mansions that lined right up to the edge the harbour water. The lifestyle Sydney offered living on the water and travelling over it to and from work each day was the ideal, but not everyone could afford it. Cassie knew she was extraordinarily fortunate to come from a family that knew the value of hard work, a family that over generations had built a substantial fortune. The rope that secured the ferry to the wharf was shaken free of the pylon by the decky, and it started out for its next stop. Cassie returned to her day in the studio.

****

Timothy Barton, Belinda's partner, was a moving ball of energy, as he showed her around the building, "For orientation," he had said. "Yes, I saw your audition from behind there." He pointed to a wall mirror at the head of the rehearsal studio. "My office and lounge are behind the two-way; that's how we keep an eye on things. Sometimes we can pick up an injury a dancer is trying to cover up and have it treated before any real damage is done." He waved his hands about as if directing traffic, pointing out various aspects of the room. "Toilets and changing rooms run off the far door. The cafeteria is further along the corridor, located on the end of the building, where you are literally suspended over the harbour. Our patrons and public also eat there, so we ask that you be discreet in your conversations and behaviour."

She had been distracted by the view of the water, which took up the entire wall of one side of the studio; he noticed immediately. "Beautiful, inspiring, yes, but you'll soon get used to it. Your focus will be on that wall." He pointed to the *barre* running the full length on the opposite side with mirrors floor to ceiling. He rattled on. "We liked your audition. Of course, we did or you wouldn't be here, humph? You certainly have the talent, flair, potential and presence, but do you have the dedication, the stamina, the heart for the hard work it takes to be great? Well, we shall see, shan't we?"

He smiled warmly and energetically rubbed his hands together. "You have six weeks, and then we will meet again and review your work. We will watch your progress with great expectation." He took her hand and patted it warmly. "Belinda called me last night. I want you to know that she and I are here for you, any time. Now, come," he said and led her out of the studio holding her hand.

He turned back along the corridor toward the land end of the building. "I want you to meet the company. They are in here," he said, turning into an open door. In the room, sitting on the floor, stretching, relaxing, and talking, were nineteen dancers. Timothy clapped his hands. "Everybody, this is the new girl I was telling you about, Cassandra Baldwin, known as Cassie, who did that stunning audition here late last year. Get to know her and make her feel welcome."

She had felt nervous and even a little sick. *They looked so fit, so confident.* "These are your peers," Timothy said, waving the back of his hand in a gesture indicating the whole group. "They form the core of the company, and they will help you settle in. Our principal dancers are among them, but we do not mollycoddle anybody here. There are no prima donnas, myself excepted, of course." He smiled. "We are family; our goal is to excel as artists, and as a great international dance company."

He gestured to a male dancer. "Please, Shamus, come." A handsome young man, in his early 20s, sprang athletically to his feet from his cross-legged sitting position in front of the *barre*. "Cassie, I want you to meet Shamus O'Brien. Shamus will be your male partner for the next few weeks; he is very experienced and…oh, how do I say this without launching his highly charged ego into the stratosphere…he is *very* good."

Cassie was slightly taken aback when the young Shamus stretched to his full height and flashed an ingratiating smile, his white teeth showing off the glint of ivory highly valued for toothpaste commercials. His long, dark hair, resembling the mane of a wild animal, fell about his muscular shoulders and ran down to the middle of his back.

G'day, Cass," he said in a broad Australian accent. "Welcome aboard, we're going to get along just great." She thought he moved like a big cat, a lion. He was obviously full of himself, his presence, overwhelming.

Nervous and defensive, she had given Shamus her best cold stare and flashed him a smile of deference, she hoped.

He had just stood grinning, understanding, assuming a pose that had his tight pants straining about his perfectly proportioned body, a pose she was unable to ignore. *God!*

The morning was filled with exercises and technique at the *barre*. In the afternoon, they moved into rehearsal mode where the dancers were responsible for self-motivation and no longer prodded to excel by the class instructor. They had to build from their creative resources, choreographing their work from any of the music Timothy had selected from modern dance favourites. Shamus awed her with his extensive range of movement and his aggressive style of performance. Once working, he was thoroughly professional, very generous and helpful in offering the benefit of his experience for subtle refinements in her technique, placement and style. He was intolerant and impatient when she failed to match his effort and intensity. Still, she had sensed a thrilling and powerful surge of excitement in the marriage of their talents, performance chemistry and perfectionist expectations.

\*\*\*\*

She was again jolted back to the present by the grinding of metal on metal, as the deck-hand slid back the safety rails of the ferry gate. The boat slowed for a smooth approach to berth alongside the Blue's Point wharf.

"Ah, hope I didn't offend ya earlier. You know, you're about the best looker I've seen around here in a long time. Me name's Jerry." He smiled, revealing a dirty line of tobacco stained teeth as he expertly flicked another spent cigarette into the water.

She gave him a gratuitous smile. "I'm sure you say that to all the girls."

The boat stopped, and Jerry tossed a rope over the pylon to hold the vessel steady for the passengers to go ashore. He watched intently, as she stepped from the loading ramp and strode off along the wharf. "You're one of those dancers, aren't ya?" he called after her, drooling as the sun shining through her light cotton dress bared the outline of her body, panties and bra.

"Yes, I am," she said airily, looking back over her shoulder on the way along the foreshore path to her terrace house.

"Uppity bitch," said Jerry under his breath. "They all get sorted, eventually." He coughed up a mouthful of phlegm, swirled it noisily about in his mouth, spat a gray-brown mass of gunk into the water and watched it drift away, fascinated.

Monty was peering over the deck railing, expecting her. "I thought you'd be home about now, heard the ferry; fully intended to walk down and meet you, but I fell asleep."

"You must have needed it. I'll be right up," she said, pushing her key into the front gate latch. Minutes later, she was on the patio, sipping a cold beer. "Hm, nice drop, what is it?"

"Tooheys, a New South Wales beer. The bottle shop fellow told me it was popular here. I'm glad you like it." Monty took a sip of his Scotch. "So, how was your first day?"

"Tough, but wonderfully exciting." She dropped into a deck chair, placed her bare feet on the footrest and drew her dress up over her knees. "I'm worn out and devilishly hungry."

"How about you take a rest, and when you are ready to eat, we scoot up to the Blue's Point Café, just three minutes from here in the car?"

"Sounds good," she said, studying the bubbles rising through the amber fluid to join the creamy froth on top. *Funny how something so refreshing can level a family,* she thought remembering the struggles and tragedy of Matt's family.

"Daddy, we don't usually keep things from each other, do we?" She waited; a pregnant pause ensued. "Is there something you ought to be telling me?"

Monty coughed and took another mouthful of his scotch. "I'm a little at a loss to know what you are driving at."

"You sound like the politicians you dislike so much, Daddy." She took another sip of beer, stood up, walked to the deck rail and surveyed the harbour, looking out toward the Sydney Opera House. "One day, I'll dance there." She smiled at Monty. "Well, Daddy, first of all Belinda indicates that I'll soon forget the island, meaning Matt, of course. And then today, I get teamed up with a bloke who could only be described as simply gorgeous. Belinda wouldn't be behind that either, would she?"

"Belinda has only your best interests at heart, Cassie," responded Monty. "From what she told me, young Shamus is an extraordinary talent and your art can only benefit enormously from his involvement. She believes that you are the perfect partner for him, and when the right work comes along the two of you will be sensational; a big draw, using the marketing terminology. Now, I would consider that a hell of a compliment wouldn't you?"

"Ah, you're ducking and weaving, a dead giveaway. So unlike you, Daddy, but he will make a sensational partner." She smiled coyly. "He's another Catholic, you know, and Irish."

Monty spluttered, coughed again and then swallowed the rest of his Scotch. A moment passed. "Cassie, I, um, I do have something else to tell you," he said hesitantly. "Belinda will be joining me for a brief stay on Kangaroo Island. She is leaving with me tomorrow night."

She laughed affectionately and hugged him. "Wonderful. I thought you two might have something going; you do look stunning together, you know."

"I, umm, she is a very wealthy woman, and the family arrangements I have made, you, the boys, the farm, will not be affected in any way, if anything should come of this."

She tickled Monty under the chin. "You are a little further along than I guessed, you sly devil. No, it's wonderful; you deserve all the happiness there is to be had, Montgomery Baldwin." She chuckled merrily. "Let's have dinner and celebrate; quick shower and we're off." Energized, she danced through the double doors with a series of swirling pirouettes, heading happily for the shower.

Monty watched her disappear beyond the patio doors. He turned to stare over the water, his face reddening from guilt and shame.

# 38

Matt was typing furiously, putting his thoughts on paper before losing them to myriad others fighting for significance. The monsignor's idea to write an essay about the island was perfect. As he researched the history and spoke to descendants of early settlers, the more he came to appreciate the unique aspects of his numinous home.

*Kangaroo Island: mysterious, transcendent, centre of enlightenment, the final destination for the seeker? There are many who come and swear they experience the presence of union with God, and the serene demeanour they reflect would evidence that such is the case. How can one not find God in the experience of the island's nature with its intoxicating scents and colours emanating from a myriad of exotic flora, or the experience of the splash and song of tumbling waters rushing pristine and unimpeded from the great Antarctic 3,500 kilometres south.*

*There are many who come afflicted with issues of health, mental and physical. Many testify that a yearly hiatus to Kangaroo Island is enough to restore them to wellness and a sense of peace, of no longer being alone.*

*Kangaroo Island is my home. Oh yes, I will explore the vastness of this world and savour all it offers, but I will come back here to sit on the Admiral's cape and look over this wild and beautiful ocean, conversing with the presence, forever grateful that this extraordinary island fills my soul with wonder and a spiritual solace.*

Matt pushed his hand through his hair and stared at the words on the black and white screen. *Hmm, it's getting there.* The essay, "*Kangaroo Island, South Australia's Mystical Secret?*" had to be in the mail by Monday with that day's date stamped on the envelope and on its way to Sydney. After putting in five nights a week for the six weeks since Cassie left, at last he had almost finished.

His thoughts turned to Cassie. Staring into the screen, the worms began stirring in his gut. The letters of the essay began to transform into dancers. They blurred and swirled into a spiral of mixing metaphors, laughing and teasing his mind. A toy plane whirled above the performers.

He attempted to put his foot on the first step to board the plane, but he kept missing it. The plane was in the shape of a boomerang. It started out heading for Sydney, but flew in an arc and kept returning to Kangaroo Island. His hand reached out, snatching for Cassie as she whirled by, circling with a hysterically laughing Shamus. The letters formed and ballooned, like the dialogue in a comic book, from the male dancer's laughing lips, "Can't catch me, can't catch me; can't leave the kangaroos, ha, ha, ha, ha, ha."

Matt slammed his fist on the desk. He had received only one letter and a phone call from Cassie in six weeks. Every time he called her, she was never in. She did not have an answer machine, something she could get. There had been no letters for weeks in the delivery that came to the ranger's house twice a week, nothing. An earlier letter that told him about Shamus did it; he knew then she had hooked up with the *bastard*.

Sure, she called once to tell him how Shamus loved his *Fire in the Centre* concept, how he would like to choreograph and dance it with her. Timothy Barton thought they might be able to fit it into an opening for a four-week season in July, the Newcomer Series, which played the same three selected works, every night at the Sydney Opera House. And yes, he was going to submit *Fire in the Centre*. "You'll be credited with the concept. Timothy can't wait to meet you, and he thinks you are brilliant. It is all here for you, my darling," she had said. *Yeah, right!*

"Matthew!" interrupted Katherine, calling from the kitchen, "dinner is on the table."

"Okay, I'll be there in a minute."

Cassie had picked up the tension in his voice then. She told him she loved him, to trust the process and not to worry about the outcome. Precise outcomes could not be forecast because they were likely to change, anyway. Participation and experience in the process, moment to moment, was what really counted. "That's how we get our answers," she said. *Bullshit!*

Angry, he looked back at his essay. Suddenly, he was flooded with a new energy and the thrill of inspiration lifted him. "Her last line; it's in her last line, the wrap, 'participation and experience in the process, moment to moment, is what really matters'. My readers must come to Kangaroo Island; it is in their experience, they'll discover the island's secret. Come to the island and experience the mystique. Yes, there it is, the answer is in her last line."

Matt tapped the beginning of the next sentence into the word processor, saved the file, closed down the machine and made his way to the kitchen.

Sean was sitting at the table when Matt came up behind him, gave him a hug and tousled his hair. "G'day, mate. How'd you do today?"

Sean's progress after the snakebite had been spasmodic. A couple of times, Katherine had to place him on the ventilator when the muscles around his throat constricted, a symptom of the snake venom that would continue to affect him for six months or more.

"I had a beaut time today, Matt. Dad, Barney and me went for a walk along the beach in Weir Cove; the tide was out." Sean's upward inflection at the end of the sentence inferred the timing of their visit to the beach was special because the beach was rarely exposed. "Got some big abalone shells and Barney went for a swim. Lots of seals in the water, there were."

"Got the silly bugger out of there, quick smart, didn't we, Sean?" said Frank. "He'll finish up shark bait, if he keeps swimming with the seals, hey?"

"Yeah," said the little fellow, happy his dad was looking out for him. Frank had been spending a lot of time with Sean since the boy got out of the hospital and had been drunk only once in six weeks.

"Good on you, mate," said Matt, sitting down to his favourite meal. Katherine had roasted a leg of lamb in the oven of the wood-fired stove. The delicious aroma had percolated through the cottage all afternoon, whipping up the Ryan family's hunger. "Thanks, Katherine," he said, picking out a half-dozen golden brown baked potatoes from a bowl in the centre of the table. He poured a generous amount of rich, dark-brown gravy over the meal and began eating. "Bloody beautiful, you're a hell of a cook, Katherine."

She smiled and wiped her hands on the front of her apron. "I know you love roasts, Matthew." She sat. "You hear from Cassie today?"

"No. she's real busy; reckons they might do *Fire in the Centre*, though, in the opera house."

"Oh, my goodness that would be wonderful; Frank, we may have a famous son sitting here at the table."

"That'll be the day; *Fire in the Centre*? Humph. You'd be better off concentrating on your footy, there's where you've got a bit of talent; take after your Oldman, yeah?"

"Yeah, I've been told a thousand times you were pretty good; reckon you could have played league, if Vietnam hadn't buggered you up I heard."

"Your mother was very talented. You take after her a lot, you know," Katherine offered.

"Whatever, it'll work out," said Matt, a fleeting moment of remembrance of his mother's death showing in the sudden edge to his voice. He looked at Sean. "We have a trial game at the Gosse oval tomorrow afternoon and a barby after that. Do you want to come with me and Pat in the Commodore?"

"Can I, Mum?" said Sean. Katherine looked over to Frank.

"Yeah, 'course you can. We're going, too, aren't we?" Katherine nodded. "We'd better take his oxygen to be on the safe side, hey, Sean?" said Frank, reaching out to the boy and giving him a pat on the head.

"Sammy Marino called last night, Dad," interrupted Pat, emerging from a meditative silence. "He said he wanted to talk to you; something about next week." He then echoed Matt's sentiment about the roast. "Meal's wonderful, Mother, thank you." She smiled; pleased her boys appreciated her cooking.

"Sam has a few things he wants done, Matt. I'll need your help," said Frank.

"I told you I wanted out of the business with Sam. Dunning warned us that Woodson was out to get us. That last visit was a close call."

"Yeah, well we've got one more load for the year, and you're going to help to get it done, like it, or not."

# 39

"That's it, you blokes, good job; you battled through and showed some guts. Finish it up with a couple of laps," shouted Jamie Walls, the Saints' football coach, as he strode onto the oval after the final pre-season match. "We'll talk about next week's opener when the team's picked Thursday night."

Matt, gasping for air, pounded out the last few meters of his laps. Despite the sweat streaming down his cheeks, the air carried the distinct chill of the coming winter. He cooled quickly under the veranda of the changing rooms, panting, the consequences of Australian football's violent, body-contact nature, the bruises and fatigue becoming apparent in his stiffening body. Drizzling rain falling throughout the afternoon had made the conditions miserable and the match a test of endurance. There was the elation of physical accomplishment accompanied by relief that the game was over; every player was more than ready for the steaming shower, the barbecue and a beer or three, bewdy.

"Any sore spots in need of a rub, Matt?" asked Jordan, wearing the white track-suit of the club trainer.

"No, I'm good." Matt could hardly believe the improvement in Jordan since he came back from treatment. He was wary, though. The old saying 'a leopard does not change its spots' flashed through his mind. Nevertheless, he worked at giving Jordan the benefit of the doubt.

"Been busy?" asked Jordan.

"It's slowing down with winter coming on, but there is always something to do; Cassie been in touch?" asked Matt.

"She's working hard on that dance idea you wrote with that Shamus stud," responded Jordan unable to stop from slipping in the dig he knew would get at Matt.

"Right," Matt said, wanting him to tell Cassie to write and get a bloody answering machine, but loathed to give the brother any inkling that he had not heard from her. He stripped, headed for the showers and joined the other naked bodies under the steaming water.

****

Frank, Katherine, Pat and Sean were sitting around their usual table in the bar area of the Gosse Hall when Matt joined them.

"Bit of a limp up there, lad," said Frank. "You young fellows wouldn't get a game in my day, too bloody soft." Frank was sipping on a coke. "My buy, what do you want?"

"I could do with a beer."

"Good as done." Frank crossed to the bar.

"We're going to have something to eat and then leave. We want to get Sean home and into bed," said Katherine. Sean was sitting on her lap, looking pale and tired.

"You played real good today, you did, Matt. That Maureen lady thought so, too, she was yelling out to you all day. I reckon she really likes you. She come over and told me and mum, too, didn't she, mum?" Katherine smiled a 'yes'. The little fella's cheeky grin went straight to Matt's heart.

"Ah, she likes all the blokes, especially good looking one's like you," teased Matt.

Frank returned with a round of drinks and handed Matt a stubby, which he drained in one magnificent gulp. "Beautiful."

"Hell, you got a thirst up, all right."

"Hit the spot that's for sure," Matt said, getting up from his seat and again roughing up the youngster's hair as he passed. "Another one would be right on the money. I'll load up a plate of chops and sausages from the barby; want to help, Pat?"

The two of them went out to the beer garden where "Plonk" Plummer was sweating over the open barbecue. Several players and supporters were standing around the hot fire, stubbies in hand, trying to keep warm in the cold drizzle. Matt bought a stubby of 'West End' beer at the bar.

"G'day, Matt, Pat," said a giggling Maureen, looking stunningly chic in her black and red tracksuit. Wet bangs teased her forehead while the longer hair strands clung to her neck and each side of her face. "I watched the game after we finished basketball." She moved closer to him; he was aware of her wet and exposed cleavage. She touched his arm. "You looked terrific out there, no doubt about it, and ooh, those short footy shorts!"

An unexpected surge of excitement and anticipation delighted Matt, along with the tingling sensation tantalizing his body. He could see Patrick at the barbecue, picking up chops and sausages from the hot grill.

"Thanks, Maureen, thanks." Surreptitiously, he looked about to see if anyone was watching. A few of his grinning teammates gave him a wink. "Look…" He paused, her effect on him overwhelming. "Um, I…you're looking bloody gorgeous tonight, mate." He paused again, the effect of the beer beginning to mitigate his caution. "I…" Jordan suddenly appeared on the garden patio.

Matt shrugged, his ardour cooling instantly. "Yeah, well, thanks, Maureen, nice of you to say so." He turned to join Patrick, but Maureen tightened the grip his arm, stopped him and whispered into his ear.

"I told you, Matt; I'm going to have you. Cassie is going to forget all about you, mate, if she hasn't already." She gestured in Jordan's direction. "He was telling me that she can't get enough of some dance stud over there. I think he said his name was Shamus; seems even the bloke's name is a bit of a pun, hey?"

# 40

Dunning bounced the police car over the cattle grid at the Kingscote airport entrance and stopped 50 meters further on at the passenger terminal. Woodson was waiting by the luggage trolley, talking to the agent.

"About time you showed up." The brusque tone of Woodson's voice left no doubt in Dunning's mind that the eight weeks of the sergeant's recovery had in no way induced a kinder, gentler Woodson. "This is Ronnie Perkins, brand spanking new, right out of the police college."

Dunning shook the huge, outstretched paw of the young policeman. "Bob Dunning," he said, as he pulled his hand back from the crushing grip of the probationary copper. "I booked you in at the Queenscliffe hotel for the time being until you find somewhere you like."

"Good, so let's get going and check this young bloke into the pub," commanded Woodson. "What did they call you in college, Perkins? The Enforcer, wasn't it?" Woodson tried to laugh, but it sounded more like the cackle of a rooster, a result of the damage to his throat affecting his voice with a discordant pitch that local wags would come to joke about in the safety of their own group. Woodson swung his suitcase from the cart to the trunk of the car. "There'll be plenty of that to do here, lad."

"Yes, Sergeant," said Perkins, "but that was on the football field, sir." Perkins looked uneasy despite being about six foot four in the old measure, weighing in at a hundred and twenty kilos and not a scrap of fat on him, but it was obvious Woodson's intimidating manner was already having its effect on the young constable.

"The missus is coming in tomorrow, being Sunday, so I'll have the day off; we'll get into it early on Monday," said Woodson. He had his hair shaved off, which made him look more like a gorilla than ever. Looking on with a wry grin, Dunning watched his sergeant vigorously attacking an obviously irritating haemorrhoid.

"By the way, Dunning, your promotion to first-class constable has been published in the gazette. Maybe we can call it even, yeah?"

Dunning knew that Woodson was referring to the accident inquiry. "We'll see, boss. The promotion was routine, anyway."

"Not without my recommendation," said Woodson, annoyance apparent in the cadence of his voice. The three of them loaded into the car. "Nine-thirty, Monday morning; we will meet at the station. There will be an interesting guest there, a bloke keeping an eye on the comings and goings of our marijuana producers." His voice was smug. "I haven't been sitting on my arse, letting the grass grow under it while I've been away, First-class Constable."

Dunning gunned the car over the cattle grid, turned toward Kingscote and pushed quickly toward the 100 kilometres-per-hour mark.

"Take it easy," said a nervous Woodson. "You could kill someone."

"Yeah, right, Sergeant," replied Dunning, easing the throttle for the turn at the intersection, and then flooring the pedal again to roar along a straight stretch of road before the Cygnet River Bridge. He turned to Woodson. "*You'd* sure as hell know all about that, wouldn't you?"

\*\*\*\*

On Monday morning at 9:30, Dunning watched the rookie copper enter the front door of the police station. "How'd our enforcer sleep in his new digs?"

"The sea breeze blowing in from the bay knocked me out right out, as soon as my head hit the pillow, Mr. Dunning," said Perkins, dumping a parcel of fruit and nuts on the desk.

"I told you to call me Bob, Ron, unless we have an official matter going on in public." The front door opened. Dunning was at first a little taken aback, and then wary. "Well, well, don't tell me you're our surprise guest this morning?"

"C'mon, Bob, let's bury the hatchet for the time being, shall we?" said an unusually fit and alert Jordan Baldwin, reaching over the station desk for Dunning's hand. "After all, we are going to be working with each other for the next few months."

"Is that right? Nobody bloody told me," said Dunning, ignoring the offered hand.

"Yeah, well I'm telling you all now," interrupted a surly Sergeant Woodson, walking into the station's front desk area from his office. "Thanks for coming, Jordan." He pointed to Perkins. "Meet our new lad, Ronnie Perkins, er, the Enforcer." Woodson cackled, as he waved them toward the interview room. "Follow me."

The four men filed into the room where a large map of Kangaroo Island was pinned on the wall alongside a whiteboard. The map was spotted with different coloured adhesive dots. To Dunning's surprise, a box of doughnuts and four paper cups of coffee were set on one of the tables.

"Help yourselves; from the deli and damn good," said Woodson, gesturing toward the refreshments while rustling through a pile of documents set on the main table.

"Okay, let's cut to the quick. This whole marijuana business has been getting out of hand over here, and the brass and politicians want to come down hard on it." He looked over his troops and smiled. "That suits me just fine, because I was going to end it, anyway." He crossed to the table, sugared a coffee, slurped down a mouthful and went to the map.

"Okay, different coloured dots; why?" he said, pointing. "The four red are priority. The half-dozen blue, I'm not too concerned about; they don't grow a lot of the grass and well, they're friends of the family so to speak."

A sceptical Dunning, aware that Woodson's nefarious past included cattle duffing in the Australian outback, thought that it was more likely that Woodson's wallet was being padded by the 'friends of the family'. Also, obvious to him was that the four red dots were placed on Cape du Couedic, Kersaint, Vivonne Bay and Kingscote; the properties of the Ryans, Mad Tom and Sammy Marino.

"The green dots represent small-time growers; they are scattered all over the island," continued Woodson. "They're slap-on-the-wrist targets; we upset too many of them, and we'll have the public coming down on the politicians, and they'd get their noses out of joint over that, believe me. We'll throw an occasional eye over them and see who is picking up the crop and paying them off; that'll be the Ryans, of course, and maybe we'll even bust one or two to give the case a perceived balance."

Their was no doubt in Dunning's mind that from Woodson's point of view this was all about getting the Ryans. And, it was pretty clear that Jordan was being used as a stool pigeon. Dunning was appalled and wondered if Oldman Baldwin could be part of it? He didn't want to think so; Monty had saved his neck once when he was nearly kicked out of college after the fight with Jordan. When the light bulb lit up, he realized that for Monty this was about Matt and Cassie, a chance to kill off the relationship for good. Dunning shook his head, disgusted, he watched Woodson pointing to white-board engrossed in the brilliance of his grand plan. *My God, these white boys are bloody merciless the way they go after their own.*

"And I have good information Marino's not coming back until August for his next load. So, here's what we are going to do. For the time being we keep an eye on things, bust the odd green one here and there and, more important, we find out where the Ryans are holding the stuff." He took a long, noisy slurp of coffee. "I asked Jordan along this morning, so we could all be on the same page. He's hanging out on the west end of the island, getting acquainted and keeping his ear to the ground. Got yourself into the football club, haven't you?" Woodson said, directing his attention to Jordan.

"Trainer," responded Jordan, obviously pleased with himself. "They tend to loosen up when I rub them down before the game, learn a lot then."

"Jordan keeps me up to scratch with what's going on. Now and again, we get some useful information. Even getting friendly with Matt Ryan, aren't you?"

"He thinks he's pretty smart," said Jordan with a measure of arrogance that caused even Woodson to wince. "I wouldn't say he's smart, as much as he's been lucky. Yes, very lucky. He's a bit of a sap, really." A touch of mirth mixed easily with his conceit.

Woodson continued, "I want to catch them when they're loading the stuff onto the *Smokey Cloud*. That way we get them all, especially the two Ryans." He smiled grimly. "We'll put them away for a long time over this."

"Don't get too carried away, Sergeant," said Dunning. "They've outsmarted you before."

"We'll have help from Adelaide," answered Woodson, deflecting Dunning's sarcasm with a little of his own. "Besides, you're here to help us now, aren't you?"

"I have some good information, Sergeant," interrupted Jordan. "Last night, I got a tip from Flecky Martin that he had two bags of marijuana being picked up Wednesday night by Frank Ryan."

"Flecky said, hey?" Woodson pointed to a dot on the map towards the south-western end of the island. "This is his place, a green. Why would he be turning snitch?"

"He follows the local football team out there. I got friendly with him, found out he was a grower, let him know you were onto him and that there was a big push coming on to find and prosecute offenders; frightened the crap out of him. I told him if he helped us, we would look after him. He was reluctant at first, but at the end of the day he was on board." Jordan punched the air in a gesture of triumph. "He called me last night."

"Good work." Woodson returned to the map and traced his finger along the South Coast Road. "All right, there is the entrance to Martin's, up along Gum Hill Lane about a kilometre." He paused, thought for a few seconds and then jabbed his finger back to the road junction. "Right off here runs an old gum cutter's track overgrown with scrub, but passable in a four-wheel drive, so the Toyota wagon will do the job. Now, here," he pointed, "is where the track leads to this ridge overlooking the Martin place. That's where we'll set up." He faced the three men. "Frank will have to come back to the junction, so we can see which direction he takes from the ridge. My bet is that it's back to du Couedic. The hide is there, I'm sure of it; any questions?"

"If he spots us, are we going to arrest him?" asked Dunning.

"No way, not yet; we let him go. I already told you, I want them all, Frank, the kid, Marino, all of them." He directed his attention to Jordan. "Jordan, we'll take it from here; I don't want you anywhere near Martin's Wednesday night. Okay, that's it."

The men began filing from the room. "I want to talk to you in my office, Perkins," said Woodson. "Jordan, give my best to your father, will you?"

"Righto."

Dunning walked out onto the street with the Judas. "It'll be nice working with you blokes, Bob." He reached out his hand.

Again, Dunning ignored the offered hand and looked hard into the grinning traitor's face. "Envy is the worst of the seven deadly sins, Jordan; it's malicious. You'd be better off picking up the booze again, fella. That way we can lock you up and keep you off the street, safe from yourself."

At that moment, a blue ute passed the police station. Dunning saw Matt Ryan was driving and looking right at the both of them. He waited until Matt took a left turn onto the frontage road.

"That was Matt Ryan who just drove by, Jordan. I'd keep to the other side of the street if I were you; he probably guessed what you're on about." He smiled grimly. "You see, I think he's pretty smart, and didn't he whip your arse recently. And that reminds me, I need to even up with you, don't I; seems you were the one who smacked me at the Gosse dance, right?"

Dunning did not wait for a response, but strode off toward the post office, leaving a disconcerted Jordan standing alone on the corner in front of the police station.

# 41

Matt tapped the large brown envelope on the passenger side seat and winked at his image reflected in the rear-view mirror. *Good on ya, mate.* An urgent honking from a car horn jerked his attention back to his driving, as he cut in front of a car about to turn into the Kingscote Area School access road. He waved an apology, but 'Donk' Dobson, a Kingscote football rival, was already heading up the school road. "Shit," he said, "glad he didn't come after me."

The mid-morning sky was clear and cool for a Monday. The back route to the post office took him near the police station. He was shocked when he saw Dunning and Jordan standing on the pavement together, talking. Dunning had looked surprised, as he drove by; and given the time of the day, Matt was immediately suspicious that something was afoot, and it probably had something to do with getting his dad and him. Matt was aware that Woodson was back in town and gunning for a showdown, and why would Dunning be at the police station with Jordan when he was thought to be off the booze? *The bastard is working with the coppers.*

The sea swept away to his right, as he rounded the esplanade corner. He took the next left and the next to finish up stopped in front of the post office. With the envelope in his hand, he got out of the ute and saw that Dunning was approaching from the direction of the police station. "What now?" he sighed.

"Matt, can I have a word with you?"

Matt noticed the new stripe on his uniform. "Get a pay raise, Bob?" he asked.

Dunning grinned, "Just shows even a darky can make some headway with the white man's kingdom." He offered his hand, and Matt took it. "I heard young Sean is doing better, good"

"Yeah, thanks. What's up with Jordan? Not back on the booze, is he?"

Dunning eyed Matt. He knew that the man looking back at him was no fool. "We might be better off if he was. Look, I saw you go by and I…well, as I've said before, I like you. I don't want to see you get into trouble. Just look out for yourself with Jordan, hey?"

"Working for you blokes, is he?"

"I didn't say that." Dunning scratched his head. "He, err… Woodson's back and on a mission. You and Frank are the targets." He looked back toward the police station. Woodson and Perkins were standing on the front step, watching. He turned to Matt. "Look, take my advice and stay away from anything to do with the weed, okay? It's going to heat up over here. Woodson is all pumped up and a few people in high places are pushing him right along."

Matt nodded. "High places…and local high places as well, hey?"

Dunning shrugged, "Both here and in the city. Like I said, keep away from anything to do with marijuana."

"Thanks, Bob, I owe you." He held up the large envelope and grinned. "I have to get this in the mail today; my essay for the writing competition the Monsignor entered me into; it's about the island. I'll send you a copy."

"Good for you, Matt. I'd like to read it, I really would."

"I'll soon find out if it's any good." They shook hands, and Matt went up the steps and into the post office. *So, Oldman Baldwin is on side with Woodson; what a prick!*

# 42

Monty was relaxed, enjoying the view he never tired of, taking in the myriad smells from the beach and seawater mixing with the morning air. This was the elixir that gave him the delicious sensation of health and well-being even when life was handing him a few slaps. From the gazebo, he could easily see all the way to Althorpe Island on the horizon. A single-mast fishing cutter was working slowly across the water heading west. Monty smiled at the woman on his right watching the same boat through binoculars.

"How profound," said Belinda, handing the glasses to Monty and returning to the chair at the table and her steaming cup of tea. "Look at that, as we watch, people are at work, hard work, harvesting fish to feed us for another day." She sipped the hot fluid and sighed with contentment. "It's good to be reminded. A lot of us city folk take for granted the food on our table. You know how easy it is, off to the supermarket and there everything we need; no more hunter-gathering for us."

"I think of our effort here, Belinda," said Monty, "being part of a hard working community, employing people, producing meat, fish, cereal and wool. I like being among these folk, being one of them. There's something to say about having to scratch a living, literally, from the dirt; it certainly helps keep my feet firmly planted on the ground."

"Yes, of course." She paused, thinking. "And there is art, which I think is hugely important: stimulates curiosity, entertains, informs, questions, and religion without art, what? The Bible, the scrolls, the poetry, the paintings, Michelangelo's great works on the walls and ceiling of the Sistine Chapel, magnificent. Art, whether the ancient Corroboree of the Aboriginal or modern movies, all of it is informing and enlivening our story." She took another sip of tea.

"I must say, I enjoy your musings, Belinda. I am reminded so much of Kristina. She touched on such insights frequently, displaying them in bursts of exuberant choreography, right here in the gazebo." He took hold Belinda's hand. "I'm glad you came."

"I am happy to be with you, my dear Montgomery." She paused, reflecting. "The same exuberance is demonstrated in your daughter's work. She is doing magnificently with Shamus, and I must tell you," she said, her speech quickening with excitement, losing its unusual affectation, a quality cultivated to blend with the affluent of Sydney's eastern suburbs, "when Timothy and I agreed to submit *Fire in the Centre* for the Newcomer Series, we could not predict the astonishing passion of their coupling." Belinda squeezed Monty's hand. "She is a very talented young woman who will cause a sensation when the show opens."

"I live for it. I owe it to the memory of Kristina," said a wistful Monty.

"Yes, well, it is only a matter of time. The two of them are bonding, and her dance is quickly becoming an all-consuming passion. Her work ethic, Monty, is extraordinary; her quest for perfection, obsessive."

"Her mother again; I am so pleased she is away from the island, that boy and his family."

Belinda looked fondly at Monty and said with a touch of concern and caution in her tone, "Oh, my dear man, that boy, as you so harshly put it, wrote out the concept for *Fire in the Centre*. He is obviously very gifted and a deep thinker. She still talks a lot about him, and she believes he will win one of the National Writing Awards to be announced in Sydney next month."

"Oh, damn, he's not going to Sydney, is he?"

"If he wins, of course, and our company will fly him to the opening of Fire in the Centre, anyway. He will be high on the list of credits," said Belinda.

"Please don't do that, Belinda, for my sake. I would like the boy to succeed in his work, but not at the expense of Cassie's future."

"What does Cassie want? That is the question, Monty. Have you really sat down with her and asked?"

"She has yet to fully understand the consequences of youthful passion," he said, his voice short, abrupt. "It is a silly infatuation and a distraction from what is truly important."

"Oh! And what of Kristina; you took a great talent from all of us to satisfy your passion."

"We loved each other," responded Monty.

"Precisely; and that is just the passion that will have its way; if anyone or anything blocks it then the consequences we bring upon ourselves are intolerable: miserable lives, insanity or even suicide are common tragedies." Her voice became that of a counsellor advising a client. "Let me tell you something, Montgomery, you are jeopardizing the future of your relationship with Cassie; that is what you are doing." She gathered her thoughts and continued speaking as a woman who understood betrayal. "Don't you see? If you destroy her relationship with Matt, she will feel terribly violated. She is, after all, the daughter of Kristina de Coronado. Imagine Kristina's ire, if you had been unfaithful to her. Cassie's revenge will be equally as devastating, cut you off in a second psychologically, and leave you feeling mortally wounded and completely alone. Do you want to risk that?"

"I will risk all for my daughter's future," he said, his earlier, relaxed posture stiffening. "If you are unwilling to help, Belinda, so be it." The hard edge to his voice surprised her.

An uncomfortable silence disturbed the earlier ease Monty and Belinda were enjoying. The light breeze of mid-morning began to pick up speed. Layers of cloud wisped across the sky, heralding the approach of a bank of black clouds lifting off the horizon in the southwest.

"Then the risk is yours, Montgomery. I do not mind intervening to test the waters, but I will not be party to a malicious mischief threatening terrible harm to both the girl and the boy. That is not right, and I'm sure your late wife is turning in her grave right at this moment."

They sat, silent. The bright light from the sun gradually faded; the clouds grew thicker. "The air has chilled, Montgomery. I'm going inside," she said, wrapping her shawl around her shoulders and getting up from the table.

She squeezed Monty's arm and went briskly up the steps to the house, disappointed, but exuding the energy of a mature, confident and independent woman.

Monty continued staring out to sea, shaken and uncertain.

# 43

"Stop here, Perkins," ordered Woodson. The police van rocked to a stop. "Not bad for a city kid fresh out of police college, hey, First-class Constable?"

"He's learning," said Dunning, tired of Woodson's deliberate use of his new title, but glad to get out of the vehicle after enduring the bruising journey along the old gum cutter's track.

"There's the Martin place." Woodson pointed to the buildings, easily picked out by scanning along the big gum creek that passed to within a hundred meters of the shearing shed. "Too bad we're not knocking them off tonight, easy target there." He raised a pair of binoculars to his eyes, "Can't see a damn thing; look out for a light from Flecky, or the Ryan truck."

"Frank's smart enough not to use lights," said Dunning.

"Doesn't matter; Jordan set Flecky up to flash his outside floodlights, as soon as Frank loads up and gets back on the road. They should be along soon." Woodson looked behind him. "Where are you, Perkins?"

"Over here, Sergeant, setting up the spotlight."

Minutes later, Dunning, who was squatting behind some brush, stood and cocked his ear to the south. "Ahh, sounds like Frank is arriving."

"I can't hear anything except Perkins shuffling about the bloody wagon," said Woodson. Perkins immediately froze.

"Well, look over there, the dust trail on Gum Hill Lane, see it?" Dunning stared into the ambient light. "Ah, he just swung into the scrub."

"Where?" said Woodson, scanning the road through the binoculars.

"Have you got them turned the right way 'round?" asked Dunning, chuckling. "Just having you on, boss; I'm using a bit of old black fella magic to see them."

Woodson scowled, and the two coppers resumed their crouching positions.

****

"I've got a real bad feeling about this," whispered Matt. The night was cold. They scrambled up the bank of the creek they had been stumbling along and paused, straining to see through the thick bush. They could barely see the outline of a shearing shed and sheep yards a hundred meters ahead. A quarter-moon emerged briefly from behind a scattering of thickening clouds, allowing them a better view of their target. A man was sitting on the shed loading dock, smoking a cigarette.

"There's Flecky," Frank, whispered. "Everything looks clear; bring up the truck."

Matt did not move. He was scanning the ridge rising up from a large, flat paddock, nearly a kilometre away. "Look, I told you, Woodson got back last Saturday, and he's setting up to come after us, big time. I told you about Dunning's warning; are you sure nobody but us and Flecky know about this?"

"Do you think I'd be out tonight, if I wasn't sure?" A sudden breeze rattled the leaves of the tall gum trees surrounding them; a thump, like the fall of a heavy foot on hard soil, startled them. "What the hell?" said Frank, as both men spun around in unison, expecting the worst. A koala looked up at them, for a moment bemused, and then scampered off through the bush to find another tree. "Ah jeez, the little creep frightened the crap out of me for a minute."

"Bit edgy for someone who's got it all covered, hey?" a relieved Matt commented with a mild sarcasm edging his voice. "You see anything on that ridge?"

"Too far away for anyone to see anything from there; get the truck, will you?"

"They'll be looking for lights," said Matt.

"Then leave the bloody lights off. Besides, I told you, only Flecky and us are in on this."

"I don't feel right, something's off. Let's give it a miss and get out of here." Matt's growing agitation was evident in the tone of his voice.

"All right, you stay here, and *I'll* get the truck. Stone the bloody crows, you young blokes just don't have it in you, do you?"

Frank moved into the creek bed to head back to the Landcruiser hidden in the scrub a 100 hundred meters from the track into Flecky's property.

Minutes later Matt heard then saw the truck coming slowly along the Martin track. He watched Flecky stub out his cigarette, walk into the shed and re-emerge a minute later, dragging two bulging woolpacks onto the loading dock. Frank arrived, and Flecky hauled the two bags onto the tray top. The men shook hands; Frank offered Flecky a cigarette.

Matt watched them light up. "Come on, come on," he said under his breath. Frank pulled a roll of notes from his pocket and passed them to Flecky. Suddenly, a bright light swept in a brief arcing flash from the ridge. Matt, instantly alert, sprung to his feet and ran toward the shearing shed.

"Get the hell out of here, Dad," he screamed. "They're on top of the ridge. Flecky's done us in, the bastard."

\*\*\*\*

"What the hell?" yelled a startled Woodson, as he spun around to see Perkins jerking the spotlight's electrical cables off the wagon's battery terminals.

"Didn't know it was turned on, Sergeant," said Perkins. "Sorry."

"Your brain scrambled?" Woodson shouted back. "The whole damn world knows we're here now."

\*\*\*\*

Frank tossed his cigarette to the ground and jumped into the truck. "You rotten little turd, Flecky!" he yelled, flooring the vehicle in the direction of the running Matt. "I'll be back for you and the money later." He leaned over to push open the passenger side door. "Here, boy, jump in!" He stomped on the brake, allowing his son time to leap into the cab.

Frank was blinded for a second, as the whole area suddenly lit up. "What the hell? The mongrel's turned on the bloody floodlights."

\*\*\*\*

"What now?" shouted Woodson. The area around the Martin buildings lit up in a blaze of brilliant white light. "Damned idiot, he was only supposed to flick the lights on and off after Frank left."

"There's a vehicle heading out of there now," said an amused Dunning.

"Of course there is. What a bloody screw up; Frank's onto us now. Let's get the hell off this ridge and go after him and see where he's heading," ordered Woodson. "Dunning, you drive. Remind me to leave you behind to do the filing next time, Perkins. I can't believe you are so damn stupid."

"Frank's not going to lead us to the stash. He's no mug, Sergeant," said Dunning.

\*\*\*\*

Frank bounced down the Martin driveway. "What the hell got into him?" he yelled to Matt.

"I don't know, but he's got a tribe of kids to feed, and wool prices are in the shitter. He needs the money, I suppose. Someone got in his ear!" yelled Matt over the screaming engine. "Jordan, I bet; seen him and Flecky talking pretty close a few times at the footy club."

The truck slid out of the Martin homestead driveway and sped toward the South Coast Road. "That's probably it. Always knew he was a treacherous little bastard. I'm going drop you off; no sense you getting caught, if that's what they want to do, arrest us. My guess is that they are going to follow us an see where we store the stuff. It'll take the coppers a few minutes to get off the ridge, that old gum-cutter's track is pretty rough. You can walk across Ritchie Meadows and head for Tom's place." He braked abruptly and slid to a stop. "Right, get out; stay at Tom's until you hear from me."

Matt jumped from the vehicle. Pushing the accelerator to the floor, and spinning the rear wheels in the gravel, Frank fishtailed into the night with the truck lights turned off.

Matt moved quickly through the roadside scrub to the wire fence bordering Ritchie Meadows pasture and then squeezed between the tight strands of wire to begin the ten-kilometre hike to Tom's place. A couple of kangaroos feeding on the pasture straightened onto their hind legs and stared at the intruder, nervous, and then scattered, two dark boulders bounding into the darkness. Matt heard the old Landcruiser slow for the intersection and then speed away on the South Coast Road in the direction of Vivonne Bay. He grinned at his father's cunning.

As they bounced down the old track, Dunning saw Frank turn at the intersection. "Seems you were wrong, boss. He just turned to the east."

Trees were a blur on both sides of the road, as Frank, speeding, looked out for kangaroos. After a few minutes, he slowed and allowed the dust behind him to ease to little more than a transparent veil, switched the lights on and kept checking the rear view mirror. It was not long before the lights of the police wagon showed up in the mirror, closing fast at first and then backing off.

"Ah, thought so. They're looking for where we stash the stuff, all right. Well, Sergeant bloody Woodson, have I got a surprise for you."

The reflectors on the mail box at the entrance to Stumpy Flats shone red in the distance. Frank turned into the driveway, opened the gate and headed for the Baldwin shearing shed, leaving the gate wide open, an invitation.

****

Dunning swung into the Stumpy Flats entrance and stopped at the open gate. The red taillights of Frank's truck, moving along the track toward the Baldwin buildings, were in clear view. Dunning slapped the steering wheel with his hand and burst out laughing.

****

Everything was quiet, as Frank ran the Landcruiser to a stop alongside the Baldwin shearing shed. He pulled the two sacks of marijuana from the tray top and dragged them underneath the elevated shed into the deep carpet of dark, pebbly sheep droppings.

****

"He's got your number, all right, boss," said Dunning. "He's dumping what he's got at the Baldwins. He knows we know Jordan has dabbled with drugs in the past. He knows, if you go after him here, you're going to be opening a whole new can of worms." He looked at Woodson. "And we know that this is not where Frank stores it; your call, Sergeant."

# 44

Sydney's early afternoon sun was having little impact on warming the unusually chilly winter day, but the mansions sprawled along the harbor shoreline still showed up spectacularly in its unaffected radiance. Belinda's mansion fronted the harbor waters of Rose Bay, a locality in the affluent eastern suburbs. The view, of course, was wonderful, although for a Sunday, few sailing boats were plying the usually busy waterway. The two-story building used one-third of the half-hectare property, while a flourishing collection of flowers and shrubs adorned a manicured lawn running to the edge of a stone wall that dropped vertically into deep water.

"It is a beautiful place, Cassie," said Belinda, looking out of the sunroom window. "There is nothing like the sea to give one perspective and serenity."

"I like it, especially the view of the Opera House from my terrace. It inspires me, too."

"Yes, dear, of course, but I was thinking of your place on Kangaroo Island. The view from the house and gazebo are out of this world."

A generously endowed, matronly woman with a jolly demeanour lighting her round face walked into the room carrying a tray laden with a pot of tea: scones, strawberry jam and a bowl of rich, thick dairy cream.

"On the table please, Molly," said Belinda, indicating the coffee table set on a large Persian rug in front of the sofa where she and Cassie sat.

"Oh, how delightful," said Cassie. "They look delicious. Thank you, Molly."

"You're welcome," replied Molly. "Tuck into them now, Miss; you could do with a little more meat on that beautiful young body of yours."

"That will do, Molly," gently chided Belinda. "The girl is perfect for her role in *Fire in the Centre*."

Molly poured two cups of tea. "I shall eat them all, Molly," promised Cassie. Molly smiled and returned to the kitchen.

"She has been with me for twenty years now. I don't know how I would get on without her. She was a tower of strength when I discovered Aaron was having an affair with the girl who replaced me after my injury; the lead ballerina, would you believe? Somehow, with Molly's help, I stumbled through it all and we reconciled before he died, thank God. He really was a good man, only a silly one at times, something most men can lay claim to." She paused, thinking. "Life can be awfully cruel, dear." She remembered Kristina's death. "But, of course, you know that already, don't you?" She patted Cassie's knee. "Do help yourself," she said, indicating the refreshments on the coffee table.

Cassie spread her scone with generous helpings of the strawberry jam and cream. "Scrumptious," she cried with delight, as she bit into the pastry. "I'm sorry, I didn't know about…about your husband." She demolished the rest of the scone and began spreading another. "I am starving." She sipped her tea. "How did you and Daddy get on at home?"

"We had a nice time, except…" Belinda considered whether she should go on. "Except, well, we had some disagreement about a matter involving you."

"Oh," said Cassie, feigning surprise. "I hope it wasn't anything to do with my personal life."

"Yes, it was, I am rather afraid to say. You see, Cassie, despite what you might believe about me interfering in your personal life, I happen to be on your side. I am not at all happy with your father's interference. We had words about that, and I left him in rather a disappointed frame of mind, I am sorry to say."

"Yes, he thinks Matt isn't good enough for me," said Cassie, reluctant to think too much about it. "Daddy will eventually come around. I think deep down he really likes him, but, well, it's the Catholic thing, as well as Matt's dad being an alcoholic. Anyway, we have a six-month agreement."

"I hope that is all it is, dear." Belinda picked away at a plain scone while taking occasional sips of tea. "Now, tell me, how do you find working with Shamus?"

Cassie attention was drawn to the view outside of the sunroom window. A large, red, ship carrying a full load of different coloured containers on its deck was navigating slowly up the harbor toward the bridge. She pondered for a moment on what might have been the ship's many ports of call on its way to Australia.

She looked back to Belinda. "You know what you said about men being silly? I find the same thing with Shamus. He is so professional when we rehearse, but the moment we are finished, he collapses into an irritating smart aleck. His focus seems to be to add me to his list of conquests."

"You are a very attractive girl, Cassie, and you will probably drive all men crazy. Timothy and I teamed you with Shamus because you are both incredibly attractive and talented. The two of you together will mean good publicity and a very profitable season for the company."

The container ship moved on to reveal a harbour maritime ferry packed with passengers, passing grandly on its way to the suburb of Manly.

"I hope so," said Cassie. "Sometimes I worry about injury, and I don't want to let you down. Six weeks and we open; I'm so excited and nervous, too."

"Is there anything we should be worrying about?"

"I've had trouble with shin splints in my right leg, but I am taking good care treating them with ice packs and bandages. The stone bruise has healed, although Shamus was less than sympathetic about my two days off."

"You have worked very hard. I was at the rehearsals yesterday, watching from Timothy's office. Your work is coming along famously. Timothy is ecstatic about what you are doing with *Fire in the Centre*. You will be a sensation on opening night; he is expecting rave reviews."

"He is so clever. His choreography of Matt's concept is outstanding."

"Yes. Now, some news for you; Timothy and I have agreed Matt should be officially invited to opening night. We will pay for his expenses, of course, but we thought we should mention it to you first."

Cassie leaned across to Belinda and hugged her tightly. "How wonderful, Belinda. Yes, of course. You are going to be thoroughly smitten when you meet him. He is handsome and brave and extremely talented."

"I shall look forward to it. Monty will be here, so I am hoping he will put his misgivings behind him and celebrate your debut. Besides, I am rather attached to him, you know."

"Thought so," said Cassie, a mischievous sparkle in her eyes as she sat back in the sofa. "He is with you, too." Cassie glanced at her watch. "Oh, my goodness, time flies. I said I would meet Shamus for coffee in Double Bay at four o'clock." She finished her tea and stood up. "Have to go. It has been such a lovely afternoon, Belinda, thank you so much."

Belinda rose and escorted the young woman to the entrance door. "It has been a delight for me, young lady; given me a chance to get to know you better. Remember, I am always here for you." She kissed Cassie lightly on the cheek. "One last thing, Cassie, fame has a way of distorting our grasp on life; think of Kangaroo Island when you feel life running away with you."

"I promise," Cassie said and began climbing the steep stone steps up to the property entrance.

"And watch out for that Shamus, he is a rascal," Belinda called after her, laughing.

# 45

The wild weather pounding the Gosse football oval had many of the islanders at the Kingscote against Western-Districts footy match, sitting in their cars with the windows up and the motors running to keep warm and dry. Except for Matt, who was out on the field playing for the home team, the rest of the Ryans had stayed home at the lighthouse. Frank needed to be on station for reporting the weather and any distress calls that might come from vessels in distress because of the seas whipped up by the gale force winds. Sean was, also, having a struggle with shortness of breath from the protracted effects of the snake bite, so Katherine put him on the ventilator. Pat decided to stay with Sean.

The rain was hammering blue and red tattoos into the exposed skin of the freezing players. Areas of the muddy oval were covered in sheets of water; the conditions were absolutely miserable, but thankfully the final siren to end the game was only seconds away.

"I'll be glad when this is over," said a mud-splattered Bob Dunning, grinning at an almost unrecognizable Matt Ryan who was lining up to kick for goal from a penalty awarded by the umpire.

"After this kick, Bob, we win, we go in."

"Just kick the bloody thing, so we can head for a hot shower."

Matt slammed his boot into the heavy, wet ball, but to the chagrin of his teammates it wobbled off the side of his boot and splashed into a lake of water a few meters in front of the goal line. Players from both teams rushed to cover the ball, but the siren sounded the end to the game, the scores even.

"Great kick for us, Matt, but a crappy one for your mob."

Matt grinned and shook hands with Dunning. "I can see why they wanted you in the league, hell've a game, Bob."

"I was told you were pretty good; they weren't wrong. We could qualify for water polo after this lot; you on for a beer after a shower?"

"Yeah, I'll meet you in front of the fireplace; you hanging around for the barby?"

"Can't; I have to be back in Kingscote for the Lodge Ball tonight. Woodson's the guest of honour, welcome back and all that bull, and he wants me and Perkins there in full dress uniform. Bit uppity, hey?" The two gladiators split and went to their respective rooms to shower and change. The storm continued to worsen.

The roaring fire in the clubhouse lounge was the most popular spot with the players, continually jostling for a better position close to the fire to thaw their 'chilled to the bone' bodies. "Ron Perkins, our new copper, Matt Ryan," said Dunning, introducing the two men who were warming their hands over the fire. "What'll it be? Schooners all 'round?"

"You play it hard," said Matt to Perkins while nodding a 'yes' to Dunning. "I bloody near drowned when you ironed me out in that puddle in front of the goal posts."

The manager of the bar was already heading to the group with a tray full of beers. "Saw you blokes come in; on the house, Constable," he said, handing over three schooners.

"Owe you for the hit you took breaking up the fight last time you were out here, hey?"

"I'll have to come out more often," replied Dunning, raising his glass to the volunteer bar manager.

"No worries," the manager responded before returning to the bar.

"Couldn't get near you, mate, too bloody fast and slippery, you are," said Perkins, downing his schooner in one go. "Like the night a few weeks ago at Flecky's, hey?"

"Ah, was that the night you made a bit of a goose of yourself, mate?" said Matt. "Someone told me about that fiasco at Flecky Martin's place; might've been Flecky himself. He has a hard job keeping his mouth shut, doesn't he?"

Dunning finished his beer. "Enough of that, Perkins, we don't mix business with pleasure here." Perkins grimaced self-consciously, a little peeved at the chiding. "Well, here's to no more days like today, for footy, anyway," continued Dunning. They raised their glasses and toasted the game. "How long is this blow on for, Matt?"

"Supposed to back off by Monday; we've got to expect more of them from now on."

The three men continued their conversation about the weather and its affect on their football. Dunning confided that he was having a hard time adjusting to island conditions because many of his games had been played in the dry outback regions. Perkins had played in the city where the ovals were perfectly groomed, the ground perfectly flat and much easier to play on.

"It evens it out for everyone," said Matt, draining the last of his beer. "That is, if you're any bloody good at all, hey, Constable?"

Perkins gave Matt a hard look, as he gathered the glasses and then went off to the bar to buy another round.

"Ease up on Perkins, Matt. You already have Woodson gunning for you; you don't need to turn Perkins into a zealot. By the way, it was you out there the other night, you and your Oldman, right?"

"You know as much as I do, Bob. You also know that marijuana is going to be legal eventually." Matt leaned closer to Dunning. "Woodson's onto it now because he wants to do us before that happens. You know he's wrong, and it gets me that you back up the bastard."

"Hang about, mate. Right now, it is the law. I am a police officer, and I have to uphold the law as it stands. I'm trying to give you blokes a break, but I can't keep doing it. Like I told you before, stay in the clear, you've got some influential interests wanting to get control of the stuff for themselves."

"You can't hold it back, Bob, it helps people out with medical problems, and used the right way it relaxes people just like the grog, and that's legal." He paused and scanned the room. Perkins was pushing his way back through the crowd, clutching three schooners and doing his best not to spill them. "No good is going to come from what Woodson is on about. Mark my words; we're all going to be sorry if he doesn't back off."

"Sorry about what?" said Perkins, offering a schooner each to the two men.

"Don't worry about it, Ron," said Dunning. They all take a beer.

The conversation returned to the football game, and the glasses were again soon empty.

"Another round, you blokes?" asked Matt.

"All right, one for the road," answered Dunning. "Then we have to get out of here, or the boss will start calling. Besides, it wouldn't look good for a copper with a DUI on his record."

"What are you going to do, arrest each other?" said a chuckling Matt, as he left to push his way to the bar.

"Cheeky blighter; I reckon the boss is right about him." The young copper, with a habit acquired during police training, braced by drawing to his full height, squaring his shoulders and tightening his buttocks. "You think we should be drinking with him?" said Perkins.

Dunning gave Perkins a wry look. "Do yourself a favour, lad, you'd be smart to take some time to get to know and like the locals. They're good people, particularly down this end, and tough, too. They have to be. But if you ride them too hard, they can make your life miserable."

Dunning glanced at his watch and then looked toward the bar. He saw Matt was ordering the beers when Maureen O'Flaherty pushed through the crowd to his side, cupped her hand about her mouth and whispered into his ear. Matt nodded in the direction of the two policemen, indicating that he was with them. Dunning turned back to Perkins. "Ryan's a good kid, trying to make the best of a tough life. A break or two will do more good than harm. Woodson thinks they're easy pickings, thinks he can salvage his career on their backs without causing as much as a ripple."

Matt struggled through the crowd, leaving Maureen at the bar. "Here you go," he said, handing over the beers. "It's a bloody tight squeeze through there, thirsty work, too." He gulped down half of his beer.

"Have you heard from Cassie recently?" asked Dunning.

"To be honest with you, Bob, not for a while…seems she's busy rehearsing for a show that is going to open in the opera house, or else the mail is not getting here," he said, unable to hide the uncertainty written all over his face. "I've tried calling her on the phone, but it seems she's never home. I figure I'll just have to wait until she contacts me."

"I bet she's as busy as hell." Dunning drained his glass and turned his attention to Perkins. "Drink up, Ronnie, me boy, time for us to go." He flipped him the keys. "Warm up the wagon, hey?" Perkins left and Dunning turned his attention to Matt. "I enjoyed the game Matt, and the opportunity to have a few beers with you. Like I've said before, I like you, but watch out for Woodson, the push is on. Say hello to Cassie for me, hey?" He shook hands and left.

Matt immediately went to the bar where the Irish redhead with the flashing green eyes was waiting.

"Here, for you," Maureen handed him a schooner of beer.

He took the drink and smiled. "Bewdy, Moe, thanks."

She raised her rum and coke. "Here's to a good time tonight, Matt; yeah, to you and me, hey?" They tapped glasses, the earlier drinks already bringing a warm, mellow glow to the quickly thawing Ryan.

# 46

"Bless me, Father, for I have sinned. It is a week since my last confession, and…" said a remorseful Matthew Ryan, beginning his confession of a list of venial infractions in the confessional box located close to the main entrance of the Parndana church. Inside the 'praying hands church,' the rat-a-tat-tat of wind-driven rain hammered against the tin roof and precluded any attempt at conversation among the waiting congregation. Matt was thankful for the noise, as he came to his most reluctant admission. "And also, Father, I, um, had sex last night."

"Ah yes, me boy, and that would be Maureen, now, wouldn't it?" The monsignor paused for a moment and sighed. "Well, I'm not surprised, she been bulling fer ya for a good while now. Tell me, were ya wearing a French letter?"

Matt could hardly believe his ears. He was well aware that the monsignor had a reputation for not pussy-footing around sexual matters in discussions with his flock, believing he served a more useful purpose when dealing with the subject in the language of his audience, particularly adolescent males, but…

"No, Monsignor."

"Well, then, we'll be finding out what the good Lord has in mind for ya before too long then, won't we, Matthew?" said the monsignor, a touch of impish humour in his voice. "Tis as well she's a good young Catholic girl, although with, maybe, a *tooch* too much excitement running through her hormones, but the good Lord is in charge, hey, me boy?"

"Yes, Monsignor," said a guilt ridden Matt.

"For ya penance, say a decade of the rosary and ask the Holy Mother if she'd be so kind as ta be quelling ya passions for the time being." He gave the boy absolution.

"Thank you, Father." Matt left the confessional and joined Katherine and Sean. Pat was waiting in the vestry for the priest. Frank was sitting in his usual place, the smell of alcohol once again on his breath. He winced, but his father's picking up of the booze again had almost come as a relief. The longer Frank remained sober, the more intolerable he became, as the demons of his dry-drunk agitated for dominance.

The spring-loaded door of the confessional slammed shut, and Monsignor Byrne hustled up the middle of the church to the vestry to dress for Mass. The O'Flahertys filed into the family pew, two rows ahead of the Ryans. Maureen was glowing, nodding to Matt, a smile on her pretty face. He did his best to ignore her and stared ahead at the altar, pretending to be deep in prayer, but feeling sick to his stomach and full of guilt. The hangover from the alcohol along with a throbbing headache was becoming unbearable, the need to vomit overpowering. Suddenly, he pushed past Sean and Katherine and, uttering a barely audible apology, dashed outside to vomit behind the church. In seconds, he was soaked to the skin.

He was dry-retching, as he ran for the ute, yanked open the door and slid into the seat, cold, wet and shaking uncontrollably. Maureen who had followed him watched from the church entrance. She waved frantically, signalling a 'wait for me,' but he ignored her, started the motor and sped away, leaving the alarmed redhead confused and staring after him. What she did not see was the ute stopping after the first turn in the road, and Matt stepping out into the pouring rain to get a six-pack of West-End Draught, stored under the rear canvas cover, and take it into the cab with him. She did not see him snatch a stubby of the beer from the plastic wrapping, twist off the cap and, with shaking hands, drain the amber contents in one gulp. She did not see him reach urgently for another as, laughing manically, he wrenched the gear stick into 'forward' and roared off toward the South Coast Road, the second bottle already at his lips.

****

When the Ryans finally arrived home late in the afternoon, the gale was approaching its worst, and what light of day left was fast retreating under heavy clouds and furious rain. Matt was sitting on the back porch, a dozen empty stubby bottles scattered around the old sofa. The family ran through the heavy rain from the Landcruiser, Katherine carrying Sean in her arms.

"Ha, the Ryan family, headed by the celebrated and chief drunk Francis O'Malley Ryan, does approach. Hail, oh, great Exemplar." Matt laughed hysterically. "It is I, your son, drunk! A chip off the old block, so to speak. The perfect fit, hey, Frank? I am the son of the father, make no mistake."

Katherine and the boys were wary and frightened. Sensing a violent confrontation looming between the two men, they scurried past, Sean wheezing severely.

Frank was still primed, having maintained a manageable level of alcohol with small nips from his brandy flask at regular intervals during the day. "Oh, you're a real charmer, lad," he said, experience telling him to be wary of the boy. "I don't know what's gotten into you, but it might be a good idea for you to sleep it off." Matt's eyes glazed over for a moment. He slapped his face a couple of times to stop from passing out. Frank shook his head, somewhat amused by the boy's suffering, and went on into the kitchen. Matt rose unsteadily to his feet and followed.

Frank was already reaching into the liquor cabinet for the half-full bottle of brandy and pony glass he kept ready. He filled the glass, tossed down the contents in one shot and then poured another before sitting at the table.

"I'd offer you one, but you've had about all you can handle," Frank said, a sarcastic edge to his voice.

Matt tried to focus. Pat and Sean moved out of the way into the lounge room adjoining the kitchen.

Katherine sensed the menace in Matt's demeanour. "Matthew, there are two letters here for you; they were at the post office in Parndana," she said, handing them over in an effort to deflect his attention from Frank.

"Thank you, my lady." He looked at the first the envelope. "Hah, it seems a letter from the National Academy of the Australian Literary Society has arrived." With a melodramatic flair, he ripped open the envelope, took out the letter and began to read aloud.

> "*Dear Mr. Ryan,*
>
> *Congratulations. We are pleased to inform you that you are to be awarded a Meritorious Newcomer Scholarship to the University of New South Wales for your poem, 'Lust: Life's Fiery Centre.' Details are to follow,*

*but the presentation ceremony will be in Sydney on the afternoon of Friday, July 5. We hope you can be at..."*

Matt looked up, eyes peeping surreptitiously over the top of his arm held up in front of his face, as if a cape lay over it. He laughed manically. "Well, well, do you think, perhaps, I, son of Frank, just might have inherited a fragment of talent from my teacher mother?" His voice rose on the last five words of the sentence.

"Seems you just might've," said Frank, aware of how tenuous the situation was becoming.

"What wonderful news, Matthew. Congratulations," Katherine said, breaking in, attempting to ease the escalating tension. "This calls for a celebration. I'll bake some nice fresh scones to have with strawberry jam and cream." She busied herself about the cooking area, pulling oven trays from the stove and bowls from the cupboards. "Who is the other letter from?"

"Ah, the other letter," Matt said, as if making an announcement of an important discovery. He noted the writing on the envelope. "Well, well, from Cassie and about time, too," although his voice revealed a ramped up level of anxiety. He pulled out two pages and a small cream envelope. From the cream envelope he took out a card with gold lettering on it. "Oh, nice, an invitation from Cassie's dance company to attend the opening of *Fire in the Centre* on July 5. July fifth, that's the same date as the scholarship award, unreal." He flipped the invitation onto the kitchen table in the same moment, as a deluge of rain driven by the force of the gale hammered the roof, making further conversation impossible without yelling.

Matt glared at Frank, and then he walked unsteadily into the lounge where a log fire set by Pat was already warming the room. He settled onto the sofa and read Cassie's letter.

*Dear Matthew,*
  *It seems such a long time since I heard from you. I miss you terribly, particularly when I think about you holding me. Everything is going well with my dancing, although minor injuries sometimes slow progress, but it is to be expected as a dancer. The opening to Fire in the Centre is fast approaching, as you will see from the enclosed invitation. I am so excited about seeing you. Timothy, Belinda, and Shamus think you must be brilliant and can't wait to meet you.*

As he ran a finger over the familiar writing, the earlier feelings of shame and guilt began to break through the anesthetizing effect of the alcohol. Switching his attention to the fire, he remembered the warmth of their couplings, a vastly different experience from his mad sexual escapade with Maureen. He took a deep breath, slowly exhaled and returned to reading the letter. Cassie described her life in Sydney, the demanding schedule that left her exhausted but exhilarated each night, and the way she coveted her Sundays to do nothing other than rest and recover her energy, or write letters, or journal the week's experiences.

  *Finally, my darling, in reply to the last letter you sent me, which seems such a long time ago, I want to say I cannot understand why you have not received my letters, there should have been at least three, or why you did not return my phone calls, two in the last couple of weeks. I spoke to your father each time, who I must say was rather short with me; surely he passed them on to you.*

Matt did not finish the rest of the letter; a dawning realization raced through his mind. Incredulity became rage; the pain of violation and betrayal tore at his heart. "God, help me!"

Frank was sitting at the table with the two boys when Matt rushed into the kitchen and slammed Cassie's letter against Frank's chest, so hard he was almost knocked off his chair. "Got the rest of my letters have you, hey? You bastard!" Katherine and the boys looked on, shocked and scared. The violence in Matt's voice was homicidal. "And the phone messages you didn't pass on, why not?" He was screaming now, shaking Frank violently by the front of his shirt. Pat moved from the table; Katherine clutched her apron; and, no one noticed Sean get up from his seat, slink through the kitchen door and out onto the back veranda.

"Come on, Frank, why did you do it?" Matt screamed, tightening his grip on the front of his drunken father's shirt. "Why did you do it?" he howled. The young man, on the verge of tears, began pounding Frank's chest with his fists.

Frank pushed up from his chair, grabbed Matt's arms and spun him across the kitchen into the cupboards, almost knocking Katherine down, as she tried to catch him.

"I'll tell you why," said Frank. "Those Baldwins will bring you no good, boy. They are rich swine and have no room for the likes of you in their family. Oh, they may say one thing, but believe me that oldman is already working at getting you out of his daughter's life."

"Cassie loves me, Dad, don't you see that?" pleaded Matt, dumbfounded, beginning to hyperventilate. His rage returned. "C'mon, come outside and have a go, if you've got the guts."

Katherine held him. "That'll settle nothing, Matthew. I'll take care of this." She turned on Frank. "The girl loves him, Frank," yelled Katherine. "What on earth is the matter with you, taking the boy's letters? Do you have no shame? You had no business…"

"Shut up, woman!" yelled Frank. "You don't understand these people. They are the scum who sent my mates to die in Vietnam; they stayed home and made money from the war. Do you think we mean anything to them? We are a commodity, cannon fodder, labour to them."

"The Baldwins had no more to do with the war than you or I. I know a lot happened to you in Vietnam, Frank, that has left you hating, but I tell you I am tired of it affecting our family. You have no right using Matt to get at them. You'd better get some help, or I'm taking the boys and leaving you."

For a moment, both Frank and Matt were quiet. Neither had heard such deadly intention in Katherine's voice. Frank realized she was offering an ultimatum, no ifs, ands, or buts about it. Matt's mind filled with memories of the many terrible ordeals his mother endured with Frank's neuroses and drinking, the precursors to her suicide.

"I was doing it for you, lad," Frank said. "I'll be in the lighthouse, if you want to take this further." He stepped around Matt and crossed to the door. "Where's Sean?"

"He must have gone to his room; he usually does when things get like this. He hates arguments and it scares the life out of him when you are drunk, Dad," said Pat quietly. "He'll be down when he knows you've gone."

"You'll find those letters in the top right drawer of the office desk, unopened. I'm sorry, son. Katherine is right, I had no business..." Frank shrugged and left.

****

Sean was scared. Matt's fury and violent confrontation with his father was more than he could handle, and his main thought was to get out, to escape. He crept through the kitchen door, took a raincoat and hat from the clothing pegs on the laundry porch wall, went onto the veranda and put on his hat and coat. The rain was coming down in buckets, and the wind at hurricane strength. Barney was out of his kennel, straining at the end of his fully extended chain, wet and barking furiously. Sean crossed to him and released the catch on the chain.

"C'mon, Barney, we're going to the cave; c'mon, boy." He started out for the south side of the cottage fence, head-on into the driving rain that stung his face and blurred his vision. "We're going to our secret place."

The last of the light was almost gone, but the small winding track to Weir Cove was so familiar to Sean he could have walked it blindfolded. *Always fighting and yelling when Dad's drunk and now even Matt's drunk. I can hide in my secret place. Nobody can find me there; then they'll be sorry.* He tripped over a piece of protruding limestone, fell forward and skidded over the sharp rock, scraping the skin off his arms and hands. Tears formed in the little bloke's eyes and ran down his wet cheeks. Hardly able to breathe, the wheezing worsening, he struggled to his feet and pushed on doggedly toward his destination.

He finally made it to the lip of the cliff where it dropped away to the old supply jetty 65 meters below. Looking down at the water, he saw the huge swells rolling toward his cliff, building into lines of arching peaks before crashing over the rocks and thundering up the steep walls of his fortress. He moved away to a large clump of scrubby bush to the right of the path, reached in amongst its prickly branches and pulled out a rope about twenty-five meters long. On one end was a snap catch, which he attached to a rusty metal clamp anchored into the side of an old concrete block a few paces from the cliff. He threw the other end over the edge and then, clasping his hands around the rope, turned his back to the sea, climbed over the edge and worked his body down the almost vertical wall. Barney barked crazily, whirled around in circles and pawed Sean's coat in a behaviour imploring him not to go down there that night. The rain and wind became increasingly violent.

"Go to the cave, Barney, that's a good boy, go on; I'll meet you there!" he shouted. Barney had a special way of reaching the cave. A track made by wild goats, too narrow for a human to traverse safely, zigzagged across the face of the cliff to the rocks at the bottom, passing the cave entrance 15 meters below the cliff top. Barney scampered off while Sean worked cautiously down the wet and slippery rope. His wheezing grew more urgent; he gasped desperately for more of the cold air; with a meter to go to the cave entrance, disaster. He slipped and burnt the flesh of his already battered hands as he clamped them tight around the wet rope. For a moment, God intervened, and his feet hit the edge of the cave floor where it protruded slightly from the cliff wall, stopping his slide. He clung to the rope, panting, desperately trying to suck more air through the tightening muscles of his throat. He probed the dirt entrance with his foot, seeking more of the cave floor. Barney arrived, sized up Sean's plight and grabbed for the bottom of his pants.

Sean's mind started to wander, and already weakened from the snakebite, what strength he had left was quickly draining. Barney managed to snare the bottom of the boy's pants between his teeth and began to pull him into the cave. Slowly, very slowly, the gallant kelpie made progress and dragged the lower part of the boy's body, centimetre by centimetre, toward safety. Rainy squalls continued to lash at Sean, hypothermia threatened. His fierce grip loosened, and he slipped farther down the rope almost beyond the safety of the cave entrance. Barney hung on tenaciously; Sean managed to tighten his grip again and stop the slipping. The faithful dog's grip held. Sean was almost hanging upside down. Barney clung to the fabric, pulling frantically, trying to drag the boy back into the cave.

An enormous, purple and white flash of lightning filled the sky; the wind howled around Sean and swung him out from the cave. He began to drift into delirium and what was left of his strength deserted him. He let go of the rope and tumbled down the steep face of the cliff wall to the rocks, fifty meters below, taking a frantic Barney with him, still latched, vice-like, onto the tearing fabric of his master's pants.

\*\*\*\*

Matt fought his way to the lighthouse. The heavy rain, driven by the fury of the sou'westly, was almost impossible to penetrate. The wind screamed around the unyielding limestone and granite walls of the tower, its brilliant light never failing, continuously pushing its sweeping signal out across the Southern Ocean. He slammed through the door. Frank was at his desk, holding a cigarette almost burned down to the filter between two fingers of his left hand. The printout of a weather map showed a low-pressure area, the isobars wound tightly together and centred over the south-western end of the island. An almost empty glass of brandy sat next to an ashtray full of cigarette butts.

"We can't find Sean!" yelled Matt.

Frank cupped his hand to his ear. "What did you say?" he shouted.

Matt leaned closer to his father. "We can't find Sean. We've searched the house. Pat and I looked all through the sheds and the other cottages."

"Did you look under his bed?" Frank picked up his glass and drained the last of the brandy. Matt slapped the empty glass from his father's hand.

"For God's sake, man, did you hear me? We can't find Sean! He may have gone to his secret place, but none of us knows where it is other than over by Weir Cove."

The seriousness of Matt's message began to penetrate Frank's consciousness. His past military experience took over, and he snapped into action. "Jesus, if he's out in this weather, in his condition, he won't last long." He started giving orders. "Get the Landcruiser: ropes, spotlights, radios, blankets and flasks of hot tea, now! We may need help. I'll call Tom; he'll round up some people." Matt was transfixed for a moment, panic and fear threatened to crush him. Frank grabbed his shoulder and shook him. "Come on, lad, brace up, we don't have much time. I'll be along after I've spoken to Tom." He pushed Matt toward the door.

Matt pulled the Landcruiser up by the cottage gate. Frank ran up from the lighthouse, one of the spotlights set up and already turned on. Pat was running from the veranda with flasks of hot tea; Frank and Pat leapt into the truck. "Go!" yelled Frank, "Weir Cove!"

"Wait," cried Pat, "Mother's coming."

Katherine was running from the veranda, carrying a flashlight and pulling a raincoat over her shoulders. She ran to the truck and threw herself onto the tray back. Frank leapt out of his seat in the front cabin.

"Katherine, it would be better if you stayed here!" he yelled.

"That's my boy out there!" she screamed. "Now, let's get going." Frank nodded he understood, leapt onto the steel tray, put an arm around her shoulders and banged on the cab roof, signalling Matt to get moving.

"Tom is getting a search party together, just in case!" he yelled into Katherine's ear.

The truck bounced over the rough limestone heading for the lip of the cliffs. Pat swept the bush with the spotlight, the beam reflecting off the shiny, wind-torn leaves, forming scary, demonic images from countless shadows. They reached the edge of the jetty drop-off and swept the area with the spotlight, nothing.

"Matt!" yelled Frank, leaning into cab-side driver's door. "Head for the Admiral."

They drove along the narrow track until it ended. All of them got out and searched along the cliff and under the arch, both spotlights on; beams bouncing off the rocks and rough water. Nothing!

"Katherine, take Pat and your flashlight, keep looking here. Matt and I will head farther around the cove. If you find him, send Pat after us."

The two men returned to the truck and searched the terrain to the old storehouse, again, nothing.

Matt stopped the truck. "Keep going," yelled Frank above the shrieking wind. "He might have gone down the path into the cove, where we went there other day. A few rocky outcrops of limestone offer some shelter along the bottom face."

"No, I know he's around here somewhere," Matt yelled back, sliding out of his seat and taking the second spotlight. "You go on into the Cove."

Frank nodded. "Okay, take this radio and be bloody careful." He handed over a handset and slid across to the driver's seat. Matt watched the truck's red tail lights bounce crazily until they were out of view further down the rough track.

Trusting the insistent urgency of his intuition, Matt started his search in the vicinity of the store ruins. A blinding flash of lightning followed by a sharp crack of thunder startled him. He looked at his watch; an hour had gone by since they started searching. "Hurry up, Tom, hurry up, you should be here by now," he yelled into the storm. Again, he swept the beam slowly along the edge of the lip of the cliff. As it cut through the wet darkness, the light picked up a narrow black shadow stretching along the ground from the old concrete block. His first thought was that it was a snake. Then, his heart skipped a beat when he realized it was a rope, leading to the edge. *It's gotta be down there.* He peered over the lip, following the rope down with the spotlight to where it ended. The narrow beam, stretched to the limit of its range, barely illuminated the jagged rocks at the bottom. His eyes strained to make out what appeared to be something moving in the retreating foam of the crashing waves. "Barney! It's Barney! Oh, Jesus God, no!" he screamed, and he made out the form of his stepbrother lying limp on the rocks. Barney was tugging at Sean's jacket, trying to keep his head above the water and away from the breaking waves that threatened to drag them both into the sea.

Matt, half-crazed with anguish, pushed the transmitter button of his radio and shouted, "He's here, at the bottom of Weir Cove jetty! It looks bad. I'm going after him! Hurry, Dad, hurry!" Breathless, he grabbed the rope and prepared to lower him-self over the lip when suddenly, a wall of light from a bank of spotlights attached to the bull bar of a truck blinded him.

"Where do you think you're going? Stop, Matt, stop!" yelled Mad Tom, running to Matt with a light in his hand.

"Tom! Thank God, you're here. Sean's down there!" he shouted, pointing.

"I heard your radio call; others are on the way." Tom peered into the deep drop, his more powerful spotlight, hooked to the truck's power system, clearly illuminating Sean's horrifying situation.

"I've got two long ropes in the back of my truck, get them," he ordered.

"But…"

"Get the bloody ropes, tie them together and hand me that radio!" Matt hesitated. "Now!" shouted Tom, brutal. Matt let go of the rope, gave Tom his radio and ran to get the ropes from the truck. Tom picked up Sean's rope and positioned himself to go over the lip. Matt returned dragging the two ropes.

"No, Tom, don't. He's my brother," He sobbed, dropping the ropes.

Tom looked menacingly at Matt. "I said, tie them together and then feed them down to me." He disappeared over the lip.

As Tom reached the end of the first rope, he quickly tied it to the rope Matt was feeding, and then slid the rest of the way to the bottom of the cliff. Matt kept the light trained in front of Tom's path over the jagged and slippery rocks. Barney was barking even more desperately, as the tough Oldman reached the boy. Sean's face, covered with cuts and bruises, was deathly white. Tom's heart chilled; blood was trickling from the corner of the boy's mouth. One of his legs twisted at a terrible angle from his thigh, obviously broken. Tom felt for a pulse. It was weak, very weak, he was close to death.

More light from above flooded the area. The radio crackled. "Tom, can you hear me?"

Tom reached for the radio slung over his shoulder. "I can hear you, Frank. It's bad down here. I don't want to move him, but these waves are getting bigger and closer. I have to get him out of here."

Matt and Frank peered over the lip and watched Tom lift Sean into his arms. Katherine and Pat arrived along with a large group of rescuers who had been listening to the radio transmissions. A frantic Katherine rushed to Frank. He held her briefly and then handed her the spotlight. "Here, keep this on Tom and Sean. I'm going down." He tossed the radio to Matt and picked up the rope. In the same moment, Matt glimpsed a large wave rolling in from the southwest and already beginning to curl into the bay. It was the one in a thousand, the one twice as large as any other, a rogue.

He screamed at Frank into the radio. "Watch out, it's a rogue, coming into the cove now!" Frank turned toward the open sea and saw the big wave arching above the rest, fast closing on the jetty. He leapt from the cliff edge, rappelling head-first down the rope, a technique from his training in Special Forces. Without gloves, the rope tore into the flesh of his hands as he plummeted, barely under control, to the bottom.

Tom, cradling Sean in his arms, heard Matt's frantic voice screaming over the radio. Barney was barking furiously. "Watch out, it's a rogue, coming into the cove now!" He glanced over his shoulder to see the giant arching above the others, still fifty meters off. He ran, jumped and slipped across the rocks, cracking his shins, clutching the unconscious Sean in his arms, Barney leading the way. He heard the roar of the breaking rogue racing up behind them.

He saw Frank, swinging off the rope, his arm reaching toward them, ready to grab for the boy. The wave hit, and Tom threw Sean toward Frank who grabbed his broken son in a vice-like grip and clutched him to his chest. He managed to scale a meter of the cliff before the overwhelming force of the water crashed over them and almost tore them from the rope. In a few seconds, it was over; the water withdrew in a swirling torrent back to its source. Frank held on to the rope, clutching his son, watching as Tom was swept by him, caught up in the receding turbulence, flailing desperately, bouncing off jagged rocks and then disappearing into the open sea.

More ropes slapped against the cliff floor next to Frank. Rescuers quickly arrived. They gently took Sean from Frank and then wrapped them both in blankets. Barney, wet and bloody, somehow managed to survive. He sat next to Sean, licking his master's face, whimpering.

The ranger from Flinders Chase tending Sean turned to Frank, tears rolling down his cheeks. "I'm sorry, Frank; he's gone."

# 47

The storm had moved on and a full moon was high in a clear sky. The police, the ambulance and the monsignor arrived within minutes of each other. Already, a huge and growing crowd of neighbours, friends, parishioners and emergency service volunteers were quietly gathering about the Ryan cottage. Parties of rescuers were continuing their search for Tom along the cliff bases, hoping for a miracle.

The wailing of the distraught Katherine who was being cared for by the local women inside the cottage, cut through the eerie calm that had settled around the cape. A murmur of greeting rose from the crowd, as the monsignor hurried into the house. Katherine's wailing faded to a quiet sobbing; the priest hugged her and then kneeled next to the small boy laid out on the sofa; he anointed Sean's body with holy oil and administered the last rites. Gently, he stroked the boys bruised and scratched face, his eyes teary. Reaching for Katherine's hand, who was clutching her rosary beads and praying at the head of the sofa, he drew her to kneel beside him and join in the rosary.

"Hail Mary full of grace the Lord is with thee…" All of those within earshot, Catholic and Protestant alike, knelt and bowed their heads.

Woodson and Perkins were conversing in the back yard while Dunning talked to the locals. Perkins split from the sergeant and headed for the lighthouse. Woodson motioned for Dunning to join him, as he went into the cottage.

Matt, Frank and Patrick were sitting at the kitchen table. As he looked into the faces of the Ryan men, Dunning's heart wrenched. He attempted to offer his condolences, but choked on the words and struggled to hold back tears. Woodson acknowledged the Ryans and mumbled his respects, adding that an inquiry into the two deaths would have to be conducted, and they "might as well get started."

Matt offered the two policemen a cup of hot tea. Woodson nodded a 'yes', Dunning a silent decline. Matt began to fill one of two cups set out on the table. Woodson sat down and pulled a notebook from his tunic pocket. "All right, let's start at the beginning. You first, Frank?"

Matt stopped pouring, slammed the pot down on the table and fixed Woodson an icy stare. "You mongrel, Woodson, we should have left you to rot in the scrub." Before Woodson could react, Matt stormed out of the kitchen.

Dunning stiffened and followed. He squeezed through the crowd outside and hurried after Matt, who was striding angrily toward the Admiral.

"Matt, hang on," called Dunning. Matt slowed, and Dunning caught up. "I'm so sorry for what just happened in there. I swear to God, I'll drag that mongrel into the scrub myself one day and off the bastard." He paused and then placed his hand on Matt's shoulder. "I hardly know what to say, what words to use to tell you how I feel for you and your family."

"It's my bloody fault, Bob, pure and simple," said Matt, tears tumbling from his eyes, their distinct blue vividly surreal despite their bloodshot backdrop. "I'm no bloody good, mate; I as good as killed the two of them myself."

"Hey, hey, lad, take it easy, take it easy."

"You don't understand. I got drunk today and went after the Oldman. Sean got scared and took off for his secret place at Weir Cove. If I hadn't been such a dickhead, he would still be alive. I really am a piece of work, Bob. Last night I went out with someone else, and I…I really stuffed up…"

"Cut it out, Matt. Go easy on yourself, for God's sake. Life's not black and white; life happens; things happen for reasons we don't understand. There is a power; God, Nature, call it what you like and it runs through our lives, taking all of us with it."

"No, Bob, no excuses. Life gives us choices, and I've made too damn many wrong ones." He wiped his eyes and took a deep breath. "I loved that little bloke. Lord God Almighty, why, why, why wasn't it me?" He glanced up at the sky, and then back to Dunning. "I need some time to myself," he said, reaching out and shaking Dunning's hand. "You're a hell of a bloke, a straight up copper and good to us out here. Thanks." He left and after a few paces, turned. "I left a message for Cassie. If she calls, tell Pat I'm down at Admiral, will you?" His head down, he shuffled off in the direction of the Arch.

"Of course," Dunning called after him. He watched the solitary figure, silhouetted against the full moon, gradually fade and blend in with the dark, rocky terrain of the Admiral and the silver ocean beyond. He turned for the cottage and saw Perkins coming out of the machinery shed.

"What are you up to, Constable?"

"Taking a bit of a bo-peep, Bob," said Perkins. "The boss told me to do a little snooping while we had the opportunity."

"Did he now?" Dunning sighed. "Why don't you get the car started, Mr. Perkins? Get it warmed up, hey? Bring it to the lighthouse; we'll meet you there. It's about time we let these people alone. We can tidy up the paperwork some other time."

Perkins hesitated for a second. "Get on with it, Probationary Constable Perkins, I'll find Mr. Woodson." The two men parted; Perkins in the direction of the police car and Dunning to the cottage.

"And you can get the hell out of here now, Woodson!" yelled Frank, as Dunning entered the kitchen.

"I want you to answer the question, Ryan," said Woodson, angry and agitated; the recent injury to his throat edged his voice with a strange eunuch-like pitch. "You'd been drinking, right? You didn't see the kid walk out into the storm, right?"

Dunning placed his hand on his sergeant's shoulder. "Can I see you outside, boss? Something you need to know," said the first-class constable, his voice tightening. Woodson glared at Dunning, annoyed by the interruption. Dunning squeezed Woodson's shoulder until it hurt him and stared into his eyes, signalling a very serious matter needed his attention right away.

"I'll be back, Ryan, and I'll want answers."

"Don't make it anytime soon," Frank replied.

Dunning led the sergeant through the swelling crowd of neighbours and rescuers, a growing murmur of disquiet and resentment followed the policemen. A couple of older men aggressively jostled Woodson. A few insults followed: "Keep going, copper; we don't need your kind around here" "Let's feed the bastard to the whites, plenty of 'em off the Admiral" "They'd spit him out" "Not a shred of decency in the man." Dunning hustled Woodson through the gate and directed him toward the lighthouse.

Perkins had the car waiting in the parking area, idling. "You wait there, Perkins; we'll be back in a few," said Dunning. They reached the tower, and he opened the door. "Here we go, Sergeant," he said, ushering in Woodson and then closing the door behind them.

"This had better be good, Dunning."

Dunning, his back to the door, braced and fixed his sergeant a stare full of contempt. "For crying out loud, have you no decency, no compassion, Reg?" His voice was icy. "This family has just lost a child, and you're behaving like you're conducting an inquisition. You even sent Perkins to snoop about."

"Who the hell do you think you are?" responded an angry, but wary, red-faced Woodson. "I'm running this game, and it's in your best interest to do as I tell you, you darky prick."

Dunning's temper detonated. Memories of insults hurled at his Aboriginal mother, his hopeless attempts to defend her, the stinging sense of shame he had felt each time he thought of his inability to end the bigotry, to stop them from hurting her.

Woodson never saw it coming, or knew what hit him. The whip-like snap of Dunning's right hand, slapped the sergeant's face and ear so violently that the man tumbled over Frank's paper-covered desk. "That's for my mother." Woodson staggered upright, his ear ringing and his face stinging. As quick as the first, Dunning slapped the man on the other side of his face. "That's for Sean." Woodson slowly straightened, bewilderment glazing his eyes. Dunning's hand snaked out again, a final slap with all his power behind it, and Woodson collapsed into Frank's chair. "And that's for the Ryans."

Bob Dunning sat on the edge of the desk. "We're even now, Sergeant. From now on, you can come after me as hard as you like, but a word of warning. If you ever call me a darky again, I will personally feed you to the whites." He bent over to within a few centimetres of Woodson's face. "And that, mister, is a promise."

"I'll have you drummed out for this, Dunning," snarled a cowering Woodson, his ears hot and ringing and his head spinning. "Assaulting a superior; you'll do time first, a long time."

"Oh, I don't think you'll try that just yet, *Reggie*. You've got too much to lose. They would reopen the inquiry into the superintendent's death, if they had new information. Racial bigotry would not sit well with your future aspirations, either, Reggie, especially with the dicey resume you have already built up in that area. Nope, you will just sit tight for the time being, biding your time. Later, if you're still around, you'll come after me." He chuckled. "But I'll be ready for you, *Reggie-boy*."

Dunning opened the door. "We'll be in the car waiting; we're going back to Kingscote. And don't take your time." He strode to the police car's driver-side door and opened it. "Slide over, Ron, I'm driving. The boss will be out in a minute." He smiled at Perkins. "He'll want to ride in the back."

# 48

The tall, square block of apartments, rising twelve floors above the harbour sat on a prime parcel of land at the end of Blue's Point Road. Isolated by its position on the jutting point, the plain, boxy design, a relic of the 60's, was a bone-of-contention among many of the local residents. The views of the harbor, however, from inside the building were extraordinary. High on the ninth floor, his balcony looking east toward the harbor entrance, was the two-bedroom apartment of Shamus O'Brien.

"What a delightful meal; you're quite a cook, Shamus," said Cassie, finishing off the last of her red wine. She placed the empty glass on the table and dabbed her mouth with a napkin, careful not to smudge her red lipstick. Flames from the gas fire reflected in the large dining room window overlooking the harbor, giving the impression that flames were dancing on top of the water. Beethoven's "Moonlight Sonata, adagio sostenuto," played in the background and fit perfectly with the evening ambiance.

"A wonderful red," said Shamus, emptying his glass.

"A South Australian Shiraz from the Penfolds McLaren Vale vineyards; their wines are popular all over the world, I thought you'd like it."

"We have some spectacular whites grown in the Mudgee and Hunter Valley regions, too." He opened the refrigerator door and took out a bottle of chilled white. "I found this at a relatively new winery on my run up through Mudgee today. I tasted it, superb, so I bought a case. Rather fruity for a Semillon; I hope you like it. Oddly enough, the winery is called the Farmer's Daughter. I thought it an apt kudos to my talented partner and a worthy complement to Chef O'Brien's dinner this evening," he said, chuckling. He placed two clean wine glasses on the coffee table set in front of the sofa, which was positioned to take advantage of the view. "Let's sit here and relax; I have a tasty dessert prepared for on."

Cassie moved to the sofa. Shamus poured a small amount of Semillon into a fresh stem glass and handed it to her. She swirled the straw-collared wine, tasted it and then swallowed the rest. "Yes, nice," she said and held out the glass for a refill. "Fill 'er up please, mister." The effect of the red wine over dinner was already causing her to feel a little light-headed and delightfully relaxed.

"Glad you like it." A very suave Shamus grinned and filled her glass to the brim. As he passed it to her, he kissed her lightly on the lips. Cassie was caught off guard, surprised, not by the kiss, but by the rush of erotic energy that tingled through her body. For a moment, she held his kiss and then pushed him back.

"Whoa, boy, I'm not up for any hanky-panky." She put the wine on the coffee table. Shamus lowered himself into the sofa somewhat pleased with himself and nonchalantly filled his glass. Cassie sat up straight and pushed her dress down over her knees.

"Ah, come on, Cassie, you got a bit of a buzz out of that, didn't you? Hell, we've been dancing together for over four months. We can't ignore the attraction we have to each other."

He edged closer to her. "We have a lot going for us that's not only professional."

"Oh, it is professional, Shamus." She paused for a moment, considering. "Look, you're very attractive and talented, but that's it for me." She reached for the glass and took another sip. "This white *is* good." The next track began, "Barber's *Adagio*, Oh, I love it."

Shamus rested his arm on the sofa, behind her shoulders. She sipped her drink warily, as he edged even closer. "No, it is much more than that." He brushed aside the hair from her ear and lightly blew on it before she could move away. The tingling sensation returned, and with her head swirling from the effects of the wine, her resolve began to weaken. The hypnotic magic of the harbor view, the Opera House, magnificent and calling her, mixed with the seductive strings and clarinet arrangement of the "Adagio" swept her toward the realm of fantasy. Shamus's warm breath gently caressed the nape of her neck.

****

The red light of Cassie's new answering machine on the bedside table was blinking urgently. It was after 2:30 am, and she was tired and angry. *The bugger wouldn't take no for an answer.* "Bugger, bugger, bugger," she yelled, flinging her bag on the bed, angry because of the part of her that enjoyed it. She pushed the play button on the machine.

"Cassie, this is Matt. I must talk to you; I have some terrible news. Please call me when you get in, no matter the time. I love you." 'Click', the machine shut off. Her heart began to pound. She picked up the phone and dialled.

The phone on the other end was answered almost immediately. "Hello, this is Frank." The passive tone of his voice sent chills through Cassie.

"Mr. Ryan, this is Cassie Baldwin. I'm sorry to bother you, it being so late, but I had a message from Matt telling me something terrible has happened. Is it Sean, the snakebite? Is he all right?"

There was a long silence; she waited, dreading the words she knew now were coming. "Ah, Cassie, love, thanks for calling. Yes, it is Sean, I'm afraid. A nasty accident; he fell off the cliff at Weir Cove. He's dead."

Cassie's heart stopped. She stared at the photo of Matt.

"Cassie, are you there? Are you all right, luv?"

She heard Frank telling Pat to get Matt quickly.

"Mr. Ryan, I'm so sorry, so sorry..." She began to cry.

"I hear you, lass. He really liked you." She heard Frank's voice beginning to break. "I've sent Pat to find Matt. I think I hear him coming...yes."

"Mr. Ryan, tell Mrs. Ryan and Pat I love you all."

Frank choked, and he began to sob.

"Cassie, Cassie, thank God you called," interrupted Matt. "Hold on a minute, my love." She heard Matt tell Pat to help his dad back to his chair. "Dad told you, hey?"

"Oh, my God, Matt, I don't know what to say. I'm so sorry." She sobbed uncontrollably.

Matt began to cry. "I know, love, everyone is devastated. And Tom Donaldson is missing, swept out to sea trying to save him. He saved my bloody life, too, Cassie...stopped me from going down after Sean. Little bloke, he was beating the snakebite...I don't understand what the hell...it's my fault,

Cassie. I got drunk and started a fight with Dad; Sean took off in the storm for his secret place and fell; because of me."

"Don't say that, Matt. You loved him, and he loved you. He idolized you. We have been together for a long time, Matt. Your family is as dear to me as my own, and I love you absolutely."

"Cassie, I have something else…" He sighed. *Get a grip, not now.* "I love you, too. No matter what happens or what you may…my heart is yours forever." Still sobbing, he paused. She heard people moving about in the background. "Cassie, they're about to take Sean out to the ambulance. The monsignor is going to say a prayer first, so I have to go. Are you okay?"

Yes, Matt, I'll call Belinda. I want to be with you when Sean is…" She sobbed. "I'll say a prayer for Tom. I love you. Bye, for now."

"Bye."

She placed the phone in the cradle and rolled face down on the bed. The bedding muted the terrible cry that came from the very core of her being. "Ahhhhhh, no, no, no, no, no!" she wailed, beating the bed violently with her fists. Eventually, she rolled over and faced the ceiling, sobbing, sobbing. Time crawled. The ticking of her bedside clock, thunderous in the silence of the room, brought with each tick a new image. Sean's cheeky smile while walking at Matt's side: his tiny hand in Matt's, Matt running from the water at Kersaint, Matt waving from the side of his ute at the airport; and Shamus, *while Sean was dying*! She gagged.

"God," she cried out, slid off the bed and rushed to the bathroom, undressing on the way and into the shower where she turned on the cold-water tap. In a trance-like state, her mind and body numb, she stepped into the icy stream and without so much as a shiver, began to vigorously soap and scrub, soap and scrub, every part of her body.

# 49

A few days later, Thursday, Tom's body was still missing despite the thorough searches out to sea and along the south-coast coves and cliff bases.

On a hill overlooking the Kingscote Township and the blue waters of Nepean Bay, the air was crisp and cool. The winter's mid-morning sun brightened the sky over the gathering crowd of mourners forming around the gravesite. Cars in the procession from the Kingscote Catholic Church where the mass was held for Sean, nearly a kilometre away, were still arriving. Most of the Islanders had gathered for the burial; schoolchildren from the Kingscote and Parndana schools lined the entire route from the church to the cemetery. Sean's classmates, boys and girls all dressed in white, formed an honour guard from the cemetery gates to his grave. The local Member of Parliament, the mayor, the district councillors and clergy from all the island churches stood a respectful distance from the Ryans. All three policemen were in full dress uniform; Bob Dunning was standing close behind Matt.

The Ryan family stood by the side of the hearse waiting for the last of the mourners to arrive. Sean's flower-covered casket was visible through the open back door of the coach. Monsignor Byrne was standing between Frank and Katherine who were both dressed in black. Matt and Pat, dressed in black suits, stood next their parents, Pat holding his mother's hand and Matt by his father. Cassie, dressed in a black dress and wearing a black hat, had her arm around Matt's waist and was continuously dabbing her eyes with a lace handkerchief. A black veil attached to Katherine's hatband covered her face; Frank's head was bowed. The boys did their best to control their emotions, nodding occasionally to Islanders who came by whispering their condolences. The six-year-old Hamilton twins from Sean's class, Charles and Rebecca, stood in front of the monsignor, holding baskets of white rose petals. The last of the schoolchildren lining the route from the church filed silently into the cemetery and formed up at one end of the grave.

The funeral director called the pallbearers forward. Frank, Matt and Pat lined up on one side of the casket; Sammy Marino, Bob Dunning and John Walls, the football coach who also coached the juniors, lined up on the other. Slowly, the men slid the small casket from the hearse and then followed the monsignor and the twins, who sprinkled the ground in front of the casket with the white rose petals. Katherine followed immediately behind and was supported by a group of local women. The cortège moved slowly through the centre of the honour-guard to the graveside. Classmates cried, men quietly wiped away tears and women wept.

The six men placed the casket gently on the cradle set across the top of the open grave. Matt released his grip on the handle along with the others, and then motioned to Cassie, who was standing with Monty and Jordan among the front group of mourning islanders, to join the family. She went to him, he took her hand, gently squeezing it and pulling her close to his side.

Monsignor Byrne walked slowly around the casket, sprinkling holy water. Then, he stood at the head of the grave and began to address the mourners.

"We cannot know the reason the good Lord has chosen *ta* draw his little lamb Sean *ta* his bosom at this time. Any reason cannot, nor should it, pacify the terrible pain inflicted on the Ryan family: Katherine, Francis, Matthew, Patrick, and all of *ya* here who loved him. In this moment, *'tis* good *ta* remember the joy he brought *ta* us all, and the lesson he leaves through his early departure. He reminds us that in our love for each other, *'tis* wise always *ta* be kind, patient, and caring, *fer* we cannot know when the final call will beckon us from this life's cycle. *'Tis* good to remember, also, the great love of Thomas Donaldson, a more humble, kindly and unassuming man one could only hope to meet, yet when he was called, *'twas* to demonstrate once again 'that no greater love has a man than he lay down his own life for another.'"

The monsignor slowly walked to Katherine and her family. He gently took her hand and gestured to the funeral director. The pallbearers picked up the canvas straps that were looped under the casket. Then, on a signal from the director, the men eased the casket down into the grave until it settled on the earthen bottom.

Katherine cried out, sobbing, "My boy, my little boy!" Cassie moved to comfort her.

The men stepped back from the graveside, and Frank turned to Katherine and Cassie. He put his arms around the two women. Matt joined them and then Pat. They stood as a group, as a family, crying, hugging and comforting each other. Then Frank took Katherine's hand and led her to the side of the grave. With a trembling hand that held the red rose, she dropped it onto the casket. Pat passed Frank a rose, and then he dropped it onto the casket. They blessed themselves with the sign of the cross, and then followed the monsignor back to the family car. Matt, Pat and Cassie, tears rolling down their cheeks, prayed silently together and dropped their roses onto the little fella's head. The rest of the mourners began filing by the graveside, each dropping a single red rose onto the casket.

It was said by the groundsmen that when the last mourner dropped her rose, a red hue could be seen rising to the sky, lifting to God's place.

# 50

The members of the Country Women's Association of Kangaroo Island organized an after-burial supper in the Kingscote Sports and Recreation Centre. The community pitched in to help; tables were loaded with meats, salads, breads, fresh baked cakes, cookies, scones, tea, coffee and cordial for the youngsters. Locals who lived on one end of the island caught up with those who lived on the other. The Ryans were inundated with offers of help: money to defray expenses, the use of vacation shacks on the island and the mainland to get away for a few days, and small things like taking care of mundane chores around the home cottage. Late in the afternoon Katherine, a sober Frank, he had not touched a drink since Sean's death, and Pat left for Cape du Couedic. Frank took good care of Katherine throughout the day, and when Monty and Jordan approached to offer their condolences, he politely accepted. Matt and Cassie did not leave until after the last of the mourners had left.

****

Matt was sitting on the sofa in the big room of the Baldwin homestead, sipping hot tea, keeping warm in front of the log fire crackling away under Kristina's portrait. Monty and Jordan had long since gone to bed.

Cassie poured herself a cup and then sat next to Matt, her eyes red and swollen from crying. "Belinda and Timothy were very kind, making the bookings and getting me to the airport. I had to be here, Matt. I couldn't sleep; I couldn't get Sean out of my mind. I kept seeing the two of you together; God, how he loved you, idolized you, even tried to walk like you and when he smiled, it was your smile." She dabbed her eyes with a wet hanky. "I think today was the worst day of my life since the day I watched Mummy die."

"You were about Sean's age then." Matt took another sip of tea and gazed into the fire. "I want to hate God for this, but it's myself I really hate sometimes, Cassie." He choked back threatening tears. "I was so full of it, not thinking about anyone else but me, me, always me, bloody pathetic. I knew the little bloke hated arguments, I hated them myself when I was his age…still do." He reached for Cassie's hand. "I can't drink, Cassie, I just have to stay away from the stuff. If I don't, I'll finish up like the Oldman."

"I'd forget about blaming you, Matt, it's not going to help, and I think Sean would be really ticked off to put it bluntly. He'd want you doing something positive like leaving the island and getting on with your writing, so you can write a story about him." She tried to smile, put down her cup and snuggled into him. "Remember how mischievous he could be? Especially with that white mouse of his, what did he call him, Snot, wasn't it?"

"Yeah, right," a smile creasing Matt's face. "Pat had him in his pocket at the funeral today. He's gonna take care of him."

"Pat is a lovely boy. He was telling me about studying to be a priest, that the monsignor was organizing to get him into

Rostrevor College next year, and that the Knights of the Southern Cross are helping to pay for it. I think it's going to be okay for you to come to Sydney now, Matt, don't you?"

"After Christmas; the next few months are going to be really tough, particularly on Katherine. Dad's broken, horse-whipped; I don't know he'll pull through. Strange, it occurred to me watching him over the last few days, I think he really loves us all; it's just he can't live without the booze; too many demons living in his head. I think I understand a little bit better about that."

"Yes, alcohol can take you places you don't want to go, I know that for sure." She stroked his cheek. "Christmas then, and I am soooo ready. Hey, you'll be in Sydney in two weeks for your award and the opening of *Fire in the Centre*. You are going to be blown away when you see what Timothy has done with your work."

"Yeah, I'm already crapping myself."

"They'll love you."

They held each other, silent, exhausted, deep in thought until they fell asleep, her head resting on his chest.

Later, Monty came into the room and placed more logs on the fire. He looked on the sleeping couple, his mind tormented with conflicting thoughts. Reaching down, he gently brushed a lick of hair from his daughter's forehead, and then picked up the knitted afghan from the back of the sofa and spread it over the sleeping couple.

# 51

"And so it is with great pleasure I present this award, the Australian Meritorious Newcomer Scholarship, to Matthew Ryan for his work, the sestina 'Lust: Life's Fiery Centre.'"

Matt got up from his chair next to Cassie and Belinda and went to the podium. The annual event was being held on the lawns surrounding the imposing white stone building of the Sydney Conservatorium of Music. Originally built on the prominent city hill during the governorship (1810-1821) of Colonel Lachlan Macquarie, it was once the stables of the then Government House. Now, the conservatorium overlooked the imposing white sails of the Sydney Opera House, a perfect backdrop for the day's prestigious occasion. Academics, producers, literary agents, city politicians and society members were in the crowd of over five hundred. Television cameras and journalists were clustered together in a roped off area designated 'Media.'

As Matt stepped onto the podium, the chairman of the judging panel shook his hand and presented him with the award certificate. "Congratulations, Mr. Ryan." There was a round of enthusiastic applause. "Now, Mr. Ryan doesn't yet know about this, so it is a surprise, but I have here a Special Recognition Certificate from the board of the Society for his essay 'Kangaroo Island: South Australia's Mystical Secret?' For those of you who do not know, Kangaroo Island is where he was born and raised, a place that is rapidly becoming an international and local tourist destination for that dream vacation." The chairman handed him the award certificate along with the microphone. "Well done, Mr. Ryan."

Matt took the microphone, his lifeline in that moment. "Thanks," he said, his heart pounding and legs turning to jelly. With the back of his hand, he wiped away the beads of sweat beginning to trickle into his eyes.

"This is such an honour…I…hardly know what to say. Um, look, first of all, I want to dedicate this award to my little brother, Sean, who…" Matt stopped, struggling to go on. "Who died a few of weeks ago back on Kangaroo Island…He was my best mate, and I miss him like hell." He paused and wiped his eyes, again; the crowd were silent, absorbed by the sudden sharing of a new intimacy with the young man standing on the podium. "I want to thank the Society for giving me this award…there are special people who encouraged me to write, who saw something in me and believed in me when I was starting out. Katherine, Cassie and Monsignor Byrne who set deadlines and made sure I kept them. You know, mentoring…makes me think of Tom Donaldson who lost his life trying to rescue my brother. He was a hell of a good bloke…made me read books and write. He left Pat and me his farm…" His mind went blank for a second, a panic attack threatened. "I think mentoring…well, it means a lot to me, and I'd be bloody useless without it. Thanks." He almost ran from the podium to his seat next to a smiling Cassie.

"That was beautiful, Matt, lovely. Sean is looking down on you now, and he is so proud of his big brother," she said, hugging him. "I am so proud of you."

As the applause subsided, the chairperson took up the microphone again. "Thank you, Mr. Ryan and God bless, little Sean. I think I can say from all of us here that our hearts and prayers go out to you and your family. Ladies and gentlemen, tonight, the Australasian Modern Dance Company will open," he said pointing over his shoulder, "as part of the Opera House's Newcomer Series Season, with the debut of *Fire in the Centre*. Ms. Cassandra Baldwin, also from Kangaroo Island, will dance to Mr. Ryan's concept, choreographed by the renowned Timothy Barton. Please, Ms. Baldwin, let us see you." A smiling Cassie stood and waved, while the crowd responded with a round of cheering and clapping.

# 52

The jaunty Hagherty ferry pushed out from Blue's Point pier and began to nose through the wash of busy boats, a course set to take it under the bridge and onto Circular Quay. Despite the chilly breeze of the July winter, Matt sat up in the bow, the combination of spray, bright colours, rattling trains and soaring buildings delighting his keen senses. A fully loaded motor cruiser cut across their bow. The ferry skipper sounded the siren and at the same time turned sharply to port to avoid a collision. Alcohol-plied diners hooted and shook fists with good-natured derision.

The Sydney Opera House, its towering white sails a familiar landmark around the world, dominated the view ahead, as the ferry passed under the harbour bridge. Matt was exhilarated, but tumbling around in his stomach was the ever threatening curse of his nemesis, anxiety. Minutes later, the ferry bumped against its Circular Quay berth, the hub for people arriving on trains, buses and ferries from all over Sydney. Buskers, street people and regulars mingled, some heading to concert halls and theatres, others joining luxury boats for harbour cruises. Pier-side food vendors offered tasty delicacies from around the world.

Matt lingered, savouring the rich blend of aromas, sights and sounds. A large station clock with Roman numerals, hanging from a beam at the end of a wharf, caught his eye. It was 7:30 pm, and he needed to hurry.

The tension inside the playhouse was electric. The chatter of the crowd grew louder, as the long awaited moment for the opening performance of *Fire in the Centre* was at hand. The pace over the last week had been insane: dancers coping with the added pressures of intense promotional activities and rehearsals, photographs and interviews, newspapers and television screens. The public was excited and hungry for the debut of a new talent. Already, the season was a sell-out.

Matt was ushered to the front row where Monty and Belinda were seated.

"Lovely to see you again, Matt. You were wonderful today and looked so handsome," Belinda said, smiling and patting his arm. "We'll be seeing a lot of you next year." She returned her attention to the stage. "Oh, I'm just so nervous, I can't stand it."

"Hello, Matt," said Monty. "Congratulations. The scholarship is quite an achievement."

"Thanks, right," said Matt, nervous, uncertain. "Bit of a surprise, really. I've got a lot to do before I can start at the university here next year."

"Right," Monty chipped in, "you can never be sure. A lot can happen."

The lights faded to black. The crowd noise settled to a restless silence: the annoying odd cough, the nose blowing and the rustling of programs. The primitive drone of a didgeridoo began to drift out into the auditorium. Blue light began to filter through the blackness, backlighting the stage to reveal the silhouettes of seven figures sitting in a wide circle, facing their centre. The raucous cry of a crow and the sharp sounds of Australian native birds preceded the slow clack, clack, clack of beating sticks. The silhouettes started to sway and bend in a worshipping motion toward the centre of the circle. Then, emerging from the stage floor, confined within a meter-wide circle, a cluster of multi-collared shafts of laser light: reds, oranges, blues and yellows pulsed upward. Theatre smoke wafted through the light of the lasers, creating the illusion of fire. Drums began to beat, slowly at first, gradually increasing their tempo.

A female dancer burst onto the stage and whirled around the lasers in sweeping *pirouettes*, flinging her arms wide, stretching her body from the balls of her bare feet into the blue hue of the stage lighting. She appeared to be nude, but a flesh-collared body liner clung to her and a short, light blue cotton skirt swirled provocatively from her narrow waist.

Matt was sweating. Belinda grabbed his arm again, her fingernails digging into his flesh. "She is beautiful," he gasped.

"I told you," Belinda whispered, first into Monty's ear and then into Matt's. "She is her mother, the goddess, Venus."

Cassie continued to circle the fire, probing the fringe, fascinating her, jumping back, reacting to the heat. As the stage lighting changed to burnt orange, the silhouettes transformed into full-bodied dancers who bare-footed, began to mimic Cassie's probing movements. Their bodies were almost nude; the four females, two of them Aboriginal, wore only mauve body liners. The males were in loincloths. Cassie became more adventurous. She reached further into the outer shafts of the fire. Suddenly, a loud clap of thunder accompanied by a blinding white flash of lightning illuminated the scene, frightened her and sent her scurrying into the wings.

The drumming intensified and Shamus sprung, with a sensational *grand jeté*, onto the stage, his black mane flying until it fell around his shoulders spectacularly when he landed, his body already glistening from the sweat of his warm-up. He launched into a series of leaping, sweeping turns around the fire. The chamois cloth covering his loins was little more than a thong. The crowd went crazy. The women moved restlessly about their seats. The seven dancers reacted, increasing the range and tempo of their movement, teasing the fire, moving to it, away from it, circling, parting, goading the inquisitive Shamus to probe further the flames. The sound of the didgeridoo grew louder; the dancers started increasing the noise from the clicking of their wooden sticks and began chanting to the rhythm. Cassie returned to the stage and advanced, warily at first, toward the fire and Shamus, the ritual of fascination and discovery soon enveloping the two principal dancers.

Matt was spellbound, caught up in a mixture of emotions: awe, fear, worship and jealousy. Time seemed to disappear, as he watched their bodies move in a blue haze of slow motion frenzy, carnal desire, the core impetus of their movement pushing toward climax, all too real.

The seven silhouettes opened their circle to the fringe of the stage, still clicking their sticks ever louder. They stretched upward, spun, bent over, weaved and high stepped to the rhythm of the raw, native sounds of beating drums and the high-pitching drone of the didgeridoo. Their chanting increased, words formed a repetitive mantra: "We are the fire. We are the fire. We are the fire. We…"

Cassie and Shamus grew bolder, testing the flames from opposite sides of the circle, springing in, springing out, gradually edging further into the flickering flames, discovering more of each other. Shamus, raging with desire, leapt toward her, a lion leaping for its prey; Cassie danced deftly around him, a young lioness, teasing, seductive and sleek, mocking his passion. They circled, their movements growing more intense, deliberate, fighting to close on each other, yet constrained as if held at the end of imaginary elastic cords. Their bodies glistened with sweat. Shamus' black mane, wet, whipped about his head, his leaping grew more urgent. He circled her. The drumming grew louder.

Cassie, now in the centre of the flame, lifted *demi-pointe* on her left foot and slowly raised her right leg above her head, stretching her right foot to pointe toward heaven, a perfect execution of *grand battement*. The audience went crazy. Cassie's mind flashed to her dance on the beach at Cape Kersaint after making love with Matt. She felt the warmth of the sand on her body, the all-consuming fire of that moment of union engulfed her. Her body trembled, as Shamus finally caught her around the waist and slowly turned her full circle, gradually taking her to the floor as she lowered her right leg until she lay on her back, for an instant, still.

Shamus leapt over her. The music rushed toward crescendo. Cassie arched her back and raised her knees, tucking her feet tight against her buttocks. Shamus stretched over her, a hand on the floor each side of her body supported his weight. He lowered his body to hover within centimetres of hers. Their noses almost touched. She cried out.

The chanting, "We are the fire. We are the fire…" grew louder, more intense. Matt watched; his eyes wild and glowing.

Blood surged through his body, arousing him. The final stanza of "Lust: Life's Fiery Centre," coursed through his mind:

> *This dark battle is, maybe, a metaphor for lust's rage*
> *When it transpires among the heat*
> *of coupling bodies, passion*
> *Intensifies the fire of orgasm and lovers scream,*
> *"We are alive!"*

Suddenly, it was over and the curtain dropped. For a moment, there was a stunned silence. Then, the audience erupted with wild applause. "Bravo, bravo, bravo," they yelled. Matt found himself clapping frantically. Belinda was thumping him and Monty. Monty, too, was clapping madly, a triumphant gleam in his eyes.

The curtain rose, and the dancers ran onto the stage and took their bow. Then Cassie and Shamus appeared down stage centre. The audience went crazy. Timothy hurried onto the stage a few moments later, carrying a huge bouquet of roses and handed them to Cassie. The crowd's applause bounced from the walls and roof of the theatre into one thunderous roar.

Cassie shaded her eyes from the glare coming off the lighting grid and looked into the front row of seats. Her smile widened, as she saw her father, Belinda and Matt. Taking a rose from the bouquet, she motioned to Matt to come to her. He hesitated, but Belinda urged him forward. As he reached the lip of the stage, Cassie, teary and smiling, bent down to hand him the rose. "For our little brother," she said. A beaming Shamus looked directly at Matt, bowed and gave him a cheeky wink.

\*\*\*\*

Matt poured Cassie a glass of red wine; filled his and took a sip. "Nice."

She raised her glass, smiling. "Here's to a fantastic day, my darling, your awards, my debut and the magnificent banquet on the promenade; not bad for a couple of Island kids, hey?"

"Yeah, I couldn't take to that Shamus bloke, though; cheeky bugger winked at me, too. In love with himself a bit, isn't he? He's got the hots for you, that's for sure; bloody tough to keep my thinking straight watching the two of you in that dance."

For an instant, Cassie was caught off guard and felt uncomfortable. She quickly regained her composure. "A touch of jealousy there, hey? Good, keep you on your toes," she teased. "Besides, I can handle him. He liked you, though; thought you were way too handsome."

"That's right," said Matt, pushing his hand through his hair and looking at his reflection in the window. He became serious. "How long before you'll be home again?"

"Good news; during the banquet Belinda introduced me to the director of the National Dance Company of New Zealand who saw the show and loved it. She wants to book us for a four-week tour over the Christmas season for the opener to their perennial ballet, the *Nutcracker Suite*. The topper is I can come home for all of August." She laughed gleefully. "I have to keep fit and be back in time for rehearsals in September. Isn't that wonderful?"

"That Shamus bloke going, too?" asked Matt.

"Of course."

"That's a bit of a worry; he doesn't seem to be the kind who would take no for an answer."

Cassie blushed, and then dismissed Matt's comment with a shrug of her shoulders. "I only need to think of us together at Kersaint. I can take care of myself, Matt."

Matt laughed and hugged her. "Hmm, that's quite an image, but I'd rather be there with you." They kissed. "I'll make sure you get plenty of exercise while you're home."

Cassie put down her drink. "Well, how about we start right now?" They laughed and fell back on the sofa. "I love you, Matt."

# 53

August, the month when the wildest storms hit the island, was living up to its reputation. It was six o'clock on Sunday evening, and the sun had long since gone down. The streetlamp in front of the Kingscote police station threw a single orb of light onto the flooded pavement; driving rain smashed against the glass of the windows, brightly lit from the inside fluorescents.

"I don't think Marino is so stupid that he'd risk sailing in this storm, Dunning," said Sergeant Woodson, as he placed the weather map on top of the inquiry desk and pointed to the centre of a tight circle of isobars twenty kilometres southwest of Cape du Couedic. "It would be lunacy; he'd run slap-bang into the worst part of this before he got to Vivonne Bay." He waved his hand toward the front door. "Listen to that wind. It's going to be full-on by midnight."

"We haven't heard from your snitch in Port Hacking for two days," said Dunning, his voice thick and rasping. "Sam Marino is the best boat skipper around these parts. If he gave it a shot and left two days ago, he'd be here and loaded by now."

"Yeah, well, Jordan has been keeping an eye on things at Vivonne. If Sammy was there, he'd let us know."

"I wouldn't count on it; he's back on the booze." Dunning crossed to the front door and peered outside into the rain. "It's getting worse." He sneezed. "This bloody flu…been around all week…can't get rid of it."

Woodson was amused by Dunning's discomfort. "What's got into you, anyway?" he said, picking up the map and pinning it back on the notice board. "It's sort of out of character for you to be concerned about those who are breaking the law, well growing weed, anyway."

"I'm still a policeman," answered Dunning. "I haven't changed my view on the law being too inflexible on the issue, though. The stuff grown here is special; it produces a drug that helps a lot of suffering people." He took a handkerchief from his pocket and blew his nose. "You know as well as I do that this is just an effort by the pharmaceutical boys to keep the lid on this so-called Island secret until they can figure out a way to control production and distribution." He coughed a couple of times and spat out a mouthful of phlegm into his handkerchief. "And, all you want to do is crucify the Ryans." He coughed again. "I want to be around to make sure you don't get way out of line."

"You and I are never going to get on, Dunning. When this is done, you'll be on your way. I've requested that you be transferred." The phone rang and Woodson picked it up. "Woodson…Yes, Jordan…What the hell? Do you know if they loaded…okay…tonight? No, you stay out of it." He slammed down the phone. "That was Jordan. He's calling from Middle River. Flecky Martin phoned him from Vivonne; Marino's boat is in the bay, can you believe that? He said he didn't see them loading anything." He checked his watch. "Get Perkins up here, fast. We'll have to do this on our own; the boys from Adelaide won't fly a chopper in this weather."

"Can't it wait until morning; Marino's not going anywhere in this tonight."

"He's here, isn't he?" Woodson shook his head. "No, I want us at Vivonne tonight. We'll stake it out for as long as it takes. They'd be flat out loading the boat in this weather, so we'll be in place to nab them when they do."

# 54

Monty pulled the homestead veranda door shut and took off his wet oilskin coat. "The gazebo is still intact," he said, leaving wet footprints on the polished floor when he crossed through the big room to the kitchen and the back porch to hang up his wet oilskin. "If this storm gets any worse, it could be on the mainland by morning."

Jordan, his back to the fire, was holding a large glass of port. "A toast to you, my dear sister; it seems that you went, conquered and now have returned." He raised his glass. "Well done."

Cassie was sitting on the sofa adjacent to the fire, looking sophisticated and beautiful. The blue sweater she wore complimented her complexion and dark hair that was pulled back into a ponytail. She smiled politely and was barely able to cover her deep disappointment over Jordan's relapse. His drinking had become much worse than her father had indicated on their drive from the airport.

Monty, pulling on a light, tweed jacket, returned to the big room. "Ah, that's better." Picking up his glass of port from the mantelpiece, he stood next to his afflicted son. "Jordan is right, Cassie, it is good to have you home. The place is not the same without you." He raised his glass. "Here's to you, my daughter, and your wonderful performances. Hmm, fruity, a great drop; yes, Hardy's Chateau Reynella, another of South Australia's finest, my favourite."

Cassie lifted her glass to touch his. "Thank you, Daddy; it is nice to be home." She finished the last of her red wine. "This one is lovely, too." She picked up the bottle and read the label. "No wonder, another McLaren Vale red, Tintara, Cabernet Sauvignon." She nodded approval to Monty. "These South Australian wines keep getting better and better, maybe we should start growing grapes here."

"I have been thinking about it, talking to a few farmers who have approached the Research Centre chaps in Parndana to work up a pilot project."

"Trust you to be right onto it. Thanks for picking me up; it was a horrible day to have to be out on the roads. Matt would have come, but his father wanted him around the lighthouse in case of any trouble. They are having a really hard time dealing with Sean's death, especially Katherine."

"Tragic," said Monty. "Burying your child is not what we sign up for when we have our kids. God forbid anything happens to any of you."

They sipped their wine, the howling wind and driving rain was getting worse. Jordan drank the last of his port and went to the liquor cabinet.

"Don't you think you've had enough, Jordan?" asked Cassie.

"No I haven't, and I'll drink as much as I like, thank you, very much," he replied, irritated and filling the glass to the brim.

"How long has Jordan been back to drinking, Daddy?" She noted that the worry lines in his face seemed deeper.

Monty shrugged. Cassie stood up and confronted Jordan. "You're killing Daddy, Jordan."

Jordan glared at her. "That comment is a little farfetched for you, isn't it?"

"I've never been more serious. I'm going to be here for the rest of the month, and I won't put up with what Daddy does from you. Either you stop drinking, or you get out of here."

"Who the hell do you think you are, little sister?" snarled Jordan, the deep scar running from the corner of his mouth, contorting his face into the tragic mask, made more grotesque by the tiny red veins beginning to show in the skin on his cheeks, spotting his pale complexion. He stepped toward her, swaying unsteadily. "You think you can dance back in here and throw your weight around like you own the place, huh?"

"I do."

"Cut it out, both of you," barked Monty. Cassie and Jordan stopped, surprised. "Enough, enough, please," he pleaded. "We'll sort it out tomorrow."

"Oh, Daddy, forgive me. I'm tired; the flight from Sydney took forever and it was bumpy, especially in the small plane from Adelaide to Kingscote. I'm going to make a cup of hot chocolate and then go to bed. Would either of you like one?" The two men declined.

"Come and say good night before you retire, Cassie," said Monty, trying to sound at ease.

"Of course, Daddy." The phone rang. Cassie went on into the kitchen; Jordan picked up.

"Yes...Flecky!"

Cassie filled the kettle with water, put it on the stove and opened the kitchen cabinet door to get the chocolate powder. As she pulled the can from the shelf, an envelope dropped to the floor, which she picked and saw that it was open and addressed to Monty with Belinda's return address. She smiled and stretched up to place it back in the cabinet, but the letter fell out of the envelope and dropped to the floor, partly unfolding and exposing an underlined paragraph in the middle of the first page that immediately caught her eye. Curious and feeling guilty at the same time, she read it.

*I urge you, Monty, don't do it. You will ruin the boy's life and cause Cassie to turn from you forever. Don't do it.*

It took a few seconds for the letter's words to register. She re-read the piece; the meaning was clear. Her heart raced, her head spun, and her breathing was short and rapid. She moved unsteadily to the kitchen door that led back into the big room and stopped. Monty and Jordan were arguing, shouting loud enough for her to hear what they were saying over the noise of the storm.

"In this weather, someone is going to get hurt. I don't want that on my conscience. Phone them back and tell Woodson to call it off!" yelled Monty.

"Look!" shouted Jordan, "they're already on their way; you can't stop it now. Those bloody Ryans have got it coming, anyway, and that smart-arse Matt…" He stopped, mid-sentence when he saw Cassie standing at the kitchen door. Monty saw her in the same instant. His eyes dropped to the letter in her hand.

She moved deliberately toward him, holding up the letter, shaking it and staring at him. "What the hell is going on?" Monty was speechless. "What have you done?" He looked away. "What the hell have you done?"

Monty's face was ashen. The noise from the rain, beating against the corrugated iron roof seemed louder. For a moment, he thought of lying. "I don't know what to say," he said, his voice hardly audible.

"You…you have betrayed me! I can't believe it, you damn well bloody betrayed me! How could you, you…"

"Jeez, calm down, Cassie, for God's sake, calm down. He did it for you, you know," said Jordan.

She ignored him and stared into her father's eyes, pleading, willing him to tell her it was all a nightmare. Moments passed. Then, her voice, colder than ice tore into his heart. "If anything happens to Matt, I will never forgive you…*never* forgive you, Daddy." Her eyes were cold and clear. "Now, you are going to tell me what is going to happen."

Monty hesitated. She screamed. "Tell me!"

He dropped his eyes and grimaced, defeated. "The police believe the Ryans are involved in growing marijuana, and they are staking out the jetty at Vivonne tonight. Marino's boat is there, he transports the stuff. They don't think it has been loaded yet, too rough," Monty said, sadness in his barely audible voice, his shoulders slumping. "They don't know where the marijuana is being held, but suspect it's at the lighthouse, or somewhere close to the boat." He bowed his head. "They are going to arrest them when they start loading the *Smokey Cloud* tomorrow."

Cassie shook her head and reached for the phone.

"Who are you calling?"

"Matt, not that it's any of your business any longer." She dialled; the phone rang twice. "Yes, hello, Mrs. Ryan…it's me, Cassie. Could I speak to Matt? It's urgent." She waited. "Yes,

Matt…I love you…it's really blowing here, too. Listen, Matt, the police are staking out Vivonne Bay; they know Sam Marino's boat is there. They know you and your dad are involved; you have to stay away from…What? So that's what you were doing today. You don't have to be sorry. I don't care, I love you…Yes, but stay away…No, don't do that, it's too dangerous…All right then, but I'm coming, too…No, I'm coming. You wait for me, you hear? You wait for me. I'll meet you at the shack. We can use the Harriet River to go by them. I'm leaving now."

Cassie dropped the phone back into its cradle, hurried to the kitchen and then on into the sunroom. As she put on her oilskin coat and elastic side boots, a despairing Monty entered. "Where do you think you are going, Cassie?"

"To meet Matt; I'm going to make sure that he and his family don't get into any more trouble." She took her keys to the Pathfinder from the key rack. "You are not who I thought you were, Daddy." She turned from him and hurried out into the storm.

Monty went back to the kitchen door. "Jordan, we are going to Vivonne. I want to talk to Woodson personally; I want to make sure Cassie doesn't ruin her life."

# 55

At Cape du Couedic, the south-westerly gale was gusting to 65 knots and getting worse. The light from the top of the lighthouse continued to sweep through the storm and, as always, the tower stood strong and unmoved against another familiar season of vicious attacks on its granite wall. From a window at its base, a shaft of light pushed through the driving rain. Inside, three men sat around Frank's office desk, drinking beer.

"I'm ahappy to be off the boat tonight, Frank. This astorm was the worst I've been in," Sammy Marino said. "Peter, here, says he's only agunna fly to Kingscote in future." Sammy laughed. "But I told him he's agunna come back with me, I needa his help."

"Should have had his regular crew in this weather," offered Peter Ferrano, still looking deathly pale from a bout of seasickness.

"It would have beena too obvious, if the crew wasn't at the pub lasa night," said Sam. "Thisa way, the snitches would've missed us. Thisa morning, was already so big a bloody storm, no one woulda been able to see if any boatsa were out." Sammy pointed to the latest weather map on Frank's desk. "By the morning the storm, she will a have eased off enough for us to get outa here."

"I'd love to see Woodson's face when he finds out he's missed the boat. This storm works in our favour," said Frank, emptying his glass and howling with laughter. "That boy of mine has got some guts. You see the way he went over the side of the dinghy to save that bag of weed?"

The radio crackled, interrupting Frank. "Cape du Couedic, this is the grain carrier Holbrook, Port Lincoln. We are fifty kilometres south en route to Port Melbourne from Esperance, Western Australia. We are encountering five-meter seas with the occasional rogue at 10 meters. Wind to seventy knots. Advise all shipping caution. Do not leave harbor, over."

Frank picked up the receiver. "Thank you, Holbrook. Advisory's are out. Safe passage, over."

"Thank you, out."

"I'm glad we're not out there tonight," said Sam's crewman.

The door opened and Pat stepped inside, his oilskin coat and hat dripping water. "Mother said to tell you dinner's on the table and to come right away before it gets cold."

"You tella your mother we are coming, Pat. Right away, thanka you very much." Pat left, and the three men put on their oilskins.

Even before they entered the kitchen, the men could smell the rich aroma of roast lamb and potatoes. The table was loaded with plates of meat, vegetables, gravy and bread.

Sam went straight to Katherine and swung her into his arms. "Katherine, you, you are a saint-a." He lowered her back to the floor and held up a thumb and middle finger joined at the tips to form a circle. "Mom-a-mi, itsa look abeautiful."

They all sat down and began to tuck into the Aussies' favourite hot meal. "Where's Matt?" asked Frank.

"He left about an hour ago," said Katherine. "Cassie called; she arrived back from Sydney today. He's off to meet her at Vivonne."

"Vivonne…tonight?...that's bloody odd."

"He left this. I read it earlier," she said, her eyes teary, as she handed him the letter.

"Pat, get us all a beer, will you?" Frank opened the letter. His eyes welled up with tears that trickled down his cheeks, as he read.

> *Dear Mum, Dad and Patrick,*
>
> *I thought I'd write this to let you know that I've arrived here in heaven. Things are pretty good. I have lots of friends and plenty of pets to play with. I know it is hard for you with what happened and all, but I can still keep my eye on you from here. Tom comes by from the big people's heaven every now and again. He likes it there, and he sees God every day. God put him in charge of the sheep and the lambs. He says to say g'day, and that he's sorry he couldn't save me. I tell him he gave it a bloody good go.*
>
> *Thanks for taking good care of me, Mum. I love you. Pat, you can have that sheep rug Tom gave me. Tom said God reckons you'll make a good priest. Dad, thanks for having a go at saving me, you were terrific. I hope your hands are better now. Look out for Matt, he loves you, too.*
> *Lots of love,*
> *Sean*
> *PS. Give Barney a hug for me, will ya?*

Frank placed the letter on the table and wiped his eyes with the napkin. "Did he say why they were going to Vivonne?"

"No, but he did say that Flecky Martin had told the police Sam's boat was in the bay and to tell you not to go near there."

"Good God in heaven, Katherine, the coppers are onto us. Why didn't you tell me sooner? God forgive me, he's going to get aboard that boat and sail her out of the bay; I'll bet my life on it. He's going to dump the load."

"Not in thisa weather, Frank, no," said Sammy. He paused. "I didn't fuel up. The tanks, they are almosta empty."

"Come on," Frank yelled, jumping up from the table. "We gotta move fast."

# 56

Matt flicked off the ute's headlights and turned onto the ironstone road that ran from the South Coast Road to the Vivonne Bay jetty. About a kilometre and a half along Jetty Road, he swung left and drove cautiously for another 200 meters to the large parking area that bordered the Harriet River and where a row of 12 beach shacks extended side by side along the river bank. Cassie's Pathfinder was already parked next Sam's shack. The difficulty of staying on the road with the headlights turned off coupled with the pouring rain for the last two kilometres had cost him time. He hurried to the shack where a single globe cast a dim yellow light over the back door entrance.

Cassie was in the kitchen busy stoking the stove fire. She saw Matt enter, yelled gleefully and ran into his arms. "Oh, Matt, you're here at last," she shrieked, kissing him hard on the mouth and taking a step back to look him over. "You've lost weight, but you look wonderful." She hugged him. "I've missed you terribly."

"Me, too, mate." Matt, beaming, pulled her tight against his body. The fire was roaring a huge welcome, competing with the noise of the rain hammering the roof and winning.

"Let me put the kettle on and I'll make us some tea."

"So, Jordan's still at it, hey?"

"It's not just Jordan; Daddy is in on it, too.

"Yeah, I thought he was up to something all along. I didn't want to believe it," he said, his voice edged with anger and disappointment. "It must have been bloody awful for you when you found out."

"Shocking, I'd say," a gritty firmness showing in the set of her jaw. "I'll deal with him after we get tonight sorted."

"I'm going to have to sail *Smokey Cloud* out of the bay and dump the load. Come morning, those coppers are going to be swarming all over it. Dad and Sammy will be arrested, if they find one plant on board, and Woodson will do his best to tie me in with them."

"I know." She loaded more wood into the stove's fire. The water in the kettle was soon boiling. "So, let's work out how to get on the boat without them spotting us."

"Hold on, Cassie, this is going to be bloody dangerous. That storm is the worst we've had in a long time. The weed will have to be dumped well out to sea, or it will wash back up on the beach."

"So? Sam's boat is one of the best. I'm ready." She picked up the kettle and poured the boiling water into two huge mugs, each with a tea bag in it and handed one to Matt. "Drink this. Oh, and by the way, I've already scouted the jetty area."

"What?"

"Don't worry, they didn't spot me. I took the old bush track that goes along behind Fisherman's Row above the jetty. Bit of a feat with the headlights off and the rain and all, but I know most of this area pretty well." She warmed her hands, cupping them around her hot tea. "One of the police cars is in front of the fishermen's shacks, set up so they can look out over the bay. I got close enough to see Woodson, easy to pick, the gorilla head and all, and the new bloke I saw at Sean's funeral. The other vehicle was hidden just off Jetty Road in the bushes on the crest of the hill overlooking the bay and the jetty."

"That would have to be Dunning." Matt took a sip of tea and let out a howl, spilling some of the steaming hot liquid onto the floor. "Yoee, that's hot."

"Try sipping it. I think if we use the Harriet River to get to the beach, we can walk to the jetty under the lip of the sand dunes and avoid being seen," suggested Cassie.

"Yeah, that could work. Ross Dennis keeps his tinny at the bottom of the boat ramp. We can use that," said Matt. "Sam usually keeps an outboard in the garage."

"It's there. I checked it for petrol; it's good to go." She watched him sip a little more tea. "Finish it off, and then we'd better get going, Galahad."

Matt heaved the outboard onto his shoulder, and then they stepped out of the shack onto the bank of the Harriet River; it cut through the sand dunes for a few hundred meters before it emptied into Vivonne Bay. During the summer and autumn months, a sandbar closed the river's mouth at the beach and formed a large lake where the locals could bring their kids for a safe place to swim, picnic and kayak. Matt and Cassie had spent many summer vacations there, taking annual swim lessons in the state-sponsored "learn to swim" classes. Little did they know then that the intimate knowledge they had acquired of the river, beach, sand dunes and surrounding landscape would be critical to the successful beginning of their dangerous mission.

Cassie led, pushing into the pouring rain, eyes alert, scanning ahead for any sign of discovery or danger. Matt, carrying and sometimes dragging the outboard through the heavy, wet sand, stopped frequently to wipe the stinging rain from his eyes; their progress was painstaking. They made it to the mouth of the river and discovered that the sandbar had been breached, and the river was gushing out into Vivonne Bay. Because of a high tide, there was only a very narrow strip of sand between the sand dunes and the seawater for the 350 meter walk to the tinny.

"It's going to be tough slog through that heavy sand, but the police won't see us," yelled Cassie.

"Yeah, well we don't have any other choice, hey?"

"Ready?" asked Cassie.

"Let's go."

The rain and the lightning were getting more violent, but they pushed ahead. It took another half-hour of hard slogging before they reached Ross's tinny, turned upside down on the sand and tucked close under the lee of the limestone cliff, which dropped off sharply from Jetty Road and where Dunning had set up his hide. They struggled to drag the boat to the water's edge, all the time aware that Dunning could spot them in a flash of lightning. "This is some workout," said Cassie, breathing heavily at the side of the boat while Matt attached the outboard to the stern. "At least we're keeping warm, wet but warm."

"We'll stay close to the shore and keep under the lee of Point Ellen for as long as we can," said Matt. "That way, we'll avoid the big waves. We'll have to make a run for it from inside the point to *Smokey Cloud*, as soon as there's a flat spot."

They pushed the boat into the water. Cassie moved up to the bow and took hold of the hitch line; Matt jumped over the stern and adjusted the fuel settings on the motor. It started on the first pull of the rope, which was just as well because a wave was rushing at the beach, a small wave, but big enough to swamp them if they were caught abeam. Just in time, he gunned the motor and the tiny craft smacked through the top of the wave as it broke; he turned to run close along the shoreline, heading for Point Ellen; a series of sheet lightning lit up the sky, as they approached the jetty.

"Nothing we can do, but pray they don't see us," yelled Matt through the roar of the surf, the wind and the rain. They slipped carefully under the solid wooden structure and kept close in along the rocky shoreline until they were under the lee of Point Ellen. They slowed and maintained enough speed to keep under way, turning in a tight circle, watching out for a flat spot in the waves.

"Keep a lookout for a break in the pattern, Cassie! Take off that oilskin, your sweater and boots. If we go over, their weight will take you straight to the bottom."

She had just finished taking the oilskin off when a searchlight beam swept across the water in front of them. "That's coming from where Dunning is located," she shouted. "I swear to God, those Aboriginal blokes can see in the dark."

"Natural instinct; they never lose it," yelled Matt. "I don't think he's seen us yet, but he knows someone is out here." The bigger waves on the ocean side of the Point were breaking over the narrowest part in the neck of land that jutted out for a couple of hundred meters into the western end of the bay, sending up huge plumes of spray that joined with the rain, some of it splashing into the couple's boat.

"We have to take a chance and go for it now, or we'll swamp," yelled Matt. "Hang on." He twisted the throttle around as far as it would go. The tinny leapt forward, bucking, bouncing and crashing over and through the waves, heading in the direction of *Smokey Cloud*'s mooring. Dunning's searchlight swept across their bow, came back, held on them for a moment and then swung away to fix on the white hull of the fishing cutter, pitching and tossing in the wild water, dead ahead.

"He's lighting up *Smokey Cloud* for us!" yelled Cassie.

Matt ran the tinny by the stern of the cutter, turned sharply along its lee side and then cut the motor. Cassie, with the dinghy mooring rope in her hand, leapt for the ship's safety rail, got a grip on it and hung on for dear life. She dangled in space for a couple of seconds before the cutter rolled away into the trough of a passing swell and helped her to scramble over the gunwale. She quickly looped the rope around the mid-ship capstan and tied off.

The tinny was almost full of water when Matt reached for the rail, but another swell lifted the hull of *Smokey Cloud*, and he missed it. Cassie was watching and immediately tossed him the overlap of her rope. He was able to catch it, just before the tinny began to sink from under his feet. The rolling motion of *Smokey Cloud* jerked him high into the air and then slammed him back against the hull when it rolled into another trough. Cassie, struggling to hold onto the rope, was able to get a couple more loops around the capstan and secure it. Matt, using his bare feet to push up against the steeply angled hull and pull up on the rope, managed edge up the side of the cutter to where Cassie was able to reach the front of his shirt and help pull him over the rail and onto the deck.

"Cassie, the wheelhouse, quick; start the engine and move ahead slowly up onto the mooring. I'll go forward and let the chain off; the moment we are free, head for the open sea."

She stumbled along the rolling deck to the wheelhouse. It was dark inside. The boat pitched forward, throwing her off-balance, sending her crashing into the ship's wheel and bruising her chest. "Shit!" she cried, rubbing her chest with one hand and searching the instrument panel with the other for the key to the ignition. She found it right away; luckily Sammy had left it in the switch. The big engine began cranking over easily, but the chambers wouldn't fire.

"C'mon, c'mon, start you bugger," Cassie yelled. A flash of lightning showed up a tag under a red knob reading, 'compression lever.' "Of course; it's diesel." She slammed the big red knob hard against the panel. Right away, one after the other the engine's twelve cylinders fired and a thrilling, powerful roar snarled above the sound of the shrieking wind. She engaged the gears and eased the throttle forward.

The pitching, rolling *Smokey Cloud* moved slowly up on her mooring chain. Standing up on the bow, Matt slipped open the shackle holding the cutter captive. As it came free, the wind started to blow the heavy cutter broadside into the waves. Cassie reacted swiftly, opened the throttle a little more and spun the wheel to starboard to swing the bow back and point *Smokey Cloud* directly into the oncoming waves.

Matt opened the wheelhouse door and shut it behind him. "Good work, mate; let's get this done."

Cassie slammed the throttle to full ahead. *Smokey Cloud* shuddered, its single screw thrashing the black water at its stern into an expanding flurry of white foam. The heavy cutter gradually picked up speed, pushing the bow deeper into the on-coming waves before it lifted, sending massive bursts of incandescent spray cascading over the bow of the little ship.

# 57

A constant flow of gases from the police pursuit vehicle's exhaust discharged as steam into the wind and rain. Inside the car, Bob Dunning had the heater fan on high, trying to keep warm. His coughing and runny nose had not improved even after taking the antihistamines picked up from the pharmacy shop on the way out of Kingscote. He unscrewed the top of a thermos flask half-full of hot chocolate and poured the steaming liquid into the paper cup that balanced precariously between his knees, and then unwrapped the roast lamb sandwich from Roger's deli in Kingscote; he took a generous bite, tasting and enjoying the fresh bread and the tenderness of the clover-fed roast lamb.

Dunning continually scanned the darkness from the stakeout position in the bush off to the side of Jetty Road where it crested before dropping down to the jetty and offered a potentially good view of the bay. In the flashes of lightning, he could see the other police vehicle 500 meters ahead to his right and at a higher elevation in front of the shacks on Fisherman's Row. There was no let up in the wind and rain beating against the car's windscreen, forcing him to keep the wipers going at full speed. He wiped his nose, looked over at Woodson's car and scratched his head. *I could be in bed.* He coughed up a mouthful of phlegm, wound down the window and spat into the rain; it blew back into his face. "Damn."

Before he could wipe the glob away, a series of lightning flashes changed night into day over the bay. "What the hell?" he muttered. Snatching the binoculars, he leaned through the open window and scanned the water, straining to see beyond the rain. Nothing! He wiped away the phlegm and took another bite of the sandwich.

He chewed mechanically no longer aware of the taste, wrestling with his thoughts. "Something's going on out there," he mumbled, and then snatched up the searchlight plugged into the car's power system and stepped out into the storm. The wind threatened to tear the Akubra hat from his head, so he jammed it tighter over his ears and raised the collar of his oilskin coat. Shivering from the cold, he flicked on the searchlight and directed his eyes along its beam, sweeping the shoreline from the jetty to Point Ellen. Nothing! Another series of sheet lightning lit up the bay.

"Yeah, something…someone's out there, all right!" The searchlight picked up the tiny boat charging out from Point Ellen. Then he saw that the tinny had two people in it and was heading for *Smokey Cloud*. "They'll never make it," he yelled, as he swung the light to the cutter and trained it on the white hull. "There you go boys, good luck."

As Dunning kept the light on the fishing cutter, he picked up the microphone. "Boss, do you copy; over?"

Perkins' voice crackled back. "Read you loud and clear; over."

Dunning was about to speak when a car roared by.

The radio crackled again. "Car just went by you; did you see who it was?" demanded Woodson.

"No, going too fast, but there is a small boat with...I think...two people trying to reach the *Smokey Cloud*," said Dunning into the microphone.

"What?" Woodson's voice crackled over the radio. "We've bloody well got 'em. Set up a road block right there, Bobby Boy, we'll go after the incoming vehicle." He laughed; the eerie whistle was prominent in the mix from his wounded throat. "We've got the bastards boxed in at last."

Dunning watched the lights of Woodson's vehicle cut through the darkness when he dashed from Fisherman's Row to the jetty. He swung the searchlight back in the direction the cutter, but he was unable to find her. Another series of lightning flashes lit up the bay for a few seconds; *Smokey Cloud* was under way. "Good, God, they're heading out to sea; they have to be crazy."

*Stuff the roadblock; we've got trouble, now, real trouble.* He leapt back into the police car, hit the gear lever into reverse, gunned the motor and backed out of the bush hideout onto the road. Slamming the gear into forward, he roared down to the jetty. As he approached, he saw Monty Baldwin standing in the rain and talking to Woodson. Skidding to a stop behind the Baldwin car, Dunning hurried to join Monty, Woodson and Perkins; he noted that Jordan was sitting in his father's car.

"I'm not going to call anything off, Mr. Baldwin. I have these blokes as good as in jail. They've been breaking the law, and now they are going to pay," Woodson was shouting.

"Enough harm's been done, Sergeant. I am warning you, if you don't call this off, I'll see to it that you spend the rest of your career..."

"It's all academic, now, Mr. Baldwin," interrupted Dunning. "The *Smokey Cloud* just left for the open sea with at least two people on it."

"What! Who?" demanded Woodson "Bloody Marino, he wouldn't leave in this weather."

"Looks like he has," said Dunning.

Suddenly, the headlights from another vehicle dropped over the crest of the hill and rushed down the road to the jetty. Frank Ryan and Sammy Marino skidded to a stop and jumped from the Landcruiser, Ferrano following.

"You blokes seen Matt?" yelled Frank.

Woodson could not believe his eyes, but Dunning realized immediately what was happening. "Holy bloody hell, *Smokey Cloud* sailed out of the bay about five minutes ago, Frank."

"It's sailed? It can't have bloody sailed already." Frank ran to the jetty and peered into the darkness.

"Looks like we got you at last, Ryan!" screamed Woodson through the rain and wind. "Where's the weed? In the back of the truck, is it, hey? Check their truck, Perkins."

Monty was under no illusion about the identity of the second person on the fishing cutter. He stepped up to Woodson, grabbed his shoulder and whirled him around to look him directly in the face. "My daughter is on that boat, Sergeant. Stuff the drugs. We have to mount a rescue effort, now," he shouted, pointing out to the sea. "*Wave Dancer* is here in the bay." He yelled to Jordan. "Jordan, get your backside off that seat and get that chain off the dinghy. The keys to the padlock and *Wave Dancer* are on the key ring in the car; and hurry, your sister and Matt are on *Smokey Cloud*." Jordan reached for the keys and scampered off to get to the Baldwin tinny, chained and padlocked to the light pole, halfway along the jetty.

Perkins returned from the Landcruiser, "Nothing, boss."

"What!" shouted Woodson? "They're on the boat. The marijuana is on the boat. You buggers loaded it today, didn't you? We've got to get that boat!"

"Yeah, that's right, Sergeant," said Frank sarcastically. "If you want us, you have to have the stuff, which means you have to get the boat, hey?"

Woodson snarled. "I've got you, Ryan."

The men hurried down the jetty to the light pole where Jordan was unchaining the dinghy. "Mr. Baldwin, our besta chance to make it to *Wave Dancer* is for only one of us to be in the tinny. It'sa less likely to swamp." said Sam. "Here, Jordan, givea me that key to *Wave Dancer*; I bring her back and picka you all up."

Jordan looked at Monty, who waved his go-ahead. "Get on with it, Sam," he said, "and be as quick as you can."

The men turned the tinny over, freed the leg of the outboard already clamped onto the stern and slid it down the jetty steps into the water. Sam jumped into the rocking boat with professional dexterity, started the little motor and pushed off into the waves, quickly disappearing into the gloom, heading in the direction of *Wave Dancer*.

The men on the jetty waited anxiously. The wind was howling and getting even stronger, driving the rain almost horizontally across the bay. The minutes ticked by, and then a glow appeared through the darkness, moving rapidly toward them. *Wave Dancer*, a thirty-meter, steel-hulled fast boat with two 360-horsepower Caterpillar Marine diesel engines, throbbing powerfully, all working lights blazing, burst into view rolling and bucking through the rough water. Sam guided the vessel expertly in a tight circle to bump broadside on against the heavy timber jetty.

Frank, Dunning, Monty and Jordan leapt aboard. Woodson yelled to Perkins to stay back and monitor the police radio. Ferrano had already returned to the Landcruiser, seasickness claiming him from his few minutes on the jetty. The moment Woodson's feet hit the deck; Sam pushed the throttles forward to full speed. The twin propellers whipped the water at the stern of the fast boat into a cauldron of white foam. *Wave Dancer* surged forward and quickly gained speed, smashing through the rolling swell and sending mountains of white spray flaring off each side of her bow. Sam set course for the open sea.

Dunning, Monty and the others joined Sam in the half cabin. He flicked on the switches to the radio and the radar. The radar's luminous screen cast an eerie green glow on the men who were immediately focused on the green dial sweeping around it. "It'll be hard to makea out *Smokey Cloud* with all the bounce-a coming back off the whitecaps, but we might getta lucky," shouted Sam.

Dunning saw through the glass that Frank had moved up to the bow, and was sweeping the ship's main searchlight through the hellish weather ahead of them. *I bet he was a hell of a soldier.* He saw that Monty was looking across at him. As if reading Dunning's mind, Monty nodded. *Tough old bugger, hey, whitey?*

They pushed ahead. Twenty minutes later, the crackling of the radio broke through the anxious thoughts of each man.

"Mayday! Mayday! This is *Smokey Cloud*. Does anybody read, over?"

"That's Cassie!" Monty yelled.

# 58

"Matt! Matt! We have to get the flares up," shouted Cassie, trying to shake Matt awake from his blow to the head. "They're looking for us; we have to get the flares up, now."

Matt's eyes flickered, opened and fixed on Cassie. Her voice echoed through his spinning head. He gradually became aware of the screaming wind and the pitching and rolling of the boat. Scattered images of *Smokey Cloud* in the storm, of the engine running out of fuel, of how Cassie had dragged him over the lip of the engine room hatch, tumbled through his mind. His eyes were drawn to the bloodstained bandage wrapped around the leg of her moleskin pants.

"Cassie, your leg is..."

"No time to worry about that," she shouted, pointing to the flare box caught near the hatch. "We've got to get a flare up."

"But your leg…"

"It won't matter a damn, if you don't get those flares up. We've a chance, not much of one, but *Wave Dancer* is out there looking for us," she yelled pulling the bandage tighter around her wound. "Get them. Get the flares for God's sake!"

"Cassie, I'm sorry, I'm sorry, I got you into this."

"Oh, for God's sake, Matt, I'll do it myself!" Angry, she turned from him and reached for the flares. "There comes a time when you have to fight, to never give up," she shouted, managing to grasp the box with her fingers. She pulled open the lid and, after two fumbling attempts, she got the pistol loaded. Another big wave hit and pitched *Smokey Cloud* into a thirty-degree roll. Cassie slid across the deck and crashed into the wheelhouse door. Matt was caught up in the cold seawater washing over the deck, and he slammed into the cabinets under the ship's wheel.

Crying out in pain with every move, Cassie pushed and pulled herself upright and lunged for the latch of the wheelhouse door. She pulled desperately on the handle. The door was stuck!

"For God's sake, Matt, don't you see? Everything comes down to right now. This is it! God will save us, but we have to do our part," she yelled, furious, desperate and struggling for breath. "He wants us to live, and I'm not giving up."

The door came loose and opened, just as another wave crashed broadside into *Smokey Cloud*. A huge volume of water blasted into the wheelhouse. Cassie screamed and dropped the flare gun; instinctively, she grabbed her wounded leg.

The cold water and Cassie's scream hit Matt like a hard slap in the face. Adrenalin surged and flooded his body; fear and pain vanished. He scrambled and slid across the water-covered deck, managing to snatch up the sliding flare pistol before reaching the door. Swaying with the motion of the boat, he pushed to his feet and wrapped an arm around Cassie.

"Can you hold on to the door?" he shouted.

"Yes! Get the flare up, Matt, get the bloody flare up!"

The shrill howling of the wind and the stinging spray hit him full on, as he stepped outside the wheelhouse. *Smokey*

*Cloud* rushed to the top of a foaming wave. A new sound alerted him, the thunder of water crashing over rocks. Lightning flashed, and there, soaring above the cutter were the cliffs of Haystack Rock a mere four hundred meters abeam.

Matt reacted with hysterical laughter, punching a defiant fist at the looming cliff. The pain from his ribs was gone, swallowed up in a heady euphoria, the storm itself seeming to empower him. An enormous exhilaration filled him, every muscle in his body readied for the fight, the primitive instinct to survive fully alerted. He yelled provocatively into the storm, "C'mon, c'mon, I can take it! I can take whatever you throw at me; I'm not done!"

He raised the pistol and pulled the trigger. The flare streaked ahead of a fiery trail, shooting through the blackness and eventually burst into a brilliant sun at a thousand feet, turning the night into a surreal daylight textured, metallic blue.

Unbelievably, three hundred meters distant, *Wave Dancer*, her lights blazing, was balancing on top of a mountainous wall of seawater and about to slide away into the next trough.

****

"We must be close if thata radar blip is them," shouted Sam from the wheel of *Wave Dancer*. "Thosa cliffs are close."

The night exploded into daylight. "There! There she is!" yelled Dunning, holding tightly to the safety rail that ran around *Wave Dancer*'s deck. The five men wiped their eyes, dazzled by the sudden brilliance of the bursting flare. He pointed. "There, by the wheelhouse door, it's them!" *Smokey Cloud* disappeared, as *Wave Dancer* dropped into the trough.

\*\*\*\*

Matt waved frantically. *Wave Dancer* fell off the wave. Moments later she reappeared one hundred and fifty meters abeam. Several figures were holding onto the side railing looking out at *Smokey Cloud*. Because of the rain and spray, Matt could not tell who they were, except for one of them who looked familiar. The flare died, plunging them again into darkness.

He grabbed Cassie and hugged her, and then stepped back into the wheelhouse to get another flare. Luckily, the box was caught tight between the hatch cover and the wheelhouse wall, the same place it had been before. *The Big Bloke's looking out for us.* He shoved another flare into the pistol. Before he could get the shot off, the night once more turned to daylight with a flare from *Wave Dancer*, which had moved to within a hundred meters of *Smokey Cloud*.

\*\*\*\*

*Smokey Cloud*'s flare fell into the water and the black curtain dropped again. "Geta flare off, Jordan!" ordered Sam. Jordan, holding the loaded pistol, pointed it into the sky and pulled the trigger. Daylight returned; Frank, Monty, Woodson and Dunning looked over the rail toward *Smokey Cloud*.

"We'll never make it," yelled Woodson. The looming cliffs were closing. "We've got to get out of here." He rushed toward the wheelhouse. Frank stepped in front of him, dropped his shoulder into the panicking man's chest and sent him tumbling. A wave hit the boat at a forty-five-degree angle and washed him across the deck, slamming him headfirst into the gunwale. Frank launched himself at the copper and managed to grab his legs, saving him from going overboard. As the boat pitched forward, Dunning and Frank dragged the unconscious and bloodied sergeant into the shelter of the half-cabin.

Sam was wrestling with the throttles and the wheel. "Jordan," he yelled. "Puta bloody Woodson in the crew quarters forward." He twisted his head skyward. "Anda hurry up about it; we'll needa more flares."

\*\*\*\*

Matt was at last able to identify the people on the fast boat's deck. A feeling of elation soared through him when he recognized Frank, standing on the stern deck of *Wave Dancer*, its nose now pointing into the heavy sea and reversing gingerly back to *Smokey Cloud* whose bow, thank God, still pointed into the storm, her sea anchor holding, a temporary respite. As the gap between the two boats narrowed, Frank held up a rope and signalled that he was going to throw it. He whirled the weighted end above his head a few times and then let go. The accurate toss landed the lead weighted rope over the top of the wheelhouse. Matt stretched up and was able to reach it; Frank waved to start hauling. Cassie held onto Matt's belt to help keep him from being washed overboard. Attached to the throwing rope was a heavy-duty towrope, which Frank and Monty fed over *Wave Dancer*'s stern.

Matt worked his way to the bow, pulling the towrope across the gap until he reached the forward capstan. With a strength he did not know he possessed, he was able to get one loop of the wet and heavy tow rope over it, just as a breaking wave crashed over the two boats. Cassie was horrified to see Frank tumble over the side of *Wave Dancer*; her grip on Matt tightened. After what seemed an eternity, Frank's head popped to the surface well clear of *Wave Dancer*'s threshing propellers. The light from the flare died and again an immediate blackout fell over the scene. Then relief, the searchlight from *Wave Dancer* switched on. The powerful beam sliced through the black curtain and began sweeping the water, looking for Frank.

Another flare from *Wave Dancer*; light returned and revealed the fast closing cliffs.

\*\*\*\*

Struggling to keep *Wave Dancer* from crushing the hull of *Smokey Cloud*, Sam watched Frank whirl the lead rope about his head. Monty held the hitch-knot to the towrope, ready to feed it over the stern. Frank tossed the rope, watched it sail over *Smokey Cloud*'s wheelhouse and then yelled to Monty, "He's got it!" They began feeding out the heavier rope over the stern rail. "Keep it clear of the props, or we'll all be done for!" Frank yelled.

Dunning was on his way back to help when the massive wave hit the two boats. Water cascaded over the deck of *Wave Dancer*. Frank lost his grip on the rope, and the swirling water carried him to the ship's side. Dunning lunged for him, but too late, Frank disappeared over the rail. "Frank! Frank! Oh, God save him!"

Shaken and soaked, Dunning's sharp eyes searched the turbulent water and saw Frank's head surface. "Thank, God!"

"We can't do anything for him now!" shouted Monty. "I need your help; we've got to keep this rope free of the props." The flare went out. A second later, Jordan who was manning the searchlight, fired another and then swung the light back over the water, looking for Frank.

\*\*\*\*

Frank's life jacket helped keep him afloat, but the turbulence would keep pulling him back under the water. Matt saw his father's struggle, but he had to get another loop over the capstan. He turned to see Cassie dragging herself along the deck with the lead line in tow. She tied one end around the bottom of the mast and threw out the weighted end in Frank's direction. On the third try, he was able to catch it and hang on. She looked for help from Matt who was still fighting to wrap the heavy towrope around the capstan. Dragging her injured leg, she crawled along the deck and joined Matt. Working together, they eventually got the rope looped twice and clamped tight.

Matt looked up at *Wave Dancer's* stern, signalled to Monty and screamed, "Go! Go! Go!" Almost immediately, the heavy-duty rope snapped taut; *Wave Dancer* took up the slack and with her propellers churning the water, slowly, ever so slowly, she began to move forward; Sam at the wheel expertly working the throttles.

The thunder from the waves crashing on rocks was deafening. Another flare soared into the sky from *Wave Dancer*. Their hearts pounded, as they looked behind and saw the looming cliffs with the boiling mass of white-water around their base. However, *Wave Dancer* seemed to be edging forward, pulling *Smokey Cloud* with her.

"Your dad, I've got him tied to the lead line!" Cassie said, pointing, trying to catch her breath. We have to hurry."

As Matt started for the rope, he saw seawater pouring through the wheelhouse door. "The hatch cover is open! It'll flood the engine room. We'll swamp!"

"I'll get it!" Cassie shouted, pulling herself back along the deck and holding on tight to the bandage around her wounded leg that had started to unravel. "Get to your dad!"

A wall of water smashed against the cutter. Matt saved himself from going over the side by grabbing the handrail and holding tight until the rushing water was gone. Gasping for air, his arms aching from fatigue, he found the lead line, taut. Frank still had a grip on the rope.

"God give me strength!" he cried. In that moment, he experienced *a presence*; a surge of energy filled him. He heaved on the rope and saw Frank's head surface alongside the cutter. Their eyes met and for the first time in a long time, Matt knew he loved his father. He reached for his dad's outstretched hand; they touched, but a breaker rolled down the side of the boat and pulled Frank with it, burying him under a mass of water. Matt was distraught and screamed to God a second time; in the next minute, the backwash literally hung Frank over the handrail. Matt got hold of his belt, pulled with all the strength he had left, and they collapsed in a heap on the deck.

Frank rolled over, his face close to Matt's, coughing up seawater. "You're one hell of a man, Matt." They hugged as they rolled back and forth on the deck.

Cassie appeared at the wheelhouse door. "The hatch cover is broken!" she yelled. "It won't shut!"

"C'mon, Matt, there's no time to waste, let's get you two out of here." Frank, bleeding from cuts all over his body, staggered to his feet, moved toward Cassie and realized she was badly injured. He pulled the two-way radio from the webbing pouch secured to his belt. "*Wave Dancer*, Frank here, do you read, Sam, over?"

"Loud and clear, Frank; I thoughta you were a goner," said Sam, his voice crackling over the radio. "We have a serious problem; we are not amaking any headway anymore. In fact, we are losinga ground. Whata's your condition, over?"

Frank looked at his two kids. "Critical. Cassie has a bad leg injury, and the boat is taking water fast. We have to get off here quickly, Sam. *Smokey Cloud* is done, and she'll drag *Wave Dancer* down with her, if we don't move fast." He looked around, thinking. "Get in tight, as tight as you can with the winch, and throw a couple of cray pots over the stern onto Smokey's foredeck."

As Frank finished speaking, *Wave Dancer* was already reversing. On the stern deck, Monty picked up the slack on the towrope with the winch. Dunning and Jordan untied two pots and held them over the stern. Sam pushed the gear lever forward and the towrope tightened and held, *Wave Dancer*'s stern was a meter from the cutter's bow. The men dropped the pots onto *Smokey Cloud*'s foredeck.

Frank lifted Cassie into his arms and staggered forward. Matt followed, holding onto Frank's belt to help keep him from falling. When they reached the pots, Frank placed Cassie feet-first through the opening in the top of the closest pot, took off his life jacket and put it on her. As he tightened the straps, he kissed her lightly on the cheek. "Good luck, Cassie. You're one hell of a gutsy woman, luv. Now, hold onto that rope tight."

Cassie clasped Frank's hand and yelled through the noise of the breaking waves and howling wind, "Thank you, Mr. Ryan! Thank you for coming!"

Frank squeezed her hand, and then signalled Matt to help him with the pot. They took a position at each side and lifted it above their heads. Dunning, Monty, and Jordan took up the slack on the rope and hauled the young woman quickly up and over the stern of *Wave Dancer*.

\*\*\*\*

Monty reached for his daughter, as they lowered the pot to *Wave Dancer*'s deck. "Thank God, thank God, we have you!" he shouted, lifting her from the pot and hugging her.

"You have got to hurry, Daddy. Get Matt and Frank; there's not much time." She pushed away from her father and fell to the deck. He moved to her. She waved him away. "Get them, get them!" she screamed, almost hysterical. Another wave crashed into *Wave Dancer*. Seawater washed over Cassie, pushing her into the stern gunwale. The water receded, and she pulled herself upright to peer over the stern. Frank was lifting Matt into the other pot. She, also, saw that the marijuana was washing out of a gaping hole in *Smokey Cloud*'s bow.

\*\*\*\*

A bigger wave smacked violently into both boats and *Wave Dancer*'s steel hull smashed into *Smokey Cloud*, splintering her foredeck and opening a hole into the crew's quarters. A large number of bags were crammed into the small space, two of them had split open. Seawater poured through the hole and the bags of marijuana began to wash out into the sea.

Frank motioned for Matt to get into the other cray pot. "Get in, get in!" he shouted, "quick, mate, quick!" Matt was suddenly aware of the stabbing pain returning to his broken ribs. He cried out and fell to the deck. Frank dropped to his knees, picked him up, held him like the child that was his and placed him feet-first into the second pot. Gasping from exertion, he handed Matt the pot rope. "Hang on tight a bit longer, son, you're almost home."

"What about you, Dad! How are you going to get off?" Matt yelled.

"No worries, mate, I'll be along." Frank winked and grinned. "I love you all, Matt; tell 'em that for me." He hugged and kissed his boy on the cheek, signalled for the men on *Wave Dancer* to pull, and then lifted the pot and his son with one final burst of energy.

As Matt cleared the stern of *Wave Dancer*, Frank knew that time had run out; *Smokey Cloud* was quickly sinking back into the white-water at the cliff base. He pulled the radio from the web pouch on his belt.

"Sam! Sam! Gun her, mate; for God's sake get the hell out of here, or *Smokey Cloud* is going to drag you with her!" He dropped the radio, kicked the ratchet holding the towrope free and watched *Wave Dancer* surge forward and away from the stricken *Smokey Cloud*.

# Epilogue

Matt, hands in the pockets of his white moleskins, ambled across the road from the hospital to the esplanade and sat on the bench overlooking the water to the mainland. A small fishing boat chugged across the bay, its wake spreading for hundreds of meters on the gray, glassy water. Seagulls hovered around its stern; some dropped onto the wake, fighting over bits of fish gut thrown out by the fisherman, as he cleaned his catch.

The Monday morning air was chilly, and Matt pulled his leather jacket a little tighter around his shoulders and neck. Behind him, way to the southwest, a dark sky signalled approaching squalls. A car rumbled up the hill from the town, did a u-turn and pulled into the curb. The door slammed shut; Matt turned to see Bob Dunning approaching over the grass.

"G'day, Matt," he said, holding up his hand. "Don't get up." They shook hands; he sat, settled and looked out over the water toward the fishing boat. "You can't beat this, hey? I often come up to the bluff to just think, sometimes for an hour or more, looking out there when I want to think through a problem, or try to make sense of this crazy world. It talks to me, the sea…you know, gives me perspective, meaning, peace. You know what I mean?"

"Yeah, I do the same at Admirals Arch. I get a lot of ideas for my writing there." Matt paused and grunted, as he reached inside his shirt to adjust the bandage around his chest.

"Sore, hey?"

"It's nothing; I'm alive. I'm trying to make sense of the last six months. Dad, Sean, Tom…Cassie's career." Matt continued to follow the progress of the fisherman. "And yet, it was me who stuffed-up, and I'm still here. Dad gave his life, you blokes risked yours, and Cassie and I get to live. There has to a lesson there somewhere."

"To me it's real simple. All our experiences should teach us to value life and use it to better ourselves and others. Yeah, and that reminds me, your scholarship. You earned it, use it. Your God given talent is a gift to be developed; you can always come back later to live here. Cassie loves you, she'll be around," said Dunning. He paused and placed his hand on Matt's shoulder. "By the way, some good news; Sergeant Woodson has been recalled to Adelaide. He's being replaced, and I know the new bloke; he's all right. The marijuana matter has been dropped. The politicians are looking for ways to modify the legislation; take out the criminal element."

"If they'd done it earlier, none of this would have happened."

"Hold on, Matt, we're all responsible for our actions. As you said, there's a lesson or two in this for all of us."

They were both silent for a moment. "You're right," Matt sighed, "a bloke could go nuts trying to figure it all out. I guess it just is, hey?"

Dunning stood up to leave. "I've gotta get going. One of my more pleasant duties, I have to take Reggie out to the airport. He's pissed, I can tell you, but he had it coming. Reggie is a prime example of someone never learning a lesson. Oh, I almost forgot; Monty Baldwin is recommending to the Royal

Humane Society that your dad receive the Bronze Medallion for Bravery. We're verifying the recommendation."

Matt's eyes were misty, as he shook Dunning's hand. "Bloody hell, makes the Oldman a hero for real, hey?"

Dunning grinned, "Your dad was always a hero, Matt. The demons got him for a while, that's what happened. He beat them in the end. I'll be at his memorial Mass tomorrow; Parndana Church, right?"

"Yeah, thanks, Bob. Thanks for being a mate…for all your help."

"No worries. Get those ribs healed; the footy finals will be here before you know it."

"Yeah, we'll have you blokes," Matt called after him.

Dunning drove off, and Matt turned back to his view of the sea. The fishing boat was gone, but its wake still lingered, and on it a few seagulls remained to squabble over the odd piece of missed offal. He took a deep breath and looked at the sky. "I'm going to make the best of the chance you've left me, Dad," he said, making fists of his hands and lightly thumping his thighs.

"I saw you and Bob Dunning together," said Cassie, arriving quietly at the rear of the bench, on crutches. The tartan-pleated skirt she was wearing ballooned over the plaster wrapped around her left leg from thigh to ankle. "I didn't want to interrupt."

Matt, excited to hear her voice, jumped to his feet. "Ahh, bugger," he groaned, grinning stupidly and clutching his chest.

She dropped the crutches, and using the back of the bench for support, hopped around to hug him carefully, laughing. "We're such a great pair."

They sat. "Bob's a good bloke, one of a kind. So, what did the doc say?" asked Matt.

"Nothing's changed; he checked to make sure the blood was circulating properly and said the Adelaide surgeon's report arrived last Friday. It confirmed what they told me before; they don't think I'll be able to dance professionally again. I'll see about that."

Matt nuzzled her neck, taking care not to put pressure on his ribs. "I'll do all I can to help, Cassie. If anyone can do it, you can. There are breakthroughs for treatment occurring all the time. Belinda told me she is checking out a doctor who is doing good work at some sports medicine clinic in Colorado. No, we won't give up."

"We'll talk about it down the road. For right now, I'm happy to be alive and with you. It has always been a dilemma for me; I love to dance, and I love my life here. Anyway, I need some time with my dad. He is a mess and needs all the help I can give him. Belinda will be here next week, and that will be good for him. Jordan is going back into rehab, thank God. I don't want to see him back here until he is well."

Ripples began to ruffle the surface of the water and a light breeze lifted over the lip of the cliff. Cassie shivered, zipped up the front of her leather jacket and rested her head on Matt's shoulder.

"I talked to Pat about Tom's farm, and he agreed it's a perfect place for the church to use as a holiday camp for orphan kids and kids from families having a rough go of it." Matt smiled. "Monsignor likes the idea, and Katherine says she would live there, be the nurse and cook for the kids. Pat will be off to the seminary, eventually, but we all want to keep the farm running. We reckon that between the three of us, we can make it work. We want to dedicate the camp to Tom."

"He loved you boys, that's for sure. What a brave, wonderful man. I could help Katherine out when you are at university next year."

"I might have to put that off, Cassie."

"No, no, no, you are going, you must go. There is our place in North Sydney for you to use, and I could come and stay some of the time."

"You would…that would be fantastic. What about Monty?"

"He thinks we might do very well together."

"Does he? Well, he's changed his bloody tune, hey?" said Matt, laughing. "I love you, mate. I will always love you."

"Hmm, love you, too, Matthew Ryan." They kissed. "Oh, there is one other thing; I want to take communion at the memorial tomorrow to honour your dad. Do you think that would be okay?"

"I reckon Dad would probably round up Sean and Tom to watch…"

"…and Kristina and Matilda, too, I reckon. That's a lot of love up there looking out for us, Matt," said Cassie.

As she finished speaking, the clouds scattered and the sun emerged, its golden sparkle dancing along the top of a suddenly very blue sea.

"Reckon they just gave us the nod, mate," said Matt.

\*\*\*\*

# About the Author

**Tony Boyle** grew up on a sheep and cattle farm on Kangaroo Island, South Australia. He attended school on the island and later Rostrevor College on the mainland. After finishing his final year at Parndana Area School, he joined Elder, Smith as a cadet stock salesman in Kingscote and was later transferred to Ororoo, a rural town in northern South Australia. Three years later his mother died suddenly, and he returned to manage the family farm on Kangaroo Island. A marriage produced three beautiful children. During this time, he was also active in rural and state politics that lead to a tilt at running for state office.

Fifteen years later, he and his family moved to Adelaide where he worked as a salesman for an insurance company. He pursued an interest in amateur theatre as an actor and supplemented his income with modeling assignments in fashion and commercials. This led him to Sydney and then London where he was signed with the famous Gary Loftus Modeling agency in Curzon Street. He eventually returned to Sydney where he played Dr. Gavin Morris in the Australian television series *Young Doctors*, appeared in many commercials and free-lanced as a writer of promotional, training and industrial scripts for various clients.

In 1986, Tony opened his own production house on Blue's Point Road, North Sydney, produced videos for corporate clients, and spent time in Africa and Pakistan filming documentaries for the refugee NGO, Austcare.

He moved to the United States in 1990 to marry Kathy (his beloved wife of 23 years) and worked in theatre, television drama, commercials and industrial productions as a producer, writer, presenter and actor. He has written several movie scripts and novels for assorted clients, including the screenplay adaptation of his novel *Kangaroo Island*.

When Tony began writing his first novel he was driving a limousine in Denver and the Rocky Mountains, opening his laptop at every opportunity. Sometimes, this would include hours of waiting outside strip clubs, restaurants or prom events; all fertile fields for stories and story ideas. He is a speaker at conferences, addiction rehabilitation centres, book stores, book clubs, schools, service clubs, and has been interviewed on radio and television. He is currently writing the novel *Under the Southern Cross*, the sequel to *Kangaroo Island* and where the locations will expand from Kangaroo Island to the Outback station country of northern South Australia.

Tony lives in Golden, Colorado and travels frequently to Australia and Kangaroo Island with his wife Kathy to research his new book and to spend time with their children, 10 grandchildren and family.

Printed in Australia
AUOC02n0845171213
259064AU00001B/1/P